Fifty Shades of Roxie Brown

A romantic comedy by

Lynda Renham

Fiftyshades: When a person has lots of different mood changes.

www.urbandictionary.com
June 24, 2012

Chapter One

'Mr Morgan will see you now.' The receptionist points at the lift where he is waiting for me. The doors slide shut and I inhale the clean smell that is uniquely him. I'm intoxicated. He could have me now, here in the hotel lift. My legs tremble and he supports me with one hand while his fingers trace my face with the other. I shudder with desire. His breath hitches, or is it mine? There seems to be so much hitching of breath when I'm with him that it is difficult to tell who it is that is doing the hitching. No, it can't be me; I can barely breathe at all. My eyes lock onto his lips. Kiss me I implore silently. Spank me until I'm raw. Take me, do what you will.

I bite my lip and he sighs.

'How many times do I have to tell you about that?' he whispers. 'You know how it tempts me.'

'I'm sorry,' I breathe, feeling my desire for him, way down below.

I lick the blood from my bitten lip. He's right, I must stop this. I already have two blisters. Anastasia Steele never has this problem. His breathing has become heavier while I'm barely breathing at all. 'Pull away,' cries my subconscious voice. 'Pull away while you can.' But I can't. I can't pull away from the muscular toned body of Ark Morgan. I'm mesmerised by him.

'You should stay away from me. I'm not the man you think I am,' he whispers into my ear.

'Who are you then?' I ask huskily, running my hand through his damp tousled hair.

My head is swimming.

'You're next,' he says.

'Next?' I repeat.

Holy crap, he really is going to initiate me. I bite my lip in anticipation and cry out in pain. 'Stop that lip biting,' scolds my inner goddess, 'or you'll have no bloody lips left. You've got more pain than this to come.'

I shiver with anticipation.

'Next,' echoes a voice. 'You want serving?'

What? Did he ask if I wanted spanking? I'm dragged from my *Fifty Shades* fantasy and come face to face with the shop assistant.

'Fifteen thirty-five,' grunts the purple-haired cashier, holding out a ringed hand that could be mistaken for a knuckleduster.

By the time she's pushed her gum into a rounded bubble through her over-painted pink lips I've dredged the depths of my little floral purse and realise I don't have enough. It occurs to me I could do a runner but who do you know does a runner from Aldi? I shouldn't have got the wine.

'Erm,' I begin, biding for time while I rummage through my bag for those odd coins that loiter at the bottom. 'I'm sure I had more. I'm really sorry.'

'Ain't you got enough money?' she says loudly, affronted, like I've done it on purpose just to annoy her.

'Ain't you sure you don't need a megaphone?' I mimic.

Don't you just hate it when shit happens? Maybe you don't. Perhaps shit doesn't happen to you. It happens all the time to me. I'm forever treading in the metaphorical shit in my well-worn twenty quid Matalan boots. Purple Head shakes her mop of hair and rolls her eyes in the direction of a Liz McDonald lookalike standing behind me. Lookalike's perfume is seriously clogging up my throat that I fear I may well have to guzzle the unpaid-for wine right here at the Aldi checkout. Lookalike groans and stares accusingly at my bulging carrier bag. I pull out a packet of custard creams and some sliced ham.

'I don't really need these,' I say with a smile. 'We've got loads at home.'

'Why you buy more then? That stupid, no?' says the Polish assistant at the next till, scanning items with such speed I feel sure I see sparks fly. I never get this abuse at Patel's corner shop.

'Doug,' yells Purple Head, 'she ain't got enough money. Can you put this stuff back?'

'Do you have to shout?' I say softly.

'Can you 'urry, I'm on me lunch break,' says lookalike, swinging her peroxide hair and showering me in a volcanic cloud of perfume.

'Can't she sodding pay?' yells someone from the queue.

I feel my face burn as everyone glowers at me. Honestly you'd think they'd keep such outrage for a shoplifter wouldn't you? I'm giving things back not bloody nicking them.

'Now look what you've done,' pouts the assistant.

'If you hadn't shouted,' I protest.

'Thirteen eighty,' she says her face devoid of emotion. 'Or do you want to give something else back that you're stockpiling?'

And have Doug make a second trip? I don't think so. I scrape together the thirteen eighty and grudgingly hand it over.

'Thanks for your patience,' I say sarcastically.

'You want patience you go to Waitrose,' says Purple Head.

'This Aldi, not 'arrods and you no Princess Diana,' quips the Polish assistant.

'And you no Aldi's queen of people's hearts,' I snap.

'What you say?'

I'm about to answer when I see through the windows two little buggers trying to remove the wheels from my Ford Fiesta. Honestly, the bloody thing barely moves as it is, and that's with wheels.

'Shit,' I grab the carrier bag and run from the store. 'Bugger off you little sods,' I shout, clouting one around the ear.

'Hey, that's abuse,' he spits, rubbing his head.

'Good,' I retort, giving him another one for good measure.

'You're bald anyway,' he says cheekily 'I 'ope you get done.'

'You cheeky bugger, I'm not bald at all.'

'Your tyres, you silly tart. You'll get done.'

'I'll do you if you don't push off.'

I sigh and watch them run off before checking my car. I'm Roxie Brown by the way, short for Roxanne. I'd like to say my name was inspired by the *Moulin Rouge* movie but it's not as romantic as that I'm afraid. My mum was obsessed with The Police. The eighties rock band that is, not the force. She was obsessed with Sting to be more precise. She still is actually. She spends more time talking about tantric sex than anyone I know. In fact, I don't know anyone else who talks about tantric sex. I only hope she doesn't spend as much time actually doing it. It doesn't bear thinking about, does it? Sting and Trudi whatserface doing it at their age is one thing, but your parents … Well, I don't like to dwell on it. It's a bit demoralising to think your parents are having longer sex sessions than you. Mind you, just about everyone must be having longer sex sessions than me and Darren. Tantric sex with Darren lasts about ten minutes and by our standards that's a mammoth session. It doesn't end with any real spiritual connection either, unless Darren mumbling 'alright Babe' counts, but I don't actually think it does. By then I'm usually out for the count. So if there was any Dalai Lama stuff going on I've most certainly missed it. Anyway, the only Tibet Darren knows is the Tibetan Palace curry house in town, so I doubt he even knows who the Dalai Lama is. He'd probably think it's a new dish on the menu. Not that we have it that often, sex that is, not curry. If Darren had his way we'd have that every night. Curry that is, not sex. Darren is more interested in looking through his telescope. He has a thing about stars, the ones in the sky that is, not those on the telly. He loves the galaxy he says, while I'm more interested in actually eating one, while in bed, reading my erotic novels and fantasising about my Christian Grey boss, Ark Morgan. Not that Ark Morgan would look twice at me. I'd be lucky if he looked once. Not that I'm unattractive or anything but multimillionaires just don't look at chambermaids do they? But there's no harm in a little fantasy is there, and if you saw him you'd understand. I've seen him in person only once and that was at the staff Christmas party. He didn't stay long but he was so close that if I'd reached out I could have touched his sensual thigh. My table was that near to the podium. He gave all the chambermaids *Viktor@Rolf Flowerbomb* perfume and a bottle of champagne. Not that I wear it much. Darren says it gives him a headache and I do get runny eyes when I wear it. But it was a fabulous gift, you have to agree. Ark Morgan is very generous to his staff. I imagine he thinks I've got sawdust for brains. People think that about cleaners. Not that I've always been a cleaner, mind you. I once worked in the pharmacy department of Boots as a dispensing assistant. I had all the qualifications and everything but the pay was rubbish and I got a bit punch drunk counting out pills all day long. At least my job has some variation now, although I can't say I like cleaning but the pay is brilliant.

I pull my vibrating phone from my bag.

'I've got carrots coming out of my ears,' says Mum.

'That's unusual. They normally come out of the ground.'

'Your dad's been at the allotment, digging up God knows what.'

'Well, as long as it wasn't bodies I really don't care,' I say, yanking the door of my Fiesta. It squeaks noisily and I cringe.

'I've packed a bag for you.'

'Am I going somewhere?' I ask, starting the engine, or at least trying to. It always needs at least three attempts.

'A bag of carrots and some of your dad's potatoes.'

'There was me hoping you'd say Majorca.'

'Your dad is really chuffed. Marge said she'd never seen one so big.'

'We're still talking about potatoes I hope?' I say.

'Well,' she says proudly, 'your dad has nothing to be ashamed of. Oh, that reminds me. I've got you a book, *Tantric for the Busy Woman*.'

'Tantric on the go is it?'

'Don't be silly dear, it's ...'

'I've got to get going,' I break in as I see a police car pull into the car park. Holy shit, that's all I need. Bald tyres, a noisy exhaust and a crack in the windscreen is not a car they're exactly going to miss. Honestly, my day can only get better can't it? I squint into the dazzling May sunlight and hope it's blinded them enough that they haven't spotted me. I try the engine again and thankfully it starts, and I edge the car slowly out of the car park only to have the damn thing stall. I curse and turn the key again when the police car flashes me. Shit. Why is this my life and on the other side of the world Angelina Jolie has hers? Why did I get Darren Smart and she got Brad Pitt? I mean, how is that fair? I undo the top button of my blouse and put on my vulnerable look.

'Everything okay officer?' I ask innocently, when it obviously isn't.

'Please step out of the vehicle madam,' says one of the policemen while the other snoops around my Fiesta.

Don't panic. That's the key. Don't give them any cause for suspicion.

I say policemen but police boys may be more appropriate from the look of them. Don't you just hate getting pulled up by policemen that are younger than you? I step nervously from the car and make a huge attempt to look confident. Not easy when you're struggling to remember if your insurance is up to date. Why can't I be more mindful?

'Can I see your driving licence please madam?'

I try to look nonchalant as the other one studies my tyres, while I rummage in my bag for my purse, only to find the damn licence isn't in there. I begin pulling things out of my overstuffed shoulder bag and arranging them onto the bonnet. The policeman's eyes widen at my well-thumbed copy of *Fifty Shades*. I blush profusely. It's not a crime to enjoy a bit of erotica is it? Erotic literature that is. Goodness, I've not got time for the real thing. Let's face it, if Darren and I haven't got time for tantric sex we've certainly not got time to tie each other to the bedposts and shag one another senseless have we, as lovely as it sounds. One half-eaten Galaxy follows the book. I'd forgotten all about that. It has bits of hair stuck to it now. Shopping receipts and an assortment of hairbands are followed by torn-out recipes from magazines, a hairbrush, make-up bag, a lipstick with the lid off, and several chocolate covered leaflets on tantric sex that Mum had given me yonks ago. I'm looking like a sex-mad chocoholic. I feel my heart hammer in my chest when I realise there is no sign of the licence and then I spot the tear in the lining, and there it is along with three pound coins. Where were they when I needed them for the custard creams? I've a good mind to go back and stick them under Purple Head's nose.

'Are you aware two of your tyres are bald?'

Not until that little sod mentioned it earlier. I wish Darren would keep a check on these things.

'Oh no,' I say dramatically and feel real tears well up. 'Is that bad?'

It's always good to feign innocence isn't it?

'When was it last serviced?'

I jerk my head up. God, for one minute I thought he was asking when I was last serviced. I must stop reading *Fifty Shades*.

'I'm not sure. My partner sees to those things.'

That's a joke. I'm lucky if Darren fills the thing with petrol.

'Looks like he hasn't seen to those things for a while,' says the policeman as he pokes the exhaust.

There are a lot of things Darren hasn't been seeing to if you want my opinion. The car isn't the only thing not getting a good service. I fight back a sigh. Please don't let them say I can't drive it. How will I get to my cleaning job? Come to that, how will Sylvie get to her cleaning job. Sylvie is my best friend by the way and she really is the best aside from saying *Jesus wept* a lot. I put that down to her Catholic School education. She's also addicted to crime; I don't mean crime like burglary or anything. That would be awful. While I'm into erotica Sylvie is into crime novels. She has visions of herself as another Detective Chief Inspector Jane Tennison. I only wish she'd used her expertise and spotted my bald tyres before the police.

'Make sure those tyres get replaced and that exhaust checked,' says one of the police boys, handing me my licence.

'Off you go.'

'Yes sir.'

Did I really call him sir? I came close to curtseying too. I give a little wave as I drive out of the store's car park and decide to stop at Patel's and buy a lottery ticket with the money I found in the torn lining.

Chapter Two

'Darren, he come in already and bought ticket, usual numbers,' says Mrs Patel.

Usual useless numbers she means. We've been doing those numbers every week for the past three years and we must be the only people I know who haven't even won a tenner.

'I thought I'd do an extra one,' I say.

She nods while arranging bags of Bombay Mix. I take the lottery slip over to the shelf in the corner and study the numbers. What am I doing? My chances of winning the lottery are 14 million to one. I've got a better chance of doing a house swap with Angelina Jolie. I stare at the ticket and curse that the numbers only go up to 49. How useless is that? My first number has to be 50 for *Fifty Shades*. I circle '49' and then '1'. I bite the end of the pen while choosing the other numbers. I suppose '3' should be another for the three pounds I found in the lining, after all, that was a stroke of luck wasn't it? If I hadn't found them I wouldn't be buying another ticket would I? Okay, Darren won't get his custard creams but that won't kill him. I circle '30' for today's date and then '4', the number of years I have worked for Ark Morgan as a chambermaid for his chain of hotels. You can't get luckier than working for Ark Morgan, not that I ever see him, at least not close up. I fight back the little stomach flutter I get every time I think of Ark Morgan. Finally, I hover over the number '2'. I'm not sure if having two bald tyres is lucky exactly, but the police did let me off so that has to be my last lucky number.

'Circle '6',' says Mrs Patel seeing me hovering. 'That's my lucky number.'

What a dilemma. I'm not sure the number 6 has ever been my lucky number but how can I not put it? Not now that she's asked me. I hate that I can't say no to people. I circle '6' and hand the ticket to Mrs Patel.

'You feeling lucky?' she asks.

'There's always a chance isn't there?' I smile.

I take the ticket, tuck it into my purse and drive to my parents' house. Mum opens the door and a hot blast of air hits me.

'Have you got the heating on?' I ask, feeling beads of perspiration form on my forehead.

'We've just got back from Morrisons,' she says, like that somehow explains it.

'It's a supermarket, not a morgue.'

'I'm checking the answering machine. We advertised for swingers. Isn't it exciting?'

Mum's wearing one of those velvet kimonos with enormous shoulder pads. If they were any bigger she'd look like the Hunchback of Notre Dame. I look at her. Did she really say what I think she said? Have they gone completely mad? My dad swinging, good God, it's too crazy to contemplate. I feel myself sway. It's like a sauna in their house. It's May for goodness' sake. No wonder all her plants die. The only thing that seems to survive is the cacti in the living room, and they get bigger by the week. I'll arrive one day to find their house looking like a remake of *Lawrence of Arabia.* I'm surprised the plastic covers on their three-piece suite haven't melted. I so wish she would take them off. There's nothing worse than sitting on plastic is there? It's the getting off that's the biggest problem. It's not normal to get stuck to a couch if you want my opinion.

I hope they didn't advertise in the *Clapham Chronicle*. This is dead embarrassing. What if they used their real names? My mum should have a degree in embarrassment. I still tremble at the memory of when I was a teenager and we lost our pet cat. Mum asked all my school friends if they had seen my pussy. I wanted to die.

'Shoes,' she barks.

Mum would have made Hitler a great wife. Even the cat is too afraid to shit in its own garden and goes to the neighbour's. I exhale and pull off my boots.

'You look tired,' she says.

'Well I do get up at five.'

'Ridiculous godforsaken hour,' she mumbles.

'At least I finish early.'

'Your cousin Helen is pregnant,' she says almost accusingly, like I had something to do with it.

'Oh,' I say.

'Everyone's having babies except you.'

Not everyone. That's a bit of an exaggeration isn't it? Jennifer Aniston isn't for one but I think better of saying that.

'There's plenty of time.'

'You're nearly thirty-two,' she says, as if I could forget.

'I'm not about to draw my pension.'

'It's getting late to have babies.'

'Lots of women have babies late in life these days,' I say.

'I hope you're not thinking of waiting until you're sixty-two like that woman in Algeria. It's a bit difficult spoiling your grandchildren when you're dead.'

I sigh and follow her into the kitchen and slump onto a stool as messages issue from their antiquated answering machine.

'Margo, it's Joan, you don't have a lemon squeezer do you? Geoff and I are trying something new for tonight.'

Lemon squeezer? Christ, what can they do with one of those?

'Only me Margo. Just to let you know Pam's husband has buggered off. We should all pop round later, cheer her up. What do you think? Call me.'

Mum's name is Margaret by the way. But she decided after watching re-runs of *The Good Life* that Margo suited her better.

'Hello, I'm responding to your advert for the garden swing. Is it still available?'

I stifle a giggle. Mum gives me a filthy look.

'Honestly, some people,' she huffs.

You have no more messages, announces the machine much to my relief.

'I'm making camomile tea, do you want some?' asks Mum, filling the kettle.

I nod, I think I need it.

'What do you mean *swingers*? This is Clapham. People don't swing in Clapham,' I say dismissively. 'This isn't Surrey you know.'

'You think we should advertise in Surrey?' says Mum brightly, popping teabags into the teapot.

'I don't think you should advertise at all. What's this?' I point to a bulky envelope on the kitchen table. It's addressed to me.

'Sting and Trudie swing.'

Frankly I could swing for Sting and Trudie for the trouble they cause me.

'Ah Roxie, how's it going? You haven't seen my sudoku book have you?' says Dad, strolling into the kitchen.

Do people who do sudoku swing – surely not?

'No,' I say, removing my cardigan and socks. It's hotter here than in the Bahamas.

'Martin, please empty the recycling and move your trough off the kitchen table,' snaps Mum.

I sigh.

'Don't you mean *trowel*?' I say.

Things are worse than I thought if Dad is drinking from a trough, unless that's part of their bondage games. I really must stop reading erotica if I'm starting to think my parents are at it. I did think about studying, English literature that is, not erotica. After all, thirty-one isn't too old to start studying is it? But Darren doesn't see the point in study.

'You've got a good job Babe, haven't you? What you going to do with knowledge, bloody dangerous if you ask me. Besides, I suppose we ought to get a baby at some point. You'll never have time then,' he'd said, making it sound like we'd just pop down to Aldi and buy one like you would buy a chicken. Talking of which ... I stare through my parents' kitchen window.

'What's that?'

'Hens of course. Sting and Trudi have them.'

Oh well, that's okay then isn't it? I only hope Trudie and Sting don't become cannibals. I'll be in fear of my life.

'Are you sure about that?'

She looks thoughtful.

'I read it in *Chat*. Besides, think of all the eggs we'll have.'

'Think of all the mess you'll have.'

'I am thinking of it,' says Dad, grimacing at the hen that is staring at us through the glass of the kitchen door.

'Roxie thinks we should advertise in *The Surry Advertiser*,' says Mum.

'I never said that,' I protest, fingering the envelope.

'Do they know a lot about chickens in Surrey?' asks Dad.

'Don't be stupid Martin, to advertise for swingers, of course.'

'Oh that,' he says dismissively. 'Personally I'd rather keep bees,' he adds, smiling at me. 'I never did like Glenn Miller.'

What has Glenn Miller got to do with it?

'I can't believe you're even considering it. You won't even know these people. How can you trust them?' I ask worriedly.

'I'm writing a list of questions. For example, *what is your favourite film?* If they say *Fatal Attraction* we'll avoid them like the plague, but there'll be lots of us. How can it not be safe?'

Lots of us. Holy crap, as Anastasia Steele would say, they're surely not thinking of an orgy?

'Why can't you copy someone safe, like Alan Titchmarsh for example?'

'Absolutely,' agrees Dad.

Mother scoffs.

'Do you see Alan Titchmarsh swinging?' she asks scathingly.

'He is in his sixties,' I say. 'And probably too busy doing normal things like gardening.'

'Well, we're far from sixty and I really don't understand why you're making such a fuss about us doing a bit of swinging. It will be fun. We need a hobby now your dad has taken early retirement.'

A hobby? Jesus, I've heard swinging called some things but never a hobby.

'It will be disgusting,' I say, pulling a face.

'I've got two left feet anyway. I'll be useless,' says Dad.

It's either too hot in here or they've spiked my tea. What has his feet got to do with anything? I really don't want to ask.

'You'll get the hang of it,' says Mum.

'I'm not sure I want to get the hang of it,' says Dad, handing me a box.

'Plenty of spuds in there, as well as carrots. If you want some broad beans I've got lots of them coming on.'

'If Dad hasn't got the hang of it by now he never will,' I say feeling myself redden.

'You have to practise, that's the thing, Martin.'

I splutter on my tea.

'Mum what do you think swinging is?'

'Dancing to big band music of course, what else?' she says, quickly spraying with Mr Muscle and mopping up my spilt tea.

Oh dear.

She points to the envelope.

'That's your book *Tantric for the Busy Woman*. I also bought you *Fifty Shades* number three.'

'Ooh,' I say excitedly. 'Thanks so much Mum. I'll hide them when I get home. Darren thinks I have too many books.'

'The little things that make you happy,' smiles Mum.

'You shouldn't need to hide anything,' says Dad scathingly. 'It's not like *you're* doing anything wrong.'

'Don't bring that up again Martin,' says Mum.

'I just don't see why he should dictate what you do when he was the one playing away from home and ...'

'We've put it behind us,' I say, pushing the package under the potatoes and carrots.

'All the same, you earn good money and if you want to spend it on books ...'

'We shouldn't get involved Martin,' says Mum.

All the same Dad is right. If I want to spend my money on books, why shouldn't I? I'm too easy-going that's my problem.

'Ah there it is,' says Dad gleefully, pulling his sudoku book from under the box.

I finish my tea and stand up. I can't leave without warning them can I?

'Mum, most people think of swinging as wife swapping. I don't think you should advertise anywhere else.'

Dad sighs.

'Good heavens,' cries Mum. 'Are you sure? But Sting ...'

'Might do all kinds of things but you don't have to do them too.'

'Ooh Martin,' she says worriedly.

Dad rolls his eyes.

'It'll be okay,' he says in a soothing tone. 'I'll sort it, don't you worry love,' he says patting me on the shoulder.

I kiss him on the cheek and make for the door. Mum hugs me.

'With your looks and figure you should have been a model. That Darren is holding you back if you ask me ...'

'I thought we weren't getting involved Margaret,' scolds Dad.

I kiss her on the cheek and lug the box to the car. They're not wrong about Darren but that's a partnership isn't it? You've got to make it work. With that thought in my mind, I climb into my Fiesta and head home.

Chapter Three

I balance the box of spuds on my arm, throw my bag over my shoulder and trudge up the ten flights of stairs to our one bedroom flat. There is a lift but having got stuck in it once with the neighbourhood's local pervert I now tend to avoid it. I assure you fifteen minutes of my panting is preferable to the five minutes of his. Before I've reached the second floor I can smell Liz Mitchell's cigarette smoke and her fragrance of eau de Deep Heat.

'I thought I heard you,' she says blowing smoke out of the corner of her red-painted lips.

Saw me more like, the nosy old biddy. No way did she hear me. I don't start panting until I get to the sixth floor. I swear to God she is stitched into that pink fluffy dressing gown of hers. I don't think I've ever seen her out of it.

'Hello Liz,' I say politely.

'What you got there?' she asks poking her nose into my box and dropping ash onto my spuds. I wrinkle my nose in disgust and turn to ascend the next flight.

'Poor Dot's rheumatism has flared up again. Blue her ankles are,' she says in her raspy voice while blowing more smoke my way. The hallway is becoming blue too. 'I thought I had troubles with my health but she's in a state poor love.'

'Oh dear,' I say, trying to sound as sympathetic as I can.

'What she needs is someone to come and do once a week,' she says looking at me pointedly.

The box feels heavier by the minute.

'I said Roxie is the ideal person. After all, you don't want strangers in your place do you? You can't trust cleaners can you? My mate had all sorts nicked by hers.'

I fight back a sigh.

'Of course I don't mean you. I know you wouldn't nick from anyone,' she says, while stubbing out her lipstick-tipped cigarette on the hall floor. 'When can you pop into her?'

Oh dear. This is all I need.

'The thing is I'm up to my eyes in work and I'm not sure I could fit her in,' I say, trying not to sound exasperated. I so hate cleaning. If the Morgan Group didn't pay so well, and Darren had more work, I would give it up tomorrow. If only the garage would give him more hours.

'I should be getting more work next month,' he said last night, but he says that every month. Still, he does go out every day looking for work so I can't really ask for more can I? Work is scarce these days isn't it?

'Not even for Dot? Her feet are that swollen I reckon she can't see her toes. That would worry me, wouldn't it worry you? They must weigh a ton.'

The weight of this box is worrying me more. I've still eight flights to go.

'I've got so much on with the hotels but I can ask around.'

'I think she'd prefer to have you. It'd only be an hour a week.'

'Well ...' I hesitate.

'She'd be so grateful.'

'I'll drop in on Monday after I finish.'

I'm too nice for my own good, that's my problem.

'Lovely,' she says, touching my shoulder. 'Ooh by the way, I saw him on the telly this afternoon, you know, that Ark Morgan of yours. Talking about his property empire, he was, and how it is expanding. I say, he's one good-looking chap. I tell you, I wouldn't kick him out of bed.'

I somehow think the chances of Ark Morgan ending up in Liz Mitchell's bed are pretty slim. My heart flutters at the thought. Not of him in Liz Mitchell's bed, obviously, but in mine. Ooh, I'm starting to pant already and I've not got to level three yet.

'It's not being repeated I suppose?' I ask breathlessly.

She lights another cigarette and says,

'Oh yes, it is. I had a look for you. I said to myself Roxie will want to see this. So I checked in my *Radio Times*. It's on again tonight at seven, called *Empire Magnets*. You can record it on that fancy telly Darren bought.'

The fancy telly that Darren got on the never-never, she means.

'Thanks so much Liz. I'd better go,' I say, 'this box is heavy.'

'Are you pregnant yet?' she asks.

Do I look pregnant? Why is everyone preoccupied with your fertility status once you get past thirty? It's not like your breasts shrink and your vagina closes up is it? You can still make a baby after thirty. I begin ascending the next flight.

'Not that I know of,' I say.

'Don't leave it much longer,' she advises.

I bet Jennifer Aniston doesn't get nagged about having babies.

'I don't know why you don't get the lift. You girls and your weight,' she says before slamming her flat door.

I plod up the next eight flights and slump outside our flat. I take a few minutes to catch my breath and finally let myself in. The sounds of Jerry Springer reach my ears followed by a screaming woman.

'I've got a job to maintain, a baby to take care of and I have to clean up after you, I'm tired all the time. Of course I don't want sex …' she screams in her Texan drawl.

God, she sounds like me but without the baby bit. I can't seem to escape babies today.

'Now you tell me you've been having sex with my best friend.'

Oh dear, she's sounding more like me by the minute. Maybe I should go on one of these shows. I wonder how much they pay. I glance at the large plasma screen and fight back a sigh. Is this why we're in debt? So Darren can watch this crap? The screeching of the smoke alarm makes me jump out of my skin and I drop the box onto the messy couch, crushing a bag of cheese and onion crisps.

'Shit and bollocks,' curses Darren. 'Is that you Babe?'

'No, it's Jennifer Aniston.'

'What did you say?' he shouts.

I walk into the kitchen and bash the smoke alarm with the broom. I wonder how often Jennifer Aniston has to do that when Justin Theroux makes toast. The screeching stops and I open a window to let out the smoke.

'The toaster's buggered,' he grumbles, reaching over to give me a kiss. 'I've had no lunch apart from a bag of crisps. You're late back for a Saturday.'

'I popped to my parents. Dad's potatoes have come up,' I say turning down the knob on the toaster.

'You always have it on too high Darren,' I say, dropping the shopping bag onto the table. 'I'll make some pasta. I bought some wine. Didn't Joey have any work for you today?'

I try not to show my disappointment. He rummages through the bag.

'Things are a bit slow.'

It seems things are always slow.

'Didn't you get the custard creams?'

Most men greet their wife with endearments. I get *didn't you get the custard creams*? Don't get me wrong, I love Darren. He is my partner after all. And although we're not married I have agreed to take him for better or worse. Admittedly it has been mostly for the worse, recently. Most days I'm okay and we're as happy as any couple could be, considering. It's just some days, like today for instance when Dad reminded me of the past and I come home to the bloody Jerry Springer debacle that I can't help remembering Darren's indiscretion with my friend. Well, obviously, ex-friend. I'm not that laid back to still have her as a friend. I might be stupid sometimes but I'm not that daft. The truth is I can't leave him. Where would I go? On my own, my salary wouldn't pay the rent on even a tiny flat, and there would be nothing left for food and bills. Darren does love me and no one has the perfect partner do they? Sylvie says I don't value myself enough and why should I settle for anything less than perfect.

'I didn't have enough money,' I say taking a bag of pasta from the cupboard.

He uncorks the wine.

'Well, I think that will be sorted later,' he says with a smile.

'You've got more work?' I say hopefully.

He pulls the cork out with a pop.

'Not work exactly. But when Joey and I bought our lottery tickets today he said he got a little tingle down his spine.'

That will be his liver. It must be on its last legs the amount he puts away every night.

'I did too,' Darren continues. 'I think we're going to win Babe. Just think. It's a big one tonight. We'll be off to Ibiza to party Babe, with all our mates until the money runs out.'

'Or we could invest some of it ...'

'Nah, we don't know nothing about investments Babe.'

'We could buy a house?' I say, dropping the pasta into the boiling water.

'Don't be daft. You can't take it with you, that's my motto.'

I'd never have known.

'You got trifle fingers,' he says accusingly, unpacking the carrier. 'You'll get fat if you keep eating those. I don't want people saying there's Darren's chubby girlfriend.'

'I'm not chubby, am I?' I ask. I confess I do eat a lot of trifle fingers. I dip them in Nutella spread. It's divine, especially when reading a bit of erotica.

'Your arse is getting bigger,' he says thoughtlessly. 'Shame it doesn't go onto your tits. You know how I love big ones.'

'Oh,' I say.

What else can you say when your loved one tells you you're getting fat. I'm not going to say thanks for the compliment am I?

'I got paid today. You want to go bowling tonight? Joey and May are going.'

'It's Halide's *last night of freedom* do, I did tell you. We're going to the Fun Palace. It came to the Common today; can you give me thirty pounds?' I say, removing empty lager cans from the bin and dropping them into the recycling bag.

'I wish you'd put things in the right bin,' I say tiredly, grabbing my cardigan from the back of a chair. I look around the kitchen and fight back the urge to nag. The last thing I need is to keep cleaning up behind Darren. What is it with men and tidying up? I scoop up the dirty dishes from the kitchen table and take them to the sink. I'm getting a dishwasher if we ever win the lottery. Of course I'd help eradicate hunger and poverty across the globe too. I imagine Ark Morgan does that every day. But a dishwasher would be my priority. I'm sick of cleaning hotel rooms and then coming home to clean mine. Flat that is, not hotel. I should be so rich.

'Honestly you girls are worse than us blokes. *Last night of freedom*? It's just an excuse for a girl's night out if you ask me. You only had the hen do a few weekends back.'

'It's not like I do it all the time,' I say, biting back the 'unlike you.' Kev's had numerous boys' nights out leading up to the wedding.

He lugs the box into the kitchen.

'Christ, are we going to live on chips for the next month, there's enough spuds here to feed an army. Your dad does realise there isn't going to be a potato famine doesn't he?'

'There are carrots too. Can you watch the pasta, I need to change,' I say, carefully sneaking the package out from under the spuds.

'Ark Morgan was on telly this afternoon,' I call, stepping out of my jeans and pulling off my top. 'A programme called *Empire Magnets.* Can you record it for me? It's being repeated at seven.'

I turn to the wardrobe almost bumping my head on the sodding telescope. I ask you, who has a telescope in a tower block? The bedroom door opens and Darren stares at me. I'm standing in my bra and knickers. His eyes widen.

'What do you want to watch that stuck up bugger for? Don't you get enough of him all week?'

Oh, if only. One cannot get enough of Ark Morgan.

'It will be interesting, I think.'

'Interesting my arse. I'm looking at something interesting,' he winks, handing me thirty quid. 'Is that enough to buy you?'

I guess it's what I'm worth.

'We'd best hurry,' I say.

What am I saying? We always hurry.

'I'm meeting the girls in an hour.'

'I don't need an hour,' he says huskily, pushing me onto the bed.

I find myself wondering how long Ark Morgan would take. I hear the pasta boil over. I bet that never happens to Jennifer Aniston.

Chapter Four

The Fun Palace is heaving. Music blares from a fairground organ and the smell of hot dogs and fried onions makes my stomach rumble. A little tremor of excitement runs through me. The Fun Palace comes to Clapham Common on the last weekend in May and Halide had decided there is no better place to celebrate her last night of 'freedom' than here. I'm wearing the one decent dress I own. I'd bought it from Zara four years ago when Darren took me for a romantic weekend in Brighton. The dress shows off my figure nicely. I am sure my cleaning job keeps me slim and I look okay, I think, that is apart from my bum if you believe Darren. I must ask Sylvie if my bum looks big in this dress. I don't get time for real exercise but I often imagine I could run my own fitness programme for busy housewives. I could call it *Suck and Tuck it with Roxie.* Ooh, that sounds a bit wrong doesn't it? I can see myself on the telly. Welcome to *Roxie's Hoover, the Fat Remover.* It's a plan, and it could get me out of cleaning work couldn't it?

I'd decided to wear my hair loose. My hair is a messy blonde bun when I'm at work so it's nice to have it free. I'd slapped on a bit of make-up, but it felt so weird that I'd scrubbed it off. I'm not really a make-up person. I've tried mascara to thicken my lashes but always end up with thickened eyelids and a bloodshot eye instead. Not quite the Charlize Theron look I'd hoped for unless it was her *Monster* look I was aiming at. Blusher is fine but after a few drinks I look like I have a bad case of Rosacea. I'm best keeping away from make-up I've decided, but looking at Halide's and Sylvie's nicely made-up faces I'm starting to regret it. But it's not like I'm out to pull is it? After five years together, Darren and I are as good as married after all.

'Isn't this fab?' says Halide, her eyes filling up.

'It's not how I would have spent the night before my wedding, but if this is what you want,' smiles Sylvie.

'We're going to have our tea leaves read,' she says gleefully, 'by The Great Zehilda.'

'Oh no, are you serious Hal?' I groan.

'It's her night,' Sylvie reminds me.

'It's a load of crap,' I say.

'No, she is really good,' Hal says, checking the time on her phone. 'Please, you've got to come. We've got an hour. She's known all the over the world.'

'Known all over the world,' I say cynically, 'for reading tea leaves? How come I've never heard of her?'

'The Great Zehilda from Italy, you must have heard of her.' She thrusts a flyer at me with a picture of a large busty woman with a scarf around her head. 'She has special cups. They're all handmade.'

Looking at those breasts I'm not surprised she has special cups. Bra cups that is, not tea cups. I shake my head.

'I've heard of her,' says Sylvie excitedly.

Buggered if I have, but then I have always got my head in an erotic book or my head in the clouds or my head and my body very close to Ark Morgan's. Just the thought makes me tremble.

'I've had to book us in, she is so popular. Nine o'clock was the only slot I could get. I'm so happy.'

God, she's emotional. It's only a night out for goodness' sake. Kev's a good catch and all that, but he's not Kevin Costner. Oh well, let's hope I have lucky tea leaves. We spend the next hour wandering around the stalls. We play the coconut shy which Sylvie does like a pro.

'Let's have a go at the rifle range,' squeals Hal rushing to grab a rifle.

She's pretty good too, which is worth bearing in mind if I ever need anyone knocking off. The guy beside her however is exceptionally good and doesn't miss a shot. We watch in awe as he wins cuddly toy after cuddly toy only to hand them back.

'He's a bit of a dish,' says Hal dreamily.

'Hey, you're getting married tomorrow,' Sylvie reprimands her.

'Even so, I know a dish when I see one,' she grins.

'You're a real gent,' laughs the stallholder, displaying the cuddly toys back on the shelves.

'I'm a man,' laughs the dish. 'You could at least have had some cans of beer for prizes.'

The only thing I manage is to hook a rubber duck, which says a lot about me. I could have taken a cuddly toy but our flat is so bloody cluttered already, that even a fluffy teddy isn't welcome. At nine o'clock we head to the world-renowned Italian tea leaf reader where a burly man stops us at the entrance to her tent. You'd think a world-renowned tea leaf psychic could afford better than this wouldn't you?

'Ave you booked?' he asks. 'No one gets in without booking.'

Hal shows our tickets and we squeeze into the tent. There is a strange smell, which I feel sure is a mix of sandalwood and cat pee. I fight the urge to gag. Everywhere is so dark and I accidently tread on Hal's foot. A curtain is pulled back and The Great Zehilda emerges, or should I say her breasts do, followed by her shawl-covered head.

'Who wishes to go first?' she asks in an eerie voice. If she meant who is going first in terms of leaving, my hand would have shot up. For a tea leaf reading this is getting pretty spooky. We look at each other and I say in a less eerie voice,

'She is,' and push Hal forward. After all, this was her idea, and it is her night. Sylvie and I sit in the tatty waiting area accompanied by an incense burner. Sylvie spends the time sneezing while I tap my feet in tune to the fairground organ. If there was a pair of roller skates handy I'd be tempted to do a Torvill and Dean party piece. Anything would be better than sitting here waiting for some stranger to hold my hand and tell me a whole load of rubbish. After what seems like an eternity Hal emerges looking somewhat dazed. At least I think she looks dazed. It's hard to see anything in the darkness. The Great Zehilda might have mugged her for all I know and she could still be reeling.

'You go,' I say pushing Sylvie in. If she comes out looking the same then I'm off.

'Well?' I ask Hal.

'Unbelievable,' she says in an awe-stricken voice. 'The leaves showed the ace of hearts. That's a sign for happiness.

She knew I was getting married and everything and she saw babies ...' She dabs her eyes.

'Uncanny,' I say. 'You didn't happen to mention it was your wedding this weekend when you booked by any chance?'

'You're so scathing,' she says irritably. 'Don't you want to know the future? After all, let's face it we could all do with a bit of luck.'

Well, I can't disagree with that.

'If she mentions tantric sex, then I'll know she's good.'

Her eyes widen.

'Are you and Darren into ...?' she begins.

'And when do you think I'd fit tantric sex into my schedule Hal? Don't you think I'm run ragged as it is? I don't even know how to do the half lotus, let alone a full one. So I think tantric sex might be a bit of a challenge and an even bigger challenge for Darren, who let's face it, only knows the couch potato position.'

If her eyes widen any more I'm sure they'll pop out.

'You're more enlightened than me. I don't even know the lotus position,' she says innocently.

'Mum gave me a book today, *Tantric for the Busy Woman,* so if this gypsy is good she should pick up on that.'

'Why would your mum give you a book on tantric sex?'

I'm beginning to wish I hadn't started this.

'Maybe Kev and I should try some tantric sex. What do you think?'

I think they'd have to give up their jobs. It's okay when you're a rock star but a garage mechanic and a Debenhams store assistant? I'm sure you know what I mean. I'm not saying normal people can't do tantric sex but if it takes that long, how can you do anything else? After all, you can't do everything can you?

Fortunately I'm not able to reply as Sylvie rolls out and looks just as shell-shocked as Hal had.

'She's good Roxie. Go on, get yours done.'

I'm shoved into the room where I fall into a chair and find myself staring into The Great Zehilda's eyes. She pushes a china cup and saucer towards me and slowly pours tea into it from a cracked white teapot.

'This ze best China tea, drink up, dearie,' she says. 'Make sure you leave about half a teaspoonful.'

I'd much prefer to leave half a cup full. It looks and tastes like cat's piss. Come to think of it, it probably is cat's piss. That explains where the smell is coming from. I wonder who last drank from the cup. I just hope I don't catch something. I down the stuff and push the cup towards her. She turns it from left to right and then very slowly, and carefully, turns it over and settles it onto the saucer. It's a good act, I'll give her that. She looks up at me, her eyes boring into mine.

'Now ve vait,'

Is that a northern twang in her voice that I hear? I fight the urge to giggle. I wonder if I should remind her she's supposed to be Italian. At the moment she's sounding more like a German.

'Focus your mind on your destiny,' she says in that eerie voice.

She lifts the cup and stares into it.

'Ah,' she says suddenly, making me jump. 'I see ze sitting hen in the bottom of the cup ...'

Well, that's my bloody mum isn't it? Crikey, she's not going to see the tantric sex next is she?

'This means wealth from an unexpected legacy.'

All that from a hen? She is bloody good.

'Oh dear,' she adds, giving me a pitying look. 'You have the sausage and the snail. I foresee a marring of your pleasant conditions.'

What *pleasant conditions* would they be? She isn't talking about our flat that's for sure.

'Your life will change dramatically. But I see a lot of confusion in the leaves.'

I see a lot of confusion right here.

'You're not sure where you're going are you my dear?'

Well I think it's probably The King's Head after this, but I know what she means.

'But wait ...' she gasps.

I pretend to hold my breath. I might as well play along I suppose.

'I see wealth but also danger. You know something. You will know something. You've seen something haven't you? Or you will see something.'

I wish she'd make up her mind. Her Italian accent has dropped completely now.

'I've seen lots of things,' I say. 'I also know a lot of things. Nothing worthwhile, mind you, but I know them.'

Her eyes roll into the back of her head. God, she's not going into a trance is she? That's all I need. I don't fancy giving The Great Zehilda CPR.

'You will see much. *Too much,*' she says dramatically. 'I see things coming closer.'

Frankly so do I. Those breasts of hers are looming closer. Too close for my liking. I wish she'd stop leaning towards me.

'The number six is showing. This is important to you. Much will change for you tonight.'

I fight back a gasp. That's Mrs Patel's lucky number, the one I put on my lottery ticket.

'Things are not what they seem. Remember that,' she says eerily, lifting her eyebrows.

Something soft rubs against my leg and I jump up knocking over the tea cup. The Great Zehilda snaps her eyes open.

'Session is over,' she states flatly.

Thank God for that.

'Wait ...' she says ominously looking at the spilt tea leaves. She's got her money's worth; can't she just let me go? 'Love is coming your way from an unexpected quarter. That's all I have to say.'

'But I'm already ...' I begin.

'Session over,' she snaps.

I leave the room looking as shell-shocked as the others.

'My God,' gasps Sylvie. 'What happened? It sounded terrible. Did she go into a trance? That's fantastic isn't it Hal? We told you she was good.'

'What did she tell you?' asks Hal breathlessly.

'Wealth and danger, you know the usual stuff. Her cat scared the shit out of me, that's what you heard. Can we go now?'

'Come on, let's go into the Fun Palace,' says Hal, grabbing me by the arm.

'It's exciting though isn't it?' says Sylvie. 'She told me I would meet my soulmate in the next month.'

'And that I'd have a baby within the year,' says Hal.

I could have told them that. Sylvie has a different bloke every month and each time she is convinced she's found her soulmate, and Hal has made it clear that she and Kev won't wait long before starting a family.

'Amazing,' I say cynically.

'And that a friend would be giving me the one thing I've always wanted. Although I can't think what that is,' says Sylvie, thoughtfully.

'Sounds like you're going to be getting some,' laughs Hal, leading us past the candyfloss stand.

We weave through the stalls until we're standing in front of the main circus tent. Bright lights illuminate the front and the words flash at us.

'Let's do it. If we lose each other, we'll meet at the entrance in an hour and go to the pub,' says Sylvie.

We step into the tent to the deafening music from the fairground organ. Before I know what is happening I am shoved through a black curtain and am surrounded by images of myself from all angles. At least I can see for myself if my bum looks big.

'Welcome to the House of Mirrors,' says a ghoulish voice.

I jump and go to grip a handrail to steady myself but find myself grabbing an arm instead.

'Sorry,' I say without looking. 'That voice scared the shit out of me.'

'No problem,' replies a very well-spoken man, a warm musky fragrance emanating from him.

I move along the mirrors and stare horrified. I look huge.

'My God,' I whisper.

'The next room is better,' says the voice.

I see his image in the mirrors. He is huge like me, but despite this there is something about him that is very sexy. He looks like a huge Ark Morgan and there's not just one Ark Morgan there must be at least ten of them reflected back at me. I must have died and gone to heaven. He looks shorter close up but that is probably the effect of the mirrors. He smiles and inclines his head. I watch him move to the next room and I follow.

'Things are not what they seem,' laughs the ghoulish voice,

Oh my God, didn't The Great Zehilda say that? I close my eyes and open them expecting him to have vanished but he is still here. The room is full of images of Ark Morgan and me. I turn to face one, he is slimmer and smaller, but so are my reflections too, but he is more gorgeous than even in my fantasies, if that can be at all possible. He is painfully handsome, dazzling, in fact, a real-life Christian Grey. His warm eyes meet mine through a mirror. Does he recognise me? What am I thinking, of course he doesn't? I've never been this close to Ark Morgan.

'We're looking better aren't we?' he says with a smile.

You certainly are. I swear my ovaries are ovulating at nine to the dozen. If ever there was a perfect daddy specimen, he surely has to be it. I can't speak. He must think I'm a dumb mute. I hope he hasn't noticed my chubby backside.

'Shall we get wider?' he asks, moving to the next room.

I spy some dark hairs just above the top button of his shirt. My loins are having a party, my inner goddess is whispering 'ice cube' and my breasts are tingling like no tomorrow. I'll orgasm right here, right now, in front of all these mirrors. Incredibly hot and sexy but not advised. I'm blushing so much I feel sure I'm going to spontaneously combust. He is about to speak when two men enter and the ghoulish voice repeats,

'Welcome to the House of Mirrors.'

'The car is here Mr Morgan,' says one.

Oh my God. It really is him, and all I've done is drool like a lovesick dog. I'm surprised I'm not panting like a bitch on heat. This is ridiculous. Anastasia Steele has nothing on me.

'Already?' he questions. 'What's the time?'

'It's ten fifteen sir. Your plane is ready to leave.'

'Right,' he says.

I spin around to get one last look at him. He gives me a smile and my legs tremble. His warm hazel eyes look at me for a second and then he runs his hands through his gorgeous thick brown hair before saying,

'Have a good evening,' and then is gone. I'm left staring at a wide vision of myself.

'Welcome to the House of Mirrors,' says the voice as more people enter. I move along to the next room which is full of fragmented images of me. This room must know how I'm feeling. I can't believe it. It just doesn't seem possible. What were the chances of me meeting Ark Morgan? I freeze as Great

Zehilda's words come back to me; *Love is coming your way from an unexpected quarter.*

Well, you can't get more unexpected than the House of Mirrors can you? Ark Morgan is my true love? Well I'll be buggered. Well, if he's anything like Christian Grey I may well be.

Chapter Five

'Oh, please, I beg you ...'

God, he's driving me insane.

'How lovely is this?' he whispers.

It would be sweet agonising pleasure, if it wasn't so torturous. I feel like my nipples have frostbite. Can that happen? Can you get frostbite in your nipples from too much ice cubing?

'Do you want to come Miss Brown?' he whispers.

His fingers are trailing dangerously close and I arch my body upwards. I'm panting so loudly. Nothing else matters except his commanding voice. Although I can't deny my feet are getting pins and needles from the leg clamps but I don't want to complain. I daren't complain.

'Shall I take you?'

'Oh please ...' I beg, staring back into his warm sensual eyes.

I'll have frostbite for sure, not to mention deep vein thrombosis if he doesn't soon.

'How many times do I have to warn you about that?'

Did I bite my lip?

'I'm sorry, Ark,' I say, panting even harder.

I'm suddenly thrown off the bed and fall with a thump to the floor.

'That was out of order,' he yells, but his voice is deeper. 'How many times have I warned you?'

I'm brought out of my fantasy to find myself on the ground with the guy from the rifle range standing over me, except now he's half naked.

'Is the lady all right?' someone yells. 'How the hell did she get there?'

I look around to see where *there* actually is and realise I'm lying on the ground at the edge of a boxing ring. A strong hand lifts me to my feet.

'Hey, I'm really sorry about that,' he says. 'You shouldn't really be here, you know?'

He has a half-smile on his face and a small cut on his lip. I gaze at his bare-chested torso and quickly lower my eyes to his blue shorts and then look up again to where the shouting is coming from. A man looks at us from a platform where a crowd of people surrounding it are staring at me curiously.

'Let's go, round six, or I'm stopping the fight,' yells the man.

I stare flabbergasted. Six? Oh this is ridiculous. I'm letting this psychic thing get to me. But The Great Zehilda did mention the number six didn't she?

'Are you okay? I'd really like to get back. I think I'm winning this one,' asks the dish, with a wink.

I realise now that in my dazed state I must have wandered from the House of Mirrors through the cordon and back out into the Fun Palace. I got knocked over when the boxer got thrown from the ring. I can't blame him I suppose. I really shouldn't be here, but he does seem rather arrogant if he thinks he's winning, especially considering he just got knocked out of the ring.

'Do you think you should?' I ask. 'It looks a bit dangerous.'

'It's just fun. I've fought worse than him. I've got twenty quid on this. Hey, you can be my lucky mascot. Come on, let's get you to a safe place to watch the fight.' He grabs my hand and pulls me to the crowded ringside. 'I'm Sam Lockwood,' he says, shaking my hand, 'very pleased to meet you.'

'I really don't think ...' I begin, while discreetly wiping the sweat off my hand.

'I only need a few minutes,' he says, giving me a broad smile.

'Well ...'

'Great.'

Before I can say another word he has jumped back into the ring. Oh God, I can't watch this. He turns to give me a wave and is punched on the chin to the groans of the crowd. I wince. Some lucky mascot I am. The crowd roar as Sam Lockwood throws a punch and his opponent staggers. Sam gives me the thumbs up before taking a punch to the jaw. The guy is mad. I find myself willing him to win and join in with the shouting crowd.

'What's going on?' yells Hal as she pushes through the throng. 'We wondered what happened to you.'

'That dark-haired one is a bit of alright,' says Sylvie. 'Have you put on a bet?'

'I'm his lucky mascot,' I say proudly. 'His name's Sam.'

'Blimey, can't leave you alone for five minutes can we?' laughs Hal.

'It's not like that,' I say.

'Isn't he the guy from the rifle range?' asks Sylvie.

'Ouch,' says Hal.

I look up to see Sam being cornered and the other boxer throwing punch after punch.

'Oh dear,' I say, 'so much for being his lucky mascot'.

'Knock him out,' shouts a man beside us.

'Come on Sam,' screams Sylvie. 'Jesus wept, he's taking a bit of a pounding isn't he?'

He smiles at us and ducks under the other man's arm. I can barely look. As his lucky mascot I feel sort of responsible.

There's a roar as the bell goes and Sam gives me a cheeky grin as they total up the points.

'He fancies you,' says Hal.

'Don't be mental,' says Sylvie. 'She's in a relationship.'

'Yes,' I agree.

There are shouts from the crowd as they wait for the result.

'Winner on points is ...' barks the referee as the crowd hold their breath. 'Joe Cooper: 180, Sam Lockwood: 200.'

The crowd roar and I am lifted in the air and spun around, feeling Sam's sweaty torso through my Zara dress and then his warm lips on mine. My body tingles from the top of my head to the tips of my toes. It's like someone has cast a spell on me. I've heard the saying *the earth moved* but my God, it really feels like it does when Sam Lockwood kisses me. He pulls back and looks into my eyes. He looks as shaken as me.

'Wow,' he says, taking a step back.

I know exactly what he means.

'Ooh,' I hear Hal and Sylvie chorus.

'You do know she's already taken?' says Sylvie. 'She's got a bloke.'

I look at him dumbly.

'I said you were my lucky mascot,' he grins, wiping at a cut above his eyebrow.

'You were very good,' says Sylvie, fluttering her eyelashes.

'Thanks,' he smiles, catching a jacket someone throws at him.

'He's a bit posh isn't he?' whispers Hal.

'You're not from round here are you?' says Sylvie attempting a posh voice but sounding like she's had a minor stroke.

'Chelsea,' he grins, 'not miles away.'

Miles apart from us lot though. My mind wanders to Ark Morgan and I fight the flutter in my stomach. If the psychic is right, then Ark Morgan could be my true love. But I'm with Darren so how's that going to work? Stupid psychics, what do they know?

'I'm Sylvie, and this is Hal. It's her last night as a single woman, and this is Roxie.'

'Roxie,' says Sam, raising his eyebrows. 'Let's take a selfie, me and my lucky mascot.'

He pulls an iPhone from his jacket pocket.

'Well, I really don't ...' I begin.

He throws his arm around me and pulls me close towards him. I force a smile and try to ignore the warmth of his body pressing against me.

'So where is this chap of yours?' he asks, releasing me.

Good question.

'He was going bowling with our friends and then I expect he'll watch the Gunners on the pub telly.'

'The Gunners?' he asks, looking puzzled.

'The Gunners, you know, Arsenal football team? He's a big supporter.'

He nods.

'I don't know much about football I'm afraid. I'm a rugby man myself.'

Sylvie tucks her arm into mine.

'We should get going. It was nice meeting you, wasn't it Roxie?' she says, nudging me.

'See you Roxie,' he calls.

'Ooh a rugby man,' says Sylvie. 'I bet he's good in bed.'

'Roxie's into tantric sex, so he'll suit her,' laughs Hal.

'I'm not into it. My mum just gives me books,' I say hotly.

'Your mum?' says Sylvie aghast.

Ever wished you'd never started something?

'He's too posh anyway,' I say.

'To the pub,' Hal declares. 'Lisa and Martine will be waiting. Let's get this show on the road.'

Chapter Six

The pub is crowded, hot and noisy. Don't you just hate pubs on a Saturday night? Martine is waving at us and I cringe when I see Lisa sitting beside her, sipping her drink through a penis-shaped straw. What is it about girlie nights, weddings and penises?

'You go over,' says Sylvie, giving Hal a shove. 'Roxie and I will get the drinks.'

We push our way through the throng to the bar and I feel perspiration run between my breasts.

'All right girls, ready for your do are you?' asks the barman.

'Yep, it's all going well,' smiles Sylvie. 'Can we have two bottles of Prosecco, two Malibu and Coke and three Smirnoff Ice Raspberry Twist flavour, and a bottle of lemonade? Hal's not drinking. She says she doesn't want a hangover tomorrow.'

I can't see Hal lasting a whole night on lemonade.

'What time is the fun beginning?' he sighs. 'Those bleeding smoke machines set the alarms off.'

I feel my stomach churn.

'Sylv, you haven't?' I groan.

'Of course. It wouldn't be the same without a stripper would it? Besides, I meant to do it for the hen weekend but I couldn't get him booked.'

'Well, that's put me off my nachos,' I say, taking the food menu and a tray of drinks, and reluctantly heading to our table. There's nothing worse than seeing some bloke parading his meat and two veg is there?

'Look what we've got,' screams Lisa, holding up bunny ears and nearly perforating one of mine. She sticks a penis straw into my drink before I can stop her. Hal is now wearing an 'L' plate sash, a bunny tail and her bunny ears. It looks like we're escapees from Watership Down. If Ark Morgan walks in now I'd have to dive under the table, or should I say hop. Sylvie pops open the Prosecco and I down a glass before donning my bunny ears. We've downed two more drinks, ordered our food when the music stops and *Satisfaction* blares at full volume, along with so much smoke that it's impossible to see the bar. A fireman rushes into the pub. For a second I wonder if he is the real thing but then he pulls a giggling Hal into the middle of the room and plonks his helmet on her head, and thrusts his Russell Love Muscle in her face ... Well, if she will get married. I'm never getting married. I don't want some dipstick gyrating his rope and tackle in front of me thank you very much. I suppose I should be grateful. Hal could have organised a spa weekend. I don't do sitting around in dressing gowns reading about celebs all day any more than I do strippers. I sip my Malibu and Coke through my penis straw in an attempt to feel pleasantly faraway and unreal. By the time the fireman is down to his underpants, the smoke has cleared and we can see everything. He isn't in great shape I have to say. We all have to pose in our bunny ears and hold up our penis straws for Lisa to snap with her phone. I suppose the pics will be on Facebook before we've even left the pub. I must remember to unfriend my mum before she gets a chance to see them.

'This is why you end up with men like Darren,' she'll say.

I suppose she's not far wrong. Lisa screams into my other ear as the fireman lifts Hal onto a bar stall and looks about to mount her. All we can see is his thrusting wobbly bottom. It's gross. Hal looks decidedly uncomfortable and I find myself wishing the smoke alarm would go off. Then it's over. The fireman offers to dance with any one of us lovely ladies. After an uncomfortable silence he clambers back into his plastic fireman's uniform, accepts his payment from Sylvie and leaves.

I lean across the table to grab a handful of peanuts when my eye catches the plasma TV screen where a small crowd have gathered to watch the lottery draw. I lean forward as the first ball rolls down. It tumbles out and to my utter amazement number '4' pops up. Number '4' was for the number of years I've worked for Ark Morgan. I've never ever had a lottery number come up. I can't believe it.

'Oh my God,' I whisper, as number '3' rolls out. That's '3' for the three pounds. My hands go clammy and I struggle to swallow.

'You okay Rox?' asks Sylvie. 'You've gone a funny colour.'

Okay, it's only two numbers. It's not like I've won the jackpot is it? But still, two numbers in a row, what are the statistics for that happening? I grab the table to stop myself sliding to the floor when '1' rolls out. My head spins, and my throat is so dry that I down half a glass of Prosecco. I must have won a tenner at least.

'You must be thirsty,' says Hal. 'Our food should be here soon.'

Their voices seem distant. I picture The Great Zehilda with her ample bosom saying *I see wealth* as number '49' pops out, that's my lucky *Fifty Shades* number. I can't breathe. That's about right isn't it? I'll win the lottery, die from shock and Darren will blow the lot.

'Here's your nachos,' says Sylvie, plonking a plate in front of me.

I nod and throw back the rest of the Prosecco. I only need two more numbers to win the sodding jackpot. I'm in a trance as the number '30' rolls out and although I hear Sylvie and Hal speaking it's like they are a million miles away. I don't believe it. I've got five numbers. Everything seems to move in slow motion as the next ball tumbles down. It moves painfully slowly and it's all I can do to breathe. All I can hear is my heart beating against my chest. The ball continues its slow descent and then there it is number '2'. I don't believe it. That was my lucky two bald tyres. Why did I listen to Mrs Patel? Why was I persuaded to put her stupid number six down? If I'd kept to number '2', I would have won the bloody jackpot. Why can't I say no? I'm about to turn to my nachos when I see the bonus ball land. I stare at it, numb with shock. Number '6', holy shit. I feel a tingle down my spine and I assure you it has nothing to do with my liver. I've got five numbers with the bonus ball. I've only gone and won the bloody lottery.

Chapter Seven

The rest of Hal's party went by in a blur. I couldn't stop thinking about those lottery balls. I arrive home to be greeted by Darren's snoring. I close the door softly, remove my shoes and tiptoe in stockinged feet to the bathroom. I step over Darren's towel which is strewn across the floor along with his socks and pants and sit fully dressed on the toilet seat. My head spins from the alcohol and my stomach churns uncomfortably from a kebab we had on the way home. I drop my head to my knees and wait for the nausea that washes over me to pass. I can't believe I won the lottery and I most certainly can't believe I saw Ark Morgan in the House of Mirrors. It's all too ridiculous. I pull my phone from my bag and see it is 3 a.m. I peel off my dress and tiptoe to the bedroom where Darren is still snoring loudly. He's obviously had a skinful too. What's new? Darren has a skinful every Saturday night. At least I only spend on special occasions. No wonder we don't have any money. Then again, if I have won the lottery ... I slide beneath the sheets and close my eyes. How do I tell Darren? More to the point do I tell Darren? His words echo in my head,

'We'll be off to Ibiza to party Babe with all our mates until the money runs out.'

That's Darren all right. Money burns a hole in his pocket. He just has to spend it. He doesn't know the meaning of *saving money*. It might as well be a foreign language to him. He blew his Christmas bonus on the latest iPhone. I wouldn't mind but he still hasn't worked out how to use the damn thing. Thankfully I'd already bought the Christmas presents. The whole holiday we lived off Mum's turkey leftovers and bread and cheese. If I tell Darren we've won the lottery he will blow the whole lot in a matter of months. But he is my partner, so I really should tell him. I lie and watch the room spin. I can't believe what happened tonight. It was unreal. First bumping into Ark Morgan in the House of Mirrors and then winning the lottery, it all seems too good to be true. I'm still gutted I didn't win the jackpot though and swear I will never be able to look at a packet of Bombay Mix again without remembering how I was almost a millionairess. Nevertheless, I must have won a lot. I didn't say anything to the others, partly because I really can't believe I've won. Anyway, it was Hal's night and I didn't want to steal her thunder. I close my eyes and try to sleep but my head is spinning so much it is almost impossible. I remember the programme *Empire Magnets* and creep out of bed. I settle myself on the couch and scan the recorded programmes. It's there. I feel my heart beat just a little faster. I click into it and there is Ark Morgan looking painfully handsome: it hurts to look at him. I lean forward, so I can drool and suddenly find myself looking at the bloody Arsenal instead. What the ...? I swear Darren's days are numbered. How could he bugger up a simple thing like a recording? What's the point of this fancy telly that we can't even afford, if I can't watch one hour of Ark Morgan? It's all I can do not to burst into tears. I angrily switch it off but not before deleting the Arsenal match. I sneak back into bed and turn onto my side but Darren's snoring seems to shake the bed. I turn over again and am just beginning to feel drowsy when Darren's phone bleeps. I snap my eyes open. It's no good, I can't sleep. I slide from the bed and sway to the loo, managing to stub my toe on the bloody telescope in the process. I swear I'll chuck this thing through the window one day. It's not like he's bloody Patrick Moore is it? Darren groans, turns over and continues snoring. I bet he doesn't know one planet from the other. The phone bleeps again and I curse. I fumble with the buttons to turn it off but find myself staring at the two text messages.

'Are you up? I thought I saw your light go on.'

This must be for someone else. I blink to see the name of the sender. Angie. Who the hell is Angie? More importantly, what is she doing texting my boyfriend at three in the morning? Even more importantly why has my boyfriend got an Angie in his phone contacts?

I rest my hand on the stupid telescope and push my eye against it expecting to see Pluto or Mars, or something astrological that Darren's been gazing at, but instead my eyes feast on a big-busted redhead doing a slow striptease, and a bad one at that. Not quite the astrological vision I was expecting. Her eyes seem to lock onto mine and she winks seductively. I'm so shit-faced that it takes me a while to realise what's going on. The two-timing shagging bastard. He's at it again. I grab his phone and tap a return text.

'Miss you,' I type.

The response is immediate.

'Miss you too. Even though it's only been a couple of hours since I saw you. I can't sleep. I've been cuddled up with one of your shits.'

God, there's an image. I really hope she means *shirts*. I can't believe it. How long has the sod been two-timing me, again? Tears prick my eyes as I watch her drop her sexy nightie. I swing the telescope away from her block angrily and find myself focused on another flat where two men seem to be having an argument. I try to focus the telescope better and then realise the blurriness is caused by my tears. Damn Darren. What the hell is wrong with him? Or more to the point what is wrong with me that he has to keep shagging around? One of the men is pacing up and down and waving his arms angrily, shaking a piece of paper he holds in one of them. I try to zoom in on his face but he's moving around too much. The other has his back to the window. He's wearing a dark jacket and a black, red and white striped scarf. This is ridiculous. I should be confronting Darren, not watching two strangers having an argument. I'm about to turn away when, oh my God, the man waving the paper throws himself at the man with the scarf and now has his hands around his throat. This is no lovers' tiff. I can hardly bear to look. I stare horrified as the one with his back to the window breaks free and pulls something from his coat pocket. Jesus Christ, it's a gun, and I'm not talking water pistol. I grip the telescope to keep myself upright. The other man sinks to his knees. He's pointing at something but I can't see what it is. There is a flash from the gun and I jump out of my skin. You'd think he'd shot me.

'Oh God,' I groan.

'What are you doing Babe?' mumbles Darren, scaring the life out of me. I spin around taking the telescope with me and almost concussing myself.

'Someone's got shot, in the flats over there ...'

I am interrupted by his snoring. He has fallen back to sleep. I grab the telescope and try to find the flat again. Where the hell is it? Did I imagine it? I can't even find stripping Angie. Did I imagine her too? But then I see him, the man with the gun. He's standing by a painting of a Buddha. My heart races as I watch him look around, the gun still in his hand. Oh sod a dog, he's only gone and killed the guy. I try to focus in on his face but my hands are shaking so much that I turn the thing out of focus instead. I finally get it back and then everything is too close. Damn it. I'm looking straight into someone's eyes, blurry eyes admittedly, but eyes all the same. Oh shit. I let out a little scream but Darren continues to snore. My heart thumps in my chest. Did he see me? I wait a few seconds and hesitantly peek through it again. There is no sign of the man now. Oh Jesus, is he coming after me? I lift my head cautiously from the telescope and look over at the block and recognise it as Somerville Place. It's impossible to see anything from this distance, but all the same, you probably can't miss the window with the sodding telescope in it can you? That Buddha isn't giving out much karma is it? I should phone the police, but then again, what do I tell them? Perhaps I shouldn't get involved. The last thing I want is the police around here, what if they spot my tyres again? And after all, the neighbouring flats are sure to report the gunshot, and I don't know the exact address. I'll get done for wasting police time knowing my luck. To top it all, I'm half pissed, who's going to believe me? And what if I report it and the murderer comes after me? He could be a drug baron, or a Mafia Godfather. I'll be hunted down as a witness. I'll probably end up on a witness protection programme and will never see Darren again. I'll be given a false name and a new life. Actually, that doesn't sound all bad does it? I don't know what to do, I've had far too much to drink and I really can't think clearly. I rush to check the door is locked. I'm being ridiculous. There is no way he'll be able to work out where our apartment is. I need to talk to Sylvie. After all, she's the expert on murder and all things criminal. Darren turns over in the bed. Tears prick my eyelids and run down my cheeks. How could he do this to me again? Once was painful enough but to do it twice. He's lucky I don't have a gun or there'd be two murders tonight. I creep back to bed and count the minutes to morning while re-running the murder scene in my head and keeping one ear cocked in case someone tries to break in.

Chapter Eight

I'm still in a state of shock the following morning. I wake early and the memory of Darren's infidelity hits me like a hammer. Although of course, the hammering in my head could have more to do with my hangover. How could he? I feel as though my whole life has disintegrated in a matter of hours.

I lift the knocker of Sylvie's little rented terrace. Don't tell me she's still in bed. Mind you, it is only eight o'clock on a Sunday morning. I'd also left two-timing Darren snoring in bed. I didn't sleep a wink and when I did I just dreamt of Angie's tits and the murder. Over and over again and trust me no one should have to see Angie's tits over and over again.

'Sylvie, it's me Roxie. Open the door.'

Not even a curtain twitches. Well, that's not strictly true. They do, it's just not Sylvie's. This is all I need. The morning after the night before is usually bad enough. But the morning after the night before where you witnessed a murder and your boyfriend's mistress stripping is ten times worse. My head thumps unmercifully.

'Sylvie, please open the door, I need to talk to you,' I call, hitting the knocker and hammering on the door.

'Where's the fire?' calls a man from an upstairs window of the house next door. 'It's Sunday morning. Ever heard of a lie in?'

What I wouldn't do for one of those.

'Sorry, I'm just trying to wake someone.'

'And you've succeeded,' he snaps, slamming the window closed.

I tap on the door again.

'Sylvie, please open up.'

The door swings open and I come face to face with Sylvie's flatmate, Felix.

'Darling,' he says calmly, 'from Monday to Friday my body is a temple. From Saturday to Sunday, a ruin, so why are you making it worse?'

'You do look a bit rough,' I say.

'And you look like death sweetie, is it Versace? I must say the look suits you.'

Gay men, they can be so cutting can't they?

'Is Sylvie here? I really need to talk to her about something. We were out for Hal's do last night and when I got home there ...'

Felix holds his hand up.

'You don't have to give me *War and Peace* love, a novella will do. She's still asleep, or at least was. We all were until you came hammering on the door like the bloody drug squad.'

'Jesus wept Roxie, do you know what the time is?' Sylvie asks as she pops her sleepy head around the door. 'The wedding isn't until three o'clock ...'

'Blimey, does it take you that long to beautify yourself,' mocks Felix.

'I ... Oh Sylvie,' I begin and then burst into tears.

'Don't stand at the door love, it looks common,' says Felix as he drags me in.

'What the hell is going on Rox? You look like shit,' adds Sylvie.

'I feel like I'm falling apart Sylvie. Darren is shagging some redhead from Eastlea Towers, although between you and me if that's her true colour then I'm Joan Collins, not that I could give a flying duck. About her hair colour I mean. I do give a fuck about her shagging my boyfriend and to top it all, I think I saw a murder last night when looking through Darren's telescope.'

Her mouth gapes open.

'Shit, no wonder you're upset. What did the police say?' Sylvie asks.

'I don't think the police would be interested in my love life,' I say miserably.

'What did the police say about the *murder*?'

'Jesus peanuts, you actually saw a murder?' gasps Felix. 'Was it a crime of passion?'

I wish they'd stop going on about the murder. Doesn't anyone care that Darren has been unfaithful again?

'I haven't told the police,' I say, ignoring Felix.

They gape at me.

'But ...' begins Felix.

'What do you mean, you haven't told them? That's the first thing you do when you witness a murder isn't it?'

'It seems you bang on your best friend's door,' says Felix.

'The thing is, I didn't actually see the murder as such. Anyway, if I go to the police now they might be suspicious of me, for leaving it so late. Do you have any aspirin? My head is killing me.'

'You said you saw the murder through Darren's telescope,' Sylvie reminds me.

'I saw two men having an argument and then one of them gripped the other around the throat. At first I thought it was a lovers' tiff ...'

'An easy mistake to make,' scoffs Felix. 'After all, lovers are always throttling each other aren't they?'

Sylvie glares at him.

'Then they pulled apart and the other man was waving a gun around. He had his back to me and ...' I hesitate as I struggle to remember what I saw. Felix stands frozen at the sink, his 'Gay as Fuck' mug overflowing with soapy water. Sylvie nods at me encouragingly.

'The other man was pointing at something but I couldn't see what it was. Then there was a flash. I presumed it was from the gun ...'

'Did you hear it go off?' says Sylvie excitedly.

'She hasn't got bionic ears has she?' Felix says, rolling his eyes.

Sylvie groans.

'Sorry, I wasn't thinking, go on, what happened next?'

'I'm not sure. I panicked and my hands slipped from the telescope and ...'

'I wouldn't like to be you under cross-examination,' says Felix. 'Denzel Washington would make mincemeat out of you.'

'Jesus wept Felix, can you shut up for five minutes.'

I drop my head onto the table. I can't believe this is happening. My life was normal yesterday. Okay, not completely normal. Parents into long sex sessions, a boyfriend who watches other women strip through a telescope and fantasising about my boss isn't exactly normal is it? But you know what I mean. It was far more normal than today is turning out to be.

'Go on,' encourages Sylvie.

'When I turned back the other guy had gone. The one with the gun was still there but … but … well the other guy must have been on the floor, right?'

Felix's mouth moves but nothing comes out of it.

'Christ,' says Sylvie finally.

'I think he saw me,' I say, my voice trembling. 'The murderer was looking right at me. I could see his eyes. It was all blurry but …'

'He couldn't have seen you,' she says with conviction.

'Really?'

Well, Sylvie is the expert isn't she?

'You can surely see a telescope sitting in our window,' I say worriedly.

'Not from that distance I wouldn't have thought,' Sylvie assures me.

'I'll make us all a cup of sweet tea. That's supposed to be good for shock,' says Felix.

'We haven't had a shock,' says Sylvie tiredly.

'You speak for yourself love.'

'Would you recognise the guy with the gun if you saw him again?' asks Sylvie, sounding like DCI Stella Gibson.

'Only by his scarf, it had red, white and black stripes like a Where's Wally scarf,' I say. 'I never actually saw his face properly. Oh, he had dark brown hair. How can I go to the police with that? They'll laugh in my face. We did drink a lot last night.'

'At least a Where's Wally scarf should be easy to spot in a crowd,' Felix quips. He places three mugs of tea onto the table and adds sugar to them.

'Do you know what block of flats it was and what floor?' asks Sylvie.

I sigh.

'It was Somerville Place I think but I'm not sure. I remember the curtains were red though.'

'With blood?' gasps Felix.

'No, you plonker,' says Sylvie. 'And anyway, believe it or not when someone is shot there isn't a lot of blood. Not once they're dead anyway. The blood starts to clot. I read that in one of Patricia Cornwell's books. Fascinating. Did you know that ...?'

'That's about all I want to know,' says Felix, turning white.

'We have to go there,' I say. 'I've thought it all through. We can go to all the flats facing south. We can tell them we're a new cleaning agency and offering a free trial. That way we can get into the flat and ...'

Sylvie holds up a hand.

'Hang on, are you suggesting we give these people an hour of free cleaning?'

I shrug.

'How else do we get in?'

'I can see how you've thought it through,' chips in Felix.

'We can work out what floor by how high or low you had the telescope. If it was level with your flat then it will be the tenth floor won't it? If it was lower it's likely to be one or two floors below and obviously if higher then the eleventh or twelfth floor,' she says.

I give her an impressed nod.

'Watching CSI hasn't been a total waste of your time has it?' says Felix.

'It was definitely pointing down, round about the seventh floor I would guess,' I say.

'Chances are the police are all over it. Someone must have heard the gunshot,' says Sylvie thoughtfully.

'I'd be a lot happier if we went over there,' I say.

'Absolutely,' agrees Sylvie. 'It'll take me and Felix ten minutes to get ready.'

'What?' says a shocked Felix. 'I'm not going. I tend to avoid men who throttle me.'

'No one is going to throttle you and anyway, there's safety in numbers.'

'That's news to me. I always thought two's company and three's a crowd.'

'Felix, if Roxie and I need to investigate then we will need a lookout, and that's going to be you,' she snaps.

'We could get shot,' he protests. 'You have no idea what kind of people live in those flats. I think Darren should go. After all, if he gets shot at least he would have deserved it.'

I feel tears begin to well up again. I'm trying really hard not to think about Darren. Five minutes later and we're ready to go. Sylvie throws a rucksack over her shoulders and Felix and I look at it suspiciously.

'What's in there?' I ask.

'Everything we need to investigate a crime scene,' she says confidently. 'Don't worry I have disposable gloves and masks for everyone.'

'Darling, I don't need either. I'm not touching anything,' says Felix.

'That Great Zehilda was pretty useless if she didn't see this coming,' says Sylvie, heading to the door.

I freeze as I remember Great Zehilda's words: *You know something. You will know something. You've seen something haven't you? Or you will see something.* She was on the ball there wasn't she? I saw a lot of things, not least of all Busty Redhead's breasts. I'll kill Darren when I get home.

Chapter Nine

The three of us stare at Somerville Place. A group of lads kick a football at the entrance and occasionally stare at us.

'We now need to work out which flat it was,' she says thoughtfully.

I struggle to remember whether I moved the telescope down or up after seeing Angie doing her striptease. After all, I was in shock. If Angie's tits weren't enough, I then went on to see the murder. It's no surprise my brain has shut down.

'I don't think I moved the telescope at all,' I say, 'I think I just swivelled.'

'So the flat is on the seventh floor,' she says excitedly, rummaging through her rucksack and pulling out a pair of binoculars. What is she doing? Isn't it enough that we're loitering in an old Fiesta with bald tyres and a dodgy exhaust, not to mention the cracked windscreen, without Sylvie watching the flats with a pair of binoculars. We'll be accused of being perverts next. Mind you, Felix doesn't look far off one with his black overcoat, fedora hat, and multicoloured silk scarf.

'We have a problem,' she says.

'You've only just realised?' sighs Felix.

'The flat on the seventh floor has green curtains.'

'Maybe they changed them,' says Felix.

'In six hours?' argues Sylvie. 'Anyway, the last thing on the murderer's mind will be the curtains.'

'Right,' he says, looking at her suspiciously. 'It doesn't comfort me that you seem to know how a murderer would think.'

'The flat below it has red curtains though,' she continues, ignoring Felix.

'That's it then,' I say. I look for the police cordon. It can't be possible that nobody heard the gunshot.

'I think we must have the wrong block. Someone must have heard the shot and called the police. Why isn't the place cordoned off?' I ask.

Sylvie chews her pen thoughtfully while Felix and I wait for her reply.

'I'm not sure. It does seem odd, but this is the right block. I'm certain of it.' she says, before turning to the back seat and looking at Felix.

'What?' he asks. 'Don't tell me Sherlock, you've just deduced that I'm the murderer.'

'I need you to go in and knock on one of the ground floor flats. Tell them you're a reporter for the local rag. Let's face it, you look like one. Say you're looking for human interest stories about what took place here in the early hours.'

'I'm not going in there on my own. Have you seen the riff-raff hanging around here not to mention those kids? I'll be mugged the minute I step out of the car.'

'It's not that bad,' I say.

'Darling, just be grateful you've got bald tyres and a hole in your exhaust. They only gave your car a cursory glance and followed it up with one of pity.'

'They're just kids Felix.'

'Ah, you say that love. They thought they were just kids in *Children of the Corn* didn't they? If they're just kids then I'll eat my arse. What's the betting they're tooled up?'

'It's *I'll eat my hat,*' says Sylvie.

'Not when I say it love.'

'And *Children of the Corn* was a Stephen King novel. This is real life.'

'There ain't much difference darling.'

'Felix, I can assure you that you'll come to no harm.'

He sighs and straightens his scarf.

'If I'm not back in ten minutes send in the SAS.'

'That'll be *School Age Services* would it?' giggles Sylvie.

'Or *Silly-R-Soles,*' I add.

'Bitches,' he snarls climbing from the back of the car.

'You could at least have four doors, this is so bloody undignified. What if someone sees me?' he grumbles, yanking his foot from under Sylvie's seat. She shoves her notepad at him. We watch him adjust his coat and walk towards the flats. Sylvie winds down her window so we can hear what's said.

'Alright granddad,' one of the boys says while winking at Felix.

'Oh dear,' mumbles Sylvie.

'I'm a reporter for the local rag,' says Felix, sounding like a robot. 'I'm looking for a human ...'

Sylvie groans.

'We're all humans 'ere mate.'

'Story,' continues Felix ignoring him, 'on what happened here in the early hours.'

'Ooh I say,' laughs one.

'A lot goes on 'ere in the early hours mate but I'm not so sure they'll want to tell you.'

Felix glances at us with despair on his face.

'Go in,' Sylvie mouths.

He disappears through the entrance and Sylvie and I wait nervously. I wince as I bite my lip and my thoughts are drawn to Ark Morgan. Was it really him last night? He's more gorgeous in the flesh than he ever was in my fantasies. If only he were my true love. My stomach drops as I remember Angie flashing her tits. What I am going to do? I can't forgive Darren, not a second time, and who knows if this is the second time. It could be the third or fourth time for all I know. I hope his prick drops off. I've a good mind to chop it off myself.

I'm pulled from my reverie by Sylvie's elbow in my ribs.

'He's coming back and he looks unscathed.'

'Well?' asks Sylvie as Felix clambers back into the car.

'I'm never going to forgive you for this, you know that don't you?' he says, taking off his hat and shaking his hair into place. 'I was lucky to get out of there alive. The woman on the ground floor is a nymphomaniac. She said a lot goes on in the early hours and can also go on later in the day if I was interested. Do I look like I'm interested in the female form?'

'What else?' I ask.

'What do you mean *what else*? That's it.'

'Did she hear a gunshot?' probes Sylvie.

'No, but she did hear someone arguing, but according to her people argue here every night, especially on a Saturday night. I think we've got the wrong block of flats or you dreamt the whole thing up.'

'Buddha,' I say, as the memory floods into my brain.

'Oh wonderful, she's now gone all religious on us,' says Felix.

'There's a Buddha painting in the flat,' I say, barely able to control my excitement.

Sylvie shuffles in her seat as if she has ants in her pants.

'There's only one way to find out,' she says. 'Let's go to the flat with the red curtains.'

With a groan from Felix, we file out of the Fiesta and head to the entrance.

Chapter Ten

'There's no one at home,' whispers Sylvie.

'If there's no one home why are you whispering?' says Felix.

'Because there could be someone in flat 102 or flat 103,' she snaps.

We watch in stunned silence as Sylvie pulls a credit card from her bag and begins using it to pick the lock.

'What are you doing?' I whisper. 'What if there is someone inside?'

'And not forgetting the fact that this is known as breaking and entering,' says Felix.

'We've knocked several times,' Sylvie says, as though that justifies breaking in.

'Remind me to always let you in,' says Felix.

'I live with you,' she snaps.

'For one wonderful moment I forgot about that. It must be the stress of breaking into someone's home.'

'I'll knock again,' she says.

'Dead bodies don't answer doors do they? But the bloody murderers can. What if he is still in there?' whispers Felix with a tremble in his voice. 'He'll slaughter us all before we reach the stairs. I've seen enough slasher movies to know how these killers work.'

'He's right. Let's call the police,' I agree.

'He's not likely to still be there,' says Sylvie.

'You don't know,' argues Felix.

My phone rings and Felix screams. I rummage in my shoulder bag with shaking hands and silence it. It's bloody Darren. Trust him to nearly get me killed.

'Oh God, I think my bowels have locked,' mumbles Felix.

Sylvie shakes her head and continues fiddling with the credit card while Felix and I struggle to breathe. There's a click and Sylvie gasps.

'I never expected it to work,' she says.

We stare at the door of flat 104 expectantly. I'm not sure what we imagine is going to happen but after what feels like an eternity and nothing does, Sylvie gingerly pushes it open and peeks inside. Felix grips my arm.

'Can you see a body?' he asks in a shaky voice. 'Is there a lot of blood?'

'I can't see anything. I'm still shocked I got the door open,' Sylvie says, awe-stricken at her own skills.

'Hello, anyone home?' she calls.

'I wish I'd brought my Imodium,' moans Felix, gripping my arm tighter. 'Do you think it would be okay to use their loo?'

I roll my eyes.

'You can't use the loo, you'll leave traces of your DNA if you do', Sylvie admonishes.

'I'll leave more than my DNA,' Felix mumbles.

'Right,' says Sylvie determinedly, pushing the door wide open. I peek over her shoulder and gasp when I see the Buddha painting.

'It's the right flat,' whispers Sylvie, prizing my hand away from Felix's.

'Keep watch Felix and whistle if anyone comes.'

'I can't whistle,' he says in a panicky voice.

She sighs.

'Well cough or something.'

He nods meekly.

'We'll leave the door open,' she assures him. 'We need to take off our boots. We don't want to leave a mess. Careful where you walk though, we don't want blood on our socks.'

Felix shudders.

'Jesus peanuts, I so need the loo,' he grumbles.

I so need to go home, back to bed, and to wake up from this awful nightmare. I cautiously follow Sylvie into the flat and stare at the Buddha painting. I turn my head towards the window expecting to see a body on the floor but of course there isn't one. The flat is more modern than I thought it would be. It's open plan. One of those *with it* flats where you can chat to your guests as you prepare dinner for them. Personally I'd hate the smell of cooking in my living room but each to their own. Leather couches sit either side of a mahogany coffee table that is piled neatly with arty type magazines. A white rug covers the middle of the floor and I stare nervously at it, looking for bloodstains.

'Is this the room you saw?' Sylvie asks, pulling my attention away from the rug.

'I recognise the painting but not much else,' I say truthfully. 'I was looking at the men.'

She sniffs noisily.

'I can smell a slight odour,' she says.

I hope Felix hasn't shit himself.

'A gun has been fired in this flat.'

Oh God.

'You're sounding more like Columbo by the second,' Felix hisses through the door.

Sylvie bends down and opens her rucksack, pulling out yellow washing-up gloves.

'I thought you were going to have those special surgical gloves,' I say. Kitchen rubber gloves are as good as useless aren't they, unless she's planning on us spring-cleaning the place.

'Ark Morgan doesn't supply us with surgical gloves does he? These will have to do. It's not like you're going to give someone an enema,' she snaps.

I gasp.

'These are Ark Morgan's property?'

'Not his personally, I can't imagine Ark Morgan wearing rubber gloves can you?'

Ooh I don't know about rubber gloves but I can certainly imagine him doing rubber. Careful, whispers my inner goddess, don't start fantasising now. It really isn't the place is it?

'Just put them on,' she says throwing a pair at me. 'Do you want a mask in case we find the body. Hopefully it won't smell too much yet.'

'Don't you think we should just call the police?' whispers Felix.

'And tell them what exactly?' snaps Sylvie. 'That Roxie saw a murder last night and then failed to report it. That she was half pissed at the time. Then in the morning she thought about reporting it but was then worried that she'd be in trouble for not reporting it the night before. And now we've come here to see if there really was a murder and …'

'Broke in with a credit card,' he finishes. 'Okay, I get the picture. I'll just keep watch and keep schtum, unless, of course I have to cough.'

'Ready?' asks Sylvie. 'You check the cupboards and I'll check the freezer.'

'The freezer?' I repeat. 'You mean that little fridge freezer?' I say, pointing. 'Have you seen the size of it? You couldn't even get a midget in there. Oh my God, you don't think he …?'

We stare at each other.

'Well, it happens but I doubt he had time for that and there would be blood everywhere,' says Sylvie thoughtfully. 'Best to check though.'

'You said there wouldn't be blood if they were dead,' whispers Felix through the doorway.

'No, I meant if he, the murderer, cut the body up,' Sylvie says. 'Of course there would be blood.'

'Saints alive,' groans Felix. 'I wish you'd hurry. My bowels really aren't enjoying this.'

I cautiously open a door and scream as something falls towards me. I flap my arms around trying to ward it off and knock a painting off the wall. It crashes to the floor, knocking a vase of flowers over in its descent.

'Fuck, have you found the body?' calls Felix.

'Jesus wept. Can you two make a bit more noise? I don't think the neighbours quite heard you. For Christ's sake Rox, it's just a broom,' snaps Sylvie.

We look down at the painting with held breath.

'Is the glass smashed?' I ask, not daring to look.

'It's okay,' she says as she sponges the carpet.

My heart pounds so loudly that I barely hear her. I push the broom back, close the cupboard door and turn to hang the painting.

'Oh God,' I mutter.

The picture hook's gone and what's worse there is a ruddy big hole where it once was. I look frantically around.

'The picture hook's gone.'

'Saints alive, it sounds like you're doing more damage than the murderer,' says Felix, peeking around the door.

Sylvie finally finds the hook but now the hole is too big for it.

'How did you manage that?' asks Sylvie.

'I don't know,' I answer truthfully, struggling to twist the hook back into the hole. I hang the painting on it. It wobbles slightly and then hangs precariously.

'It's lopsided,' I say. 'And the water's marked the carpet'.

'They won't notice,' says Sylvie. 'Men never do.'

She opens the tiny freezer.

'Christ.'

'Oh my God, what's in there?' I say, wanting to hear while at the same time not wanting to hear.

'Frozen peas and enough vodka to sink a ship, this guy sure likes his booze, or should I say liked?'

'You couldn't pass a bottle out here could you,' says Felix.

'We're going to need to re-enact the crime,' says Sylvie. 'That way we'll know where to search for evidence.'

'It was near the window,' I say, 'shouldn't we start there.'

'I'll be the murderer,' she says, 'unless you want to.'

'No, I'll be the victim,' I say, thinking it matches how I am feeling at the moment.

'So, where were they standing?'

'A few feet from the window,' I say. 'My man was waving his hands around and pointing at something over there, and then he threw himself at the other guy and went for his throat.'

I imitate the actions and lurch towards Sylvie putting my rubber gloved hands around her throat.

'Then what happened?' she asks.

'You push me away and pull out the gun.'

She rummages in her rucksack and then tells me to attack her again.

'Masochist,' quips Felix.

I grab her by the throat and she pushes me away, reaches behind her and points a tin of pledge furniture polish at me.

'This is so unrealistic,' I say.

She gives me a sour look.

'Sorry,' I mumble.

I fall to my knees dramatically as I'd seen the man do and wave my arms around.

'Now you shoot me, or in your case, spray me to death. That's when I swung the telescope away and when I looked back all I could see was the gunman. He wandered about a bit and that's when I saw the painting.'

'Right, so we need to work out what the victim was pointing at.'

I point in the direction that I had seen the man do and realise I am pointing at the fridge freezer.

'Not helpful,' says Sylvie.

I sigh. He must have been pointing at something. It's then I see it. It's about the size of a pea so I'm not surprised we missed it.

'Oh my God,' I say breathlessly.

'What is it?' asks Sylvie, taking a sharp breath.

'There's a bloodstain under the coffee table,' I whisper.

'Right,' says Sylvie in that authoritative tone of hers. I watch with a sinking heart as she dives into her rucksack again. I'm really not happy that we've taken stuff from the hotel's stock cupboard. She pulls out freezer bags, baby powder and a blusher brush that's covered in coral pink blusher.

'We need to get some fingerprints.'

At that moment Felix starts coughing.

'Someone's coming,' he whispers.

Chapter Eleven

It takes seconds for us to spring into action. Sylvie scoops up her bag and I hurry behind, almost knocking over Felix in my panic. Sylvie throws a duster at me and another at Felix and we all make a show of polishing the stairwell. An elderly gentleman comes puffing up the stairs.

'Bleeding lift is out,' he grumbles.

'Disgraceful,' says Sylvie.

He stops and studies Felix.

'You look like Boy George,' he says finally.

'Oh really, thank you very much,' says Felix.

'Nice and quiet here isn't it?' prods Sylvie.

'If it's not I take me 'earing aids out.'

He grunts and fumbles in his pockets. Felix looks at me and mouths *shit.*

'Bleeding keys,' grumbles the old man.

'We're the cleaners,' says Sylvie, while Felix and I stand there like two frozen kippers. 'Can we help?'

'Cleaners,' he says, giving us the once over. 'What you sodding cleaning?'

Before she can answer he whips out his keys and Felix and I hold our breath. Oh God, he isn't going to open the door of 104 is he? He pushes them into the lock of 102 and I think Felix is going to faint from relief.

'We heard it was noisy here last night,' probes Sylvie.

'Was it? I wouldn't know. I turn me 'earing aids off at eight,' he says, before slamming his door.

'Nice chap,' says Felix.

'You attract too much attention. I knew I shouldn't have brought you,' says Sylvie.

'Both me and my bowels wish you hadn't,' he shoots back.

We return to the flat and Sylvie starts dusting everything with baby powder. She pulls her phone from her handbag and taps into it. Meanwhile I've got one ear cocked for Felix's signal. My mouth is dry and my heart is hammering nine to the dozen. I'm convinced we're going to get caught.

'What are you doing?' I ask.

My neck and shoulders are aching from the tension and I'm craving chocolate. A shot of that vodka wouldn't go amiss either.

'I'm getting confused. I don't think I'm supposed to do it like this.'

'You're joking right?' I say incredulously. 'We've broken into someone's flat and you've covered the place in bloody Johnson's baby powder and now you're saying that you're not supposed to do it like this.'

'I'm looking for the YouTube Video,' she snaps.

'YouTube?' I echo.

'Maybe you've got time to watch a DVD darling but my bowels are on a deadline,' Felix chimes through the door.

'Shit, I need to start again. Dust off the powder. I need to apply it gently with the make-up brush. I got muddled. I thought that the ...'

'Christ, this is painful,' sighs Felix. 'Kojak just walks in with a lollipop and solves the whole thing. I never saw him with baby powder.'

'Kojak?' I exclaim. 'How old are you Felix?'

'I like watching the re-runs. The old ones are the best.'

'Can we get on,' snaps Sylvie. 'You can share your TV viewing habits later.'

I watch Sylvie gently brush a wine glass and then photograph it with her phone. She does the same to the coffee table and then tells me to clean up. It's beginning to feel like a normal day at work for me. She kneels by the bloodstained carpet.

'I'll try to lift some of this,' she says. 'There must be a thousand clues in this rug. Look for stray hairs and bag whatever you find.'

'How the hell am I supposed to pick up a strand of hair with these?' I complain, holding up my yellow rubber marigold hands.

'Remind me never to have you as my assistant again,' she says irritably as she picks at the dried stain. I struggle to grasp a hair on the carpet but it's almost impossible in my Marigolds. It takes me all of five minutes and I manage to take some carpet fibres at the same time. Well, you never know do you? They might be useful. In the far corner of the room on the floor beneath the Buddha painting is a card.

'What's that?' I say, crawling towards it.

'Don't touch it,' hisses Sylvie. 'We may be able to get some prints off it. Here use these. Bag it.'

She's bossy when she's got her detective hat on isn't she?

She throws a pair of tweezers at me. How the hell am I supposed to hold those with these bloody Marigolds? The card is a Starbucks reward card, which after much fiddling with the tweezers I manage to drop into a freezer bag. I'm struggling to zip the bag up when Sylvie groans.

'Bugger it.'

I turn and gasp. The pea-sized bloodstain is now a potato sized bloodstain.

'God Sylvie, it stands out like a sore thumb. There's no way they'll miss that,' I say, panicking.

'I hate to be a wet blanket and spoil your fun, but isn't this tampering with evidence,' whispers Felix.

'Does it look *very* different?' she asks.

'Of course it looks different, are you insane? About three inches different. Men or no men, there is no way they are going to miss that,' I say, struggling to keep the panic from my voice.

'Felix, go and get some stain remover. There's a bottle in the car.'

'What?' he croaks. 'You can't possibly be serious. Why don't you spring-clean the place and be done with it.'

'Felix, just go. Roxie will keep watch.'

I will?

'I don't know what it looks like,' he whines.

'Jesus wept. Jane Tennison doesn't have to put up with this shit.'

'That may have something to do with the fact that she's a fictional character,' I remind her.

'Roxie will go,' she snaps. It sounds like an order and I don't like to argue.

'Don't be long,' says Felix as I rush past him.

This is a nightmare. I thought we'd just have a quick look around and leave. If you ask me, we're leaving more evidence than we're finding. I have never run so fast in my life. I fly back past Felix and throw the stain remover to Sylvie along with a scrubbing brush. Minutes later, like magic, the stain has gone. Even the small pea shaped stain has gone.

'Shouldn't you have left just a little bit?' I ask.

'They won't notice,' she says, 'they're men.'

'In which case they won't notice if there is a bottle of that vodka missing will they?' says Felix. 'God knows I need something.'

'That's stealing,' says Sylvie.

'You've got strange ideas on right and wrong, love.'

'We need to get this into a fridge as soon as possible,' she says, holding up the blood specimen.

'Whose fridge?' squeals Felix.

'Ours of course.'

'Over my dead body.'

'That can be arranged Felix.'

'Can we go now?' I ask anxiously.

The last thing I need is to be found on my hands and knees in the middle of a crime scene. It really won't look good will it? A Boy George lookalike gay man standing guard and two hapless women in Marigolds attempting forensics, and as for the baby powder, I'm not even going there. We look as guilty as hell. I'm not sure what of, but we certainly look guilty. I wish I hadn't mentioned the murder. It seemed like a dream but now it's a nightmare. I just want to be home in my flat with a jar of Nutella, a packet of trifle fingers and *Fifty Shades* book three. I'd so love to be sitting cosily on the couch with my boyfriend as if none of this ever happened, just like things used to be. But things can never be the same now, can they? Before I have time to fall into a depression, Detective Sylvie is at me again.

'We need to check the bins before we go. You'd be amazed at how much evidence is in rubbish bins.'

She hands me a black bag.

'Empty everything onto the sack. Take out anything you think is relevant.'

'What am I looking for?' I ask. All I want to do is get out of here.

She shrugs.

'Suspicious things.'

Oh right, that's very helpful isn't it? I empty the kitchen bin onto the sack and stare at the contents. An empty tin of baked beans doesn't count as suspicious does it, unless you count the fact it should be in the recycling bin. I carefully poke through potato peel, leftover food and torn up letters. I shove the letter pieces in a plastic bag. Not because they look suspicious but because I don't know what else to put in there and I somehow think my life won't be worth living if I don't produce something. The sound of a police siren immobilises me.

'Shit, that's it,' cries Felix. 'I have to use the sodding loo. I can't be dragged to the cells with my bowels in this state.'

'Shove that rubbish back into the bin,' she orders, 'and let's get out of here.'

Chapter Twelve

We make a beeline to Costa Coffee. Felix dashes to the loo while I order and sit watching a loved-up couple feeding each other strawberry cheesecake. Darren and I have never fed each other anything, period. Not at home or in public.

'The cheesecake is off the menu then,' says Felix as he joins me after what seems like an eternity. 'I can't tell you what a relief that was. The loo that is, not the cheesecake. I feel like a new man. In fact if you spot one, let me know.'

The loved-up couple are now kissing in between feeding each other. I hope they don't start having sex on the table.

'Right,' says Sylvie, joining us. 'I've contained the blood sample.'

'Oh good, I have to admit it was bothering me,' says Felix sarcastically.

'I wish we had found more evidence.'

'We're not going back,' says Felix. 'We should think ourselves lucky the police weren't coming for us.'

The loved-up couple are now sharing coffees and calling each other by pet names. Felix mimics putting his fingers down his throat and all I can think of is Darren. The Great Zehilda has been amazingly accurate. She said she saw a hen, or was it a chicken, oh well it's one and the same thing isn't it? That the hen predicted wealth from an unexpected legacy and let's face it, I had no expectations of winning the lottery. Even now I can't believe it. Then there was the sausage. The sausage tea leaves means the marring of my pleasant conditions. Okay, maybe things with Darren and I weren't a hundred per cent pleasant but I was reasonably happy with my lot, at least I think I was. Perhaps I wasn't and it was just too complicated to leave. The truth is I could never afford the rent on a flat myself and it was nice to feel loved. Well, that's all gone out of the window. But her words *I see wealth but also danger. You know something.*

You will know something. You've seen something haven't you? Or you will see something. Let's face it, she couldn't have been more accurate about the murder than if she planned it herself, and even I don't believe a tea leaf reader would go that far just to prove her predictions. She even got the number '6' bonus ball. I mean, that is really impressive isn't it? Who'd have thought it? Me, Roxie Brown, having my life changed overnight? I'm still sceptical that I've won anything on the lottery though because let's face it, apart from meeting Ark Morgan in the House of Mirrors, only bad things have happened since I saw The Great Zehilda.

'Roxie, are you listening?' Sylvie says, breaking into my thoughts.

'Where are you going to go? You can't possibly forgive that little shit again,' says Felix.

I gape at Sylvie.

'You told Felix about the first time?' I say shocked.

'It just came up one night,' she says defensively.

'Over spag bol,' adds Felix. 'I was crying into it to be precise.'

I let out a sigh.

'Felix was having boyfriend troubles,' says Sylvie.

'And Darren screwing my friend helped with that did it?' I say feeling hurt, although I'm not sure why as right now the more people that hate Darren the better.

'He's a prick and you're better off without him,' says Sylvie. 'He's a spendthrift and frankly a layabout. I don't believe he can't get more work. Why do you stay with him?'

I shrug helplessly.

'I'm not sure. I guess I just felt I ought to try and make it work. He was very remorseful after the first time.'

God, that sounds like there have been numerous times doesn't it? Well, for all I know there has been. Bloody men.

'And well, where would I have gone and who would have watched DVDs with me and ...'

They look at me.

'I know. I guess it was easier to stay than to leave. After all, we've been together five years and he really was remorseful.'

'So remorseful that he's done it again,' says Felix, grimacing at the loved-up couple at the other table.

'If you need somewhere to stay you can bunk up with us, can't she Felix?'

Felix chokes on his Caramel Frappuccino.

'It depends what you mean by bunking up.'

'She can have the couch,' says Sylvie, bunching up her hair and donning her cap. 'Right, we all need to get ready for Hal's wedding. I'll get this blood in the fridge and then we need to get it analysed.'

'Are you sure it needs to go in a fridge?' asks Felix with a shudder.

'Yes. We also need to regroup *soon*. Is everyone free tomorrow night?'

I've never heard Sylvie talk like this before. It's like she really has metamorphosed into Detective Chief Inspector Jane Tennison.

'And just where do you suggest we go to get blood analysed? Forensics-R-Us?' says Felix, rolling his eyes. 'If you ask me the whole thing was a waste of time and not to mention an enormous strain on my poor bowels. It's going to take days for them to recover.'

'He's got a point,' I say, checking my phone and seeing five missed calls from Darren.

'Since when were you worried about Felix's bowels?' Sylvie asks.

'I'm talking about the Forensics-R-Us bit, not his bowels. Anyway, I should go home. Have it out with Darren.'

She nods sympathetically.

'Good idea. Come round when you're ready. Meanwhile Felix, you and I need to google. There must be someone who can do the analysis. You're good on the computer – that can be your job.'

'Ooh, you're really gorgeous when you're masterful. I could share a strawberry cheesecake with you while you're like this.'

'Although I guess it will be expensive,' says Sylvie.

'It's two pound thirty,' he says looking at the menu.

'I meant the analysis, not the bloody cheesecake. They're bound to charge us a fortune.'

'I've got money,' I say, the words coming out before I can control them. 'I think I won the lottery last night.'

Sylvie's mouth drops open while Felix continues scanning the menu.

'What, you mean like ten quid?' he says. 'Lucky old you, I never win a bean.'

'I got five numbers and the bonus ball. At least I think I did.'

Felix's head snaps up.

'Close that darling. Who knows what might drop into it. There are enough germs in this place to sink a battleship,' Felix admonishes Sylvie, pointing accusingly at her mouth.

'You are kidding?' Sylvie says finally.

'No, these places are known for it,' says Felix. 'You can't trust those hygiene certificates they stick on the wall.'

Sylvie sighs.

'You honestly won the lottery, you're not kidding?'

I shake my head.

'The Great Zehilda predicted everything from the break up with Darren to the lottery and even the murder.'

I don't mention the Ark Morgan bit.

'Have you double checked?' asks Felix, pushing his Caramel Frappuccino to one side.

'No. I'm too afraid to.'

'What were your numbers?' he asks, tapping into his phone.

'49, 1, 3, 4, 11 and 6,' I say before holding my breath.

Felix stares at his phone.

'Bloody hell,' he says. 'You really did win.'

Chapter Thirteen

I can't believe my life has changed in just a day. I'm all geared up to confront Darren only to find a note telling me he's gone to watch Arsenal play a friendly, and the cheek to ask where the fuck have I been all morning and don't I check my phone any more? He's totally forgotten the wedding. I could cry. What a wanker. Who forgets his friend's wedding? I'm going to look a total idiot sitting alone at the reception.

The lottery people confirmed I'd won. My winnings total seventy-five thousand. I'm gutted that I put Mrs Patel's number six instead of my lucky number two, but hey, I'm seventy-five grand better off than I was on Friday, so I can't complain. They are sending someone to see me, to check I am who I say I am. Not that anyone would ever pretend to be Roxie bloody Brown.

I'm terrified I've left my DNA at the murder flat. It wasn't until I got home that I discovered my socks were fraying. That will teach me to buy from Poundland. I had a sodding great hole in the big toe, which means I've probably left toe prints all over the place. Then, to top it all I've also lost an earring. I daren't tell Sylvie, she'll go absolutely ape shit. The chances are I've lost the earring somewhere else but visions of it laying on the floor of the murder flat haunt me. I'll most likely just get the lottery money and then be incriminated in a murder. I throw the frayed socks into the bin and rummage through the kitchen cupboard for some camomile tea. Typical that we don't have any isn't it? There's only green tea with lemon. God knows why I bought that. I hate green tea and it certainly isn't going to calm me down. I unscrew the Nutella jar and scoop out a large dollop with my finger. Fifteen minutes and half a jar later I'm feeling a whole lot better. I pull my phone from my bag and send an angry text to Darren.

'It's Hal's wedding in …'

I check the time and see that, shit; it's in an hour and a half. Fuck it. I've not even showered.

'An hour and a half, honestly Darren, you are such an arsehole at times.'

I send the text and fly into the bedroom and throw shoes, make-up, hair tongs and the wedding present into a carrier bag. There must be more I need. Oh yes, the card. Bugger, this couldn't have happened on a worse day.

I skid out of the front door. I don't have time for the stairs so I run into the lift only to find the damn thing is out of order. I dash down the stairs and sprint to the Fiesta where I finally slump into the driver's seat. Please start, I beg and, miracle of miracles, it actually does.

'Christ, I was about to send out a search party. Where have you been?' Sylvie greets me.

I can't see her face for the green avocado mask. If I didn't know better I'd think she was going to the wedding disguised as Shrek.

'I've not showered,' I say, trying not to panic.

'Bloody hell Rox.'

She pulls me upstairs and bangs on the bathroom door.

'Are you going to be much longer in there? It's Hal's wedding not Cannes bloody film festival.'

Felix opens the door with steam and Dior aftershave billowing behind him. He lets out a shriek.

'Are you trying to give me heart failure? Jesus peanuts, Sylvie love, your face is a shock most mornings but you've never looked like Kermit the frog before.'

'Just get your arse out of the bathroom. Roxie is all behind for a change,' she says rolling her eyes. 'I'll get our dresses ready.'

I don't think I've ever showered so fast in my life. By the time I reach the bedroom Sylvie is dressed in her pink satin bridesmaid dress.

'Oh,' I say. 'You look lovely.'

'Don't get carried away. I'm not the bride. I'll blow dry your hair while you do your make-up.'

'Won't that be awkward?' I say.

'We've got forty-five minutes, have you got any better ideas?'

'Darren's gone to see the Arsenal,' I say fighting back tears. 'He forgot about the wedding.'

I rummage in my bag for my phone.

'And my texts haven't been delivered.'

'Bastard,' she snarls, blow drying my hair wildly while I struggle to squeeze my eyelashes between the eyelash curlers.

'I'm making a brew,' calls Felix.

'Throw some whisky in it,' yells Sylvie.

'Drunken bridesmaids are not the done thing darling,' he calls back.'

'Just do it,' she screams.

'You're getting tense,' I say, spitting out bits of hair.

Felix bursts in with the tea and whisky and Sylvie takes a gulp from the bottle. I stroke Vaseline onto my lashes and curl them again. I step into my dress and Sylvie pulls the back together.

'Breathe in,' she says.

'I am breathing in.'

'Are you sure?'

'She's turning a purple colour, so I think she's telling the truth,' says Felix, standing in front of me, high heels dangling from his hand. He looks quite appealing in a dinner jacket and bow tie.

'Christ, it won't zip up,' she says.

'What do you mean it won't zip up?' I shriek. 'It's got to zip up.'

'When did you last try it on?' she asks, pulling it so tight I'm beginning to sympathise with Victorian women.

'If you pull much tighter I won't be able to breathe at all.'

'Her tits are looking a bit squashed,' says Felix, taking a swig of whisky.

I grab the bottle out of his hand and take a swig myself.

'Shit,' says Sylvie pulling so hard I have to grab Felix to stay upright.

'Right, there's nothing for it. Felix you'll have to pull it together while I zip.'

'Jesus peanuts.'

'And can you stop saying *Jesus peanuts*, it drives me insane.'

'She's stressed,' I say.

I take a deep breath as Felix pulls and Sylvie tries again. I feel my bra pinch my nipples and Sylvie sighs.

'It's done. God knows how you won't burst out of it.'

'The taxi is here,' says Felix, throwing my shoes at me.

Sylvie chucks our evening bags, presents and cards into a carrier bag.

'Let's go,' she says, pushing a diamante slide into my hair and shoving a bouquet into my hands.

'I'm never getting married,' I say. Not to Darren anyway. That's now a certainty.

Chapter Fourteen

'I don't believe it,' says Sylvie. 'It's Sunday, why aren't people enjoying their sodding gardens instead of clogging up the roads?'

'The Queen is passing through,' says the driver. 'It's on the news.'

'Did somebody mention me?' pipes up Felix.

'Christ,' mumbles Sylvie between gritted teeth, 'Why did she have to choose today of all days?'

'We've only got five minutes,' I say.

'Bloody royalists,' Sylvie snaps. 'Stop the taxi.'

'You're not suggesting we walk from here?' blubbers Felix. 'I look like a prize penguin.'

'You always look like a prize penguin, why should today be any different?' she scoffs.

'Ouch,' says the taxi driver.

Felix fumbles in his wallet to pay, and then we're left stranded in the middle of Swiss Cottage looking for all the world like spare parts that *haven't* made it to the wedding.

'Which way do we go?' asks Sylvie.

'You don't know?' I say.

I lift my dress and follow Sylvie down the street, trying to ignore the looks from passers-by.

'Excellent Sylvie, bloody excellent,' groans Felix as a group of Chinese tourists take a picture of us. 'It will be on twitter in a few seconds. We'll most likely be viral by tonight.'

We turn the corner and stop as we see Hal's car approaching.

'Shit,' says Felix, pointing to a side door in the church.

'This is your fault,' says Sylvie, nudging me.

Darren's bloody fault more like.

'Through here,' says Felix leading us into the vestry.

We stop and stare. The vicar is donning his cassock and a dubious looking wig.

'Oh,' he says, quickly adjusting it. 'Welcome. The wedding party usually come through the main door.'

The wig is askew and I wonder if I should say something. I wouldn't want him going out there looking like a half-pissed vicar.

'Yes, we did think about it,' says Felix with a smile. 'Personally, I'm used to entering by the rear.'

'Jesus wept,' says Sylvie. 'I mean, heavens, oh shit.'

'Maybe best not to speak at all,' I whisper. 'Is it okay if we go through, we'd like to make it before the bride?'

We dash through the vestry door and into the church.

'Bloody hell, I really cocked that up didn't I?' groans Sylvie as we hurry to the entrance. We watch as Hal approaches in her flowing white dress.

'She looks beautiful,' I sigh.

'She looks frumpy if you ask me,' says Sylvie. 'I'm sure that dress looked better on her at the last fitting.'

Hal smiles at us with tears forming in her eyes.

'I'm so happy,' she says, hugging us and squashing her bouquet.

I feel myself come over all tearful. I doubt if I'm ever going walk down the aisle, apart from now of course, but you know what I mean.

'Don't start,' says Sylvie, dabbing her eyes. 'I bloody hate weddings.'

God, this dress is killing me. I can't feel my breasts any more. I'm terrified to do anything more than take a shallow breath in case something pops at the back. *Air on a G String* begins to play and Sylvie and I lift the train and follow Hal into the church. Hal said she wanted to walk down the aisle to Air on a G String because that's all she would be wearing under the dress. I look for Darren. There's no sign of him. We reach the vicar and lower the train. I take Hal's bouquet and for the rest of the ceremony try not to sneeze. Everything goes smoothly aside from an awful moment when Tony fumbled in his pockets for the rings. Then it is all over and we're heading back outside for the photos, confetti and hugs. There is still no sign of Darren. I only hope he turns up for the reception. Then again maybe it would be best if he didn't. I really don't want to stab him with the cake knife. How can I tell Hal that Darren forgot about their wedding and went to the Arsenal instead?

Chapter Fifteen

I must look like the jilted bridesmaid. I'm on my fourth glass of champagne and my dress popped during the speeches. I must have finally taken a breath to avoid collapsing with asphyxia. Fortunately someone lent me a safety pin. I'm at that point where I couldn't care less if I've gained weight. If a man can't love you for who you are then they're not worth having are they? On that note I decide to get another bowl of profiteroles when I spot her, redheaded Angie. I really do see red and I don't just mean her hair. She's one of those late guests, the ones who aren't good enough for the reception but get an invite to the party. And right behind her is the bloody unfaithful dipshit Darren. He sees me, waves and sheepishly trots over. I exhale and finish the champagne. It's most probably best if I stop knocking back the booze now he is here. At least he turned up. Better late than never I suppose.

'Ooh the wanderer doth return,' says Felix, strolling to our table with a plate of smoked salmon sandwiches.

'What's she doing here?' I say nodding to Angie.

'That's Kev's cousin isn't it?' says Felix.

'That's bloody Angie,' I say, fighting back my anger, 'shagging Angie from Eastlea Towers.'

'I'm so sorry Babe, I totally forgot and signal was crap and …' says Darren in a pathetic voice as he reaches me. He leans down to kiss me and I quickly lift my glass to my lips.

'Don't worry, we've coped without you,' says Felix, offering him a sandwich.

'They're a bit curled around the edges I'm afraid.'

'You should apologise to Hal,' I say, struggling to control my anger. I let my eyes stray to Angie on the other side of the hall.

'I'll catch her now,' he says.

I glare at Angie and she struggles to avoid my eyes. The music is turned up and Hal and Kev slide onto the dance floor to lead Gangnam Style. Darren slopes to the bar. That's about right.

'Come on love, let's have a dance,' says Felix, pulling me up. 'Let's show Ginger Spice what we're made of.'

'She's a redhead,' I say miserably.

'If she's a real redhead, I'll eat my arse.'

I laugh and let him lead me onto the dance floor.

'Hey,' shouts Sylvie as we join her, Hal and Kev, 'Let's do it.'

And we do. At one point it is the five of us leading the dancing. Darren looks on dejectedly, working his way through his pint while Angie looks decidedly uncomfortable every time I glare at her.

'Enjoy yourself,' shouts Felix. 'Have it out with the toerag later, but for now let him see you can have a good time without him.'

'He's right, and I don't often say that about Felix,' laughs Sylvie.

'Charming,' smiles Felix.

Two Gangnam Styles and fifteen minutes later and I can barely breathe. I join Darren and his pint at the table.

'Another drink darling?' asks Felix.

'I'll have another beer,' says Darren.

'I think these are on Darren. Isn't that right, Darren?' asks Sylvie.

'Well ...' mumbles Darren.

'I'll have a white wine spritzer love,' says Felix. 'I'm parched, how about you Sylve?'

'I'll have a spritzer too.'

'A shame you weren't here earlier,' says Felix. 'The bar was free up until eight.'

'Are you buying a round?' says Lisa as she joins us.

'Well ...' repeats Darren.

'What are you having Sylvie?' she asks.

'We're all having white wine spritzers. How about you Roxie, love?' says Felix with a wide grin.

'I'll have the same,' I say.

That will teach the two-timing little sod. He hates spending money on others.

'Martine, do you want a spritzer?' Lisa yells.

'This is ridiculous,' Darren whispers, leaning across to me.

'Do you have any money?'

Oh yes, plenty but you're not getting any of it.

'I didn't bring any Darren,' I say, biting into a sandwich and not feeling in the least bit guilty for lying. He fishes his wallet from his suit pocket with a groan.

'Well, I can't carry that lot back on my own,' he grumbles.

'Just give us a wave and I'll come over,' winks Felix.

Darren fiddles with his shirt collar before heading to the bar.

'I can manage,' he mumbles.

'What's going on?' asks Lisa.

I shake my head. I don't want a scene at Hal's wedding. It's her big day after all.

'He's in Roxie's bad books,' says Felix.

'Oh, Single Ladies,' squeals Lisa as Beyoncé belts from the speakers. She grabs Martine and they disappear to the dance floor with Sylvie.

'I'm going to chat up that gorgeous bloke. He's been giving me the eye all evening,' says Felix.

I watch Darren weave his way back from the bar with the tray of drinks to an empty table.

'That's bloody great. That lot cost me an arm and a leg and now everyone has buggered off.'

'They'll be back,' I say, feeling Angie's eyes on me. How could I have not known about her? I'm too trusting that's my problem.

'Christ, that disco is loud. I can't hear myself think. You're in a funny mood,' he says downing another beer. I notice he got himself two. God forbid Darren should go thirsty.

I sip my spritzer and ignore him. I'm not going to have it out with him here, it wouldn't be right, not at Hal's wedding reception

'You'll never believe this but Joey only went and won the bloody lottery.'

'No, really?' I say, widening my eyes.

'Thirty quid, he got four numbers. I told you when Joey gets that tingle it means something's up.'

Something's up all right. The DJ lowers the volume.

'In a few moments the gorgeous bride and her groom will be cutting the cake,' he yells excitedly. 'What a cake it is too. Then we'll be waving goodbye to Hal and Kev as they head off into the sunset.'

'Or Devon more like,' says Sylvie, joining us. 'Thanks for the drink Darren.'

'I got you more profiteroles,' she says, handing me a bowl.

'That's why you keep gaining weight,' Darren mutters.

'Oh piss off Darren,' says Sylvie drunkenly. 'You can talk. Looked in the mirror lately, you've got a nice little paunch there?'

'Sylvie,' I say firmly.

'You're a bad influence on her,' says Darren.

'I'm a damn sight better for her than you are,' she says before burping in his face.

Oh dear.

'Ooh drinkies,' says Felix, joining us. 'All right our Sylvie?' He looks at her questioningly and then to me. I just raise my eyebrows in response.

'Shall we get a bit of air?' he asks delicately.

Thankfully she allows him to lead her outside. Darren and I sit silently watching the dancing. I sip my spritzer and pretend not to hear him over the music. Meanwhile he downs his beer and struggles not to look at Angie. It's all I can do not to tip the beer over his head. There is a drum roll and a distorted Frank Sinatra's *Love and Marriage* is played too loudly as Hal and Kev cut their three-tiered cake.

'I'm getting another beer,' says Darren.

I help myself to a large slice of cake. How dare Darren say I'm fat? He strolls to the bar while I wander outside to wave Hal and Kev off in their old battered Peugeot. An hour later I shove a very pissed Darren into a cab.

'Will you be okay?' asks Felix, kissing me on the cheek.

'Yes, thanks Felix.'

I hug Sylvie and hold her up until she regains her balance.

'She'll regret this tomorrow when she drags herself out of bed for work,' smiles Felix.

I climb into the cab beside Darren who is slumped in his seat. I somehow think tonight isn't the time to talk about Angie.

Chapter Sixteen

I spend the night snivelling and mumbling while Darren snores as usual. I'm sure he's got a nasal problem. I bet Justin Theroux doesn't have a nasal problem. I finally got up, swore at the bloody telescope, drank half a bottle of wine and polished off a pack of trifle fingers with a jar of Nutella. At one point, I called a live radio phone in, and asked, what was the point of winning seventy-five thousand pounds if you have no one to share it with? I think the phone lines got jammed after that with people offering to share with me. Christ, I hope I didn't give my name. I'm almost afraid to look out of the window in case there's a posse of people wishing to share. I know sharing is caring but there are limits. A quick peep behind the curtain tells me all is safe. I feel like crap. My head thumps. I should never have had the wine, not after all the booze I drank at the wedding. My eyes feel like they've got sawdust in them and my shoulders ache from the tension of searching the flat yesterday. I run a hot bath and throw in some lavender oil. I'll make a cup of tea and relax in the water.

'This bloody toaster's had it,' shouts Darren as the smell of charcoaled toast wafts into the bathroom.

'You always set it too high,' I shout.

I bet Jennifer Aniston's mansion doesn't stink of burnt toast.

'It doesn't bloody toast otherwise,' he says in a whiny voice, popping his head round the bathroom door. 'Aren't you going to work?'

'I don't feel great.'

He's good looking is my Darren. Women notice him and I know he looks at them but just because we're not married doesn't mean he can touch does it? He brushes back his hair and grins at me.

'That was a bloody boring wedding wasn't it? Christ, I've had more laughs at a funeral.'

'You were late.'

'I'm never going to forget it either am I? Talking of which, I'd better get going.'

'Darren, are you shagging that busty redhead in Eastlea Towers?'

Someone more posh than me would ask 'Are you having an affair?' Frankly I haven't got time for that tosh. He chokes on his burnt toast and coughs. I suppose I should thump him on the back but I'm afraid if I do I may not be able to stop. He points to my tea with watery eyes and I reluctantly hand it to him. He gulps it down before wiping his eyes.

'Are you?' I repeat.

His mouth opens and closes and his shoulders jerk nervously like a goldfish that has leapt from its bowl.

'I read your text messages, so there's no point in denying it.'

His face turns red.

'You read my text messages?' he says hoarsely. 'That's an invasion of privacy.'

'Are you shagging her?' I ask, more loudly this time.

Darren opens his mouth and then his shoulders sag.

'Well, you're never up for it are you? Either you're too tired or too busy reading that erotic rubbish. You're always knackered these days and ...'

'I've got a job Darren. I never stop. Then I come home and clean up after you. I'm exhausted by nine ...'

I sound like that woman on the Jerry Springer show.

'If you gave me as much attention as you give those bloody books it would be a start.'

I really don't believe I'm hearing this. Is he saying it's my fault he had to shag some busty redhead because I work hard and like to relax with a book?

'Maybe if you got off your arse and worked a bit harder yourself I wouldn't be so tired.'

'I do my best,' he snaps. 'Maybe if you had a more lively personality like Angie and lost a bit of weight and stopped eating those sponge fingers dunked in sodding Nutella ...'

'You bastard,' I say, tears running down my cheeks. 'Her personality has bugger all to do with it and you know it. It's what's in her knickers you're interested in. You always did like redheads.'

His world will fall apart when he discovers it comes out of a bottle. The hair colour that is, not her personality.

'Come on Rox, we can sort this out. I'm sorry,' he says, jumping up and trying to take me in his arms. He's lucky there isn't a knife on his plate because I swear to God I'd plunge it into his chest.

'Don't touch me with your filthy unfaithful hands,' I scream.

A rap on the door stops us in our tracks.

'Roxie, Darren, I've got water coming through the ceiling. Are you trying to drown me?'

It's our downstairs neighbour, Craig. Shit, I'd forgotten about the lavender bath. I dash into the bathroom slipping on the wet floor. I can't say the smell of lavender is doing much to calm me. I pull the mop from the cupboard and throw it at Darren.

'Here. You can clean this up and when you're done you can pack up your stuff, and that includes that bloody telescope, and then you can hot foot it over to busty Jayne Mansfield.'

'Who?' he says, looking confused.

I bloody hate men.

'But you can't pay the rent on your own,' he says stupidly.

'If you're not out when I get back Darren, I'll hire some heavies to throw you out.'

Although I'm not sure who the heavies will be at the moment as the only men I can think of are my dad and Felix.

'You'll regret this,' he says, fumbling with the mop.

I somehow don't think so. It's well overdue but it still bloody hurts.

'Sod off Darren,' I say, slamming the door of the flat behind me.

Chapter Seventeen

I stand outside the flats with a tear-streaked face, hair askew, in my tatty tracksuit bottoms and scruffy cardigan. I couldn't look any worse if I tried. I certainly don't look like someone just flush from winning the lottery. I rummage in my bag for a tissue and noisily blow my nose. After much deliberation I head for the park near the flats. It's either that or my parents and I really don't think I can take the stress of being with them right now. It's all I can do to keep the tears at bay. How could Darren blame this on me? I really can't believe I've wasted five years of my life with the wanker. What is wrong with me, anyone else would have dumped their boyfriend the first time they strayed. The truth is, I do, or at least did love Darren. I see the good in everyone that's my problem, and Darren does have a lot of good qualities. He would sit through the corniest rom coms with me. How many men do that without complaining, and go out of his way to get my favourite sweet popcorn? He may be untidy but he always put the rubbish bins out on time and always bought me a jar of Nutella when I was premenstrual. I suppose that was more for his sake than mine come to think of it. If only he didn't have a straying eye, or more to the point, a straying dick.

I find an empty bench and fall into it. I dab my eyes. I won't cry. I won't let the cheating little bugger get to me, but minutes later I'm thinking of all the disgusting things he and redheaded Angie may have done together and I'm the quivering wreck I vowed not to be. I pull my phone from my bag and text Sylvie to say I'm going to be late.

'Don't worry chick, I'll get the train. I'm that hungover,' she texts back. *'I won't even notice the difference. Keep your pecker up.'*

Well Darren is sure to have his pecker up and I don't need reminding of that. I'm finished with men.

'*Big Issue*?' says a guy with a woolly hat. 'Help the homeless.'

'I've just made someone homeless,' I say, standing up. 'And he's the last person in the world I want to help.'

'It's people like you ...' he begins.

'That everyone walks all over,' I say miserably, rummaging in my bag and handing him a couple of quid.

'Make sure that doesn't go on Darren Smart,' I say, walking towards Starbucks. I'll get a takeaway camomile tea and then I'll head back, and if the two-timing little bastard hasn't left I don't know what I'll do. I wipe at my tears and enter Starbucks, the fresh smell of coffee beans reviving me.

'Roxie, isn't it?'

I turn from the counter to see the boxer from the Fun Palace smiling at me. My morning couldn't get any worse. I might be finished with men but that doesn't mean I'm happy about one of them seeing me looking like Nanny McPhee. He looks different to when I last saw him, but that may have something to do with him being half naked then. He's looking quite dapper in a dazzling white shirt, blue tie and suit. He's sitting alone at a table with his laptop in front of him.

'Do you remember me from the Fun Palace?'

The truth is you couldn't forget someone like him. He is quite stunning. All his features perfectly chiselled. He's giving me his cheeky impish grin. He's quite difficult to resist, even in my fragile state.

'You don't remember me do you?' he smiles.

'Sam Lockwood,' I say, trying to pat down those bits of hair that stick out at all angles except the right one.

He smiles.

'You've a good memory. I don't recall your surname I'm afraid.'

'Brown, Roxie Brown,' I say, wishing I could be alone. I can't seem to pat down these stupid bits of hair and I can't seem to stop my mind having visions of Darren and Angie doing disgusting things together. I feel tears well up and quickly brush them aside before Sam Lockwood spots them. I must have a traumatised expression on my face because he gives me a pitying look and says,

'Won't you join me?'

'I really should get back,' I say, when the last thing I want to do is go back.

'Let me at least buy you a Danish? They're pretty good here and it's the least I can do to thank you for being my lucky mascot the other night.'

'I really should ...' I begin.

'They're very comforting,' he says with a wink.

Well I certainly need comforting that's for sure. While he gets the pastries I make a quick trip to the loo to see if there is anything I can do with my wretched hair and tear-stained face. I conclude that aside from plastic surgery there isn't much that can be done. I twist my hair into a hairband and return to the table where he is waiting with the pastries.

'I thought you'd abandoned me. I was just thinking how all was not lost and how I get to have two pastries when hey presto, you returned.'

He has a lovely voice. I can't imagine why someone like him would want to have coffee with me. He pushes the pastry towards me and then fiddles in his pockets.

'Do you have a reward card?' he asks.

I shake my head.

'Ah well,' he says throwing the jacket over the back of his chair. 'I can't find mine and seeing as points mean prizes, you were welcome to have them.'

Oh my God. I stare at him. He is the right build of the murderer and he has dark brown hair. Maybe it was his eyes I saw through the telescope. This meeting was probably not even accidental. He most likely followed me from the flat. My hand is trembling and I put the cup down before I spill the tea. I don't want him to know I know, do I? Once he knows that I know he knows ... Oh God, my brain is going around in circles. My heart races as I think of ways to escape. He looks at me, both our pastries untouched in front of us.

'Are you going to eat that? They really are to die for,' he says.

I hope he doesn't mean that literally.

The Danish looks innocent enough but supposing he has poisoned it? He could have sprinkled it with cyanide when I was in the loo. No one would have noticed. Who would be suspicious of a clean-cut guy like Sam Lockwood? I'm going to die in Starbucks.

'Well ...' I begin.

Then a flash of brilliance enters my head.

'Would you mind swapping? I don't really like cinnamon and that one seems to have less.'

The truth is I love cinnamon.

'Sure,' he says, exchanging plates.

What if he's poisoned both of them? Or what if he guessed I would be suspicious and knew I would want to swap, then he would have the safe one and the poisoned one would be in front of me now. He takes a bite of the Danish and I feel my heart rate slow. I'm being ridiculous. There must be thousands of people with Starbucks reward cards and hundreds who would have lost one. I'm being stupid. I bite into the Danish feeling a little more confident.

'I thought you lived in Chelsea?' I say, while wondering how long it takes for cyanide to have an effect.

'I have a meeting. In fifteen minutes actually, but I like to prepare so I usually sit here, have a coffee and a Danish. It sets me up nicely,' he says with an impish grin. 'What about you?'

'Me?' I say, widening my eyes.

'Where do you work?'

I'm not going to tell him I'm a chambermaid. Not that I'm ashamed or anything, not really.

'In Chelsea actually,' I say. 'I work for Morgan Hotels.'

His face darkens.

'Ark Morgan?' he asks.

His mouth tightens and a frown appears on his forehead. I nod.

'Do you know him?'

'Unfortunately,' he says flatly.

There is an uncomfortable silence and I shift in my seat. I can't imagine anyone disliking Ark Morgan. He does a lot for charity, eradicating hunger and poverty across the globe, you know the sort of thing.

'He's a good boss,' I say. Don't ask me why I said that. I just felt I should stick up for Ark Morgan. The cloud lifts from his face and he smiles again. He's much better looking when he smiles.

'So, why aren't you working today?' he asks, popping the last of his Danish into his mouth. Neither of us has collapsed convulsing to the floor yet, so that's a relief. He must have seen I'm a quivering wreck, it's impossible not to notice my puffy eyes and blotchy face.

'I had an argument with my boyfriend,' I say.

'Ah, the one who likes the Gunners,' he says, seemingly proud of himself for having remembered.

'He also likes redheads,' I say miserably and instantly regret it. I could bite my tongue.

'I'm sorry,' he says touching my arm. 'I could tell something was wrong.' He looks into my eyes for a moment and is about to say something when my phone rings.

I glance at the screen expecting it to be Darren but it's my mum. I hastily reject the call.

'It's time for me to go,' he says softly, removing his hand. 'It was nice seeing you again.'

'Thank you for the Danish,' I say.

'Next time I'll get you one without cinnamon,' he says, closing his laptop.

My phone bleeps with a message. I really don't need this now.

'Someone is keen to get hold of you,' he smiles.

'It's just my mum. She's probably found a book on tantric sex she wants to give me ... Not that I'm into that,' I add quickly. 'Tantric sex, I wouldn't actually ... Well, it's my mum ... not that she's into it either, not exactly. She just reads books and things. Seriously, who's got the time?' I laugh nervously.

Christ. Get me out of here.

My phone bleeps again. I've never been so popular.

'I'd best leave you to it,' he says, with a broad smile. He holds out his hand. 'It was nice seeing you again Roxie Brown.'

I feel something in his hand and look down.

'My number, if things don't get sorted with the Gunner guy. We could maybe do another pastry.'

His eyes meet mine again and for a second I feel hypnotised.

'See you Roxie,' he says as he heads for the door. My phone rings. It's Mum and she's in floods of tears.

'Your dad has left me. Can you believe it? I've given him the best years of my life and now he buggers off.'

That's all I need.

Chapter Eighteen

'A project should have a code name and from this point on this is to be known as project *That Night*,' says Sylvie.

'That doesn't make any sense. How about project *Bad Buddha*?' I suggest.

'Project Bad Buddha doesn't exactly roll off the tongue,' says Felix. 'It conjures up crime busters with huge bellies and evil smiles on their faces.'

Sylvie shakes her head.

'Why do we need a code name anyway?' asks Felix.

'Because that's what you do,' says the all-knowledgeable Sylvie. I've also set up a *That Night* WhatsApp group so we can stay in touch and share evidence. Our mission is to find enough evidence to solve this crime and then hand it over to the police so that justice can be done.'

'Is *That Night* the best you could come up with?' asks Felix.

'It's cryptic,' says Sylvie.

'You don't say,' mocks Felix. 'Right, who's for wine?' he waves a bottle of Gallo Grenache Rose.

'Ooh yes,' I say.

I could so easily become a lush right now. My partner of five years has left me and is probably shagging the life out of the bottled redhead. My dad left my mum, not to shag a bottled redhead I should hasten to add, and admittedly only got as far as the garden shed, but all the same. He couldn't face swinging. Who can blame him? Mum had been playing lots of Matt Monro apparently, and that tipped him over the edge. I think it would tip anyone over the edge, frankly.

'She kept playing Walk Away,' he'd said. 'So I did.'

I've completely given up men and I don't mean for Lent either, not that I know when Lent is mind you. So I may as well take up booze. Wine and Nutella, that works for me.

'Here you go love,' says Felix, pouring a nice measure.

'Not while we're doing forensics,' snaps Sylvie.

'Going through someone's rubbish is not exactly forensics,' argues Felix. 'It's more like an invasion of privacy, and I'd much rather be pissed doing it if it's okay with you. Who knows what we're going to find.'

'Breaking and entering someone's house is an invasion of privacy,' argues Sylvie, 'and that didn't seem to bother you.'

He gasps.

'Oh, such words. Like a thorn to my heart they are. I'll have you know I'm taking Buscopan like no tomorrow thanks to that little trip. I fear my bowels will never come out of spasm.'

I down half of the wine before Sylvie can take the glass out of my hand.

'This is serious what we're doing. A man has been murdered. Have both of you forgotten that?' says Sylvie crossly.

'Of course not love. I just think you're getting a bit intense. After all, we're just going through some rubbish, not cracking the enigma code,' mocks Felix.

'I haven't forgotten but I have had a bit on my mind,' I say, trying not to sound too defensive. After all, Sylvie is just trying to help.

'I wouldn't mind having seventy-five grand on my mind,' says Felix. 'Does shagging Darren know about that?'

'I never got around to telling him,' I say. 'I told him to bugger off and he did.'

'*Result*,' says Felix, downing his wine while giving Sylvie a challenging look. 'At least you won't be bunking down here.'

Sylvie shoots him a dirty look before placing all the evidence from the murder scene on the carpet in front of us.

'Okay, so this is the situation. We know there was a murder because Roxie saw it.'

I shudder at the memory.

'So, we have one specimen pot containing what we can presume is the blood of the victim. Photographs of the fingerprints, a Starbucks reward card which I'll lift for prints in a bit. Plus we have carpet fibres, hair, and the contents of a rubbish bin taken from the murder scene. So what should we be looking for?' asks Sylvie.

Felix shrugs, 'Colonel Mustard and the lead piping?'

'A tall dark stranger who likes coffee,' I offer.

'Clues,' Sylvie sighs. 'Did you have any luck with your internet search for a blood analyser, Felix?'

'There are some cheap ones in India.'

'India?' Sylvie echoes.

That's a thought, now I have some money I could pop off to India couldn't I? I've never really travelled much unless you count the Isle of Wight and a budget break in Rimini. It's not that I haven't wanted to travel. It just didn't happen. India seems very colourful doesn't it? Well it does if *The Best Exotic Marigold Hotel* is anything to go by.

'We're not going to sodding India are we?' barks Sylvie irritably. 'Didn't you find anyone?'

'As it happens I was visiting this friend and I happened to mention I was looking for a blood analyst and ...'

'You just happened to mention?' I say.

Sylvie rolls her eyes.

'Anyway,' continues Felix. 'He has a friend who has a friend who knows this guy who happens to know someone who knows this chemist ...'

'Jesus wept,' moans Sylvie. 'Is there anyone now left in Clapham who doesn't know we're looking for a sodding blood analyst?'

'Anyway, we can go tomorrow night. I've got his address,' he says proudly handing over a scrap of paper to Sylvie. 'He'll be expecting us.'

Sylvie pops it into her bag before handing us latex gloves.

'These aren't Ark ...' I begin.

'No, they're not from the hotel stock cupboard. What would Ark Morgan be doing with latex gloves?'

Ooh I shudder to think.

'Can we please concentrate? Try to focus,' orders Sylvie.

'Shall I light some candles?' suggests Felix.

'We're not holding a bloody séance, unless you were thinking of making contact with the victim.'

'We don't know who he is,' I say. Not that I believe in séances and all that nonsense. Then again, Madam Zehilda was pretty spot on wasn't she?

'Was,' Sylvie corrects. 'We have to refer to him in the past tense.'

I shudder again.

'Ah,' Felix says. 'I do know who the victim is, I mean, was.'

'What?' Sylvie says.

'I looked up the address from the electoral roll on 192.com.'

'Does it tell you if he's deceased?' Sylvie asks.

'Don't be mental. Its 192.com, not find-a-corpse.com.'

I refill my glass. This is getting too gruesome for me. The past few days have been hideous, apart from winning the lottery of course, which was far from hideous but it would have been much more enjoyable had there not been a murder in the midst of it.

'His name is …'

'Was,' corrects Sylvie.

'Actually we don't really know if he … well you know?' I say nervously, wishing we could move off the subject of the victim. It's enough I've got my mum's problems on my mind not to mention my own relationship break up.

'I can't believe he didn't tell me how unhappy he was,' Mum had sobbed. 'He said it was the Sting stuff.'

That's understandable. Who could cope with having tantric sex and chickens rammed down their throat? I don't mean literally of course, having chickens rammed down your throat would be awful.

'He said the chicken shit is ruining the garden and the tantric sex books are an embarrassment when Duncan comes round.'

I don't imagine Duncan even knows what the missionary position is let alone the 'lust and thrust' position. He's not a bachelor at fifty-seven for nothing.

'Apparently Duncan picked up my copy of *The Galloping Horse* thinking it was a Dick Francis novel. Your dad said it's my fault that he's now on blood pressure pills.'

'Dad is taking blood pressure pills?' I'd said alarmed.

'No, Duncan. I do wish you would keep up.'

'All because he looked at one of your books?'

'*The Galloping Horse* is a graphic description of that sex position dear. Don't you read any of the books I give you?'

I've probably been far too busy to indulge in the galloping horse or any other animal type sex position. I didn't think it was the time to tell her about Darren, or about the lottery win come to that. I drag my mind back to Felix.

'His name is …' Felix says, pausing for dramatic effect as if announcing an Oscar winner, 'Victor Wainwright.'

'Victor?' Sylvie and I whisper.

The door to the kitchen creaks open and Sylvie and I scream, scattering latex gloves over the carpet. Polly, Felix's cat, strolls in and rolls on them.

'She loves latex,' says Felix, 'but then don't we all?'

Sylvie scoops the cat into her arms.

'Don't let it near the evidence,' she cries, throwing the cat at Felix.

'Christ Sylv, I'll have to give him a double portion of cat treats now,' says Felix.

'We don't actually know if Victor was the victim though, do we?' I say. 'He could have been the murderer.'

'She has a point,' says Sylvie. 'You need to find out more about Victor.'

'Why me?' asks Felix petulantly.

'Because you do it so well.'

Half an hour later, we have consumed the bottle of wine and worked our way through two bags of tortillas while sifting through the contents of the bin, which much to Sylvie's disgust consist of two takeaway menus, a card from a local electrician, a Waitrose receipt, a torn letter and the remnants of two tickets for the Fun Palace. The disjointed letter is now crudely sellotaped together and sits pride of place on the floor. We stare at it with bemused expressions on our faces. It's on headed notepaper but it's impossible to see the whole address.

'All I can see is *Chelsea*. It could be anywhere.'

'It says *Mansions*,' I say.

'There are loads of blocks in Chelsea that have *Mansions* in the address,' says Sylvie.

'These tortillas are fab darling. Where did you buy them?' asks Felix.

Sylvie looks angrily at him.

'Please remind me why you are here?' She asks.

'You tell me love. If I could get out of it I would.'

I study the torn pieces of the letter. It's impossible to decipher. The figure of one thousand pounds is mentioned.

'Do you think it's a blackmail letter?' I ask, looking at the words *failure to deliver*.

'It's usually the heavies they send round darling, not letters on headed notepaper,' laughs Felix.

'She could be right though,' says Sylvie, nodding in agreement. 'The words *unforeseen circumstances* and *failure to deliver* could all be considered threatening.'

'You'll be saying Break clause is code for *break a leg*,' he laughs.

'Or kneecap,' says Sylvie animatedly.

'If you ask me it's simply a demand for money, legal money that is. Like a tax bill or something. Frankly I think you should stop reading Ruth Rendell, darling,' says Felix. 'And maybe read the local rag instead. Has anyone considered doing that?'

'Ah yes, I thought of that?' says Sylvie and I have to agree with Felix that she is sounding more like Columbo by the day. 'Nothing on the local news, so I don't imagine there will be anything in the local paper but we need to check that on Friday. That can be your job Felix.'

'Everything seems to be my job,' he moans. 'Don't forget I have a real job love, as an air steward. EasyJet won't accept my part-time activities with project *That Night* as an excuse for a day off.'

'I think Felix is right,' says Sylvie.

'Yes, it wouldn't be good if he lost his job,' I agree.

'I'm not talking about his job. I'm talking about the letter. I think we should dismiss it as evidence,' Sylvie says before slapping her hand to her head in the manner of Columbo.

Felix winks at me.

'I think we should buy her a rumpled raincoat, what do you think?'

'We need to go to the local shops. Find out if a lot of bleach has been bought recently.'

'Bleach?' says Felix.

'Why bleach?' I ask, feeling sure I should know the answer. After all, I watch just as much CSI as Sylvie, or at least I did when Darren was around. I come over all melancholy again. I'm in my early thirties. I don't even have a mortgage. Not that I want one of course. I mean, who wants a mortgage? But I should have one by now right? I should have a husband and stretch marks. I should really have huge leaky boobs with a baby hanging off the nipple while I'm watching CSI. That's what women my age are doing isn't it? Not watching CSI with babies hanging off their nipples, I don't mean, but settling down to married bliss. I'm not sure how bleach led me to married bliss, but I'm sure there must be a connection somewhere.

'The fact we didn't find the body leads me to suspect someone of speeding up the decomposition of the ...'

'The de what?' questions Felix.

'The decomposition.'

'I'm still none the wiser love,' he says, offering round custard cream biscuits, reminding me again of Darren's infidelity.

'It means the decaying of the body. Bleach can speed up the process as well as disfigure the body so it is unrecognisable.'

He lowers his custard cream.

'There are lots of things I don't need to know before I die and that was one of them.'

I am about to confess about the hole in my sock and the lost earring, when Sylvie says,

'And on the subject of being unrecognisable I think we must congratulate ourselves for not leaving any trace of our visit. We have some good fingerprints and the Starbucks card too, and I'll lift those prints from the card and see if they match the ones on the glasses.'

She has a short memory. I somehow think she is overlooking the lopsided painting and the water stain on the carpet. And I've not even mentioned my big toe print, which the police could be lifting as we speak. I really don't have the heart to tell her.

'Right, on that Starbucks note, who's for coffee?' asks Felix. 'Who'd like a dot of cream in theirs?'

Dot, oh damn, I forgot to clean her flat. That's all I need.

If only it was Ark Morgan's flat. Just imagine ...

'Miss Brown, can you please come here?'

I walk slowly towards Ark Morgan, my heart pounding.

'Did you deliberately miss this bit, Miss Brown?'

He points at a thin layer of dust on the huge dining table.

'Are you wanting me to punish you, is that it?'

I blink rapidly, praying that he will be kind to me.

He whips his tie off, almost whipping himself in the face with it. I almost remind him it is me he is punishing not himself but

think better of it. He fastens it around my wrists. Holy Moses, he's knotting it a bit tight.

'I have scissors,' he says.

'But your tie,' I whisper huskily.

'I have hundreds,' he whispers, 'hundreds to tie you with. Now lean over the table Miss Brown. I'm going to take you hard from behind.'

'Oh God,' I groan.

'Roxie, are you okay?'

I shake myself from my fantasy and come back to reality.

'I forgot to clean Dot's flat,' I say with a sigh. 'Better go.'

'I found this in the flat,' says the man at the bar. 'Nothing to do with you is it?'

The other man laughs.

'Do I look like the earring type?'

He takes a sip of beer and studies the earring.

'Although, it does look kind of familiar but I couldn't tell you where I've seen it.'

'Well I can assure you it wasn't there before Saturday, so this could be a clue as to who broke into the flat ...'

'And rearranged the furniture ...'

'The burglar's *calling card* perhaps?' he laughs, dangling the earring between his fingers.

'So we're looking for a woman then?'

'One who cleans carpets and pick locks,' says the other man thoughtfully.

They sip their beers in silence.

'Another?' says the man before pocketing the earring.

Chapter Nineteen

His finger is poised over the lift button, his eyes meet mine and my legs almost give way. If it wasn't for Henry I don't think I would still be upright.

'Going down?' Ark Morgan asks.

Now there's a thought I daren't dwell on. My heart is pounding as I step in beside him, his delicious fragrance wafting over me. The doors slide shut and I'm alone in the lift with him. He exudes power, wealth and oh God, sexual tension that is so potent that I'm feeling heady. Damn, I'm only wearing my chambermaid overall with *Morgan Hotels* neatly embroidered on it and my name badge over my left breast. My hair is scrunched up into a bun. I'm carrying a Henry and a bucket of cleaning supplies. He's certainly going to notice *me* isn't he? He'll probably have me in the lift any second now. Let's face it, how can he not find me irresistible? The lift moves slowly and I fiddle with Henry's hose and feel my breathing quicken as he moves closer to me, his musky fragrance making me heady.

Suddenly he lunges towards me, the paperwork in his hand flying around the lift like confetti. His hands are pinning me to the wall of the lift, his hips grinding against mine.

'Henry,' I mumble, as the hose is pushed against my breast. I know Henry and I are quite intimate but this is taking things too far.

'Fuck Henry,' he says. 'I'm having you now Miss Brown.'

Holy shit, Ark Morgan wants me. He wants me right here in the Crescent Hotel lift. He must have remembered me from our meeting at the Fun Palace.

His lips move closer to mine. I'm so wet. At least the front of my overall is wet. Oh God, what is he doing to me? I can feel his erection hard and stiff pushing against me. My breath is coming in short sharp gasps. His eyes are burning into mine and his hardness is pressing against my hip bone. He removes his tie, licking his lips slowly as he does so.

'Loosen your top,' he demands.

I'm so afraid the doors will open and people will see us. Ark Morgan and me doing it in the lift.

'Did you hear me,' he says sharply. 'Your top is loose.'

His arm shakes me by the shoulder and I'm dragged out of my fantasy. Ark Morgan is pointing to my overall. Holy crap, I'm covered in Johnson's floor polish and Henry's hose has somehow got hooked under the hem. Holy smoke, what must Ark Morgan think of me? I look like a lactating mother jerking off to a hoover hose. I feel myself grow hot.

'The top of the floor polish bottle has come loose,' he says, his voice abrupt. 'I hope it isn't going to stain the carpet. You'll need to see to this before you do anything else.'

'I ...'

'In future can you use the stairs? It really doesn't create a good impression if cleaners use the same lift as the guests. I'll have a word with someone about it. We have top-class clientele here.'

Use the stairs? He surely isn't serious. I couldn't possibly carry all this up fifteen flights of stairs. I'm not a bloody female Russian commando. The doors slide open and he marches out. I'm left standing with Henry between my legs. Maybe this is the only thing I'll have between my legs from now on. The doors slide shut again and I fight back my tears. I look at myself in the lift mirror and cringe. My overall is soaked and my face is redder than a beetroot. The doors open again and I drag Henry with me. I'm sick to death of this job. I spend half my life with my hand down a shower drain pulling out other people's hairs and when I'm not doing that I'm replacing bog rolls. What kind of job is that? I'm always being judged by what I do for a living. It's not fair. I bet Ark Morgan wouldn't have spoken to me like that if I wasn't a cleaner. Just because I wear an overall and carry a feather duster doesn't mean I'm stupid does it?

I hate men. They're arrogant sexist liars. I'm going to become one of those self-sufficient women. Perhaps I'll even take a course in plumbing. Yes that's it. I'll become an emancipated woman, free from the restraints of men. I'll be empowered and eat as many Nutella-tipped sponge fingers as I like.

'Where have you been?' asks Sylvie when I finally arrive on floor eight. 'I think I know who that frigging biscuit thief is. I saw …' she stops at looks at me, 'What happened to your overall?'

'Ark Morgan had me in the lift and during our sexual tussle I spilt the floor polish,' I say facetiously. 'In a nutshell I had a run in with Ark Morgan and ended up with the moustache up my skirt and Johnson's polish down my front. He'd prefer it if the chambermaids used the stairs in future. We're an embarrassment apparently, and he doesn't want their clientele to see us.'

Especially not with Henry hoovers up their skirts, it does after all give the wrong impression doesn't it?

'The moustache?' she asks curiously.

'The dusting brush attachment,' I explain.

'I suppose we should be grateful it wasn't the extended nozzle,' she giggles.

'I think that would have got me the sack.'

'And more,' she laughs. 'Anyway, he is a stuck-up prick. Don't let it bother you. Now you've won the lottery you can chuck his job in his face if you want to.'

She's quite right of course and it is something I've been thinking about. In fact only today the money was transferred into my account. But I've already decided to use it as a deposit to buy my own flat. I can't just chuck in my job. I'll have a mortgage and will have to keep up the repayments. But I could take some classes and maybe eventually get a better job.

Sylvie points to the trolley which carries biscuits, teabags, bottles of complimentary shower gel and shampoo.

'I found this among the biscuits,' she says holding a toy train. I expect her to add, 'Mark as exhibit B.'

'I'm not sure I get it,' I say. The truth is I'm not getting much at all since Darren revealed his big indiscretion. How do I tell my parents? I haven't even told them about my lottery win yet. Do you want the good news or the bad news? The bad news is Darren has been shagging the redhead in Eastlea Towers and the good news is I've won the lottery. Winning the lottery hasn't eased my pain at all, and now Ark Morgan has turned on me. I'm beginning to know how Jesus felt. It's too much betrayal at once isn't it?

'It's obviously that Horrid Henry brat in number six. You know the ones. The parents get through shower gel like no tomorrow, not to mention teabags. I bet all your lottery money that they've got bottles of the stuff stashed in their Primark suitcase. Either that or they spend all day in the shower. It's easy to work out that's not happening because their room never smells that great,' she says self-righteously.

'Right,' I say, following her into number eight. The bed is a jumble of sheets.

'Dirty weekenders,' says Sylvie.

I'm not sure how she has deduced that and really don't want to ask. I change my overall and chuck the other one into a bin liner before stripping the bed.

'Ooh Jo Malone, Earl Grey and Cucumber, how weird is that?' she squeals as she sprays it onto her wrists.

'You'll get caught one day,' I say, sniffing the air and realising I could afford to buy a bottle for myself if I wanted. A little thrill runs through me.

'I'll do the shower in this one,' Sylvie smiles. 'I'm sure there are all sorts of goodies in here.'

An hour later we are at Lady Harle's penthouse suite where she lives for half of the year. I wait as Sylvie unlocks the door before saying,

'I really fancy Ark Morgan.'

There, I have finally admitted it.

'Tell me something I don't know,' she says.

'You knew?' I say dropping Lady Harle's post beside a pile on the hall table.

'You dribble every time you mention his name. You know he's available?'

'No way,' I gasp. 'I thought he had a girlfriend.'

'For a big fan, you don't keep up with the gossip do you? There was an interview with him in one of those *Tycoon* magazines. They put one in every room; where have you been? Anyway, they parted six months ago. He doesn't like to talk about it, claims he's had no time since for a new relationship. So he's available.'

'Not for someone like me.'

'I'm not so sure of that,' she says holding up a gilt-edged invitation.

'Lady Harle is on her world cruise isn't she? Who will notice she's missing? You have to admit it's a shame to waste the ticket.'

She thrusts it into my hand.

'It's this Saturday.'

I look down at the invitation.

Mr Ark Morgan requests the honour of your presence at a Cocktail Party aboard 'Morgansong,' Saturday, June 6th[h] *from 7 p.m. until midnight. Embarking from Dock C, Slip No. 27 at Royal Victoria dock. Dress formal.*

'I can't possibly,' I say. 'What would I wear, and supposing he recognises me as the chambermaid with the hoover brush up her skirt.'

She claps her hands together.

'First, we know that Ark Morgan only invites a handful of guests to these functions. Most of them he's never set eyes on. The rest are business contacts. I'll bet you anything he has never met Lady Harle. You can be whoever you want to be. We'll take you to the top beauty salons in London. You can afford it now Rox. By the time they've finished with you I won't recognise you, let alone Ark Morgan. We can go to a fancy designer dress shop and get you a really posh outfit. And you can have your hair done. You'll look like a million dollars.'

'But the invitation is for Lady Harle,' I point out. 'I can't pretend to be someone I'm not.'

'It hasn't got her name on it.'

'I've never been on a yacht in my life,' I say, placing the invitation back on the hall table.

'Now's your chance, and you'll meet lots of rich and handsome strangers, I only wish I could come with you,' she sighs. 'It's the stuff of Mills and Boon.'

'You can come to the beauty salon with me,' I say, knowing how she has always wanted to treat herself. 'In fact I was going to arrange it for you.'

She claps her hand to her mouth.

'The Great Zehilda got everything right. She said someone would give me something I've always wanted,' she says tearfully.

Blimey, it's only a beauty treatment, not Ryan Gosling covered in whipped cream and melted chocolate.

'I'm not making any promises though. I'll have the beauty treatment and everything, but I'm not sure about the yacht and all that stuff.'

Ooh, champagne and canapés with Ark Morgan on his private yacht. His glass touching mine, his lips pink with desire, his eyes full of lust and his husky voice whispering *laters Baby*. I suppose I could. What harm could it do?

Chapter Twenty

I turn the ignition one more time. The engine splutters and dies.

'That's it love. It's reached its final destination,' says Felix, 'the great car park in the sky. Good job you won the lottery.'

'I forgot to put petrol in,' I say apologetically, 'and I didn't *win* the lottery, I had a lottery win. There is a difference you know.'

You'd think I'd become Victoria Beckham overnight the way Felix talks.

'We'll have to get a taxi,' says Sylvie as she clambers out.

We stand on the pavement and watch a stream of black cabs file past, not one with their light on.

'We could be standing here all night,' says Sylvie, clutching her carrier bag with the blood specimen inside. 'We'll have to get the bus.'

'I'm not getting on one of those,' says Felix, flinging his scarf around his neck. 'Those bell pushes and handles are covered in germs.' He throws himself into the road and waves frantically at an oncoming cab.

'Lonsdale Street,' says Felix as the cab screeches to a halt. 'Number 23.'

The cab driver peeps at us through the rear-view mirror. Even I have to admit we look an unlikely threesome. Felix in his fedora, silk scarf and velvet jacket looks like he has stepped out of the Bohemian twenties, and Sylvie looks no better in her multicoloured shawl and crinkled skirt. I'm the only one looking normal in my jeans and blouse. Lonsdale Street is not a place you would park a car. Even my Fiesta wouldn't be safe here. The cab driver pulls in behind a burnt-out Honda.

'I don't suppose you'd consider waiting?' asks Felix.

'You're dead right there mate. I wouldn't,' replies the driver.

We pay and try to ignore a group of yobs on the street corner. We deduce they're yobs by their immediate greeting of

Whadda lookin' at? And by the number of tattoos and earrings that adorn their bodies.

'Just ignore them,' Felix advises.

'We are,' says Sylvie. 'It doesn't seem to be helping though.'

'Where's the fancy dress party?' calls one.

'I think we should answer them,' I say.

'Are you insane?' asks Felix.

'She's right. They're more likely to get aggressive if we ignore them,' agrees Sylvie.

'Pay them off,' suggests Felix. 'You've got enough. If you spend your winnings on saving our lives then it must be worth it.'

'I'm not giving three yobs seventy thousand quid,' I say.

'Christ, keep your voice down. We don't want them mugging us,' whispers Sylvie.

'Ya looking for some good shit?' one asks before making a gurgling sound and projecting a piece of phlegm which lands close to my foot.

'Don't open your mouth,' Sylvie hisses. 'I've got a feeling they may be homophobic, as well as racist and misogynistic.'

'Can you be all three?' asks Felix in a hushed tone.

'We're looking for number 23a Doctor …' she says in a sing song voice.

'Winters,' I say, helpfully.

They laugh.

'Meow meow you're after is it?'

I'm beginning to wonder what it is that Dr Winters does. I'm only now hoping it isn't something to do with cats and the local Chinese takeaway.

'Yeah, they look the type,' laughs another. 'We can do you a good bit of blow.'

They spread themselves across the path as we try to pass.

'Whose great idea was this?' I whisper.

Felix opens his mouth, thinks better of it and closes it again. I see number 23 is across the road. I tug at Felix's sleeve and nod in that direction.

'It's fine, thank you very much,' I say boldly. 'We can see the house. We don't need any blow today.'

I'm not giving the buggers a penny of my lottery money.

'Sure we can't get ya to change ya mind,' says one menacingly.

'Not unless you want D.I. Rennard here to arrest you. We're undercover, chaps. We're going to raid Dr Winter's pad and sort out the meow meow, so why don't you make yourself scarce before we throw you into the back of our police van.'

I'm hoping meow meow is something illegal otherwise I'll be looking a right plonker. Felix gazes at me in wonderment and admiration. Meanwhile the yobs look confused. I hope they can't see my trembling hands. Sylvie nods confidently.

'Move on you little pricks. I don't want you on my turf. This is a big one I'm breaking here and I don't want you in my way. Now scuttle off before we do you for that bit of blow you're trying to flog us.'

One slides his hand into his pocket and I feel sure Felix is hyperventilating. Sylvie crosses the road and I follow on my wobbly legs. We follow Felix down the stone steps to the basement flat, and knock on the door of 23a. Meanwhile the yobs have legged it, much to my relief. The door creaks open. A dishevelled man wearing goggles on his forehead stands on the threshold waving a taser gun at us.

'Oh,' he says. 'I thought you were those little fuckers again.'

'We have an appointment,' says Sylvie with a tense smile.

'Charlie arranged it,' says Felix.

I'm not sure which is worse, the yobs or the chemist. He's most likely in the middle of making a batch of meow meow. We're ushered into the hallway, past piles of newspapers and science magazines and into a room at the end of the hall.

'My laboratory,' he says proudly.

I'm afraid to look. I have visions of cats hanging from the ceiling or struggling in cages with pleading eyes begging for release. I shudder. I look around cautiously and am relieved to find there isn't a cat in sight.

'Your neighbours mentioned meow meow,' I say nervously. 'I'm just keen to know what it is.'

'If it's mephedrone you're after, you've come to the wrong place and can bugger off now. I'm not into drugs,' he says walking back down the hallway. 'Everything is in the power of the mind,' he adds mysteriously.

'We don't want drugs,' Sylvie says, shooting me a dirty look. 'We've got blood.'

'We've all got blood,' he retorts crisply.

'We need the blood analysed,' says Felix.

'For what?' he asks.

That's a point. We all look at each other.

'For DNA,' says Sylvie.

'If it's blood it will have DNA. You will need a DNA sequencer if you want me to find out anything about the donor,' says the doctor dismissively.

'Do you have one of those in your Tardis, doctor?' Felix asks.

He looks at us like we're mad.

'No sense of humour,' whispers Sylvie.

He leads us back to his laboratory. Felix peers at a test tube bubbling over a Bunsen burner. It wouldn't surprise me if Dr Winters is building Frankenstein the second in another room. The place gives me the creeps.

'Dr Winters ...' Sylvie begins as she hands over the specimen.

'Phil,' he says, studying the container.

We all fidget uncomfortably. The thing is we didn't have proper specimen bottles so Sylvie had to stuff it into a coleslaw tub. We washed it out first, obviously.

'Have you been a scientist long?' asks Felix, peering at bottles on a shelf.

'I'm a biochemist,' barks Phil. 'I'm doing a post doc. This is free of coleslaw isn't it? I bloody hate coleslaw.'

Dr Winters looks puzzled as he studies the sample. He takes the coleslaw tub over to the table, pushes the goggles onto his head and replaces them with a pair of thick-rimmed spectacles and studies the specimen under a microscope. We wait patiently

'This is an oil-based pigment,' he says suddenly.

'Is that a particular type of blood?' asks Felix.

'It's not blood at all,' says Phil, pushing the goggles further back onto his head. 'But there are tiny particles of what looks like skin mixed in with it.'

This is getting more gruesome by the minute.

'What does that mean?' asks Sylvie.

'I've no idea,' says Phil handing back the coleslaw pot. 'But it points to something odd if you ask me.'

'I knew it,' says Sylvie triumphantly.

My heart sinks. I was so hoping I had imagined the murder. Now it seems I didn't. Somewhere out there in the midst of Clapham is a murderer. I don't know who he is but he probably knows me and it's only a matter of time before he catches up with me.

Chapter Twenty-One

'I can't bear it,' he whispers into my ear, his hot breath against my cheek. 'I can't resist you in this dress. I've got to have you.'

'But we can't leave yet,' I say.

Holy crap, we've only just arrived. He fingers the ice cube in his glass and gives me a wicked smile. It doesn't matter what all the sex manuals tell you. I can assure you all you need is an ice cube and you're done. He pushes me against the railings of the boat. I look down at the rippling water. I wonder if I should mention that I only ever got as far as my 10 metres swimming certificate. I mean an ice cube is one thing but the freezing cold water of the Thames is another. I hardly think a 10 metre proficiency badge is going to hold me in good stead.

'Make your excuses Miss Brown,' he whispers, 'or I'll have to take you right here and if you struggle I'll have to tie you up, and you know how you dislike that.'

'You're always so in control of me,' I whisper.

'I exercise control over all things Miss Brown as you well know.'

My legs give way and his hands are there to support me. My breath hitches as he strokes my bottom. I wince and make a mental note to buy more arnica. This whipping malarkey is all very well but I do have to sit down occasionally even if it's only on the loo. It's lucky I don't have an office job.

'Are you ready for me?' he asks, his hand lifting my D. Von Furstenberg dress and sliding up my thigh.

I gasp. It's bloody freezing out here. I've got goose bumps where I didn't know I could get goose bumps. My hair is getting blown all over the place. I'll never get it back looking the way it was. Why can't I be all sophistication and grace like Jennifer Aniston? And now the wind is blowing right up my dress and there is nothing sexual about a cold breeze hitting you in the crotchless knickers area. I struggle to remember if I had signed up for this in my contract.

'Do you want to touch me, Miss Brown?' he whispers huskily, pressing his hardness against me.

I'm on the brink. I really am. I'm on the brink of falling into the bloody Thames. I can't see him for the hair in my eyes. I feel his lips close to mine and open my mouth to eagerly receive his, only to get a mouthful of river spray from a passing speedboat. I splutter and he thumps me on the back.

'Are you all right darling,' he asks.

Darling? He never calls me darling.

'Roxie, are you okay?'

Sylvie's voice pulls me from my fantasy as a Harrods' shop assistant pats me on the back. I'm standing in front of a mirror in a D. Von Furstenberg black cocktail dress and choking after seeing the price tag.

'Yes, I'm fine. I can't believe how fabulous this dress is.'

I can't believe the fabulous price either.

'You look beautiful my lovely. It was made for you,' says the assistant offering me cashew nuts from a silver tray.

'It does look spectacular,' agrees Sylvie. 'You have to take it. It makes you look really trim.'

Is she trying to say I usually look fat?

'It's very expensive,' I say, holding back a fart. I really shouldn't eat nuts, but when they are offered like that it is hard to refuse. Darren used to guess how many nuts I could eat before I started. No, I must not think about Darren. I've got to bugger on haven't I?

'One thousand five hundred is a small price madam, when it transforms you into a million dollars.'

'I'll take it,' I say. After all, I can afford it and I can't possibly attend Ark Morgan's function in my Zara dress. Sylvie claps her hands excitedly.

'We need to get you a matching clutch bag,' she exclaims as the assistant thrusts one into my hands.

'A match made in heaven,' gushes the assistant, 'and at eight hundred pounds, an absolute bargain.'

She's certainly on commission.

'Oh my God,' utters Sylvie as we waltz out of Harrods. 'I can't believe you spent all that money.'

Nor can I, but Ark Morgan is worth it. Let's face it; this is my one and only chance to get Ark Morgan to notice me. Although I can't believe I actually bought a dress from Harrods. Who would have thought it? Me, Roxie Brown of all people, it really is unbelievable. Sylvie says we should go to a show after our beauty treatments.

'Make a night of it. I always wanted to see Les Misérables, we could go to one of those fancy theatre restaurants for dinner,' she says.

Sylvie certainly knows how to spend my money.

'Right, next stop, beauty spa,' she says excitedly.

I don't know about you but I always feel slightly guilty at being pampered, like I'm not entitled to it or something. Sylvie has no such qualms and I'm dragged to a top London beauty spa and kitted out in a dressing gown which is nowhere near big enough for me. I spend the whole time checking my boobs haven't popped out which is not quite conducive to relaxation, and as hard as I try I really can't see the benefits of the mud wrap. Being covered in mud and wrapped in cellophane by a total stranger feels more like a form of torture, unless of course Ark Morgan is doing it, then I imagine it is a sweet agonising torture. Ooh, he can wrap me in cellophane any time. Sylvie loves every minute of it and doesn't seem at all fazed being covered in mud. Then, of course, there are the other women at the beauty spa. You know the type, all fur coats and no knickers, you've seen them. Those women who waft past you smelling heavenly and looking sensational and have never had a bald tyre in their life, or lost their boyfriend to a busty redhead. I've probably fished a few of their hairs out of the hotel shower drain in my time.

Darren came back last night to collect his speakers. Bloody nerve as they never were his to start with but I couldn't be arsed to argue. He said Angie's hair absolutely does not come out of a bottle. And that it is Titian not red. If she's a natural Titian then I'm Jennifer Aniston, although I'm starting to look like her, Jennifer Aniston that is, not Titian Angie.

After the mud bath is the pedicure and foot massage. Having a stranger fondle your feet is a bit disconcerting especially if you're ticklish like me. When Sylvie mentions the sauna I put my foot down good and proper. The last thing I want to do is sweat in a hot room with a bunch of strangers. It's bad enough having Sylvie see me red as a beetroot and dripping sweat all over the floor. I really don't get the appeal of pampering. It's a loss of dignity if you ask me. It's like going into a communal fitting room. Don't you just hate those? You stand there comparing how you look against everyone else. You either come away feeling ten times better about yourself or ten times worse. The latter is normally true for me. But now, after the mud bath, pedicure and manicure I have to admit to feeling twenty times better about myself. I'm sitting in front of a mirror and for the first time I don't mind looking at my reflection. My skin is glowing and looks all dewy fresh and is totally free from blemishes. Lionel the hairdresser looks at me through the mirror, his blonde Rod Stewart hair as stiff as meringue peaks.

'I'm going to be creative honey,' he croons.

Sounds good to me, the more creative the better, in fact the more unrecognisable I am the better. Then there is less chance of the murderer spotting me.

'She wants to show Darren what he's lost,' Sylvie says, staring at her own reflection.

'Let me tell you something honey,' chirps Lionel, pulling my hair around like there's no tomorrow. 'Ooh split ends my love. I'll sort those little bitches out for you.'

A girl places a green smoothie in front of me. That's the trouble with these places isn't it? Everyone's on a health kick. What I wouldn't do for a mug of tea with a sponge finger.

'Men are like toilet cubicles my love,' Lionel is saying. 'They're either taken or full of shit. I should know I've had my fair share. There's plenty more fish in the sea and I bet your ex had a face like a mackerel didn't he? No offence of course.'

'No offence taken,' I say.

'This is fabulous Rox, thanks so much,' says Sylvie, coming over all emotional and dripping tears into her smoothie. 'You should have had the waxing, everything feels so smooth now.'

If I'm going to have someone whip hot wax off me, then that someone is going to be me. Okay, it may take hours but at least I get to control the pain. I did try an epilator once, but Christ, that made my eyes water. If you want my opinion they're weapons of torture. *You vill tell us vat ve need to know or ve vill epilate you.* There's a limit to what I'll do in the name of beauty.

Meanwhile Lionel is talking nine to the dozen. I swear he's stoned. I hope he doesn't get too creative with a hairdryer and a round brush because there is no way I'll be able to repeat the look no matter how many round brushes and sprays I'm given. It's always the way isn't it? You look sensational as you walk out of the hair salon and pray that you don't get caught in a gust of wind, because that's it, no matter how hard you try it just won't go back into that perfect style you saw in the salon's mirror. I watch in awe as Lionel transforms me. I've never had such sleek hair in my life. I'll be sliding off the pillows. I can't help wondering what Darren would say if he could see me now, that's if Darren recognises me. I barely recognise me. Jennifer Aniston, eat your heart out. I haven't felt this good about myself in months. I should do this more often, well as more often as the lottery money lasts. I imagine life must be heaven when you have money.

After our treatments we have tea in a French cafe off Regent Street.

'Unless you're John Paul Getty the third, of course,' says Sylvie, 'and you get kidnapped and they start cutting off bits of your body and sending it to your dad. Then I don't imagine it is heaven somehow.'

Dad would not like that at all. He practically faints when Mum plucks her eyebrows. Just the thought of that puts me off my rhubarb tart. I push it to one side and check my phone. I stupidly keep hoping that Darren will message me to apologise for his stupid behaviour and beg to be taken back, but there is nothing. How can he prefer Titian-Bottle-Angie to me?

'Could we have some more tea please?' Sylvie calls in that voice she reserves for posh tea shops. It never works. She always sounds like she's just had Bell's palsy. Not that Sylvie and I spend much time in posh tea shops. The last time we had a posh tea was when Ark Morgan arranged afternoon tea at Claridge's for his staff when one of the hotels won an award. He does things like that. He thinks of his staff and is very nice to them. Not many bosses do that kind of thing do they? I'm sure something must have been wrong this morning for him to be so sharp with me. I can't believe he has broken up with his girlfriend. I read about her in the Sunday paper once. That's another perk of the job; you get the magazines the guests leave behind. She was featured in one of the glossies. I remember looking at her dreamily and wishing I had skin that glowed like hers. I expect she goes to a beauty spa every day. I would too if I could afford it and had the time. It's not so easy when you've got a job.

'Of course you'd have to have tons of security and stuff. Think of all those burly men that would have to follow you around,' giggles Sylvie.

'All the same, it must be nice to have money. You'd never have to worry would you?'

'You've got money,' she smiles.

'Yes, but I won't get more will I? And it won't last forever. Once it's gone that's it.'

'You should invest it.'

'Ooh,' she says, picking up her cup. 'I meant to tell you, the fingerprints on the Starbucks card matched those on one of the glasses. The other glass had different prints, but those prints were all over the coffee table. I'm guessing the Starbucks card belonged to a visitor and not the owner. But of course we don't know which set of prints belongs to the murderer or the victim.'

Why does she have to tell me this now? I was just about to tuck into my rhubarb tart again.

'What do we do now?' I ask.

'I'm not sure. Wait until a body pops up I suppose. It must do eventually. We should have another *That Night* meeting I guess.'

I'd much rather put this whole murder business behind me. Right now I'm thinking only of myself. Very narcissistic I know, but it's not my fault there are mirrors all around the tea shop. I'm glowing brighter than a light bulb. My mind wanders to the cocktail party on Ark's boat. I hope Ark notices me. Sylvie seems to think he won't be able to resist me.

'Roxie.' I turn at the sound of my name to see Sam Lockwood. The guy seems to be everywhere. One minute he is in Clapham and the next in Knightsbridge. He's like Superman, popping up when you least expect it. There was me thinking no one would recognise me.

'It is you isn't it?' he asks, looking at me closely.

Charming, there's no need for him to sound so surprised is there? Sylvie flutters her eyelashes and puts on her posh voice.

I do wish she would stop doing that. I'll have to record her one day, so she knows how odd she sounds.

'Fancy seeing you here,' she says.

How he gets time to work when he seems to spend his life in coffee shops is beyond me.

'Hello, how are you?' I say.

'You look …' he hesitates and I widen my eyes. 'Different,' he finishes.

Surely he doesn't think I walk around in track suit bottoms, with bloodshot eyes and a blotchy face all the time? He points to a chair.

'Mind if I join you?'

'Please do,' says Sylvie.

'If I remember, I promised you a Danish without cinnamon. This is my chance.'

'Without cinnamon?' says a surprised Sylvie, 'but you love …'

I kick her under the table.

'Can I get you one too?' he asks Sylvie.

She nods dumbly.

'I'll get a menu,' he says as he walks to the bar.

'Why did you kick me? And why does he think you don't like cinnamon? You love cinnamon,' says Sylvie.

'Yes I know, but the last time he bought me a Danish I was convinced he'd laced it with cyanide,' I say, lowering my voice.

'Why would he lace it with cyanide? And more to the point why would you even think he would lace it with cyanide?' She stares at me in disbelief.

'Because I thought he was the murderer,' I whisper while watching him talk to a waitress.

She raises her eyebrows.

'Why would you think *he* was the murderer?'

'Shush,' I say. 'Why do you ask so many questions?'

'Because people just don't go around thinking their Danish pastries are laced with cyanide.'

I sigh.

'Because he couldn't find his Starbucks reward card,' I say, feeling my face redden.

She shakes her head.

'Do you know how many people have Starbucks reward cards?'

'I know,' I say hastily, seeing him walking back to our table. I have to admit he doesn't look like a murderer. He's dressed more casually today but still looks smart. He's not carrying a laptop this time but has a sports bag.

'There you go ladies,' he says handing us a menu while not taking his eyes off me.

It's nice to get all this attention but I'm sure if he knew I was a chambermaid he wouldn't give me a second glance, with or without the beauty treatment. I glance shyly at the menu so I don't have to meet his piercing brown eyes. What I wouldn't do for a cinnamon Danish, damn it.

'I'll have the cinnamon roll,' says Sylvie, grinning at me.

I swear she does this on purpose. I love cinnamon rolls. I opt for a custard tart. What else can I do?

'He's really gorgeous,' whispers Sylvie as he gives the order to the waitress. 'But it's you he fancies.'

He can fancy all he likes. I'm off men and I am certainly off posh pricks, apart from Ark Morgan of course. They soon change their mind when they discover you haven't got a high-profile job in business or some other fancy occupation and let's face it, being a chambermaid isn't a high-profile job. Anyway, I'm starting to think Sam Lockwood is a bit too smooth for my liking.

'So what are you girls up to in Knightsbridge?' he asks.

'We've been having beauty treatments. Don't say you can't tell?' she says teasingly.

'I don't imagine either of you ladies needs a beauty treatment,' he says with that cheeky grin of his. See what I mean? He's nauseatingly smooth. He's a bit pushy too, shoving his phone number at me as soon as he heard I'd broken up with Darren.

'You're such a tease,' flirts Sylvie, putting on a sexy pout. It never works with Sylvie; she just looks like Donatella Versace.

I nibble my custard tart and covet Sylvie's cinnamon roll as I do so. Sam Lockwood reclines in his chair and appraises me.

'What are your plans for the rest of the evening?' he asks between sipping his latte.

'We were thinking of going to the theatre, unless you have something better in mind?' says Sylvie, changing her posh voice to her sexy one, which sounds ten times worse but it's no good telling her.

'I'm fighting in an hour,' he says, checking his watch. 'I was thinking you might like to watch. Roxie is my lucky mascot after all.'

Oh yes, sure. Like watching two men bash each other about is my idea of a great evening.

'Are you a professional boxer?' says Sylvie. 'That's awesome.'

'I don't see what's awesome about beating each other up,' I say.

He's far too arrogant for my liking. How dare he presume we'd want to watch him and some other guy beat seven bells out of each other?

'Amateur,' he smiles. 'It releases a lot of tension and they're friendly fights,' he says, looking into my eyes.

'We could go,' says Sylvie, 'it might be fun.'

I thought she wanted to see Les Misérables. Mind you, that's not going to be a bundle of laughs either is it? The waitress hovers over us, or should I say hovers over him, and Sam nods pleasantly at her.

'Would you ladies like anything else? Or would you like to join me in a cab to Stepney?'

Stepney, now there's a night out. I look at Sylvie. Surely she would prefer the West End.

'Sounds fab,' she says.

Great. Bloody great, and I didn't even get a cinnamon roll.

'We're not really dressed for a boxing match are we?' I say, sounding like a real killjoy, but let's be honest, I've just spent a fortune to look like Jennifer Aniston and I'm not going to have it ruined by sitting in some sweaty smoke-filled hall watching Sam Lockwood get the shit beaten out of him. I don't imagine Jennifer Aniston has been to a boxing match in her life. Even Les Misérables with all its misery seems preferable to that. At least my hair would stay in place for a bit longer.

'Besides, I ought to get back to ...'

'The Gunner supporter,' he says cheekily. 'How is he by the way?'

'Very well thank you,' I say as Sylvie interrupts, 'She's broken up with him.'

I roll my eyes. Why do I bother?

'You're not rushing back to wash your hair are you?' he says with that grin that is starting to get on my nerves.

'We'd love to come, wouldn't we Rox?' says Sylvie, giving me a kick under the table.

Felix

'You okay love, can I help with that?' I ask.

What I'm doing loitering outside the murder flat I do not know. That dolly Sylvie gets me pulled into some things but this has to be the pits. Dealing with her and Roxie's wanker boyfriend issues are bad enough, but bollocking murder ... At least those irksome little buggers aren't hanging around today. The last thing I need is for them to see me. I wish that bitch Sylvie would answer her phone. I've got so much to tell her.

Last night I was happily surfing. The net that is, you'll never get me near the bloody water to do the real thing. I'd much prefer to lie on a sunbed watching other hunks doing it. Anyway, I'd been happily chatting to this gorgeous hunk on Gaydar when up it pops. The local news that is, I should be so lucky for anything else to pop up these days. A body had been found. Well it has to be ours. Not ours literally, we didn't murder the poor bugger, but it does feel kind of personal now. It has to be the guy Roxie saw get shot. I haven't been able to stop thinking about it since we saw Doctor Whatsisname. It came to me in a flash that night. Well let's face it, not much else comes in the night these days. The doc said the blood specimen was oil-based pigment. That's a no-brainer, it's clearly lipstick. I'm surprised Sylvie didn't think of it. The murderer must be a jealous husband or possibly a transvestite, although I think that a bit unlikely as I feel sure Roxie would have clocked that one. Maybe the woman had legged it by the time Roxie looked through the telescope. Jealous husband finds wife with lover and then shoots him. You read about it all the time, but whichever way it goes there must be more evidence. I tried to phone Sylvie the next morning before work but was she answering the phone? Like hell she was. Then today she disappears to some beauty salon with Roxie. I can see between the two of them they are going to spend, spend, spend that lottery win.

The old dearie smiles at me.

'Hello,' she says her rosy red cheeks blooming. 'If you could lift this bag of rubbish for me dear, that would be lovely. I don't know why they make these bins so high do you?'

'No problem love, which one is yours?' I ask.

'No 103,' she says, pointing.

She lives right opposite the crime scene. What a stroke of luck. I take her bag of rubbish and lift the lid of bin 103 which is right next to bin 104.

'Mrs Williams at twenty-two says it's disgraceful how tall the bins are these days. By the way, isn't it awful about Larry the postman? You'd never know would you? Still, Laura says it doesn't show. Her husband just got his degree. First-class honours it was. I said he'll be running that place soon. It needs a shake-up and he's the man to do it.'

I'm not sure if Larry the postman is the one who just got the first-class degree honours, if so why is he still a postman? And if she means the post office needs a shake-up then I have to agree with her. It took almost ten days for my frigging *Strictly* DVD to come. She stops and looks at me.

'You're one of them aren't you?'

I'm not sure if she means a postman, or a graduate with a first-class degree. Unfortunately I'm neither.

'You know, a queer,' she adds before I can answer. 'One of those bum boys. We have one living at 104.'

I try not to gasp. After all, I don't want to frighten her off.

'So you live next door to Victor Wainwright,' I say.

'Oh no dear, not now. He's dead.'

'Do the police know?' I can't hide my shock.

'Oh no, lovie, because Laura said I was to throw all the evidence in the bin, lovely brooches they were.'

I stare at her. This old biddy is the murderer? No, that doesn't make sense. She must have been an accomplice. She can't be the one he was having an affair with. I know an older woman has a lot to offer but this is going too far. I pull out my phone and try Sylvie again while the old girl continues to ramble on.

'I said to Laura that there were big signs on the window.'

Signs, what kind of signs?

'Everything must go, it said. There were some lovely brooches too and …'

Yes, I think we've covered the brooches.

'About Victor,' I say. 'Do you know how he died?'

'Victor who, lovie?'

'Your neighbour, Victor, the one who died.'

'That was two years ago dear. The bum boy lives there now, buggered if I can remember his name though. Are you one of his friends?'

'I have his interests at heart,' I say. I need to get in touch with Sylvie. Honestly, while those two bitches sit under a tanning lamp, I'm doing all the investigative work.

'Do you think I should tell the police then?' she asks worriedly.

'Did you hear the shooting?' I ask gently.

'Shooting,' she squeals. 'Who's been shot?'

'You said about getting rid of the evidence, was that from the shooting?'

She places her hand on her heart. Jesus Christ, I hope she's not going to have a heart attack. There's no way I'm pumping that chest and my lips are most certainly not touching hers. I have strict boundaries regarding who touches my lips, and an eighty-year-old woman is way off limits.

'Laura said it was just the blings that had to be got rid of. That just because the window signs said *Everything Must Go,* it didn't mean I could just take it. But you have to admit it isn't very clear is it? But Laura never told me someone had been shot. Was that my fault?'

'You took blings from a shop that had a closing-down sale?' I say widening my eyes.

'It said *Everything Must Go*.'

'I don't actually think that means you just take it.'

'That's what Laura said.'

Laura talks a lot of sense if you ask me. I lift the lid of bin 104 and glance inside.

'If you want the blings dear, they're in my bin,' she says helpfully.

The last thing I need is to go home with a pocket full of stolen blings.

'Oh no that's fine,' I say, peering into the bin. God it stinks.

'I just want something I threw in here by mistake.'

'What about the man that was shot?' she asks.

'Did you hear it?' I ask eagerly.

She shakes her head.

'No, I only know about it because you told me.'

I sigh and carefully retrieve an estate agent's letter from the bin. A good dollop of anti-bacterial gel is needed after this. Honestly, the things I do for that mare Sylvie.

'Well I'd better get going,' I say. 'By the way, what is the name of the gay man in 104?'

I might as well try again. You never know she might just remember it this time.

'Ooh, I don't know if he is gay dear. He always seems pretty serious to me.'

'Yes but what's his name,' I say patiently. 'The bum boy?'

I thought those words went out with Oscar Wilde.

'I've no idea, dearie. Did I tell you about Larry, the postie?'

'You most certainly did. Anyway, I'd better be off. Have a nice day.'

Wait till I tell Sylvie. I think I'll get a book on forensics. I'm getting into this crime solving malarkey.

Chapter Twenty-Two

The only good thing about this boxing scrum is that the auditorium is large and airy. Sam points to the bar.

'Get yourselves a drink. It's on me. Enjoy the fight. Aiden will show you to your seats.'

Even with a few drinks in me I really don't think I am going to enjoy this fight.

'Two glasses of champagne,' Sylvie says to the barman. 'It's on Sam Lockwood,' she adds giving him her sexiest smile.

'I'll bring a bottle to you,' says the barman appraising Sylvie. Honestly, I can't take her anywhere.

'We shouldn't take advantage,' I say.

'I'm sure he can afford it,' says Sylvie. 'And if not we can give him the money for it.'

She means I can. My winning the lottery has really changed Sylvie. We follow Aiden through a throng of excited spectators.

'Ever been in the front row before?' Aiden asks. 'Prime seats they are.'

Front row? Oh shit. I've just spent a fortune on beauty treatments and now I'm going to be splattered with blood. I so hate violence, I hate it even more when I have to watch it.

'Could we not sit somewhere further back?' I ask.

'Have you had a lobotomy?' asks Sylvie. 'These are the best seats.'

She's full of tact is Sylvie. Hopefully after a couple of glasses of champagne I'll be past caring who kills who. The auditorium is packed with people. I throw back a glass of champagne and pour another.

'This is the life,' whispers Sylvie. 'How often do we have champagne?'

'Never, and don't think we're starting now just because I had a win on the lottery.'

There's nothing wrong with good old Aldi wine.

'You're such a spoilsport,' she mumbles.

A bell rings and a hush descends over the auditorium before the crowd explode with cheers as the referee introduces the boxers.

'In the right corner we have Sam Lockwood.'

He enters the ring to *Eye of the Tiger*. The crowd roar and some women throw knickers into the ring. I must admit to feeling a little tingle in my own loins at the sight of his well-toned physique. I feel my face grow hot as he smiles at me. I'm not throwing my knickers into the ring if that's what he's hoping. Sylvie jumps from her seat and whistles when he appears. His opponent's name is announced to a mixture of cheers and boos. I gasp as he enters the ring. He's huge with lanky black hair hanging down to his shoulders and a grin that reveals a number of missing teeth. There's no need to wonder how he lost those. There's no way Sam Lockwood can beat this guy. It will be like fighting the Incredible Hulk.

'Jesus wept,' gasps Sylvie. 'He's a massive bugger isn't he?'

By the time the bell rings for the first round, I am on my second glass of champagne. Sam gives me the thumbs up and I feel terribly responsible for what happens to him. I'm his lucky mascot after all. I need to have a word with him about this lucky mascot thing after the fight. They seem to dance around each other for ever and I am tempted to jump into the ring and lay out the other guy myself and get the whole thing over and done with. By round three I'm close to throwing in the towel, well my scarf anyway, although I'm not sure if a Topshop scarf is an eligible fight stopper. Sam is taking a beating and I'm watching it through half-closed eyes. Sylvie is hoarse from shouting and the woman in the seat behind me is yelling *kill him kill him,* which I think is a little bit harsh. I only hope she doesn't mean Sam Lockwood or I'd be tempted to give her a black eye.

'You need to shag him,' says Sylvie, the shock almost knocking me off my chair.

'What?'

'Sam Lockwood, you've got to shag him. Get that two-timing dipshit Darren out of your head.'

There's a roar and we look up to see Sam has the Incredible Hulk cornered. I jump to my feet spilling my champagne.

'Yes, yes,' I hear myself screaming.

'Kill him, kill him,' yells the woman behind me. She's on Sam's side, that's a relief. I won't need to give her a black eye after all.

'Shagging Sam Lockwood is not going to make me forget Darren.'

'For about fifteen minutes you will.'

Sam takes a punch to his head and reels backwards. I feel myself reel with him and fall back into my seat.

'Jesus wept,' groans Sylvie. 'That was bad.'

'Shouldn't they stop the fight?' I say, giving the referee daggers. The bell sounds to end round 3. God, how many more rounds are there? More to the point, how many more rounds can I take? There is a cut above Sam's eye that is bleeding badly.

'I don't think I can take much more of this,' I say.

This is the last time I agree to one of Sylvie's suggestions. I'm off men. They're nothing but trouble, apart from Ark Morgan, of course. There is no way I'm shagging anyone and most certainly not Sam Lockwood. I'm resolute. I shall look at flats tomorrow. I'll then take up yoga and buy loads of self-help books. I'll buy some lavender oil and an oil burner and practise mindfulness. I'll ...

'*Come on*,' screams Sylvie.

The crowd goes wild as Sam shoots into the ring for the fourth round and with a sudden burst of energy throws a right hand punch that knocks the Incredible Hulk to the floor. There are cheers as the referee counts. Sam is animated and dances on his toes as he waits for the count. The Hulk struggles to his feet and wobbles before lurching himself at Sam.

'Oh God,' I groan, tipping up the champagne bottle only to find it empty. 'That big hulk just won't go down will he?'

'He's so damn sexy, how can you not want to shag him?'

I hope she means Sam and not The Hulk.

'I can't believe you can talk about shagging while two men are killing each other up there,' I say hotly.

'Ooh talking about killing,' she says, handing me her phone. 'It looks like the police have found a body. Felix sent a WhatsApp.'

Sam is now wedged against the ropes and the Incredible Hulk is laying into him.

'Totally unrecognisable,' Sylvie says.

'Come on Sam, you can do it,' I yell. He turns and smiles at me and my heart does a little flutter. He's galvanised into action and ducks underneath The Hulk and throws a heavy blow to his jaw. For a minute I think he will go down but the guy seems indestructible and comes at Sam with a vengeance. I turn my face away and read Felix's message.

They've found a body. In a dumpster by Sainsbury's bottle bank. What a way to end up? Waitrose would have been better wouldn't it? Still, it might have been a lot worse. It could have been Lidl. Anyway, I've just been watching Hot Fuzz and I think we should stake out the flat. Oh and Sylv, can you answer your bloody phone.

'Do you think it's our guy?' I say, wincing as Sam takes a blow to his shoulder.

'It's too much of a coincidence,' says Sylvie, before screaming. 'Come on ref that was out of order.'

'Kill the bastard,' yells the woman behind me. The crowd go wild as Sam corners The Hulk but the bugger just keeps on coming back. It's like one of those horror movies where the bloody villain just keeps going even though he's been pumped full of bullets. My hands are sweaty and my face red from the adrenalin. The Hulk has Sam pinned against the ropes and it's not looking good. The cut above Sam's eye is bleeding heavily now and I'm sure he's limping. Surely they will stop the fight soon.

'I'm throwing my scarf in,' I say as Sam takes another blow to his jaw. 'This is barbaric.'

The bell goes to end the round. I collapse into my seat. There are so many men around Sam that I can't see how injured he is. The crowd are baying for blood but I can't tell whose blood they want. I really don't think I can sit through another round. My bag vibrates against my foot and I pull out my phone. This must be Darren. He's finally realised what he's lost. Well, if he thinks I'm forgiving him a second time he can think again.

'It's me,' says Mum. 'I hate to tell you this but we've just seen Darren in Wetherspoons with some bottled redhead.'

'He hates Wetherspoons,' I say.

'We're absolutely livid darling. Your dad is all for taking him behind the bicycle shed.'

Ooh, I think that would look a bit suspicious in this day and age wouldn't it?

'Mum, can I call you back?'

'No Martin, of course not, it's just a figure of speech.'

'What?' I hate it when she tries to conduct two conversations at the same time.

'We thought you should know.'

'I do know.'

'You know?'

I just said that didn't I?

'How can he prefer her over you? What is it with men and redheads?'

I've no idea. I wince as Sam takes a punch below the belt.

'Out of fucking order ref,' yells someone behind me.

'When were you going to tell us?' she asks in that hurtful tone that she saves for occasions such as these which is supposed to make me feel like the worst child since Damien.

'A lot's happened,' I say. That's putting it mildly.

'He's probably suffering from sex addiction.'

Are we still talking about Darren?

'I don't think ...'

'No point getting upset. Sex drives men. It's not their fault. Their brains are in their ...'

'Mum, I really have to go.'

'Shit, he's winning, he's only bloody winning,' yells Sylvie.

I look up to see Sam knocking a hundred and seven bells out of the Incredible Hulk. The crowd are on their feet and cheering him on. Meanwhile the Incredible Hulk clings onto Sam until the referee parts them.

'Where on earth are you?' shouts Mum.

'At a boxing match, a friend of mine is fighting.'

'I hope you're not getting involved with a boxer,' she says primly. 'There's no future in that. He'll end up with Parkinson's disease and then you'll never get any sex.'

If you ask me it's my mum who's obsessed with sex.

'He's a friend. I've only just broken up with Darren. The last thing I need is another man and I'm certainly not going to have sex with him.'

'There are decent ones out there Roxanne. If Darren wants a slummy mummy then let him have one. You'll ...'

'Slummy mummy?' I stammer. She's got to be joking.

'Two little brats, although there could be more, but that's all she had with her in Wetherspoons.'

'She has kids?' I say, trying to get my head around it.

'Most women of your age have got babies,' she says in her accusing voice. 'Come for Sunday lunch. We can talk about things then.'

If by things she means babies, then forget it. She'll have me booked in for IVF if I'm not careful. After finally agreeing to go for Sunday lunch I get Mum off the phone just in time to see Sam throw such a punch that The Hulk loses his balance and hangs onto the rope for support. This is too awful for words and Sylvie thinks I would want to shag someone who enjoys beating the hell out of people? The referee counts to eight, studies The Hulk and finishes the fight. Thank God for that. The cut above Sam's eye is bleeding badly and he has another on his lip, but the bugger is still smiling. Does he ever stop? He gives me the thumbs up and attempts a wink.

There is a buzz from the crowd as they wait for the result.

'More champagne for sure,' says Sylvie gleefully.

The crowd roars as Sam is announced the winner. Some men clamber into the ring to congratulate him. He raises his arms in celebration and Sylvie climbs into the ring before you can say boxer shorts. I glance at my phone again and resign myself to the fact that Darren isn't going to ask for forgiveness.

'Did you enjoy the fight?' Sam asks, before taking a gulp from a bottle of water.

'It was brilliant,' enthuses Sylvie.

'It was okay,' I say shyly, conscious of his half-naked body.

'Roxie doesn't believe in living dangerously,' says Sylvie.

'That's not true,' I say.

'Would joining me for a drink be a bit too dangerous for you?' he says looking into my eyes.

'Well I ...'

'My friend will be there too and I am sure Sylvie will come, won't you Sylvie? We're going to a little private club. I guarantee to see you home safely.'

'Thanks, but I can find my own way home and I really have to get back.'

'You have my number if you change your mind.'

Sylvie and I watch him walk away as the crowd cheer him and reach to pat him on the back.

'God, he's so gorgeous. How can you not want to shag him? You're mad not going for a drink.'

'I wish you'd stop talking about shagging,' I snap. 'And the fact I don't like him is one reason not to shag him, but also in case you have forgotten I'm just getting over a broken relationship.'

She scoffs.

'You're crazy if you let that arsehole get to you.'

Well the truth is I am letting the arsehole get to me. He's left me for a slummy mummy bottled redhead. Of course it's getting to me.

Chapter Twenty-Three

'You what?' says Sylvie.

'I've looked everywhere. I was really hoping I didn't drop it there but I can't think where else it can be. I wasn't going to tell you ...'

'You weren't going to tell me?'

'I didn't think it was that important but now they've found a body I thought I should mention it.'

We're outside the murder apartment block sitting in my Fiesta. I can think of better ways to spend a Friday evening, like preparing for Ark Morgan's party for instance. There is a lot to do if I'm to be the kind of woman that Ark would notice. The kind of woman Ark would make a beeline for. I've made a list:

1) Get an early night. One needs to be fresh faced and glowing. I'd bought some expensive face cream for this very reason. Slap on loads of oil and then tons of moisturiser and drink gallons of water. Obviously not too much as don't want to be peeing every few minutes while at posh yacht party.

2) Shave under arms, wax legs and bikini line, obviously. Check thoroughly for downstairs hair.

3) Douche downstairs just in case.

4) Douche the other downstairs too, just in case. After all, one can't be prepared enough with the likes of Ark Morgan, especially if he is anything like Christian Grey.

5) Book a blow dry with Lionel. Best to be safe than sorry – don't want to see Ark Morgan with bird nest hair.

6) Spend fifteen minutes reclining with Glam Glow mud mask, but refrain from wrapping face in cellophane as may be a touch dangerous.

7) Choose appropriate underwear. But just what is appropriate underwear? Supposing I do get off with Ark Morgan? It'll be *Pretty Woman* all over again. Except I'm a chambermaid not a prostitute of course. If I wear the Ann Summers sexy lacy Brazilian undies Sylvie made me buy, then I'll look like I was expecting it. Of course my Marks and Spencer firm control high leg panties are wonderful and will make the dress look even more perfect but not so appealing when in Ark Morgan's playroom. This is tricky, extremely tricky, as I want to get everything right. After all, this is my only chance. I don't want the red room of pain stuff ruined because we can't get the sodding pants off.

8) Practise being chic, sophisticated and alluring. The bathroom mirror is the best place for this.

9) Spray lightly with Jo Malone's Earl Grey and Cucumber perfume and hopefully knock him dead. With my allure that is, not from the perfume.

10) Practise walking on new three inch heels. I can't think of anything more disastrous than falling arse over tit in front of Ark Morgan …

'Roxie, are you listening to us? What have you done with the other earring?'

'It's in my jewel box, why?'

'We need to dispose of it,' says Felix dramatically. 'That way no one can trace it back to you.'

'I bought them in Topshop. Loads of women must have them.'

'It will have your DNA on it you dope,' says Sylvie.

'Yes, she's right,' says Felix, thumbing through his copy of *Forensics for Dummies*.

Honestly, it was bad enough with Sylvie acting out episodes of *Waking the Dead* but now Felix is at it too. I'm not sure I can bear it. All they talk about is DNA and fingerprints. Oh well, I may as well spill the beans.

'I also had a hole in my sock. I didn't realise until I got home.'

'Jesus Rox,' groans Sylvie.

'They were from Poundland, so I may have frayed everywhere too.'

'It would have been easier to have left a business card love,' quips Felix.

'Jesus wept,' groans Sylvie.

'I imagine he would if he were here,' says Felix.

'I didn't see any sock bits,' says Sylvie, 'so hopefully that won't be a problem, but get the earring and give it to Felix as soon as possible so he can get rid of it,' she instructs.

'How am I supposed to get rid of an earring?' Felix asks.

'Can't you throw it out of your aeroplane or something,' she says.

I roll my eyes.

'What do you expect him to do, open the door at thirty-thousand feet?' I say.

'Christ, I know EasyJet has a bad reputation, but I didn't know it was that bad,' laughs Felix.

'Can't you flush it down the loo,' suggests Sylvie. 'They're not going to go through all that shit and spot an earring.'

'Yes, well thanks for that image love. Anything else you want me to do? I seem to be doing just about everything. I tell you, I never want to see another bottle of Parazone. I must have gone in every shop from here to Land's End asking about bleach.'

'A slight exaggeration,' sighs Sylvie.

'Anyway, only normal amounts have been sold, whatever they are. So maybe they only used a couple of bottles.'

I shudder.

'Honestly,' I say, 'I really think you two are getting carried away. We don't even know if that body is our victim.'

'I feel it in my water,' says Felix.

At least we're not talking about his bowels for a change.

'It's too coincidental, here's what we know so far,' he says as he hands around the evidence that he took from the bin.

'First, we know that Victor Wainwright is not now the occupant of the flat. He died two years ago. The electoral role hasn't been updated, but what we do know is that the tenant in 104 is gay, at least according to the old girl in 103. Now, the question is, can a light-fingered eighty-year-old be trusted ...?'

'Light fingered?' I interrupt.

'Walked off with a whole bag of blings from a clear out sale because she thought an *Everything Must Go* sign means exactly that. You just shift the gear. However, if she can be trusted that means that either he is a transvestite ...'

'Transvestite? ' I query. 'How did you work that one out?'

Felix sighs.

'The so-called bloodstain was oil-based pigment, or in other words ...' he pauses for effect, 'lipstick.'

I check the time on my phone while Felix isn't watching. I really want an early night. I want to look my absolute best tomorrow.

'Oh,' I say, still not really getting the point.

'Or, there was a woman there. The murderer could have been a jealous husband,' he finishes before opening a bag of doughnuts.

'They always have doughnuts on stakeouts,' he says. 'Anyone for coffee?' he asks producing a flask and three plastic mugs. 'It's decaf.'

'I though the whole idea of coffee on a stakeout was to keep you awake. Don't you think decaf slightly defeats the object?' sighs Sylvie.

'I don't get it,' I say.

'Don't get what?' asks Felix.

'The transvestite thing. I'd have noticed if one of the men was dressed up like Eddie Izzard wouldn't I? And surely if the murderer is a gay transvestite then he wouldn't be having an affair with a married woman would he?'

Felix nods.

'That's the point. If the lipstick didn't belong to a woman then we have to presume he's a cross-dresser.'

We do?

'Anyone fancy a Domino's pizza? I'm starving. We could be here hours. They always have pizza on stakeouts.'

'Is that what it says in your book?' I say scathingly.

'You can scoff darling, but if you hadn't been a peeping tom in the first place we wouldn't be here.'

'It could have been a crime of passion,' says Sylvie. 'You know what gays are like. They're so over the top sensitive. He probably glanced at another guy at the Fun Palace and his partner became insane with jealousy and shot him.'

'This is all supposition though isn't it?' I say.

'Ooh, hark at her with the long words,' laughs Felix. 'Of course, there's still the question of the piece of paper the victim was holding, which brings us to this, exhibit A.'

He's only gone and marked it too. We look with interest at the crumpled estate agent's details.

'Where did you find that?' I ask.

'It was in the rubbish bin,' he says proudly. 'It was right on the top. I think the killer threw it in there so it wouldn't be found in the flat. There's handwriting at the top. Whoever sent this was with the victim on Saturday.'

I lean over the seat to get a look at the scribbled writing. *Good price, see you Saturday for the Fun Palace and we can discuss.*

'So he could be an estate agent,' I say and my heart sinks. I've got to go and see one to view a flat. What if the murderer shows me around and then recognises me. I know the chances of him actually having seen me are slim but then again so were my chances of winning the lottery, and that didn't stop me did it? The last thing I need is to be alone in a flat with the murderer.

'Unlikely, there's only two people working at that office and they're both ancient,' says Felix.

'It says the flat is in Rommel Mansions,' I say, looking at the photo on the agents details.

'Except that doesn't really help us, does it darling?'

'Can you get pepperoni?' asks Sylvie, 'and maybe some beers. What do you want Rox?'

To go home sounds good.

'Ooh, here we go. He's definitely gay isn't he?' says Sylvie, nodding at a guy walking towards us. I sink down in my seat.

'Act natural,' snaps Felix, quickly hiding the doughnuts and flask.

Act natural? How is it natural for three people to be sitting outside someone's flat stuffing their faces with doughnuts? You have to agree it is an odd place to have a picnic. It's not exactly the most scenic place in Clapham. You'd be hard pressed to find a blade of grass anywhere.

'You've got the gay radar, is he one of your lot?'

'He doesn't look the murdering type,' I say, not that I have any idea what the murdering type looks like. I don't suppose Jack the Ripper looked the murdering type, not that I know for sure of course.

'He's not gay,' says Felix, taking the doughnuts from the glove compartment as the guy passes.

'I really don't understand why we're doing this,' I say finally. 'Even if someone does go into the block how will you know if they go to flat 104?'

'Ah,' says Felix gleefully, grabbing Sylvie's binoculars from under the seat. 'We can follow them up the stairs with these. The lift is broken remember?'

'Plus they will put the lights on when they get into the flat,' adds Sylvie with a roll of her eyes.

'We need to get this handwriting analysed,' says Sylvie. 'That way we'll know if we're looking for a gay guy won't we?'

'I suppose that's my job too?' says Felix.

'I'll do it,' I say. 'On the condition you let me go home and get some sleep. I've got a big evening tomorrow.'

'Oh yes, Sylvie told me. What are you wearing?' asks Felix.

'Sylvie,' I say exasperated.

'What? I only said you were going to a posh do.'

'They do a pepperoni with anchovies,' says Felix, flicking through the Domino's Pizza menu.

'Okay, you two can play Charlie's Angels, minus one,' I say angrily.

'Charlie's Angels were all girls,' mumbles Felix.

'Precisely,' I say.

'Oh cutting dear.'

'Just another hour Rox and then we'll head home,' says Sylvie.

I sigh.

'Okay, can you get garlic bread with the pizza then.'

I'm so easily swayed when food is involved.

Chapter Twenty-Four

Ark Morgan is playing the piano expertly in the yacht's dining room where waiters circle the guests with canapés on silver platters.

'Quail egg madam?' offers one.

I decline and accept a glass of champagne, of which there seems to be a never-ending flow. I move hesitantly towards the piano and am mesmerised by Ark Morgan's slim elegant fingers as they skilfully slide across the keys. He lifts his eyes and meets mine. I chew on my lip nervously. His hands pause and his audience sigh as he stops playing. He stands and walks towards me. His hand grasps my arm and I look up at him. I could stare at him forever. He whispers,

'Don't bite your lip. You should save that pleasure for me.'

It might be pleasure for him but its bloody agony for me.

'Miss Brown isn't it? We've met before?'

I don't like to remind him it was when I had a hoover up my skirt.

He grins, the unspoken words, 'Laters Baby,' hang between us as does a waiter who is determined to stuff quail eggs into us.

'I'm going to give Miss Brown a tour of the yacht,' he says.

I shiver.

'The ship has a safe room,' he says. 'I'm going to show you it.' What he really means is his playroom. I may look stupid but I'm not naive.

'Why?' I ask breathlessly.

'Because I want to be alone with you, where no one can reach us.'

I grab a glass of champagne from a passing waiter and knock it back. I need something to calm my loins, let alone my nerves.

'Why?' I ask again, sounding like a pestering five year old.

'Because I'm going to spank your little bum raw. That's why.'

Well at least he said little bum. Up yours Darren Smart.

'Why?' I ask. I'm sounding like a retard now.

'Because you're my submissive Miss Brown and then I'm going to fuck your brains out.'

I struggle to breathe and totter on my heels as he pulls me along. I trip and his arm reaches out to support me.

'Are you okay? You know what they say, take more water with it.'

I look up at Ark Morgan, except it isn't Ark Morgan at all. It's a grey-haired gentleman and he's offering me his hand. I'd only gone arse over tit on my stupid heels. Me and my fantasies, honestly I'm lucky I didn't end up in the river. That would be a great start to the evening.

'Thank you, I'm not used to high heels.'

I cringe. Not something one should say at a do like this is it? There can't be a woman on board without a wardrobe full of Jimmy Choos.

'Are you making your way to *Morningsong* by any chance?' he asks kindly. 'I'm happy to escort you. Save you tumbling on those heels again.'

I open my mouth to reply when he spots the invitation in my hand.

'How remiss of me, of course you are. Allow me.'

This is a terrible mistake. I realise that now. As soon as I saw the limousines and waiters in their dinner jackets milling around the yacht I knew I was out of my depth. I should never have come. What if Ark Morgan recognises me as the chambermaid that spilt Johnson's furniture polish down her front? I'll get fired. He's not stupid. He'll know I nicked the invite. Chambermaids don't get invitations. Keep calm. The chances of him recognising me are really slim. In fact, the chances of him even noticing me at all are even slimmer. I'd opted for the lacy Brazilian undies though, just in case. I rather think the Marks and Spencer's pants may well be a penis reduction job.

I watch as limos pull up and women dripping in diamonds pour out. I'm going to stand out like a sore thumb. I can't say my name is Roxie can I? They'll think I'm the bloody cabaret for the evening. If only I could turn back but there is no turning back and anyway the path is blocked with a posse of yuppie upstarts. I doubt I'll make it without a gas mask as the heady perfume and aftershave could knock someone dead at fifty paces. So, I am led along the gangplank by the grey-haired man and onto the yacht. I feel my stomach churn with fear. I must keep calm. There is nothing on the ticket to say who it belongs to. I hand it over and attempt to smile confidently.

'Thank you madam, enjoy your evening.'

'Buck's Fizz?' says a waiter, approaching with a tray. I accept one and sip at it nervously. A tray of savouries are thrust in front of me. I decline politely. I feel so sick with nerves that there is no way I can eat. The last time I had Buck's Fizz was at my gran's wake. That wasn't the real thing either. It was Babycham and orange juice, and it tasted better than this stuff, which just goes to show just how out of my depth I am.

I follow the grey-haired man into the crowded foyer as a roaring noise sounds behind us. I turn to look as a shiny motorbike comes to halt beside a white Rolls-Royce.

'What the devil?' says the grey-haired man. 'Who's that on the Harley Davidson?'

This could be the perfect opportunity to escape. While all eyes are on the yob on the motorbike they're not going to see me, unless I go 'arse over kettle' as my grandma used to say, on my dash down the gangplank. I wish I hadn't worn these damn shoes. A quick getaway is impossible.

'This way madam,' says a waiter.

'Oh,' I say.

I wobble on my new Jimmy's and fall straight into the arms of Ark Morgan. I guess that's one way of getting him to notice me.

Chapter Twenty-Five

I stare into his dreamy eyes as *Nothing's Gonna Stop Us Now* plays in the background. His arms are around my waist and I can feel his hands burning through my dress. I can't believe I am this close to Ark Morgan and what's more he's smiling at me. A waiter mops up my Buck's Fizz, but I'm unaware of anything other than Ark Morgan's beautiful eyes and sensual lips. I could be standing on the broken glass and I wouldn't notice. I can stand any pain for Ark Morgan.

'I'm so sorry,' I mumble. 'I don't know what happened.' Speak clearly for goodness' sake. Poise and confidence, remember.

'No problem,' he laughs. 'The boat rocks occasionally. Let me get you another drink.'

He acknowledges some passing guests and gestures to a waiter.

'Lucinda, Jeremy, lovely to see you. Do go through. I'll catch up with you later, beautiful dress Lucy.'

He looks stunning in his white shirt and bow tie. He could be a walking advert for Daz, his shirt is so white. I'm struggling to keep my eyes off him. He slaps a man on the back, 'Lovely to see you George,' and then passes me another Buck's Fizz.

'I'm Ark. I don't recall us having met?' he says, meeting my eyes.

I'm saved from answering by another guest who glides towards us.

'Mwah,' she says, kissing those gorgeous Ark Morgan cheeks, 'Lovely to be here darling.'

She glides away leaving a trail of heavy musk in her wake. Ark turns to me and rests his hand on my hip. Oh my God, this is surely one of my fantasies.

'Which hotel are you staying at?' he asks as he leads me into a room overflowing with people, food and drink. I'm so dying for a pee. These Brazilian lace panties aren't helping. Or it could be that my loins are throbbing so much that the Brazilian lace just isn't coping. I feel it slowly disappearing up the unmentionable and it is all I can do not to shove my hand down there and pull them out. I'm uncomfortable enough without that too.

'I spend a fair amount of time at the Crescent,' I say. Well it's not a lie is it? I spend half my week at that one.

'Ah, that's one of my favourites. I'm sorry, I missed your name.'

Bollocking tit basket.

'Roxanne Brown,' I say, and struggle not to wince.

'Roxanne,' he repeats. 'That's an unusual name.' He leads me to the buffet table.

'Please help yourself Miss Brown,' he says, looking into my eyes.

'You smell heavenly by the way,' he adds before moving off to greet another guest.

Oh my God, Ark Morgan said I smell heavenly. I've got to text Sylvie. Five minutes later I am mingling around the dining table as waiters serve lobster with salad and garnishes. There is roast beef, roast pork, roast duck and would you believe it, quail eggs. There are whole poached salmon, prawns, oysters and just about every seafood you can think of. I'm standing by an assortment of rice dishes when my eyes meet Ark's across the room. I look behind to check he isn't looking at someone else, but no, he is looking into my eyes. I smile nervously and look away.

'Is there a loo I can use?' I ask a waiter.

That was a stupid question. He isn't going to say *no you've got to piss into the Thames* is he? As it happens there is a choice of three bathrooms. I choose the nearest and burst in only to find three glamorous women parading in front of the mirrors, their Chanel make-up and hair tongs strewn across the marble top sink unit. Honestly, there are three loos here and they have to choose this one.

'I told him if he fucks that little slut again it's over. I can't keep firing the bloody nanny can I?' says one of the women.

They turn and glare at me. You'd think I was the little slut the way they look at me. I consider doing a U-turn and finding the other loo but then think better of it. I really don't think I can hold it in much longer. Doing a little wee in your knickers at a posh do like this just isn't the thing is it? The yuppie women give me another look and continue talking in their posh voices. I imagine they have names like *Beatrice* or *Theodora* but most definitely not *Roxie*. I close the door of the cubicle and lean against it. All I can think of is Ark Morgan's hand on my hip. I thought I was going to multiple orgasm there and then. I find myself visualising him pulling off my Brazilian panties, staring down at me, his eyes sparkling with anticipation as I throb in readiness. I feel myself sliding down the door. I pull my phone from my bag and text Sylvie

Ark Morgan thinks I smell heavenly.

The bathroom door slams as the yuppies leave and I venture out of the cubicle. I check my reflection. Everything still looks perfect. I wash my hands with the luxury soap and tap my red cheeks with a cool cloth from a basket by the sink. The towels are soft and white. I've seen all this stuff in the hotels of course, but I never thought I'd be a guest expected to use them.

I venture back to the dining room and look for Ark Morgan, but there is no sign of him. I expect he is greeting his other guests. I can see a guest holding a crash helmet. He has his back to me but I guess he must be the motorcyclist. I can't imagine why Ark Morgan would invite someone like that. It just seems so out of place. He turns, ruffles his hair and it is then I see his face. Holy shit, what the hell is Sam Lockwood doing here? I swear to God the guy is stalking me. What if he knows Ark Morgan really well, he'll give me away. What to do? I need to phone Sylvie. Why is he here? I thought he didn't like Ark Morgan. I glance over the shoulder of the man in front of me and see Sam Lockwood hand his things to the cloakroom assistant before accepting a Buck's Fizz. He's dressed very casually in a pair of jeans and white shirt and stands out like a sore thumb. He sips his drink and glances around. I move my head so he can't spot me.

'Are you fish or meat? What tickles your taste buds?'

I jump at the sound of Ark's voice and blush. I can think of many things about Ark Morgan that tickle my taste buds.

'Oh, I didn't see you,' I say stupidly.

'I smelt you,' he says with a smile.

As long as he's talking about the perfume then that's okay.

'You still haven't answered my question, are you fish or meat?'

'Fish please,' I say with a quiver in my voice.

'The oysters are good,' he smiles, placing some onto my plate. 'Oysters are good for you in more ways than one. Do you like them?'

Holy crap, I should pinch myself. Oh God, did my breath just hitch? I wish my heart would stop thumping. I feel it will burst out of my chest like a scene from *Alien.*

'Try one,' he says, holding a shell in front of my mouth.

'Is this sensual or is this sensual?' whispers my inner goddess. Its mind blowing is what it is. I do as I'm told. I don't need telling twice. I've read enough *Fifty Shades* to know how to submit. I open my mouth to take the oyster and pray like a religious zealot that I don't choke on it.

'Let the juices slide down your throat,' he says softly.

That was it. With those words, it's like the ache in my loins explodes and I begin choking like no tomorrow.

'Killing off the guests now are you Morgan?' says a familiar voice.

I accept a tissue from Sam Lockwood and dab my watery eyes.

'Well well, if it isn't Sam Lockwood. Correct me if I'm wrong but I felt sure it was your manager I invited?' says Ark, his eyes hard and his tone caustic.

'He couldn't make it I'm afraid. I'm here on behalf of Lockwood Estates,' responds Sam with a grin.

'Hello Roxie,' he says turning to me. 'How are you? Fully recovered from the boxing match I hope.'

I cringe and pray Ark didn't hear him.

'Hello,' I say shyly. 'Yes, fully recovered thank you.'

'Are you okay Miss Brown?' Ark asks, turning his back on Sam Lockwood.

I nod.

'Perhaps a little water,' he says, gesturing to a waiter.

'I'd avoid the oysters if I were you,' smiles Sam, 'they're not all they're cracked up to be.'

I sip the water and try to avoid Sam Lockwood's eyes. Ark hooks my arm through his.

'If you'll excuse us, there is something I wish to show Miss Brown.'

Ooh he can show me his something any time.

'It's Roxanne,' I say.

Sam Lockwood raises his eyebrows. I'm whisked past the throng of guests. The place is brimming with people.

'Oh we bloody roared didn't we Luce?' a deep-voiced man is saying to the laughter of his audience. Ark leads me past a champagne fountain.

'Would you like another?' he asks, glancing indifferently at the fountain.

'It's beautiful,' I say.

'Not as beautiful as you,' he says softly, moving closer. Heavens, someone needs to pinch me. I can't believe that Ark Morgan has noticed me. Should I tell him I work for him? It's always good to be honest at the start of a relationship.

Whoa there girl, whispers my subconscious, *nothing's happened yet. It will though,* says my inner goddess. *It won't be long before he gets those nipple clamps out. You go girl.*

I shiver.

'Are you cold?' he asks, removing his jacket and draping it around my shoulders. His touch has me verging. I'm like a nympho. Still, that's not a bad thing with someone like Ark Morgan is it?

'Just a little,' I say.

He leads me away from the noise of the party and into a mirror-panelled ballroom. Chandeliers hang from the ceiling. I stare in awe. I've never seen anything like it. I thought the hotels were stunning but this is breathtaking. Everywhere I look are reflections of Ark Morgan and me. He smiles at me through a mirror.

'Actually, we have met before,' he says, clicking his fingers. 'I remember where it was.' He gives me a smile that melts my heart while his words nearly stop it beating all together. Oh no, please don't say he remembers me from the lift with Henry up my skirt and polish spilt down my overall.

'The House of Mirrors,' he says, 'do you remember?'

I'm speechless with relief. My body feels like it is vibrating until I realise it's my phone. It has to be Sylvie. I'm about to reach into my clutch for it when Frank Sinatra's *Witchcraft* croons around us. Oh my God, it's the same as in the *Fifty Shades* movie. It has to be a sign doesn't it?

'I believe this is our song Miss Brown, after all, you have put a spell on me,' he murmurs, tracing his fingers along my arm. I tell you my loins think it's Christmas and my birthday all rolled into one.

'Dance with me,' he says huskily, pushing the remote button and increasing the volume.

He's turned up my volume all right, and everything else. My breasts are bursting out of my lacy bra. I fear the back clip will snap and I'll burst forth. It'll be like an upmarket porno film. Linda Lovelace will have nothing on me. He takes my hand and I hold my breath. He places it onto his shoulder and circles my waist to pull me closer. We glide effortlessly around the ballroom, our reflections bouncing back at us from all angles. It's a good job he is holding me up because my legs certainly aren't.

'So, why are you here alone? Surely a woman who looks as gorgeous as you has someone in her life?' he asks curiously.

This Jo Malone is potent stuff. I'll have to buy a job lot.

'We broke up,' I say honestly.

Let's face it, Darren wouldn't be seen dead here unless they had lager on tap and a barrel of custard creams.

'His loss is my gain,' he says. 'So how do you know wanker Sam Lockwood?'

I flinch.

'I don't really. I kind of bumped into him at the Fun Palace. I don't think he's a wanker.' Why I'm defending Sam Lockwood I do not know. His face darkens as he twirls me around and then back into his arms.

'You seemed very friendly with him.'

'I barely know him.'

'I should tell you that the Lockwoods are corrupt and can't be trusted,' Ark says his face hardening. 'We had a dispute last year over a plot. The Lockwoods were trying to buy the land for cheap warehousing which would have devalued the area terribly. Fortunately their usual tactic of ignoring planning rules was discovered and the sale fell through. I was able to buy the site and bring employment to the area with one of my hotels. Sam is, of course, very bitter about it.'

'But surely that kind of thing happens all the time in business?' I say.

He stops dancing.

'Sam Lockwood hits below the belt. He tried to steal everything from me and when that didn't work he stole the love of my life ...' He breaks off and struggles to compose himself.

'I'm sorry. It's silly of me to be so upset. I'd just hate you to be misled by him. He has that Mr nice-guy manner about him. Women are often enticed by it. Please don't be fooled.'

There is silence for a moment before my phone vibrates again.

'Someone wants you,' he says huskily. 'I really can't blame them. I wish we could stay here all night but I fear I have to get you back Miss Brown and it really is rather rude of me to neglect my other guests just because I prefer this very fragrant one.'

He twirls me again and then clicks off the music.

'Shall we?' he asks offering his arm.

I take his arm and then freeze when he asks.

'So what brings you to the Crescent?'

Chapter Twenty-Six

'Oh shit. What did you say?'

I'm huddled in yet another loo cubicle. The lacy Brazilian knickers really haven't done well under pressure. I really should have brought a spare pair.

'I didn't. He had a call on his mobile and I left him in the ballroom. What am I going to say if he does ask, and what about Sam Lockwood? I'm living a dream and nightmare all at the same time,' I say trying not to panic.

'Stop panicking for a start and whatever you do, don't say you're a chambermaid. Jesus wept, that would be romantic suicide.'

'But what if he sees me at work?'

'Come on, Rox, how often has that happened?'

'You can't very well hide me in the cleaning trolley can you?'

'I'll shove you in a cupboard if I have to.'

See what I mean about Sylvie being a true friend. How many would go the extra mile like that?

'As for Sam Lockwood, why should he mention you working for the Morgan Group? He'll probably think as you're there at the party that you have a high-profile position.'

I sigh with relief. She's quite right of course. I'm just panicking. In fact the boat is so huge I can easily avoid Sam Lockwood for the whole evening.

'Stay calm,' instructs Sylvie. 'You look fabulous. I told you Ark Morgan wouldn't be able to resist you. Now go out there and party-party-party.'

With a final yank of the panties I obey Sylvie's instructions and venture back to the dining area. I do a quick check that Sam Lockwood is not around and fill my plate with roast beef and salad. It's then that I see him. He's picking the raspberries off the garnish of a beautiful pavlova. How rude is that? He should at least cut a piece. I feel like giving him a piece all right, a piece of my mind. After all the trouble Ark must have gone to and to think he even kindly invited a representative from Lockwood Estates even though they have treated him badly. That's integrity in business isn't it? Before I know what I'm doing I'm marching around the table to confront him, catching snatches of snooty conversations along the way.

'He read history at some obscure place in Wales, I ask you,' snorts a man with an uncanny resemblance to Boris Johnson.

'Well you should read the *Telegraph* darling, then, you'd understand. One has to make a stand,' another woman is saying.

I quite agree. I'm about to take a bloody stand with Sam Lockwood.

'I'm voting Tory. I mean what else is one to do?'

Huh, I vote green. You can't go wrong then can you? Not that I'm into Greenpeace or anything, although, I did make an effort to sort my clothes out one weekend with the intention of selling them on eBay and giving the proceeds to Greenpeace, but finally decided I needed them much more. I wasn't flush then. I'm about to approach Sam Lockwood but stop in my tracks when I see he is talking to a long legged blonde. She is laughing and her white even teeth sparkle. She's like a woman out of a toothpaste advert. She's wearing a light blue velvet dress with a plunging neckline. Her arse certainly doesn't look big in that and I bet my lottery win that her lacy undies haven't got all screwed up in her unmentionables. I can pretty much guarantee that her boyfriend isn't screwing a bottled redhead either. Above the swell of her breasts are a string of pearls which match her pearl stud earrings perfectly. She flicks her hair provocatively. What am I doing? I spin around to make a quick exit.

'Roxie,' he says.

I'm like a rabbit caught in headlights. I so need a rabbit hole. I cough nervously.

'Hello,' I say, feigning innocence. 'I'm trying to decide what to have for dessert.'

I'm holding a plate of roast beef and salad. I must look a right glutton.

'This is Verity Robinson, she writes for the *Guardian*,' says Sam.

'Oh,' I mumble, putting down my plate. Please don't ask me what I do for a living.

'He makes it sound so grand,' she laughs, pretending to be modest.

It's grander than being a chambermaid.

'I write a column for the property supplement,' she adds, acting not in the least modest. In fact it wouldn't surprise me if she shoved the latest edition under my nose next.

'I should be getting back, Calvin will be wondering where I've got to,' she says in her silky soft voice.

Calvin? Oh well, I suppose it's better than Darren. She kisses Sam on the cheek and gives me a little nod.

'I thought you'd gone on a boat expedition with Ark Morgan,' he says, scooping up more raspberries.

'There are fresh raspberries on the table,' I say irritably. 'Why are you taking them from here? You're totally ruining the garnish.'

'You're worried about the garnish?' he asks with his irritating grin.

'It seems very rude when there are raspberries already on the table.'

'Are you on a *Save the Raspberry Pavlova Campaign*?'

I sigh. The man really is impossible. He slices through the pavlova and places a piece onto his plate.

'Does that help? Am I allowed them now?'

'I never said you weren't allowed them, I just ...'

'Told me off for helping myself to dessert,' he says, his tone sharp.

I straighten my shoulders.

'I just feel if someone has made all this effort then it is important to be polite.'

He nods.

'I agree totally. I'd hate to think of poor Ark Morgan working his fingers to the bone over all this food just to have me thoughtlessly massacre his pavlova.'

'Enjoy the evening,' I say, turning away.

'You're not having dessert?' he says mildly. 'There are plenty of cinnamon-free choices.'

I hear the smile in his voice. He's mocking me.

'I'm well aware of that,' I say, putting down my plate to accept a glass of wine.

He reaches across me to take a glass from the waiter, his hand accidentally brushing my breast. His touch sends a shiver through me.

'So, how do you know Ark Morgan then?' he asks, before clicking his fingers and adding, 'Oh, I remember. You work for the Morgan Group don't you?'

Oh no.

'Don't tell me,' he says, holding up his hand. 'You're in charge of catering. That's why you're so devastated about the pavlova.'

I watch as he slices into it.

'I'm more involved in the domestic side of the hotel's upkeep,' I say before taking a large gulp of wine.

'Oh really,' he says, taking a bite of pavlova. 'How does that work exactly?'

I'm doomed. I open my mouth to tell the truth when there is a drum roll scaring me half to death.

'Ladies and Gentlemen, please welcome our host, Mr Ark Morgan.'

Ark runs his hands through his hair, nodding confidently at everyone as he walks to the centre of the room. He gives his guests a dazzling smile and I can almost smell his fresh fragrance from here. He holds up his hands for quiet. I'm mesmerised. It's then I see it, as he looks down to the floor. Is that a small bald patch on the top of his head? No, surely not. It must be a trick of the light. Ark is perfect. Anyway, bald men can be quite sexy can't they? Not that Ark is anywhere near bald.

'Thanks everyone. I just want to thank you all for coming tonight. Eat, drink, dance and be merry. I'll be chatting to each and every one of you before the night is over. So without further ado, I'll leave you to it.'

There is applause and I watch enraptured as he mingles with the guests crowding around him.

'Party has got off to a good start for old Ark hasn't it? He's a natural charmer, I'll give him that.'

I'd forgotten Sam Lockwood.

'At least he isn't corrupt in business,' I say, my voice dripping with sarcasm.

'Ha, now that's the funniest thing I've heard all year,' he says, his eyes twinkling.

'I hope you enjoy your raspberries,' I say. 'If you'll excuse me, I see someone I know.' Like the loo. Let's face it I'm getting to know that very intimately.

'Maybe I'll see you for a dance later?' he grins. 'After all, we've been told to dance, and be merry.'

I give a nod and make my way to the loo. The bloody Jimmy Choos are feeling more and more like stilts with each glass of wine. I must keep count of how much I'm drinking. There are waiters with trays of wine, champagne and Buck's Fizz everywhere I look. Of course they are also carrying trays of water but I don't somehow think I'm going to get through this on water.

'I hope you've had plenty to eat Miss Brown. You need to stay fit and healthy.' Ark says, appearing from nowhere and blocking my path to the loo.

'You don't seem to be eating very much,' he smiles.

My breath quickens.

'He's a fast worker,' whispers my inner goddess. I reckon those nipple clamps and hot wax will be out before you can say *sex addiction*. 'He's preparing you. I'd stuff a few more of those oysters down your throat if I were you but that's just my opinion.'

My subconscious shivers.

'I hope you'll save a dance for me this evening. Meanwhile eat. There's plenty.'

With a heart-stopping smile he moves on to greet his other guests. Flushing from head to toe I continue to the loo passing the cloakroom as I do so. I freeze, and take a sharp intake of breath. Hanging on one of the racks is a Where's Wally scarf, identical to the one the murderer was wearing.

Chapter Twenty-Seven

'The murderer is here,' I say, my trembling hands almost dropping the phone down the loo.

'Jesus wept Rox, are you going to spend the whole evening in the loo?'

'Did you get the photo I sent to *That Night?'*

'It's upside down and blurry but we can see it.'

'What if he recognises me?' I say anxiously.

'Are you mad? First he would have needed telescopic eyes to see you from that distance. Have you forgotten that you were looking through a telescope at the time? You've got to get a grip. And secondly, any number of people could have the same scarf. It doesn't mean it belongs to the man you saw in the flat.'

I sigh with relief. She's quite right of course, but all the same …

'It's a strange coincidence don't you think? Maybe it would be safer if I left.'

'What's happening love?' I hear Felix ask in the background.

'She's thinking of leaving because of that Where's Wally scarf in the cloakroom, the one in the photo.'

'Ah, that's what it is.'

'It wasn't that bad,' I say defensively. 'Anyway it was taken in a hurry and with trembling hands.'

'Don't worry love, we won't be entering it into The International Photography Awards,' says Felix.

I shake my head in exasperation.

'Oh God,' I say, an awful thought occurring to me. 'You don't think Ark Morgan is the murderer?'

'Roxie, come on …'

Yes, of course, it's highly unlikely. What would he be doing in Clapham and he wouldn't be seen dead in a Where's Wally scarf.

'She's losing it,' says Felix.

'Sylv, have you got your phone on speaker?' I ask.

'Well Felix is kind of involved in the murder,' she mumbles.

'I'd prefer you didn't put it like that,' says Felix.

I bite my gel-painted manicured nails.

'I suppose dying on a yacht is better than at Starbucks,' I say.

'What is she on about?' asks Felix.

'Roxie, stop panicking. The chances of that scarf belonging to the murderer are a hundred to one,' says Sylvie.

'I suppose you're right,' I say, pulling at the Brazilian lace panties and feeling them rip.

'Ooh I've just had an epiphany,' says Felix.

'I'd never have known,' quips Sylvie.

'If she gets a bit of the scarf we can check it for DNA and stuff.'

Is he mental? I can't go cutting up bits of people's scarfs at a do like this. It's most likely a Zandra Rhodes or something. She designs colourful things doesn't she? It's not from Topshop that's for sure.

'I can't do that,' I say.

'Just snip off a bit. Then we'll know if it was someone at the party.'

'Snip a bit off the scarf?' I repeat. 'You're surely not serious.'

'You'll need to be careful not to get your DNA on it. Pop it in a freezer bag or something ...'

'Where am I supposed to get one of those?'

'Ask for a doggie bag,' suggests Sylvie.

Oh great. If I didn't look like a glutton earlier, I certainly will after asking for a doggie bag.

'People don't ask for doggie bags at this kind of do,' I say.

'Don't be a dopey donkey,' says Felix. 'They're the worst.'

'Improvise,' says Sylvie.

'If we can match the DNA on the scarf to the DNA we found at the flat then we'll know that scarf belongs to the murderer,' says Felix, brimming over with forensic knowledge. I wish he'd never bought that book.

'But I thought that chemist guy said he couldn't analyse DNA?'

'Ah, the good news is Felix has found someone who can and it's not that expensive,' says Sylvie.

I'm going off Felix.

'How expensive is *not that expensive*?' I ask.

'About five thousand,' says Sylvie without hesitation.

'Five thousand from my lottery win you mean. I'm not doing it,' I say resolutely.

'Stop worrying, Felix knows someone who will do it as a favour so hopefully we won't have to pay the five thousand.'

'I've just had another thought,' says Felix. 'We'll need the guest list. If the scarf belongs to the murderer then he will be on the guest list won't he?'

'Great idea,' exclaims Sylvie.

I wish she'd stop agreeing with him.

'Oh yes, brilliant idea. Except silly me didn't come equipped with scissors,' I say irritably. Or a needle and thread come to that, which would be far more useful right now. 'And perhaps you'd like to tell me how I actually get close enough to the scarf to snip it without anyone actually noticing?'

'She's got a point,' says Sylvie.

'It's all right for you two, you're not here,' I whisper as I hear someone enter the cubicle beside mine. Oh shit, what if it is the murderer? For goodness' sake, I must stop panicking. This is the ladies. The murderer was a man wasn't he? *But if he's capable of murdering someone, he's more than capable of entering the women's loo,* my inner goddess reminds me. Although why she's getting involved I don't know. She's only supposed to advise me on Ark Morgan stuff.

'He's right though Rox, you need to get a piece.'

'I guess she should snip a bit from the middle,' say Felix thoughtfully. 'We want to be sure his DNA is on it don't we?'

My hands turn clammy and I come over all hot.

'So you do think he is here? Oh my God, I'll be scared to eat anything.'

'Of course you can eat, you dopey donkey,' says Felix.

'Yes,' agrees Sylvie. 'He can't poison everything.'

'He could lace a few things with cyanide. If he's watching me he'll know what I'm going to eat next,' I say.

'Are you mad?' Sylvie asks.

'I'm starting to feel it,' I mumble.

'Sorry, did you say something darling?' asks the lady in the next cubicle.

Holy crap. Anastasia Steel never had these problems when she met with Christian Grey.

'No, I was just thinking aloud.'

'What did you say?' asks Sylvie.

'Brilliant do isn't it?' says the voice from the cubicle. 'Ark never fails to impress does he?'

'Mmm,' I mumble. I can't disagree with that.

'We can't hear you love,' yells Felix.

'Is this your first time?' asks the woman.

'Yes, my first time.'

'Have you been shooting up darling? Felix asks.

'How much have you had to drink?' says Sylvie.

I can't deal with this. A three way conversation is one thing but a four way one is a whole other matter.

'Enjoy it. Ark will chat with you later. Staying at one of the hotels are you?' she asks, pulling the chain.

'The Crescent,' I say.

Her cubicle door opens.

'What about it?' asks Sylvie.

'Lovely, have a good time,' calls the voice and then the toilet door slams.

'Christ,' I groan.

'What's happening to you?' asks Sylvie.

'There was someone in the cubicle next door. They were talking to me.'

'We thought you'd finally lost it. As for the scarf, you can cut it with a knife.'

'Won't it look jagged?' I ask.

'There must be scissors there somewhere. Say you've had a wardrobe malfunction.'

'Okay,' I say meekly and hang up. It's not far from the truth.

I check my reflection in the mirror and quickly dab my flushed cheeks with powder. I need a stiff drink for courage and then I'll head to the cloakroom.

Chapter Twenty-Eight

'Can I help?' asks a prim lady at the cloakroom counter, her eyes studying me through her black-rimmed glasses.

'I wonder do you have a sewing kit? I've had a little wardrobe malfunction', I ask politely.

'Of course madam, can a member of staff help?'

'It's rather delicate,' I say shyly.

'I assure you madam we've seen everything,' she says smugly, sounding like a bowel screening advert. *Your doctor has seen them all.* Well, they've not seen mine and they're not going to either. She'd make a great airport security guard. I can imagine her doing the frisking.

'I'll be fine,' I say. 'I just need some scissors for the job.'

Oh dear, that sounds like a line from a horror movie.

'Oh, I thought it was a sewing kit you needed,' she says, standing her ground.

'They have scissors don't they?'

'No, they don't. So is it scissors you actually need or scissors and a sewing kit?'

Holy Christ, what is it with the cross examination?

'Just the scissors please. That would be great.'

'Certainly madam, I'll fetch you a pair.'

I nervously totter on my Jimmy Choos, refusing three offers of a drink as I wait, although I could do with one. Another waiter approaches with a tray of salmon tarts. I take a deep breath, force a smile and say,

'Ooh they look lovely. My grandmother would love one. She's resting in a cabin at the moment, but I'd love to take her one. You don't have a little doggie bag by any chance?' I struggle to keep my voice sounding natural. I so hate lying.

'Of course madam,' he says whipping out a bag from a pocket. 'How many would grandmother like?'

'Oh just two,' I say, thinking I can scoff those quickly enough. As soon as he moves on, I stuff them into my mouth and empty the crumbs from the bag. Then I see my tousle-haired dreamboat Ark, walking my way just as Miss Prim returns with the scissors.

'Here we are madam. Kindly return them when the job is done.'

'Miss Brown, you're not leaving already?'

I turn, the scissors in my hand pointing menacingly at him.

'Whoa,' Ark smiles. 'Was it something I said?'

'Madam has had a little wardrobe malfunction,' says Miss Prim.

'I'll be two secs. I just need something from my coat,' I say, diving past her before she can stop me. I hack the scarf with the scissors and stuff a small piece of wool into the doggie bag. The scarf looks like it has been attacked by a starving moth. I drop the package into my clutch bag and rush back, tripping ungainly but gratefully into Ark's arms, almost stabbing him with the scissors as I do so. He removes them from my hand and says sexily,

'I should introduce you to less dangerous toys.'

Oh yes please.

'Dance with me again,' he says, taking the clutch bag from me.

'Put this with Miss Brown's things please,' he instructs Miss Prim before taking my hand.

I find myself back in the ballroom. It is crowded now. *I've been waiting for a girl like you* begins playing and he sings the lyrics into my ear, albeit slightly off key, as he leads me effortlessly onto the dance floor. I feel like I'm floating when with him. My stomach suddenly rumbles and he looks concerned.

'Have you eaten Miss Brown? I'll be cross if you haven't.'

'It's Roxanne,' I say again, the name sounding strange even on my own lips.

'You seemed very friendly with Sam Lockwood,' he says as we glide around. 'Did you not heed my warning?'

Is that a pimple on his cheek? I didn't notice that earlier. I expect it's the stress of the evening.

'He really isn't my type,' I say, the wine making me bold.

'What is your type Miss Brown?'

My heart thumps in my chest. I'm feeling more like Anastasia Steel by the minute. I'm about to answer when the music changes tempo and Cheryl Cole's *A Million Lights* begins, and I find myself in Sam Lockwood's arms.

'My turn I think,' he says.

The leggy Verity adds, 'Yes I agree. My turn Ark.' And she swings him away, his eyes blazing at Sam Lockwood.

'How dare you,' I say angrily.

'Now we're equal,' he says, mirroring my tone and interlinking my fingers through his. He wraps his arm around my waist. I reluctantly place my hand on his shoulder. He leads me slowly, pulling me closer as he does so. I can feel the heat from his body. He smells clean and fresh. His cheek is close to mine and I see a faint bruise on his.

'I hope you enjoyed your strawberries,' I say, trying to avoid his eyes.

'They were raspberries actually,' he says, pulling me closer so we don't collide with another couple. As we turn my Jimmy Choo twists under me and I feel myself fall. It all happens so fast. The ground comes up to meet me and then I'm pulled back into the security of his arms. I can feel his heart beating against mine. I inhale the fresh smell of soap and a warm comforting fragrance that emanates only from him. I remember his scent from our meeting at the Fun Palace.

'Are you okay?' he asks, holding me tightly.

He looks into my eyes and I can't look away. I feel like the world is standing still.

'Yes,' I whisper. My eyes drop to his lips and I feel an overwhelming desire to have him kiss me again. I'm torn between pushing him away and pulling him closer but I am paralysed, unable to do either. His breathing quickens as he moves me around the dance floor.

'Time's up Lockwood.'

I realise the music has stopped and Ark is standing in front of us, Verity by his side. Sam runs his hand through his hair.

'I rather think that is for Roxie to decide.'

Ark's eyes blaze.

'Miss Brown?' he says firmly, holding out his hand. He looks frustrated, his eyes flashing angrily.

'Ooh he's masterful,' whispers my inner goddess. I take his hand and avoid Sam's eyes. Ark pulls me through the throng of dancers and away from the pounding music. I find myself on deck, the chilly night air cutting through me. I shiver and Ark again places his jacket around my shoulders. He points to the stars.

'I wanted to show you this beautiful vision. Come see them through my telescope.'

Not another telescope. I allow him to lead me forward and reluctantly look through the eyepiece.

'It's breathtaking,' I say, feeling him move closer.

I can't believe a beauty makeover, a top designer dress and some Jimmy Choos are having this effect. It can only be the Jo Malone that's doing it.

'You smell heavenly,' he whispers into my ear. 'You intoxicate me. I hate it that Lockwood has touched you,' he says angrily. 'He always wants what doesn't belong to him.'

I hate to point it out but I don't really belong to anyone. Not even unfaithful wanking Darren. I'm about to tell him that when a voice behind us stops me.

'Your brandies sir.' I turn to see a waiter. When did Ark order these?

'Thank you,' Ark says, handing me a glass.

'There's so much I want to show you Roxanne. More than Sam Lockwood ever could.'

I wish he would stop mentioning Sam Lockwood. I sip the brandy, the liquid warming me.

'Did I hear my name?' says a familiar voice. Ark sighs and I feel his body tense beside me.

'Why are you here Lockwood?' he snaps.

'I told you, representing the company. You did send an invite. Oh, is that brandy? I wouldn't mind one.'

Ark gestures to the waiter.

'I don't recall your name on the guest list,' he says.

'You're right, but as Nick couldn't make it I thought I'd stand in.'

I so wish I could escape to the loo. It must be time for another visit mustn't it?

'I really should ...' I begin.

Ark grabs my arm and I shiver. Ooh this is more like it.

'Stay Roxanne,' he orders, using my Christian name for the first time. Sam throws back the brandy and hands the glass to the waiter.

'As great as this is Morgan, it somehow leaves a bad taste in my mouth. I find it difficult to swallow something bought with immoral money.'

'That's rich coming from you. You'd do anything to get what you want.' The two men stare at each other before Sam turns to me.

'See you Roxie,' he says. 'Don't believe everything you hear.'

'Sorry about that, a little too much to drink I fear. Let's get you back into the warm,' says Ark his fingers stroking my arm. I shiver but am not sure if it is from his touch or the cold draught running up my dress and blowing on the unmentionables where the lacy Brazilian knickers have totally disappeared.

'I'd like to see you again,' he whispers sexily into my ear, his brandy lips touching my ear lobe ever so gently.

'Yes,' I reply, trying not to pant.

'Can I phone you Miss Brown? I'd like to take you somewhere special.'

Here it comes says my inner goddess. *This is what you've been waiting for* and it's not even a fantasy.

Chapter Twenty-Nine

'It's a mother-in-law's tongue,' says Dad. 'I just thought it might cheer up the new place a bit.'

'It's probably the closest you'll get to a real one,' grumbles Mum. 'So you might as well take it. Not that there will be much room in your bedsit.'

Dad smiles uncomfortably. They'll be giving me a sympathy card next.

'I'll only kill it,' I say. 'I'm rubbish with plants. I'll never remember to water it.'

Mum shakes her head.

'Just as well you never had a baby,' she says, manically turning the roast potatoes.

A baby and a plant aren't quite the same thing are they, but I don't have the energy to argue. The roast smells heavenly. I only get a decent roast dinner when I visit my parents.

'I'm resigned never to be a grandmother,' she says in that, why did I give birth to the she-devil, tone.

'I can't say I'm sorry,' says Dad, carrying cutlery into the dining room. 'He wasn't an ideal son-in-law if I'm honest.'

'At the rate your daughter is going there won't be any son-in-laws left, let alone an ideal one,' she says, hacking through the roast beef. 'You do realise she's thirty-two.'

I rush to turn off the boiling over vegetables.

'That's not exactly ancient is it dear?'

'Try telling her ovaries that. And to think my daughter is going to end up in some pokey bedsit in Clapham. Oh, I can't bear it,' she says, weeping over the Yorkshire puddings. 'What man will be interested in a chambermaid in a grotty bedsit in Clapham?'

She sure knows how to cheer me up. I don't know where this pokey bedsit in Clapham came from. I've never said anything about a bedsit.

'I'll open some wine,' says Dad, pretending everything is normal. 'Red goes with beef doesn't it?'

'I had a lottery win,' I say, nibbling a Yorkshire pudding.

'At least you've had some luck,' she says miserably, dabbing her eyes with her apron.

'Ooh that's nice love. I don't think we've ever had a win have we Margaret?' says Dad.

She shoots him a dark look.

'Margo,' he corrects.

'I won seventy-five thousand,' I say.

Dad continues pouring the wine until the glass overflows.

'Seventy-five thou ...' stammers Mum, before grabbing the overflowing glass and knocking it back.

I nod.

'You don't need a man in a hurry then?' she says.

'I didn't anyway.'

'Oh dear,' she mumbles as the doorbell chimes.

'Who can that be?' asks Dad, 'Sunday lunch time too.'

'Rudy Green from no. 23, I invited him for lunch,' stammers Mum while wiping her tear streaked face with a tea towel.

'You did what?' I gasp. 'Have you seen him recently? He's almost bald these days and ...'

'Yes, well that was his ex-wife. A terrible stress that was.'

'He's nearly fifty.'

'In my defence, I didn't know you were now in a position to be choosy.'

'Choosy is an understatement, I'd need to be desperate to go out with Rudy Green.'

'He's anxious to marry again,' she says.

'There are agencies for that kind of thing,' I say impatiently.

'I don't even know who we're talking about,' says my confused dad. 'Do I let him in or what?'

The doorbell chimes again.

'And this is all because you want me to have babies?'

'Can someone please tell me what to do,' says Dad, raising his voice.

'You can't wait much longer,' says Mum wringing the tea towel.

'I know,' says Dad.

'Not you Martin,' she snaps. 'And don't mention the lottery win,' she says tapping her nose. 'We'll have men queuing at the door and all the wrong kind.'

'I'm been asked out on a date with Ark Morgan, so I'm certainly not going to choose Rudy Green over him am I?'

Mum's eyes almost pop out of her head. The truth is Ark didn't actually set a date, he just took my phone number and promised to be in touch, but I daren't tell her that.

'The multimillionaire Ark Morgan? Oh my Lordy, why didn't you tell us?'

'He only asked me yesterday.'

'How did you meet Ark Morgan? Oh Lordy, did you hear that Martin, our daughter and Ark Morgan ...'

The doorbell chimes again, this time with an added thump on the door.

'All I can hear is that doorbell,' says Dad, getting agitated.

'Perhaps he'll think we're out,' says Mum hopefully.

'The place smells of roast beef, the living room windows are steamed up and Roxie's Fiesta is parked in the drive, so unless he thinks we've all died from gas fumes he's unlikely to believe we're out,' groans Dad. 'Now do I let him in or what?'

'Oh God,' mumbles Mum. 'If only you were like a normal daughter we wouldn't be having this,' she throws back the last of the wine in her glass.

'I am normal,' I argue.

'Good, so we're agreed that everyone is normal. So I'll do the normal thing and open the door,' grunts Dad marching out of the kitchen.

'*Ark Morgan*?' repeats Mum. 'I don't believe it.'

'*Rudy Green*?' I mimic. 'I don't believe it.'

Chapter Thirty

'More roast potatoes Rudy?' asks Mum.

'I wouldn't say no, Mrs Brown. I have to say they really are the best roast spuds I've ever tasted.'

I stuff another into my mouth and wash it down with wine.

'I'll open another bottle, shall I?' asks Dad, looking at Mum.

This will be the third bottle but who's counting.

'Do you cook as well as your mum Roxie?' Rudy asks after shovelling some roast beef into his mouth so it sounds more like *do you fuck as well as your mum Foxie?*

I look at Mum and raise my eyebrows. Hopefully she can translate that to 'great manners he has'.

'Ach,' says Mum, suddenly turning Scottish. 'Roxie, cook, that'll be the day won't it dear? She can't even boil an egg, and that's with a cookbook.'

'Oh yes dear,' she says turning to Dad, 'another bottle would be nice.'

Another bottle would be necessary more like. Rudy laughs dismissively, showing his crooked teeth.

'I don't believe that.'

That's a shame.

'Work keeping you busy is it?' asks Dad who has no idea who Rudy is, let alone what he does for a living.

'It's a bit of a dying trade,' smiles Rudy.

'Oh dear,' says Dad, topping up our glasses. 'I'm sorry to hear that.'

'Rudy works for Aycocks Funeral Parlour,' says Mum.

'Aycocks?' I say finally, trying not to choke on my wine.

'Dessert?' says Mum, jumping up. 'Come and help me love.'

She nudges so hard I almost fall from the chair.

'You've got to put him off,' Mum dictates, pulling a trifle from the fridge.

'I think you're doing a pretty good job without me. Anyway If he asks me out, I'll just say no,' I shrug.

'You have trouble saying no,' she says, scooping up bowls.

'Not always.' But I have to agree, most of the time I do.

'Well, just in case. We have to make you so unlikeable that he won't want to ask you out.' Before I have time to reply, she has dumped the dishes in my hand and waltzed back into the living room. I sigh. This is going to be a very drunken Sunday lunch.

'Then there was the one that moved when we were laying him out,' laughs Rudy.

I grab another After Eight.

'I was thinking about those cardboard caskets for Martin,' slurs Mum. 'He's always trying to economise.'

'I've some lovely ones,' says Rudy. 'You should come over one night Roxie, and I can show you my stock,' he says fidgeting uncomfortably on the couch. I imagine his arse is stuck to the plastic. It makes a change from etchings, I suppose and it might not be a bad idea. If the murderer catches up with me at least I'll be prepared.

'That's nice,' I say. 'But I've never really been that interested in coffins. Or death come to that.'

'It's inevitable,' says Rudy. 'Go out in style is my motto.'

I may well do.

'I prefer gun carriages,' says Dad.

'I don't know how you think we can afford that,' says Mum. 'You'll have to depend on Roxie's lott ...'

'Who's up for a game of something?' I interrupt.

What the hell made me say that? There must have been hundreds of things I could have said to stop her saying the lottery word.

'I'll always play games with you,' says Rudy with a wink.

Holy shit. Only my mother could get me into this mess.

'We've got Cluedo,' says Dad, fumbling in the coffee table drawer.

No thank you. Not while I'm playing the real thing.

At that moment my phone rings and I pull it from my bag gratefully. It's Ark Morgan. My heart thumps and I become breathless. Please don't let me slur my words. I rush into the hall and answer it.

'Hello,' I say.

'You took a long time to answer,' he says in his sexy voice.

'Sorry,' I say quietly.

'You sound breathless, are you in the middle of something?'

'Not exactly,' I mumble.

'Anything I can help with?' he asks huskily.

My legs give way and I slump onto the stairs.

'Well ...' I begin.

'Let's start with something French shall we?' he asks.

He's flirting dangerously with me and I'm getting so turned on, it's unbelievable. *Not on your parent's stairs,* whispers my inner goddess.

'Are you free tomorrow night?'

'Yes,' I say breathlessly. Oh God, I so am.

'Good, I'll collect you at seven, what's your address?'

Holy shit, I can't say 106A Braden Mansions can I?

'I like to keep that private for now,' I say, attempting to sound sultry, 'until I know you better.'

He laughs.

'Well, I'll have to make sure you get to know me better then won't I? Meet me at Knightsbridge station and Miss Brown ...'

'Yes,' I whisper.

'Wear that perfume.'

With that he hangs up. I force my trembling body upright and struggle to walk back into the living room.

'Something important?' says Mum, frowning worriedly.

'I'm afraid so,' I say solemnly, leaning across to my mum to whisper *Ark Morgan.*

'What's happened?' asks my clueless dad, only to get a look from Mum that seriously could have had that cardboard casket delivered instantly.

'Oh is it that?' he says mysteriously.

'Yes,' I say.

Rudy looks from one to the other of us, confusion etched on his face.

'Can I help at all?' he says finally.

I suppose he could supply the satin tie-ups.

'I think I'm beyond help,' I say in a pitiful tone.

'Yes,' agrees Mum.

I pour some wine and we sit solemnly for a few minutes until Rudy says,

'I should be getting back. I'll phone you Roxie.'

'Yes okay,' I say, looking at him over my wine glass. He hesitates for a second.

'I don't have your number.'

'Can we drop it in to you at a better time?' asks Mum.

'Oh yes, of course. Well, you all take care.'

'I'll see you out,' says Dad.

Mum and I sit with our ears pricked until the front door slams.

'Perhaps one of you would now like to tell me what all that was about?' asks Dad.

'Ark Morgan is a multimillionaire, that's what it's about, and he's asked your daughter out. And, he's as sexy as hell,' says Mum.

Chapter Thirty-One

Avoiding Ark Morgan at work is more difficult than Sylvie had imagined. Mondays are Crescent days and this Monday Ark and a group of Japanese delegates are in the hotel.

'You look different so the chances are he won't recognise you,' says Sylvie without any conviction in her voice.

'I've not had plastic surgery. I can't look that much different.'

'No, you're probably right,' she concedes.

And that's a point. I can't go through that whole beauty regime malarkey every time I see him, just so I look the same as I did on Saturday. It's not only tedious but bloody expensive. We wheel the trolley out onto the twelfth floor and my stomach flips. Right opposite the lift is the conference room, and strolling out of it are the Japanese delegates with Ark Morgan.

Holy shit. I look at Sylvie in panic. The promised cleaning cupboard is not on the twelfth floor.

'What do I do?' I whisper.

The nearest rooms all have their *do not disturb* signs hanging from the doorknobs. I'm about ready to die on the spot when I hear Ark say, 'Excuse me gentlemen, I've left my jacket.' He turns back to the conference room and Sylvie pushes me into the lift.

'Wait in the cleaning cupboard until I text you,' she instructs as the doors close.

I feel like I'm on the run.

'That was a close call,' Sylvie says as we leave the hotel. 'Where's the flat we're viewing? I can't wait.'

I'm about to tell her when I see Darren standing on the steps, holding a bouquet of flowers. Why is this happening to me? I bet Jennifer Aniston didn't have Brad Pitt standing on her steps with a bouquet of flowers after they broke up.

'Bollocks,' says Sylvie.

His face lights up and he pushes the bouquet at me shoving petals up my nose.

'I thought I'd missed you Babe,' he says.

If only you had. What a dreadful shock not just Darren, but Darren with a bunch of flowers. I can't remember the last time Darren bought me flowers. Come to think of it I can't remember Darren ever buying me flowers. What's worse, he has that sorrowful look on his face that I hate because I can never say no when he looks at me like that.

'I've been a prick,' he says flatly.

'A bit of an understatement,' says Sylvie.

'I've lost everything,' he says miserably.

'I think you're mistaking yourself for a tsunami victim,' snaps Sylvie.

I glance at the time on my phone. My first viewing is in fifteen minutes.

'You know it didn't mean anything. I was just desperate for love.'

I'm standing like a spare part, with a bouquet in one hand and my mobile in the other.

'You don't think you overreacted a bit?' he says.

'What?' says a flabbergasted Sylvie.

'You know how you blow things out of proportion when it's the wrong time of the month?'

Am I really hearing this?

'And you were eating a lot of Oreo's that week,' he adds, as if that clinches it.

'That was because I'd run out of sponge fingers, and it had nothing to do with my period,' I snap.

'... But more to do with you screwing some tart behind her back,' says Sylvie.

'You know I'm overdrawn at the bank,' he says pitifully, ignoring Sylvie and leaning towards me.

'You do overspend Darren,' I say, barely able to control my anger.

'You should have saved your money and bought a bunch of daffs then,' quips Sylvie.

She's a hard cow is our Sylv.

'I've missed you Babe. You were quite right too. It's all out of a bottle.'

'Even the kids? Sylvie pipes up. 'Test tube are they?'

'Sylvie, this is between me and Roxie.'

'Not when I'm supplying the Kleenex it ain't mate,' she snaps.

'I heard you had a win on the lottery,' he says, his tone changing.

I wondered when he would find that out.

'Why didn't you tell me?' he asks accusingly, struggling to see me behind the bouquet.

'I think it had something to do with you screwing the bottled redhead,' repeats Sylvie.

'I wish you'd shut up,' says Darren.

'And I wish you'd sod off.'

And I wish we could do this somewhere else. Supposing Ark Morgan comes out?

'The thing is, that's my money too,' he says firmly.

'You what?' laughs Sylvie.

'I lent you a tenner on Thursday night. You said you didn't have any money so you bought the ticket with my money. Joey says that entitles me.'

'Entitles you to shit, Darren,' says Sylvie indignantly. 'Don't listen to him Roxie.'

I shake my head.

'I've lent you more money than you've ever lent me Darren. It was probably ten quid you owed me.'

Sylvie pulls me by the arm.

'Come on, we're going to be late.'

'Don't you care about me Roxie? I made a big mistake. I know that now. I just need you to be more loving and attentive and ...'

'And I just need you to stop or I'm going to throw up.' groans Sylvie.

I feel myself hesitate. He looks so lost and forlorn. I suppose I could share some of the money with him, just to help him get on his feet. Sylvie pulls me harder.

'Don't even go there Rox,' she warns, snatching the flowers and plonking them back into Darren's hands.

'Give them to the bottled redhead,' she says.

'It's Titian actually,' he retorts.

'Titian my arse,' I say, cynically.

'Who gives a shit? Come on Rox.'

'You and your guilt, you really need to get that sorted,' she mumbles as she drags me away. We climb into the Fiesta and head towards Chelsea.

'Christ, I thought you were going to cave in.'

The truth is if Sylvie hadn't have been with me, I most likely would have done.

'Going upmarket aren't we?' she smiles. 'Chelsea can't be bad.'

'You do think Darren will be all right?' I ask.

'Come on Roxie, he's treated you like shit. Anyway, getting off the subject of two-timing bastards, while you were lording it at your parents yesterday ...'

'Lording it was far from what I was doing. You have no idea,' I say.

'Anyway, Felix got the handwriting analysed from that estate agent leaflet. Although may I remind you that was supposed to be your job.'

'I have been a bit busy, Sylvie.'

'Anyway, the guy who wrote it is confident, successful, and most likely a risk taker. He likes a challenge and enjoys danger.'

He sounds like Ark Morgan. I wonder if the analyst said he was hot, sexy and irresistible too. Honestly, these past few days I've thought of nothing but sex. Well, sadomasochistic sex to be more precise. Pity Mum never bought me books on that.

'Felix feels sure it has to be the murderer. I think we're closing in on him. He's either connected to those flats or the estate agent. Plus if the scarf DNA matches some from the flat then we'll know he was at Ark Morgan's party and ...'

I gulp.

'It's Ark, I know it is. He's confident, successful and you have to take risks in business don't you, and he loves a challenge, I can tell and ...'

'He's not the type to wear a Where's Wally scarf,' adds Sylvie. She's quite right of course. I pull into a parking space and the Fiesta judders.

'I hope you're buying a new car,' she says over the squeak of the opening door. 'So what flat are we looking at?'

'No 62 Woodlands Park, this must be the guy from the estate agent.'

'Miss Brown?' he says, grabbing my hand and squeezing it so tight I almost squeal. 'I'm Justin, pleased to meet you.'

'This is my friend Sylvie,' I say. He grabs her hand too and I can tell by her wince he's giving her the squeeze as well.

'I'm so sorry to tell you that 62, Woodlands Park went about an hour ago,' he informs me.

'Oh,' I say.

'You don't have her phone number?' says Sylvie accusingly.

The guy blinks and says,

'There is a nice one in Rommel Mansions; I thought you might like to see that one. It has all the same amenities as Woodlands Park, in fact in my opinion …'

'Rommel Mansions?' repeats Sylvie. 'But I thought that was with Masons' estate agents.' A cold shudder runs down my spine. Rommel Mansions was the property on the estate agent's letter we found at the murder flat.

'It's also with us,' he says, clearly affronted. 'But obviously if you've booked an appointment with Masons …' He stops, allowing the full extent of our shame to hit us.

'We haven't booked anything through Masons,' I say. I don't add because we think the murderer may work for them.

His face brightens.

'Oh well then, shall we look at that one after the two you are viewing in Newton Street?'

'Absolutely,' says Sylvie brightly, unable to hide her excitement. 'We might find some clues.'

We get back into the Fiesta and follow Justin. I really don't want to go to Rommel Mansions and I certainly don't want to live there.

'We're closing in,' says Sylvie, transforming into Detective Chief Inspector Jane Tennison.

I'm actually quite taken with the flat in Rommel Mansions. It's exactly what I've been looking for. The previous two were a bit grim compared to this.

'Better than Woodlands Park don't you think? Nice properties but the area is a bit, how shall I say? Not an area a woman of your means would be accustomed to, whereas this is more fitting to your requirements.'

He sounds like a character out of a Dickens' novel.

'Only last week I was at Woodlands showing someone around and a tranquiliser dart just missed me. Ambulance sirens going off everywhere, it was pretty frightening. Don't get me wrong, it's an ideal area for a single woman such as yourself if you don't mind the odd protest. It is just for yourself is it? Not moving in with a boyfriend or anything?'

Sylvie and I stare at him.

'Or anything?' Sylvie repeats. 'Do you mean like a cuddly toy?' He flusters and blinks rapidly.

'I'm not keen on being tranquilised every time I visit her,' says Sylvie, strolling into the main bedroom, 'so I'll encourage her not to take one near Woodlands Park. Beside this one has a garage doesn't it?'

'Oh yes, perfect for a car,' he says, following her into the bedroom.

'Well, we weren't thinking of putting a bus in there,' she says, rolling her eyes.

'Room for a six foot in here,' he says.

'I'm presuming you mean a bed and not a bus?' quips Sylvie. I can't take her anywhere.

'This is a good buy. Came back on the market a week or so ago I believe.'

I look at Sylvie.

'Oh really. And why did it come off the market?' I ask nervously.

'It had a buyer but they dropped out.'

Or dropped dead.

'Really, I wonder why?' says Sylvie, putting on her Columbo hat.

'It was through Masons,' he says, trying to hide the venom from his voice. 'So I really couldn't tell you.'

'It's perfect Rox. The shops are just up the road and the chippy is just around the corner and it's upmarket for when you bring you know who,' she says lowering her voice.

I somehow think I'd need to be a lot more upmarket than this to impress Ark Morgan. But it's a hundred times better than 106A Braden Mansions, and it will take a six-foot bed. What more could you want? There is one small problem in that the victim was going to buy it, which means the murderer knows of it, and if he knows of me too then I'm a sitting duck at a shooting range aren't I?

Chapter Thirty-Two

He looks so gorgeous. He's standing relaxed and self-assured outside Knightsbridge station. All I want to do is take him back to my new flat and shag him senseless on my six-foot bed, except I don't have a flat or a bed to shag him on yet. But I have made an offer for the Rommel Mansions flat. He rushes over as I pay the cab driver. I couldn't pull up in my Fiesta could I?

'I'll get this,' he says, giving me his heart-stopping smile. 'You're a few minutes late Miss Brown.'

'Sorry,' I whisper, wishing my heart would stop beating so fast.

'I'll let you off this time,' he says, grinning wickedly at me. He pays the driver and slides his arm around my waist and leads me to a waiting limousine.

'You smell glorious,' he says, opening the door for me. I slide along the sweet-smelling upholstery. He slips in beside me and I shyly avoid looking at him. I'd chosen a simple blue button up dress with a silk pashmina. I'd splashed out on some Jo Malone body lotion and look as gorgeous as I possibly can. Ark places his hand on mine and strokes it rhythmically with his thumb.

'I hope you like French cuisine,' he says in that soft but firm voice of his.

I'm flying so high. As for my hormones, well, they don't know if they're coming or going. They've sniffed the perfect daddy material and are completely out of control. It's all I can do not to jump him in the back seat of the limo and rip off his perfectly ironed jeans.

'It's my favourite,' he smiles, leaning forward to push a button. I imagine he's run out of mine. He's pushed just about every button I have.

A minibar slides towards us.

'I hope it's yours too,' he says huskily.

I've never had proper French food before, not unless you count French fries from McDonalds.

'It's not something I've had much of,' I say truthfully.

'What *have* you had much of, Miss Brown?' he says, turning laughing eyes on me. I blush. 'Or will I need to teach you everything?'

Ooh yes please.

'Martini or champagne, you choose. I find a drink before flying calms me.'

Flying? He didn't say we were flying. Can he drink and fly? Did Christian Grey drink before flying his helicopter ...? I think not.

'We're flying somewhere?' The chauffeur catches my eye in the rear-view mirror and winks.

'Where better to enjoy a French meal than in France,' smiles Ark as he clinks his glass against mine. 'We're flying to Paris.'

I fight back a gasp. Poise and confidence at all times I remind myself. Jennifer Aniston wouldn't gasp would she? Then again maybe she would if Justin Theroux was half pissed before he flew their helicopter.

'Paris?' I repeat. I've got to be at work in the morning. I can't even swallow my champagne, I'm that nervous. And it doesn't help when I see him refill his glass. I know in theory dying in a private helicopter with a millionaire by your side is as romantic as it gets but I'm just not ready to go yet.

We drive into the underground car park of the Mercier Hotel, Ark's biggest and best. I've never cleaned this one. He gently takes my glass and strokes my hand.

'Follow me Miss Brown,' he says, leading me from the car to the lift. My legs turn to jelly.

'It's Rox ... Roxanne.' I say.

'We're taking off from the helipad on the roof,' he smiles. The lift doors close behind us and he turns to face me.

'I'm so glad you came Roxanne,' he whispers, my name sounding so sexy on his lips. He's not as glad as I am, although I admit I would be just a little more ecstatic if we were going to a restaurant in London. The lift doors open and waiting on the rooftop is the helicopter.

'Come on,' he says, taking my hand. 'We can have another drink on board.'

Another drink? My God, hasn't he had enough already? Surely there are rules about drinking and flying. He opens the door of the helicopter and gestures for me to get in. I hesitate. I can't get into a helicopter with a drunken pilot can I? He'll most likely fly us over Iraq and get us shot down.

'The thing is ...'

'You don't like flying do you?' he smiles, the wind blowing through his hair. He looks dead sexy when windswept.'

The truth is I don't like flying when the pilot's half pissed, but I can't say that can I?

'No, it's just ...'

'I'm terrified of flying too. So that makes two of us. We'll have another drink. These help too,' he says, pulling out a foil of Valium, 'makes all the difference.'

All the difference between flying into the dome of St Paul's and not flying into the dome of St Paul's does he mean? Jesus Christ, he'll be comatose over the controls at this rate. Christian Grey is never afraid.

'We could get the Euro Tunnel?' I say dumbly. He laughs wickedly.

'Miss Brown, afraid or not I am forcing you into the helicopter so I can take you for a French meal.'

For goodness' sake, there must be hundreds of French restaurants in London. At least in a car in London we're not likely to get shot down by terrorists, or even shot at as terrorists. Either way, it's not appealing. After all, it's not acceptable to crash into a London landmark even if your name is Ark Morgan.

'Into the helicopter Miss Brown, if I can do it then so can you.'

But I'm not flying the bloody thing am I?

'I assure you Bernie will take good care of us. He's an excellent pilot. I only use the best.'

'You're not flying it?' I ask.

He laughs.

'Me, fly a helicopter? I'm terrified of heights.'

'Oh,' I say. Christian Grey isn't afraid of heights. Christian Grey isn't afraid of anything.

'You don't go gliding then?' I ask.

He looks at me like I've grown horns.

'Are you insane, why would I want to go in one of those? Come on Miss Brown, in you go.'

'Brandy Mr Morgan, and for the lady?' Bernie asks, handing a glass to Ark.

'I'm fine thank you,' I say. I really think I need to keep a clear head, especially if contracts are produced. I want to be careful what I consent to. Although knowing me, I'll sign up for everything. I never was good at reading the small print, but I really don't want to get my soft and hard limits muddled up do I?

Moments later we are in the air and the lights and sights of London are beneath us. I see St Paul's and am grateful that we fly over its dome.

'It's a beautiful sight isn't it? Paris is even more remarkable from the air,' says Bernie.

I look at Ark as he sits uncomfortably in his seat. He takes a gulp of brandy. My mind wanders to Sam Lockwood and I remember his arrival on the Harley Davidson. I feel quite sure he wouldn't be afraid of flying. In fact, I feel quite sure that Sam Lockwood wouldn't be afraid of anything. *And why would you be thinking of Sam Lockwood when you've got the hunk Ark Morgan sitting beside you?* scolds my inner goddess.

My phone bleeps with a text and I look nervously at Ark.

'I forgot to turn it off,' I say apologetically.

'That's fine Miss Brown. I hope it's not a love rival, I would be very jealous.'

I check my phone. It's a *That Night* message from Felix.

Great news, we managed to get DNA from the scarf. Sylvie is excelling herself. All we have to do now is see if they match the DNA from the hair. If it does then we'll know our guy was at the yacht party and then we'll know if you were living it up with the murderer. What a breakthrough don't you think?

Holy shit. I bite my lip and give Ark a sideways glance. I remember Sylvie's words about the handwriting analysis. The writer is confident, successful, and most likely a risk taker. He likes a challenge and enjoys danger.

I look again at Ark and he smiles at me while rigid in his seat. Ark Morgan is not the murderer. Of that I can be certain.

Chapter Thirty-Three

Paris in springtime is truly beautiful, and it is the most romantic place to be in the world. Not that I know of many other places but right now this seems like the most romantic place ever as I walk arm in arm with Ark Morgan. We stroll along the Champs-Élysées, our eyes feasting on the sunset. Heads turn as Ark passes them and I feel so proud to be on his arm. We stop at the entrance to a restaurant.

'Le Taillevent, the best in Paris. After you Miss Brown,' he says as the doorman greets us. Ark pushes me forward, his hand lingering on my hip and feeling like a red-hot poker.

'Bonsoir Monsieur Morgan, a pleasure as always' says the waiter greeting us at the door.

'Bonsoir Pascal, may I present Mademoiselle Brown,' Ark says in perfect French. I shiver as Ark slides my pashmina from my shoulders, his hand caressing them as he does so.

'I think you'll be warm enough,' he says softly.

'Your table is ready monsieur, this way.'

The restaurant is buzzing with people. Traditional French music plays in the background and I have an overwhelming urge to run. I should tell Ark that I'd made an awful mistake and that I'm just a simple chambermaid from Clapham, but we're now in Paris and I'm just a little bit stuck aren't I? After all, one doesn't hail a plane in the same way as one hails a cab. *And you're complaining?* whispers my inner goddess. *Some women would give their Boots Protect and Perfect to be where you are right now.*

We're led to the back of the restaurant and the waiter pulls aside red satin curtains to reveal our private dining area. For a moment I thought he was leading us to the red room of pain. I'm not sure if I'm happy or sad. The table is laid for two and in the corner of the room is a huge bouquet of roses.

'Thank you for coming,' he says simply.

His sultry eyes meet mine and I melt under his stare.

'I hope you don't mind this,' he says, waving his arm to show me the room. 'I didn't want to be public with you. Selfish of me I know.'

He looks innocent and boyish, but still as sexy as hell. The waiter pulls back a velvet covered chair for me and drapes a napkin across my lap.

'I shall send your waiter to you immediately. May I get drinks Monsieur Morgan?'

'Merci Pascal, we'll have a bottle of Château d'Yquem, as we'll both be having the chicken.'

Ooh Christian always ordered for Ana Steele. He also discussed the contract over dinner. Is that what Ark is planning to do now?

'I take it you're happy if I order,' he smiles, reaching into his jacket pocket.

This is it, this is the contract ... But instead he produces a pair of black-rimmed glasses, which he puts on to study the menu. He looks a bit like Colin Firth in *A Single Man*. Less gay of course, and far sexier, but glasses ... Ark Morgan is not quite the Christian Grey that I imagined him to be for as he bends over the menu I see the bald patch on the top of his head, and this time it isn't a trick of the light. Still, it could be worse couldn't it? He could have zits all over his face. But then again he has got one. I glance at the bouquet in the corner. Darren never bought me flowers until today, let alone a huge bouquet. Although in all fairness I don't suppose he could afford it.

'Food is very important Miss Brown,' Ark says, looking at me seriously. 'If you're not happy with my choice then please say. Open your menu,' he instructs.

I glance at the menu and feel my breath catch in my throat. My maths never was that great but even I can work out that, with wine, the meal is going to cost around eight hundred euros. How can I justify eating that when there are people starving in developing countries? But then Ark does give a lot to charity so I suppose that makes things okay. All the same, I'd much prefer Prezzo. They do a great carbonara at a fraction of the price. *A man doesn't spend that on dinner without expecting something in return*, barks my subconscious. My breasts ache at the thought.

'I thought we'd have the Crab with Remoulade Sauce and Dill fleurette cream with lemon for entrées. And for main I've chosen Chicken from Bresse Country on the Spit, Mushrooms and Jura Wine Butter under the skin. Pudding, Miss Brown, is a delectable feast which I shall tease you with throughout dinner.'

I'm sure he can tease me with better things than a dessert. The waiter returns with the wine and uncorks it while Ark sits silently studying me. He samples the wine expertly. Once the waiter leaves Ark leans his elbows on the table and looks at me over his clasped hands.

I sip my wine.

'There's something I want to ask you Miss Brown.'

'Roxanne,' I whisper.

'Roxanne,' he says sexily. 'How well do you know Sam Lockwood?'

'Sam Lockwood?' I repeat. Is that the something he wanted to ask me?

'How long have you known him?'

'I don't really know him. I met him at the Fun Palace and bumped into him a few times since.'

'That's it?' he asks, his eyes piercing into mine. 'Didn't you go to one of his boxing matches?'

I gasp.

'How do you know that?' He's just like Christian Grey. He knows everything I do and everywhere I go.

'He mentioned it on the yacht,' he smiles.

I nod nervously.

'Oh,' I mumble. 'I just bumped into him when with a friend and he invited us.'

He nods.

'And that's it?'

'Yes.'

'Good,' he says after a few moments. He relaxes in his chair. 'He's bad news. I hope if he tells you anything that may affect me or my business you would tell me?'

I have no intention of seeing Sam Lockwood so there is no fear of him telling me anything.

'Let's enjoy dinner,' he says.

The dinner is indeed delicious. In fact the best dinner I've ever had. Mind you, that's not hard to do considering the most upmarket place Darren and I have been to is Jamie's. Dessert is placed in front of me and I almost die from pleasure.

'Are you pleased with my choice?' he asks, his foot gently sliding up my calf. I nod. After all, I can't possibly speak.

'The Andoa Chocolate is superb. I want to watch your pleasure,' he smiles.

I struggle to breathe as I take a spoonful and wash it down with wine to calm my pounding heart.

'Will you share Miss Brown, just a spoonful?'

He takes my hand and guides the spoon to his mouth. If his hand wasn't holding the spoon we'd have chocolate all over the show. He licks his lips seductively, his foot still rubbing my calf. I don't think I can hold out much longer.

'A good dessert, you agree?'

A good dessert is an understatement, more a mind-blowing orgasmic dessert. He stands up and walks around the table to me. I drop my spoon clumsily as he spins my chair around and leans down to kiss me. He looks into my eyes before his chocolate lips touch mine. His hand grasps the nape of my neck as his tongue explores my mouth. I savour his lips, wanting more while wondering why those magical feelings I'd been expecting aren't bursting within me. I could be kissing Darren. Obviously I know I'm not, but it doesn't feel any different. It's pleasurable enough but surely there should be more? It's Ark Morgan after all. Am I expecting too much?

'Stay the night in Paris,' he whispers, his hand sliding along my thigh.

'I ...'

'I'll show you luxury you've never dreamt of,' he says, reaching for my lips again.

I can't spend the night in Paris. I've got work in the morning and I need to get furniture for the new flat and if I'm honest Ark Morgan is not at all how I imagined him to be. I pull my lips from his.

'I need to get back,' I say quietly.

'I can't persuade you?'

His hand moves higher along my thigh. We'll be doing it in the restaurant in a minute. It wouldn't surprise me if the waiter opened another curtain into a bedroom. Nothing seems to be out of the reach of Ark Morgan.

'I'm not ready,' I say.

'I always get what I want Miss Brown, one way or the other. You can't escape me forever but if work is pulling you back I fully understand.'

He strokes my head, tops up our glasses and returns to his seat.

'So, just what is that you do Miss Brown?'

Chapter Thirty-Four

Of course I didn't tell Ark the whole truth but as I find it so hard to lie I simply said *I'd prefer to be secretive about a few things until I get to know you better*. He seemed to like that. He said it made me more alluring, although obviously not that alluring as it has been over a week since our romantic dinner in Paris and I've not even had a text from him.

My mum is panicking more than me and has shot more arrows my way than Cupid could ever have managed.

'Do you remember Colin Markson? You had a crush on him when you were seventeen,' she says excitedly down the phone. I don't even remember being seventeen.

'He's divorced,' she says. 'Had a terrible time by all accounts, horrid woman tried to take him for every penny. He's got a few apparently.'

'Wives or pennies?' I say sarcastically.

'He's just back from Thailand. He was working out there. His parents are having a little welcome home do. You must come. Tonight at seven.'

'Oh that's a shame,' I say with relief. 'I'm getting a takeaway with Felix and Sylvie.'

It's a meeting of project *That Night* which I can't possibly miss.

'You'll never get a husband if you don't make some effort,' she snaps. 'That Ark Morgan isn't going to get in touch is he? A man doesn't take a week.'

She's quite right. I'm sure if Ark was interested he would have been in touch by now. I park outside Sylvie's terrace and make a determined effort to put Ark Morgan out of my mind.

'We thought you weren't coming,' says Felix, opening the door. 'Come on hurry up, we're just about to start.'

'The DNA guy is here,' says Sylvie quietly. 'He's studying everything now.'

The doorbell rings and Felix whoops. 'Pizza at last, we ordered without you love. But I got anchovies and garlic bread.'

I follow Sylvie into the lounge where a small, bald spectacled man is leaning over our bits of evidence. I still can't believe Ark has a bald patch and wears glasses. Ark will be looking like this guy in a few years' time, not that looks are that important or anything.

'This is Milo, he's a DNA expert. Has all the tools and stuff,' says Sylvie.

'Hello,' I say, holding out my hand.

'Not while I'm working,' he says sharply. 'It affects the results if you know what I mean?'

I don't really.

'Prosecco darling?' asks Felix. 'We thought we should celebrate your new flat and the fact that we're closing in on the, you know who.'

'What are we talking about?' I ask.

'One evening with Ark Morgan and she totally loses the plot,' sighs Sylvie. 'You know,' she adds raising her eyebrows.

'The murderer,' whispers Felix.

'How are you doing love?' he asks Milo. 'Can you stop for pizza? We've got hot Americano or a veggie one if you prefer, with anchovies. And lots of garlic bread if that's your fancy.'

'I'm a vegan,' says Milo. 'I don't eat anything that's died unnaturally.'

We look at each other.

'Ah,' mumbles Sylvie.

'How about fish then?' asks Felix.

'They're killed unnaturally aren't they?' says Milo, studying the piece of scarf. 'The most tortured of all if you ask me.'

'Right, couldn't agree more,' says Felix, turning to us and pulling a face.

'I could remove the anchovies from the veggie one,' suggests Sylvie.

'They've got cheese on them though haven't they?' says Milo, looking at Felix over his glasses.

'Oh,' says Felix.

'Did you know that the dairy industry causes the death of countless male calves that are of no use to the dairy farmer, as well as the premature death of cows slaughtered when their milk production decreases?'

I look at the pizza and feel nauseous.

'That's terrible,' says Sylvie.

'Horrendous,' says Felix, biting into a slice of Americano. 'How about some garlic bread then? I don't think anyone murdered the garlic.'

Sylvie and I look at each other and take a gulp of Prosecco.

'Right,' says Milo, removing his spectacles. 'I'll have some bubbly now.'

'Okay,' says Felix, munching a piece of garlic bread. 'Obviously not worried about the grapes being crushed to their untimely death,' he mumbles.

'So, the Starbucks loyalty card and the scarf remnant belong to the same person. The fingerprints on the Starbucks card also match those on the estate agent's letter and one of the glasses. The strand of hair found also has the same DNA as the scarf.'

'He was at the party,' shrieks Sylvie.

I shudder.

'However, the DNA on the oil-based pigment doesn't match that person. The fingerprints on the other glass are also on the estate agent's letter.'

'Oh my God, do you think that was the paper I saw, you know, *him,* holding before he was, *you know'*, I ask.

We stare in silence at the estate agent's letter.

'Right, I'll have a slice of garlic bread and I'll be off,' says Milo.

'Are you sure we can't pay you something?' asks Sylvie. 'We can afford it.'

She means I can afford it.

'I'm grateful for the experience. Thanks for the bubbly.'

We wait until the door has closed behind him.

'I can't believe it, we're homing in on the killer, and I've got this,' she waves a piece of paper.

I stare wide-eyed at the guest list for Ark Morgan's party.

'How did you get that?' I ask, taking a slice of pizza and forcing Milo's words to the back of my mind.

'She's a real trooper,' says Felix. 'She sacrificed her body.'

I gasp.

'My God, you didn't? Who with?'

'Mitchell Wilson, one of the chefs at the Crescent, and I wouldn't call a kiss sacrificing my body.'

'Right, let's cross all the women off this list,' says Felix, 'and move even closer to the murderer. He has brown hair, so we can cross off the blonde, dark, ginger and grey-haired men. That should narrow it down a bit.'

We top up our glasses and work through the list.

'Mervyn Robshaw,' says Felix.

I punch the name into Google.

'Sixty-five and head of the Rotary club,' I say. 'Has a beard. I think I would have seen that.'

Sylvie scratches him off the list.

'Mark Bellingham?'

'He was jet skiing at the time of the murder,' says Sylvie.

We both stare at her, our glasses hovering at our lips.

'It was in that *Tycoon* magazine. Am I the only one that reads it?'

'I prefer *The Gay Times* love,' says Felix.

'Sebastian Lucas-Rynall?'

'Seventy, and looks about ninety. On Viagra apparently,' says Sylvie.

'That was in the *Tycoon* news?' I say aghast.

I really should start reading it.

'Of course not, you silly cow. It's common knowledge, everyone at work knows about him. He has all these women at the Manor where he has the penthouse suite. Keep him on the list. He could have a motive, a blow up with a jealous husband perhaps?' says Sylvie.

'Christ, how the other half live,' says Felix, pouring the last of the Prosecco into our glasses.

'Isn't he a bit old?' I say.

'Let's face it Rox, you can't really be sure how old the guy was that you saw?'

'Well, I think I would have noticed if he looked ninety ...'

'He dyes his hair,' Sylvie interrupts.

'I think Sylv is right. We should leave him on the list,' says Felix.

An hour later we have six suspects.

'Eight if you count Sam Lockwood and Ark Morgan,' says Felix.

'I don't think Ark Morgan would be seen dead in Clapham,' says Sylvie.

'Besides, he has an alibi,' I say. 'I saw him at the Fun Palace in the House of Mirrors ...'

'You never told me that,' exclaims Sylvie.

I shrug.

'Anyway his bodyguards came to tell him his plane was ready so he clearly flew somewhere that night.'

'All the same, he should stay on the list of suspects,' says Felix.

'Eight suspects then. So, now we have to chase them up,' says Felix. 'Sylvie you can have Nigel Forrest, the actor, and Roxie can have Sebastian Lucas-Rynall. I'll take the psychiatrist Gordon Walker. We'll meet back here on Friday, compare notes and then look into the others. Everyone agreed?'

We nod.

'Great,' says Felix 'So we're looking for a confident, successful risk taker, male, who likes a challenge and enjoys danger. He wears a Where's Wally scarf and goes to Starbucks a lot. He's also somehow connected to Rommel Mansions and knows Ark Morgan.'

'We'll nail him,' says Sylvie and we all clink glasses.

Chapter Thirty-Five

'Oh,' I gasp.

Sebastian Lucas-Rynall is half undressed. Well actually, I wouldn't even say half, he's almost naked. He is wearing purple satin underpants and a bow tie. He's holding a golf club in one hand and stands in front of his enormous desk looking like a proud peacock.

'Hello my dear,' he says appraising me.

I avert my eyes.

'It's a photoshoot,' he says, leering at me.

'Oh,' I say turning to the photographer who is crouching behind lamps and studio equipment.

'You're rather in the way,' says the photographer.

'I'm sorry,' I say trying to find a place to go where I would be spared Sebastian Lucas-Rynall's nakedness.

'I'm the new face of Harrison's golf range,' says Sebastian Lucas-Rynall proudly. 'Do you want me to swing it?' he asks the photographer.

God, just what is he going to swing?

'Just lift it slightly,' says the photographer.

I really can't look.

'Something to drink?' asks Sebastian. 'We've got everything.'

'Just water,' I say.

'Water?' he bellows. 'Good God woman, that's not a drink.'

'Marlene,' he barks, 'Drinks.'

A petite blonde woman rushes in with a trolley, her face flushed.

'Three martinis,' he barks.

'Not for me, I'm ...' begins the photographer.

'Damn it man, you'll have a drink.'

I accept the martini and Marlene drops in a cherry. Sebastian gestures for me to come closer.

'We'll do a few more with the club held up,' says the photographer.

'What do you think?' asks Sebastian, pointing to his chest. 'Pretty good shape huh, and it hasn't come easily.'

I imagine a lot of plastic surgery has helped.

'Exercise, that's the key. I've got the stamina of a thirty year old,' he adds with a wink.

'That's it,' says the photographer, relief evident in his voice. 'Thank you so much. We'll send you the proofs.'

'It will be front page of course,' says Sebastian.

The photographer opens his mouth.

'It's not debatable,' snaps Sebastian.

The photographer makes his retreat and I'm left alone with a half-naked Sebastian Lucas-Rynall. He flexes his muscles and smiles at me.

'Impressed?' he asks.

Repulsed more like.

'Aren't you hot in all those clothes?' he asks, his eyes turning sultry.

Is that a bulge in those purple satin underpants? Holy shit.

'Tell me, why are you here again Miss ...?

'Brown,' I say. He sips his martini and lights a thick cigar before reclining on a chaise longue. He pats the seat beside him.

'The charity *Moonbeams and Stardust,*' I say, feeling more like Angelina Jolie by the minute.

'*Moonbeams and Stardust,*' he repeats, patting the seat again.

I reluctantly move a little closer and stop at the window.

'Ooh, what a lovely view,' I say.

'All the women say that. I assure you you're not the first.'

I turn back and almost faint on the spot. He's removed his purple satin underpants.

'Oh my ...' I say breathlessly.

This is gross. He clicks a remote by his side and I hear the door lock. I'm five flights up so climbing out of the window isn't an option.

'Tell me, how much would you like for *Moondust and Starbeams?*'

Right now a pass out of here would be good.

'Moonbeams and Stardust,' I correct and straighten my shoulders.

'We're rather disappointed you didn't attend our function on the 30th May. We had every reason to expect you. Of course we understand if you had something more important on that night but as we're just about to publish our monthly newsletter it would be excellent to have a quote from you. We had a lot of disappointed patrons.' I struggle to fight back the tremble in my voice.

'Function, what function?' He jumps up and I step back. I really don't want to get walloped by his Viagra induced swelling.

He flicks through a big black book on his desk.

'I've got nothing in here about *Starbeams and Moondust*,' he says firmly.

'Moonbeams and Stardust,' I correct.

'That neither. I was rather busy that night.'

I try to picture Sebastian wearing a Where's Wally scarf and it somehow doesn't work.

'I see. Its rather disappointing that you were too busy to help disadvantaged children,' I say, holding my head high so I don't have to look at his meat and two veg. 'I shall report back to our patrons and assure them that you would have been there had you not been busy elsewhere.'

I turn to leave and gasp as his hands grope my breasts from behind. I struggle to keep my balance.

'I was at an exclusive sex club Miss Brown. I think you'd like it there. What do you prefer, to dominate or be dominated? Don't tell me, you like to dominate don't you?'

I pull myself away and lean across for the remote. This is like a bad dream.

'You're a naughty boy Sebastian,' I say teasingly. I so hope there isn't CCTV in here.

'Oh yes, I am, I really am,' he says excitedly.

'You've let me down haven't you?'

'Yes Miss Brown, I have. Am I to be punished?'

'Are you telling me the truth about the 30th?'

'Yes yes, I can prove it.'

'I'm very disappointed,' I say.

He grabs a bottle from the table and swallows a blue pill. Good God, the man is sex mad.

'I need to get something with which to punish you. Open the door Sebastian and then bend over that chaise longue until I get back.'

He grabs the remote and there is a click. I dive out into the foyer where Marlene is sitting at her desk.

'Mr Lucas-Rynall needs you,' I say. 'He's got his dick stuck in the chaise longue,' I call as I exit through the office revolving door.

Chapter Thirty-Six

At least we can cross Sebastian whatsisface off the suspect list. I make my way to Portobello Market. Felix said I would be able to get some great furniture there for a good price. I'm about to ask about a beautiful dresser when, from the corner of my eye, I see him. I gasp in disbelief. One minute he's in Clapham and the next Chelsea, he moves faster than Superman. I feel a fluttering in my stomach when I remember he is one of the murder suspects. Supposing he is the murderer and he saw me that night? That would explain why he would be following me. I duck behind the statue of a female Zulu warrior. She's so huge that you don't have to be Ronnie Corbett to disappear behind her. My nose touches her breast as I peek to see Sam Lockwood. He is browsing through some antique books. He's wearing shorts and a light blue shirt. God, he's got hairy legs. I didn't notice that at the Fun Palace although I was reeling from the House of Mirrors at the time. He's got hairs everywhere. His veins must be so full of testosterone I'm surprised he hasn't got a permanent erection. He turns and I duck, hitting my nose on the warrior's nipple. He wanders to the other side of the shop and browses through some old vinyl LPs. I consider making a dive for the door.

'Interested in the warrior are you? I'll have to admit, you'll be the first.'

The shopkeeper's voice makes me jump and I almost knock the warrior over. We both clutch a breast to steady her.

'She's not really my thing,' I say, keeping my voice low.

The last thing I need is her staring at me from the corner of my new living room.

'Roxie Brown,' says Sam Lockwood, 'I would never have taken you for an antique browser, let alone a warrior enthusiast.'

'I always was a big fan of Zulu,' I say moving out from behind the warrior and trying to keep my eyes off his hairy legs.

'Great film,' he agrees. *'Don't shoot until you see the whites of their eyes,'* he mimics.

'I wouldn't have taken you for an antique browser either.'

'I'm actually looking for a wedding present. They're both keen on the forties era, don't ask me why.'

'I've got some great Hitler books, a couple of swastikas too,' says the shopkeeper. 'I've got lots of Nazi memorabilia somewhere. Oh, here you go. A pair of gas masks.'

He holds them up for us. I raise my eyebrows and Sam smiles.

'I'm not sure two gas masks are the best wedding presents, or swastikas come to that.'

I fight back a giggle.

'What about you?' he asks, 'What brings you here, apart from female Zulu warriors.'

'My friend Felix said this was the best for second-hand furniture. I've just bought my own flat ...'

I stop, realising I'm giving away too much information.

'With The Gunner?' he asks, looking questioningly into my eyes.

'Without the Gunner,' I say, turning to the dresser.

I glance at his reflection in an antiquated mirror. He's extraordinarily handsome, even with a five o'clock shadow. He's hairier than a werewolf.

'Seen anything you fancy?' he asks, giving a wink.

I blush and turn to the dresser.

'How much is this?' I ask the shopkeeper.

'That belonged to a titled lady so I can't let that go for less than seventy-five quid.'

'A better choice than the warrior if you want my opinion,' says Sam.

'I'll take it,' I say.

'You're decisive' he grins. 'What else do we need?'

'We?' I repeat.

'Just a figure of speech,' he smiles.

Ooh that smile is doing things to me that it really shouldn't be doing. Only Ark Morgan is supposed to make me feel like this. Important to remember that Sam Lockwood is Ark's enemy and business rival.

'Got some lovely bedside cabinets,' says the shopkeeper.

'Do we need those?' asks Sam.

'Shouldn't you be browsing the forties memorabilia?' I ask.

'Quite right,' he says, wandering back to the LPs. 'Give a shout if you need any advice.'

'I'm sure I can cope, thank you.'

He looks at a jukebox on the other side of the shop and I sigh with relief.

'These are quality,' says the shopkeeper showing me the bedside cabinets.

I picture my six-foot bed. I then find myself imagining Ark lying on it and come over all hot. I grab a fan from on top of the dresser.

'That looks forties style,' says a voice behind me. Oh for goodness' sake.

'Most likely,' says the shopkeeper.

'Can I see it?' says Sam, sliding the fan from my hand and stroking my fingers with his as he does so. Sensations flood through me and make my body quiver. *He has that Mr nice-guy manner about him. Please don't be fooled,* Ark's words echo in my head.

'These cabinets are great, are you taking them?' Sam asks.

If I had time to think I might be able to make a decision.

'I'll let you have both for thirty quid, seeing as you're buying the dresser and all.'

'How much for the jukebox?' asks Sam.

'Oh yeah, that's forties for sure,' says the shopkeeper.

'Actually it's more fifties,' I say, although why I'm getting involved I do not know.

'It's got forties records on it,' says the shopkeeper determinedly.

'Sounds perfect,' says Sam.

Oh good, maybe he'll buy it and disappear. I try to visualise the bedside cabinets next to my six-foot bed and decide to take them. At that moment my phone bleeps with a text. I pull if from my bag to see it is from Ark.

I hope you're keeping out of trouble Miss Brown. I have missed you. Work has kept me busy and away from you.

I stare at the screen feeling Sam's eyes on me. Before I can type a response, another one bleeps at me.

Are you alone?

I'm just buying beside cabinets, I message back.

Oh God, I couldn't have sent a more boring text if I'd tried could I?

I hope they match your bed Miss Brown.

Yes,' I reply, *they do.*

I hope you're going to bed alone Miss Brown.

I feel my legs go weak and grab the warrior's breast for support.

'I see you're quite taken with that,' says the shopkeeper.

'Yes,' I text back with trembling fingers.

'You've not been seeing Sam Lockwood have you?'

Good God, it's as if he's in the shop with us. Honestly, if I didn't know better I'd think it was Sam Lockwood he was interested in and not me.

'Do you like to cook Miss Brown?'

'I love cook ...' I begin.

'Seen anything else you like?' asks Sam, from behind me. I jump out of my skin and my finger hits *send.* Holy shit. I look down at my text message and almost die from shame.

It reads, *I love cock.* I could kill sodding Sam Lockwood. My phone bleeps again and I'm too afraid to look.

'Sounds wonderful Miss Brown. I look forward to our next meeting. I will be in touch.'

My face must be scarlet. Sam hands me the fan.

'You look hot. Not bad news I hope?'

'I'll throw that in for thirty quid,' says the shopkeeper.

'A bit pricey for a fan,' I say. The shopkeeper and Sam look at me and I realise I'm still grasping the warrior's breast. I quickly pull my hand away.

'Oh, you mean the warrior? Thank you but as lovely as she is I really have nowhere to put her.'

I wait for another text from Ark but nothing comes. What must he think of me? Surely he will know I meant to say *cooking.*

'You seem attached to it,' smiles Sam. I ignore him and turn to the shopkeeper.

'When can you deliver?'

'That's the thing,' he says, whipping my credit card from my hand, 'The van's got a bit of a problem.'

'Oh,' I say, trying to collect my thoughts.

He shoves the credit card machine under my nose.

'What kind of a problem?' I ask, slowly punching in the pin.

'It's broken down. I reckon it will be two weeks before I can promise delivery, unless of course you've got other means of getting them home.'

I don't think they will fit into the Fiesta. The card machine whirrs as my purchase goes through. Damn it.

'Do you know where I can hire a van?' I ask.

'Where's it to?'

Sam hovers over us and I can almost see his ears twitching.

'Rommel Mansions,' I say softly.

'I can help you with that,' pipes up Sam. 'I know it well.'

He would wouldn't he? My phone bleeps again and I peer at it cautiously. It's Hal.

'The Great Zehilda got it right. I'm pregnant. I did the test an hour ago.'

I rather think The Great Zehilda picked up on Hal's swollen breasts and tearfulness. No wonder her wedding dress looked tight.

'Wonderful,' I respond. *'I'd never have guessed.'*

'I did struggle with the dress,' she texts back.

'Congratulations.'

'You really shouldn't leave it too long.'

I really don't know what everyone expects me to do aside from go home and inseminate myself.

'I can do it for you this afternoon,' says Sam.

'What?' I say my head still full of thoughts of insemination.

'I can deliver your stuff this afternoon. I've got the company van today.'

'Sounds grand,' says the shopkeeper

'Isn't there a job you should be doing?'

'This is my job,' says the shopkeeper.

'I meant him,' I say, tipping my head towards Sam, who, by the way has hairy toes as well. Good God, the man is a gorilla.

'That's the beauty of being your own boss. You can take a day off whenever you want to.'

It's very tempting. At least I'll get everything into the flat today. Then Ark's words come back to me, *He's bad news.*

'That would help us out,' says the shopkeeper, as if it's all done and dusted. Excuse me, doesn't anyone ask the customer any more?

'Sure you don't want the warrior? I can knock her down to twenty-five.'

'You do go well together,' grins Sam. 'You'll never be lonely.'

I glare at him. I notice the bruise is not so prominent on his cheek today.

'Isn't there someone you should be beating up?' I say turning away from him.

'I don't think of boxing as beating people up,' he says in that soft, crystal clear voice of his. 'So what do you say about the delivery? You can't still be cross with me about the pavlova? It was only a few raspberries.'

'It has nothing to do with the raspberries,' I say.

'That's a relief,' he smiles. 'I hate falling out with people over fruit.'

'Shall I book you in for delivery?' asks the shopkeeper. 'There's a charge of twenty-five quid.'

'Whereas I'll do it for free,' adds Sam.

'Sounds good to me, and I'll throw her in for twenty quid,' he says pointing to the warrior.

'I really don't ...'

'Fifteen,' he pushes.

'It's meant to be yours,' grins Sam. 'I'll tell you what. I'll buy it as a flat warming present. I'll have the jukebox too.'

'Great,' exclaims the shopkeeper, taking Sam's cash eagerly.

'Have you got the whole day off?' Sam asks.

I give him a sharp look.

'I can't get anything right can I?' he grins. 'Everything I say is wrong.'

'He has that Mr nice-guy manner about him. Please don't be fooled.' Ark's words echo in my head.

'I'll bring the van round. You're welcome to come in the van too,' he says, giving me a sidelong look.

'I've got my car.'

'I'll follow you then.'

And see my tatty Fiesta? No thanks.

'I'll meet you there,' I say. 'How much do I owe you?'

'I've got a better idea. Why don't I take you and the furniture in the van and come back later for the car, and if you really want to pay me then have a bite to eat with me.'

'Maybe I'll just pay the shopkeeper for a delivery,' I say hotly.

'Now what have I done? I'm just being friendly. Ah,' he says, holding up a finger. 'Ark Morgan is your new boyfriend. He wouldn't want you going out to dinner with me would he?'

I glare at him.

'Ark Morgan is not my new boyfriend. I'm getting over a break up.'

He nods.

'Not that it's any of my business, but I agree it's a bit quick to have a new boyfriend. I only saw you about a month ago crying into your camomile tea over the Gunner and his redhead …'

'Bottled redhead,' I interrupt.

'Ah, that's bad taste,' he agrees.

'And a slummy mummy at that,' I continue. I don't know why I'm sharing all this with Sam of all people. He sucks in his breath.

'Bad taste to totally bad taste,' he agrees, giving an impish grin. 'Talking of bad taste, what are you doing with Ark Morgan?'

I shake my head in exasperation.

'Okay, not my business,' he concedes.

'So who's doing the delivery?' asks the weary shopkeeper.

Sam looks at me. It really would be rather petty to say no and it is only dinner.

'Okay, thank you very much,' I say. 'And dinner would be nice.'

'Great.'

I only hope he changes out of those shorts.

Sylvie

This is going to be harder than I imagined. I don't know what made me think I could just stroll in and chat to the guy. He may not be Tom Cruise high profile but he's high profile all the same. I couldn't believe he was all over Google. There's bound to be bodyguards and all sorts. I hover at the stage door, straighten my poncho, adjust my hat and gently turn the handle prepared for it to be locked. Good God, it opens. I wasn't expecting that. I look into a dark musky corridor. For all I know there may not be anyone here. On Google it said he was rehearsing his new play at The Majestic in Chelsea between filming his first movie. Knowing my luck today will be the day he is filming his movie. I let the door close behind me and walk gingerly down the corridor towards the sound of voices. Blimey, if it's this easy to get to a celeb I'll have to work my way up to Jude Law. I wish there was some light here. I can't see a thing.

'Can I help you?'

'Jesus wept,' I shriek, almost jumping out of my skin. I turn to see a burly man with a crew cut, staring at me. He's wearing a smart black suit with a crisp white shirt. I knew they'd be bodyguards.

'You certainly didn't help me just then,' I say crossly. 'What's your job, scaring people to death? because if it is, you're bloody good at it.'

'I'm sorry,' he smiles, 'but this is not for public access.'

'I'm looking for Nigel Forrest. I work for the Morgan Group.' I pull out my Morgan Group badge and flash it at him like DCI Jane Tennison and before he has time to open his mouth, I add, 'Mr Forrest was at a function on Mr Morgan's yacht last week. Some rather nice cufflinks were found after the party ...'

'Cufflinks?' he repeats in a disbelieving voice.

'Well these parties get a bit hairy after a time and a lot more than cufflinks can come off.' Jesus, what am I saying? I'm not doing much for Ark Morgan's reputation.

'You want to check with Mr Forrest if they're his.'

Come to think of it, I'm not doing a great deal for Nigel Forrest's reputation either.

'If that's okay,' I say.

'You're checking with all the guests are you?' he asks suspiciously.

'Only those with the initial NF matching the engravings on the cufflinks,' I say, not missing a beat. 'There were only three guests with those initials. Of course, I could phone Mr Forrest but Mr Morgan prefers the more personal touch.'

It will certainly be personal if he finds out. In fact it will be that personal, I'll no doubt get the sack.

'What the fuck is going on out there? Some of us are trying to have a bloody rehearsal,' yells a voice from beyond the closed door. 'Christ, do you think you can make a bit more noise?'

'Brian Moody, the director,' says the burly man. 'He doesn't like interruptions.'

The door is flung open and a man in a bright striped scarf glares at us. I study the scarf and decide it is nowhere near a Where's Wally one and smile warmly at him. He pushes his glasses onto his head and peers at me.

'Do I know you?' he says in an Ian McKellen voice. In fact for all I know he may well be Ian himself.

'The lady is here to see Nigel.'

'Did someone mention my name?' calls another voice. Then standing in front of me is Nigel Forrest, ten times better looking than the photos on Google. He's actually quite gorgeous and doesn't look in the least like a murderer to me, but then looks can be deceiving. He's wearing a fab cap and I find myself looking at it enviously.

'Nigel darling, we really don't have time for you to ingratiate yourself with groupies.'

'Excuse me, I'm not a groupie and I rather resent being called one,' I say firmly.

Groupie, my arse, surely they come looking more appealing than me.

'I love your hat,' smiles Nigel Forrest

'Thank you. It's my favourite. I love your cap.'

'For Christ's sake, Can we have less of the mutual admiration society here and more bloody acting,' snarls Brian Moody. He's a cheerful bugger.

Nigel Forrest checks his watch.

'It's four Brian. We have been at it for some time and frankly I'm famished. Never mind the play; if I don't eat soon I'll die from starvation.'

'Darling, you never stop eating, but I agree, we could all do with a break. My nerves are frayed.'

'Great,' says Nigel, smiling at me. 'Fancy a bite.'

I am peckish. I'd worked right through lunch. I could kill Roxie for taking time off. I hate working with Kitty. She needs a firework up her arse she's that slow. It took us forever to get the rooms done and then she buggers off early. I wouldn't mind but she didn't arrive until seven so I was working the first hour alone anyway.

'That would be great, thanks.'

'There's a burger bar around the corner, do you know it?' he asks, grabbing a jacket and thankfully without a Where's Wally scarf. I shake my head.

'I don't know Chelsea that well,' I say.

'You don't sound like a Chelsea girl,' he laughs.

'My friend lives here,' I say, hoping that will impress.

'Oh yeah, where?'

'Rommel Mansions.'

'You're kidding me?' he says, surprised. 'I know Rommel Mansions.'

Oh my God. That's one strike. He leads me back down the corridor and out of the door back into the bright sunlight. He dons a pair of sunglasses and points to the end of the road.

'Just up here and round the corner, so anyway how can I help you?'

I'm so enamoured by his good looks and Rupert Everett voice that for a minute I forget why I came.

'You were at Ark Morgan's yacht party.'

'That's right,' he says opening the door to the burger bar for me. 'How do you know that?'

'I work for Ark Morgan and someone left cufflinks there with the initials *NF* on them.'

'Ah well that wouldn't be me. I've never worn cufflinks in my life.'

He's a real gentleman and pulls out a chair for me.

'The blue stilton burger is out of this world as are their sweet potato fries.'

I agree to both and he orders.

'Great night though, not that I'm over keen on the bloke, but he supports the arts supposedly and well …' he trails off. 'Good boss is he?'

'He's okay.'

Our drinks arrive and I sip my diet coke and make a huge attempt not to drool over him.

'Did I see you at the Fun Palace the other night?' I ask.

Please say no.

'Yeah, I was there with some friends. Geez I'm sorry, I haven't even asked your name?'

Two strikes.

'Sylvie,' I say.

It's going to be quite hard asking him if he's into danger isn't it? He's confident, certainly successful. Question is, does he like to take risks and is he the owner of a Where's Wally scarf? Not quite the kind of questions you ask someone you've only just met.

'The Fun Palace was good wasn't it? Did you stay long?' I ask.

He takes some fries from the bowl.

'I can't remember to be honest,' he says casually.

Surely if he'd killed someone that night he wouldn't be quite so casual about the evening would he?

'It's nice here,' I say, 'I usually grab a bite from Starbucks. It's useful with my loyalty card and everything.' God, could I sound any more boring?

'Yeah, Starbucks is good too. I agree. The reward card is useful isn't it?'

Strike number three.

I hold my burger and watch him eat his. He really is superstar material.

'Sorry to interrupt your rehearsal,' I say. His smile lights up his face.

'The break was well overdue. Sorry Brian mistook you for a groupie by the way.'

'Oh, it happens all the time,' I say, shrugging it off. 'Get many do you?'

'Groupies?' his eyes widen. 'God no, you must be joking. You're the first person ever to come backstage looking for me.'

He checks his watch and finishes the last of his burger.

'I'd best get back. Brian is a bit of a taskmaster but I'm free tonight if you'd like to catch a film or something.'

'Oh,' I say taken aback.

It will be chillier later won't I? I find myself praying he doesn't come wearing a Where's Wally scarf.

'That will be great, thank you.'

'Meet you outside the Phoenix at seven. There's a new Tarantino showing. Starts at 7.15 I think.'

'Great,' I say.

I'd better look up Tarantino and do my homework before tonight.

Chapter Thirty-Seven

We're squashed into the front of the van with the Zulu warrior's nellies wedged between us. By the time the dresser and bedside cabinets were in, there was just enough space for the jukebox, which meant Madam Zulu had to balance her lower body on the dresser and her upper torso was pushed between us at the front.

'She's a bit in the way of the gearstick,' grins Sam. 'I guess I'll just have to touch her up every time I change gear. Good thing is she can't slap me.'

I smile. He does have a great sense of humour. Unlike Ark, who is very intense and in that respect is very like Christian Grey. Aside from that I'm disappointed to admit he doesn't have much else in common with Christian. I somehow imagine a playroom would scare the shit out of Ark Morgan.

'You never did tell me what you do at the Morgan Group,' he says with a wink.

Bugger it, in for a penny in for a pound. After all, do I really care what Sam Lockwood thinks of me?

'I'm a chambermaid for the hotels,' I say, pushing the warrior towards him.

'Hey, she's yours remember, don't try to foist her onto me.' He gives me a quick look before saying, 'I didn't imagine Ark the type to invite his chambermaids to his fancy yacht do's. Nothing personal, of course, before you whack me with your fan.'

'Well, he invited me,' I say.

'I can understand why but what I really don't understand is what you see in him.'

I give him the 'I don't talk about Ark Morgan' glare.

'Okay, I've got the message. You're very protective of him aren't you?'

I remember Ark's words: *You've not been seeing Sam Lockwood have you?*

'Not really,' I say.

'He's not all he seems you know? He didn't get where he is today by being honest.'

'I rather think he would say the same about you,' I say.

'Ah,' he grins, 'indeed he would. The only difference is I'm the one telling the truth.'

He pulls into the car park of Rommel Mansions.

'Please don't tell me you're on the top floor,' he laughs. 'That will teach me for not checking.'

'Ground floor,' I say.

'Right, how are we going to do this?' he says, looking around.

He's only thought of that now? I don't believe it. He spots a gardener working in the grounds and waves.

He grins. 'Hey Geoff, how are you mate?'

'Hello Mr Lockwood, lovely day.'

'Glorious,' says Sam. 'I've got some stuff in the van, would you mind giving a hand?'

'Sure,' says the gardener.

'You'd better tell us where you want everything,' says Sam as they manoeuvre the dresser through the main doors. 'You don't want me coming back to move it do you.' He gives me his cheeky grin.

The warrior is the last to come.

'Lifelike isn't she?' Geoff says, looking at her breasts.

'Never having seen a real-life warrior woman I wouldn't like to say,' says Sam. 'But I'll take your word for it.'

Geoff laughs.

'Anything else?'

'That's great thanks,' says Sam, peeling a fifty-pound note from his wallet.

'A pleasure Mr Lockwood.'

'Cup of tea would be nice,' Sam says as he closes the door. 'Do you have a mug, aside from the Gunner of course?'

Darren may have been a wanker and all that but I don't need to hear Sam's insults.

'Darren was not …' I begin, but finding it impossible to defend him.

'He was playing away from home in more ways than one,' he says, strolling into the kitchen. 'He's an idiot if you want my opinion.'

'Do you have anything nice to say about people?'

'Yes, if they deserve it. I just happen to think Darren and Ark Morgan don't.'

'How do you know the gardener?' I ask, trying to change the subject.

'He works for me,' he says leaning against the kitchen counter.

'You have a gardener?' I say, squeezing past him with a milk carton in my hand.

I hadn't realised how small the kitchen was until now. His big hairy body seems to fill it.

'Lockwood Estates have a gardener,' he says.

My hand hovers over the milk jug for a second.

'I wouldn't worry about a jug just a splash in a mug will do me.'

I turn to face him. He's grinning as usual. He's so handsome. I really hadn't realised quite how good looking he was.

'You own Rommel Mansions?' I say, feeling my stomach churn.

'Lockwood Estates own Rommel Mansions.'

'Do you own a lot of properties?' I ask.

'My father's company, Lockwood Estates own quite a lot, yes.'

'It's not your company?'

'Are you trying to sell me insurance or something?' he laughs.

I blush. He points to the milk carton in my hand.

'Can I help you with that?'

'No,' I snap, pouring it into the mugs.

I grab the sugar, my heart pounding. You can't have more of a connection to Rommel Mansions than owning it can you? Shit, this is unbelievable. I tip sugar into one mug.

'Not for me,' he smiles, 'sweet enough.'

'Why didn't you say?' I ask.

'I just did.'

'I mean about owning Rommel Mansions.'

'I couldn't see a reason to. We own a lot of properties.'

I pour hot water onto the teabags and hand him a mug.

'I think its hot water first and milk last isn't it?'

'Oh,' I say, not realising what I'd done.

'No biscuits?' he asks. 'You can't have tea without biscuits.'

'This is all I have,' I say, reaching for the sponge fingers. 'I've not really been shopping yet.'

'I thought you had these in a trifle.'

'You're mocking me,' I say bravely.

'I'm not, seriously. The tea is great as it happens.'

I get my Nutella jar and put it on the counter.

'You dip them in this, at least I do.'

I'm not sure why I'm sharing my Nutella sponge fingers with Sam Lockwood. He dips one into the jar.

'Mmm, good combination, I like your style.'

That's more than Darren did. My mind is reeling. It doesn't mean he is the murderer just because his company owns Rommel Mansions, and I've never seen him wearing a Where's Wally scarf and let's face it, I've been seeing him often enough. Oh God, that doesn't bode well either. He could be following me. He has got a few things going against him. The Starbucks card for one, Rommel Mansions for two and his dark brown hair for three and let's face it, he has plenty of that.

'I'm in the amateur championship next week. I don't suppose you'd be interested in coming to watch. I think I may have a better chance with my lucky mascot there.'

My heart sinks as I remember the handwriting analysis. *The writer is confident, successful, and most likely a risk taker. He likes a challenge and enjoys danger,* I hear Sylvie saying. No man could be more confident than Sam, apart from Ark Morgan, of course. But Sam Lockwood matches the handwriting analysis perfectly. He's successful, and most certainly a risk taker, you only have to look at his boxing history to know that. Oh God, and the Harley Davidson, that's danger isn't it? Holy shit, I have the murderer right here in my flat and I'm all alone with him.

Chapter Thirty-Eight

Sylvie

He's standing outside the Phoenix waiting for me. I can hardly bring myself to look in case he's wearing the Where's Wally scarf. I've been trying to decide what to do if he is. I can't very well phone the cops and say *you'd better nab him because there is absolutely no doubt. He's wearing a Where's Wally scarf.* Fortunately he isn't wearing any kind of scarf and I feel a great sense of relief. Felix had WhatsApped to say that he'd just spent an hour on the couch with the psychiatrist.

'Not in a sexual way,' he'd added. 'More's the pity. He's actually quite gorgeous. Anyway, we can tick him off. He was at a seminar in Brighton that whole weekend. How are things with the actor?'

I didn't like to say *looking suspicious* as I'm hoping Nigel will be able to vindicate himself.

'Hey,' he smiles on seeing me. 'You look terrific.'

'Thanks,' I say, adjusting my shawl.

I'd make a big enough effort so I'd have been a bit pissed if he hadn't noticed. I'd chosen my green velvet dress with antique earrings and a red silk shawl. I'd bought them at Victorian Treasures online. I feel very arty in them and as he's into the arts I'm hoping it will make him feel comfortable with me. I'm not sure I'm going to enjoy the Tarantino movie though.

'I hope you like Neo-Noir films,' he says, crooking his arm so I can slide mine into it.

He's wearing a bomber jacket with jeans. His dress sense certainly matches mine. I can't say that about many men.

'Oh yes, I love them,' I say.

Honestly, I'm such a liar. Truth is I haven't got a clue what a Neo-Noir film is but I'm not going to admit that. My task this evening is to find out if Nigel Forrest likes danger. He's confident, so that ticks one box. He's successful at his career so that ticks a second box. He has dark brown hair. If you ask me he's ticking lots of boxes and is most certainly ticking all of mine. He hasn't admitted to a Starbucks card and so far there hasn't been a Where's Wally scarf in sight. I've got to find out what he was doing in the early hours of the first of June following his visit to the Fun Palace.

'*Inglourious Basterds* is my all-time favourite by Tarantino,' he says, leading me into the cinema.

'Mine too,' I say.

Not that I've ever seen it of course. I only hope it's not full of blood and gore, not the most comforting thing to watch when you think you may be sitting next to a murderer.

Chapter Thirty-Nine

I'm feeling really panicky. Adrenalin is pumping through my body faster than a speed train. It's quite exciting in an odd way to be this close to danger.

'Do you think I should call the police?' I ask Felix.

'And tell them what you dopey donkey?'

'That Sam is the murderer,' I say.

'Excellent love, I can see you've given this a lot of thought. I can hear you now. *He's guilty of being confident and successful and what's more he likes danger, but more importantly, he has a Starbucks card ...*'

'But it's all true isn't it?' I interrupt.

'Maybe, but it's not enough to make him the murderer.'

'What about the Rommel Mansions thing?'

'A lot of people will know of Rommel Mansions won't they?'

He's quite right. I'm panicking unnecessarily.

'You have to admit, he does seem to be popping up a lot where I am.'

'Maybe he fancies you darling. For a simple chambermaid you're doing really well in the man stakes these days aren't you?'

I wiggle my toes in the warm lavender bath water. A delicious tingle runs through me. Sam Lockwood is very appealing, of that there is no doubt.

'So you think it would be safe to have dinner with him?'

'Of course, just make sure you're always in a public place. I've got to fly love, literally. I'm off to Barcelona. Good luck.'

With those words of wisdom ringing in my ears, I climb from the warmth of the bath and get dressed. I choose my Zara dress and a pink fluffy bolero. I decide against make-up and am just finishing curling my hair when there is a knock at the door. Sam stands there in a brilliant white shirt and faded blue jeans. He pushes his hands into the jeans pockets and smiles.

'Ready?' he asks.

I can't believe that Sam doesn't have a girlfriend and it's even more unbelievable that he would want to go out with a simple chambermaid. I hesitate in the doorway and then say boldly.

'Are you taking me out because you think Ark Morgan wants me?'

He pulls his hand from his pocket and leans against the doorpost.

'I don't covet what Ark Morgan has and I certainly don't steal other men's girlfriends. Felicity and he had parted weeks before we started going out together. I wouldn't have asked you out either if you hadn't have told me that you were separated from the gunner. You said that the other afternoon when I met you with Sylvia.'

'Sylvie,' I correct.

He smiles.

'I'm a chambermaid,' I say. *Is it possible to put yourself down any more?* whispers my inner goddess. *Don't stop now, you're on a roll.*

'What's that got to do with anything?' he shrugs. 'I was a window cleaner once.'

'You weren't?' I say widening my eyes.

He nods.

'I didn't want to go into the family business. It seemed a bit bourgeoisie and all that. So I rebelled and became a window cleaner. I was quite good at it if I do say so myself.'

I stare at him.

'However, I do have one question, and it's not a put down of any kind, but what is Ark Morgan paying you that you can afford a flat in Rommel Mansions?'

I open my mouth to reply.

'Not that you shouldn't buy one, so don't get all defensive,' he adds quickly. 'But we own them and I know the price.'

'I had a lottery win,' I smile.

'Brilliant, I bet that put the Gunner in his place. Now shall we? I do believe you owe me dinner for delivering your furniture.'

'You're not going out with Felicity any more then?'

'Nope, I'm not going out with anyone in fact, except with you, for dinner this evening.'

I close the front door. Stay in a public place. That surely isn't hard to do. The problem is I've got to get to the public place first.

Chapter Forty

Sylvie

There was more blood and gore in the movie than I've ever seen in my life. I spent most of the time staring down at my popcorn. I swear I couldn't eat any of it without throwing it up later. Give me a romantic comedy any day.

'Brilliant, don't you think?' says Nigel as the lights go up. 'So realistic.'

It was realistic all right. Too realistic for my liking and what's more worrying is how does Nigel Forrest know it's realistic.

'There's a curry place around the corner, do you like Indian food? I could murder an Indian.'

Let's hope he doesn't mean that literally. How can he even think of eating after that film? All I need is a stiff drink, never mind the food.

'Sounds great,' I say, feeling sure I'll barely get past a poppadum.

'Brilliant, we can discuss the film.'

Christ, do we have to. Fortunately by the time we reach the restaurant I've regained by appetite and the film is a distant memory. Now if I can just keep him off the subject I may be able to enjoy a korma.

'Did you like the Fun Palace?' I ask after we'd ordered drinks and our poppadum's arrive. He looks at me curiously.

'It's always a laugh. You obviously enjoyed it.'

I nod.

'We went there for my friend's last night of freedom. It was her wedding the next day.'

'Ah, I can see why you had so much fun,' he smiles.

Ooh, he's going to be a heart-throb if he makes it into films as long as he isn't arrested for murder before he makes it big.

'What do you do for Ark Morgan?' he asks after placing our order.

Shit, I've been so busy preparing for the Tarantino movie that I forgot about any other questions. I wonder if I can pass and say my chosen subject is Tarantino.

'I work in the domestic department.'

God, that sounds bloody vague doesn't it?

'How do you know Ark?' I say deflecting and wishing I could turn on the voice recorder on my phone. I'm just not sure I could do it without him noticing.

'I don't know him personally,' he says pouring wine into our glasses. 'He supports the arts. Apparently he invites an assortment of people to these dos. But hey, you know that, don't you?'

I nibble on a poppadum, all memory of the blood and gore movie forgotten. I'm more focused on real blood and gore. The question is how can I find out what Nigel did after the Fun Palace without seeming (1) Obsessed with the Fun Palace and (2) Obsessed with his movements. I know I am but the key is not to let him know that.

'How long have you worked for Ark Morgan?' he asks.

'It feels like forever,' I say.

You can't get more honest than that.

'I didn't see you at the do,' he says, looking at me closely.

Fortunately our food arrives then and I don't have to answer.

'Looks good,' he says, his eyes lighting up and I feel my heart flutter.

I'm so hoping he isn't the murderer. Although, if he is, I suppose I could visit him during his time at Her Majesty's pleasure.

'We saw the psychic at the Fun Palace,' I say, steering the conversation back to my favourite subject. God, he must think me so shallow. All I've talked about so far is the Fun Palace.

'I have to admit to spending a fair bit of time at the rifle range,' he smiles.

'Did you win anything?' I ask, taking a swig from my glass.

'It was more for the fun than to win a prize,' he says, offering me some of his vegetable curry.

'This is good, try some.'

His phone rings and he fumbles in his jacket pocket. He pulls something out with the phone and it flutters onto the table. I stare at it with wide eyes. It's a membership card to a gun club.

Chapter Forty-One

'Where are you,' Sylvie whispers.

'In Desperado's Mexican just off Chelsea Bridge Road, where are you?'

'In Manjub's Balti just off Clapham Junction.'

In fact, we're both in the restaurant loos.

'At least we're getting fed,' I joke.

'He belongs to a gun club,' she says, fighting down her hysteria.

'Who?'

'Nigel Forrest, Jesus wept Roxie. Who do you think I'm talking about?'

'I don't know. I'm losing track of the suspects. I thought you meant Sam.'

'What has Sam got to do with anything?'

'I'm having dinner with him.'

'Oh,' she says. 'Anyway, it isn't a good sign is it?'

'You mean, me having dinner with Sam? I don't understand.'

'No, Nigel Forrest belonging to a gun club you wally.'

'It doesn't necessarily mean he shot our guy,' I say without conviction in my voice.

'It makes him a more likely candidate as the murderer though doesn't it? I mean, don't people in gun clubs have gun permits.'

'I don't know. I've never met anyone who belonged to a gun club. How do you know he does?'

'His membership card fell out of his pocket. We need to WhatsApp Felix. Get him to google it.'

'He's on a plane to Barcelona,' I say.

'What the hell is he doing in Barcelona?'

'He's working.'

'Shit, of course, I keep forgetting he's a bloody air steward. Can you google it?'

'I'm on my phone talking to you and I can't do it over dinner with Sam.'

'Why are you having dinner with Sam?'

'It's a long story. If we stay in the loos much longer they'll think we've got Deli Belly.'

'You don't get Deli Belly from Mexican food.' I sigh.

'You should shag him. I'd better go. I may well be with the murderer so I'll make phone contact every fifteen minutes. If I go over time and you don't hear from me you'd better call the police. I'm in Manjub's Balti, will you remember that?'

It all sounds a bit melodramatic.

'I'll make a note as soon as I come off the phone but I don't think he's going to do anything to you in a public place,' I say, remembering Felix's advice.

'That didn't stop Michael Corleone in the *Godfather* did it? Shot them at point-blank range,' she says earnestly.

'That was a film,' I remind her.

'Yes, but all the same.'

'Clapham Common is a bit different from gangland New York don't you think?'

'I know that,' she sighs, 'I'm just stating the fact that it could happen.'

'Right,' I say.

We hang up and I tidy my hair in the mirror. Of course, if Nigel Forrest is the murderer then that means that Sam Lockwood isn't. I leave the loo and head back to our table where sweetcorn and chicken wings await me. Sam offers me chilli sauce.

'It this doesn't blow your head off, nothing will,' he laughs.

Blimey, that's a bit close to the knuckle isn't it? I hope he doesn't mean that literally.

'I think I'd prefer to keep my head where it is.'

He grins and bites into his sweetcorn. There's something very honest about Sam Lockwood. I can't help but believe his story about Ark's girlfriend, but why would Ark keep saying that Sam wants everything that doesn't belong to him? The waitress brings our main dishes and Sam tucks into his chilli con carne.

'How much did you win on the lottery?' he asks.

'Seventy-five thousand,' I say honestly.

He whistles.

'That's amazing. Does Ark know?'

I sigh.

'What is it about you and Ark Morgan? He's always asking about you and you're always asking about him?'

He reclines in his seat.

'I don't ask about Ark Morgan, I ask about you and Ark Morgan, which is totally different. However, I think Ark Morgan probably does ask about me.' He pauses to sip his wine.

'I wouldn't tell Morgan about your lottery win,' he says cautiously. 'He'll try and get you to invest it, and his investments aren't all they ought to be.'

I've no intention of telling Ark Morgan about my lottery win. If I do, I'll then have to tell him the truth about myself and I'm not sure I'm ready to do that yet. In fact, I'm not too sure how I feel about Ark Morgan. He isn't at all like Christian Grey, or my fantasies, and if I'm honest, since Darren and I parted I haven't felt inclined to read erotica or fantasise, or is that since I met Sam Lockwood? My phone blings with a WhatsApp message, has it been fifteen minutes already? At least that means the actor hasn't murdered her yet.

'You haven't said if you'll come to the championship next week?'

'I don't know,' I mutter.

'I'll feel a lot more confident if you're there.'

'I don't believe that,' I say.

'Do you believe what Morgan tells you about me? That we ignore planning rules? That we try to buy land for cheap warehouses? Has he been feeding you that crap?' His eyes harden and his tone is sarcastic.

'Something like that.' I say, avoiding his eyes.

'And you believe it?'

'I don't know what to believe,' I say honestly.

'We had a dispute last year over a plot, that much is true. It originally was a run-down centre for street kids. Dad puts a lot of money into education and backs a lot of these places to get kids off the streets. My dad was like a street kid. He believes these places give kids a chance that wouldn't normally have one. We wanted to invest in the place but Morgan wanted the plot for a hotel. Felicity was appalled at his corruptness and told me about it. He didn't bargain on the fact that she would finally see through him. He's very bitter about her leaving him. He blames me for that. He deliberately did some shady deal with someone on the council. He told them we were planning to build warehouses on the plot, which was a complete lie. We were applying for permission to use the site as a social centre and Ark managed to block our application. He used all his contacts. He then bulldozed the site and then bought it at a cheap price.'

He stops, exhales and finishes his wine before waving to the waitress for another glass.

'That's the truth,' he adds. 'He believes I stole Felicity from him.'

My phone bleeps again. Time really flies when you're enjoying yourself, I glance down at it to see both are from Sylvie and both have thumbs up signs.

'Everything okay?' asks Sam.

'Fine,' I say, accepting a dessert menu from the waitress.

'There's a brilliant ice cream place around the corner, shall we go there?' he asks.

'I believe you,' I say.

He smiles.

'Good, I'm never wrong when it comes to ice cream.'

'I meant about Ark Morgan and the property deal.'

He nods.

'I'll pay shall I, and we'll get that excellent ice cream.'

I message Sylvie while he goes to pay.

Sam Lockwood is not the murderer. I click send and it bleeps immediately with a response. I smile and look at the message except it isn't from Sylvie, it's from Ark.

I have the perfect gift for you. I want you to wear it at the opening party of my new hotel in Knightsbridge. I've had it delivered to your flat in Rommel Mansions. I hope you like it. I'll send a car at seven to collect you tomorrow night for the opening.'

Tomorrow night? My heart jumps into my mouth and I can hardly breathe. How does he know where I live? My heart races and my mind whirls. I'm about to message Sylvie when my phone bleeps again. I'm almost too scared to look.

And Miss Brown, wear that perfume. You know how it intoxicates me.'

I shudder and send a WhatsApp message to the *That Night* group.

Sam Lockwood is not the murderer but Ark Morgan is looking very suspicious.

Chapter Forty-Two

I'd tried to get Ark Morgan out of my head for the rest of the evening but found it impossible. All kind of crazy ideas were going through my brain. Is my car bugged? Is the flat bugged? How could Ark know where I live? Does he also know that I'm one of his chambermaids? Has he had me followed? He must know I saw him through the telescope. Oh God, my life is in danger. Should I phone the police? I escape the ice cream parlour and head to the loo again. Sam must think I've got a bladder problem.

'Okay keep calm,' Sylvie says. 'I don't believe for one minute that he saw you through the telescope, that's if he is the murderer.'

'But he knows where I live?' I say, panic rising in me.

'Keep calm Rox. Someone with his contacts could easily find out where you live. It doesn't mean you've been followed. If he had had you followed he would know you work for him and he doesn't seem to know that. I think he just checked out your address. You must be on the electoral roll, then all someone had to do was ask around. That busybody you asked to forward your post probably told them.'

I take a deep breath. She's quite right. I'm letting my imagination run away with me.

'The important thing is to meet him. We can talk about it at work tomorrow. I've got to dash. We're going onto a club.'

I go back to the ice cream parlour where Sam has ordered triple chocolate sundaes with hot fudge sauce.

'I hope you're not dieting,' he says, handing me a spoon.

I'm so not and I so need chocolate. Ten minutes later I feel a whole lot better. We finish the sundaes and wander along Chelsea embankment, our hands barely touching until his hand slides into mine. The low sun warms us and sparkles on the

Thames. We pass loving couples on the benches and smile at each other.

'Ark Morgan has invited me to the opening of his new hotel tomorrow night,' I say.

'Ah,' he says. 'He's invited me too.'

'He has?' I say surprised.

'I don't think he sends out the invites to be honest, more likely it's his publicity manager. He'll probably be none too thrilled to see me, if I go of course.'

'Oh please go,' I say and bite my lip.

We sit and watch the sun go down. I can feel the heat of his body and when he drapes his arm across the back of the bench onto my shoulder I move closer to him. There are less people around now and Felix's advice seems no longer relevant. The air feels chilly and I wish I had brought a shawl with me. I try not to shiver.

'You're welcome to my jacket but it's not that warm I'm afraid,' he says, draping it over my shoulders.

'I'll be fine,' I say.

'Let's get your car,' he says, waving to a passing cab.

I don't want the evening to end but I can't think of a way to drag it out any longer.

He studies my Fiesta.

'Don't often see a Fiesta in such good condition,' he says teasingly.

'I know. I really should buy another car.'

'That's a healthy squeak,' he laughs as he opens the door for me.

'I wouldn't be comfortable with a car without a squeaky door,' I laugh.

I'm conscious that we're the only people in the street. I'm alone with him. If he's going to do it, this would be the time. He puts his hand into his pocket and I almost stop breathing.

'I guess this is goodbye Roxie Brown,' he says.

Oh my God. I don't know whether to scream or faint. In fact I don't think I have much choice in the matter. It's going to be a faint because my throat has closed up. He whips out a piece of paper and I feel myself sway and have to lean on the car to stay upright.

'This is the flyer for the championship match next week. Think about it.'

'Oh,' I say hoarsely.

'Hey,' he says, 'do you fancy a ride on my motorbike. I can take you for a spin before the do at Morgan's. In fact we can go there on the bike.'

I hesitate. What if Ark Morgan sees me? He'll be really angry. And if he is the murderer it might just tip him over the edge. Then again, if he knows Sam's protecting me he might be more cautious. But, a Harley Davidson, that's dangerous right?

'Okay,' I say.

'Great,' he says leaning towards me. 'I look forward to it. Thanks for a fun evening.'

My body buzzes with anticipation. I turn to him and our lips meet like magnets. My hand rests on his hip and his kiss consumes me. For a moment I am floating in heaven, unaware of anything except his body wrapped in mine. Forget the ice cubes, Sam's lips are enough to send the sparks flying. I stroke his neck, pressing against him for just that bit longer. He pulls away from me gently, looking into my eyes and I'm totally lost. This is not like the kiss Ark Morgan gave me and I have never felt this whenever Darren kissed me. I feel complete in his arms but wanting more all at the same time.

'Too soon?' he whispers.

'Yes,' I reply.

His phone bleeps and I remember Sylvie. I haven't heard from her in almost an hour.

Chapter Forty-Three

'You could have messaged me earlier,' I say sulkily. 'I almost phoned the police and then realised I couldn't even describe what you were wearing.'

'That's a point. In future I'll need a description of your outfits. It will make it a lot easier for the *Crimewatch* reconstruction if one of you is murdered,' says Felix.

'God, you're cheerful,' grunts Sylvie. 'Shame it wasn't a stopover you had in Barcelona.'

'You would have missed me love, and you know it.'

'Besides, I did message you. So, I don't know why you're complaining?'

'Because you said every fifteen minutes,' I argue.

'Christ Rox, I was busy doing other things.'

'Slut,' quips Felix.

'How was I to know that?'

Felix unscrews a bottle of cider and hands us a glass.

'Drink this and shut up. God, I'm glad I'm not a woman.'

'You're more woman than we are,' says Sylvie.

We turn our attention to the dress that hangs like a shroud on Zena the warrior in the corner of my living room and stare at in silence for a few minutes.

'If I'm honest she doesn't really do that dress justice does she?' says Felix, breaking the silence.

'That's because Zulu women don't make a habit of parading in cocktail dresses,' says Sylvie.

'They don't parade in any kind of dress do they?' queries Felix.

'Why are we even discussing what Zulu warriors wear?' I say sharply, feeling my nerves will give way any minute.

'Blimey, keep your thong on,' says Felix.

'How did Ark Morgan find out where I live?'

'Does it matter, I think you're both getting a bit carried away,' says Sylvie, dipping a sponge finger into Nutella and then into a tub of double cream. I have to say it's divine. I wish I'd thought of it. It seems such a shame to have discovered it just as I'm about to pop my clogs.

'You've only latched onto Ark Morgan because he found out her address ...'

'In an underhand way,' interrupts Felix.

I nod in agreement.

'And because he bought her a lovely black silk gown for his do tonight,' she finishes. 'It sounds like he's desperate to please her, not kill her.'

'Do you think?' I ask hopefully.

'Surely if he planned on knocking you off, he would have done it before now. Anyway, I still don't believe that the murderer saw you that night,' she says dismissively.

I so hope she's right.

'Anyway, he isn't a suspect any more, is he? You said yourself he has an alibi for the night of the murder.'

'Ah,' says Felix.

I hate it when Felix says *Ah*.

'What?' I ask.

'I checked the flight records with my friend in air traffic control. Ark Morgan's aeroplane was scheduled for a flight to Munich that night but the flight plan was cancelled at the last minute.' I stare at him, my mouth turning dry.

'He has no alibi and he's still a suspect,' Felix finishes.

'Oh God,' I groan.

'Oh shit,' says Sylvie.

I throw back the cider in one go. I don't want to go to the party. I feel sure this will be where I meet my untimely death. Ark Morgan has already sent me a message in the guise of the perfect dress. The Chanel box wrapped in black ribbon had been placed outside the flat when I'd arrived home. Inside were the dress, a bottle of Chanel No 5 perfume, and a very cryptic note.

We need to talk Miss Brown. I need to warn you. I've seen into your eyes and I'm concerned for your wellbeing.

Like hell he is.

'Wasn't that all Marilyn Monroe was wearing when they found her body?' says Felix pointing to the perfume bottle that is wedged between Zena's breasts.

'Yes,' I say. 'You think that's his way of telling me?'

'Strange thing to buy you, especially as he loves your other perfume so much,' says Felix thoughtfully.

It's as though he bought it to mark the event. I'm sure Rudy would consider it the perfect burial outfit. Ark Morgan is clearly some kind of psychopath. As soon as he sees me with Sam Lockwood that will no doubt tip him over the edge. Ark Morgan is only interested in me because he knows I saw him kill the man in the flat. After all, he's corrupt in business. That's what Sam said isn't it? He probably wouldn't think twice of knocking someone off if they stood in his way.

'I've seen into your eyes,' I quote. 'He means the telescope doesn't he?'

'Not necessarily,' says Sylvie.

'Most likely,' says Felix.

'This is ridiculous,' I say, in an attempt to calm myself down. 'The handwriting analysis doesn't match Ark Morgan at all.'

'Ah,' says Felix.

'I wish you'd stop saying that,' I say miserably.

'There's nothing to say that the handwriting on that leaflet was the murderer's. It could easily have been the victim's, or anyone else come to that. You have to find out what Ark did after he left the Fun Palace.'

'But why would Ark Morgan want to kill someone in a flat in Clapham?' asks Sylvie. 'It's not quite his style is it? Someone with his money would hire a hitman wouldn't they?'

'Ah, you say that love, but hit men have a habit of coming back to haunt you,' says Felix who is becoming a pain in the arse too knowledgeable. 'Perhaps he was being blackmailed,' he adds. 'Anyway, I'm on it. I know how to wire your phone. I've downloaded this fab app. We'll be able to track your whereabouts using the GPS.'

I choke on the cider.

'You what?' says Sylvie.

'We can wire her through her mobile. We'll know everything that is happening. And when ...'

'He goes to wipe me out,' I interrupt.

'We'll be in there,' says Felix.

'Only if we're sitting outside,' says Sylvie sensibly.

'Perhaps we should get the police involved,' I say. 'I could go undercover.'

What the hell am I talking about? I don't have a clue about going undercover.

'Christ, what's in that cider? You're talking out of your arse,' says Sylvie.

'I'm not Micky Blue Eyes,' I say. 'He's not going to admit to the murder before he blows my head off.'

'I think the sound of his hands around your throat might be a tad incriminating love,' says Felix.

I pour more cider into my glass. I'm really not feeling comforted.

'I'm not going,' I say resolutely.

'But you have to,' says Felix. 'This may be our one chance. You'll be okay. Sam will be there ...'

'Who is also another suspect,' Sylvie reminds us.

'It's unlikely by all accounts isn't it?'

'And there are three more suspects to chase up,' I remind him.

'Ah yes,' he says, pulling papers from a folder.

'Michael Nunn was on a flight to Geneva on the night of the murder. It was in all the papers apparently. He flew to some fashion designer's funeral, which leaves us with Clive Marsham, and Hugh Richards, both who seem unlikely murderers ...'

'But they could be,' I say.

'Hugh Richards is gay,' says Felix, like that automatically crosses him off the list.

'I never realised that gays didn't murder people,' says Sylvie, her voice dripping with sarcasm.

'Can we keep to the subject,' I say irritably.

'But he's a suspect and so is Sam so I'm wiring her phone all the same,' says a determined Felix. 'And until you can prove Nigel Forrest has an alibi, he's still a suspect too. You liking him are not grounds to scratch him off the list.'

'Okay, keep your frilly pants on.'

'Let's get you wired up,' he says. 'You'll need safe words. That way we'll know whether to go in or not.'

'We're not the bloody SAS,' says Sylvie.

I knew I'd need safe words with Ark Morgan but hadn't quite bargained on this.

'Maybe I should wear a bulletproof vest?' I say, not being in the least bit serious.

'That's something I didn't think of,' says Felix.

Now I really feel comforted.

'Shall we say *yellow* for *things aren't great* and *red* for *get me out of here.'*

'So *yellow* for when he seems to be threatening you and basically *red* for when he has his hands around your throat,' says Sylvie, pouring more cider.

'You can mock darling, but I don't see you coming up with anything better.'

'I've got to be ready by seven, Sam is picking me up,' I say.

'I know how to do it. It won't take me ten minutes.'

'Listen to Jack Reacher,' scoffs Sylvie. 'How did Ark take it when you told him you were coming with Sam Lockwood?'

'He doesn't know,' I say sheepishly. 'I'm just going to send the driver away when he arrives.'

'I'll be two secs, love,' Felix shouts as he disappears into the bedroom with my phone.

An hour and a bottle and a half of cider later and we're still waiting.

'How much longer?' shouts Sylvie.

'I'm still fiddling,' he calls.

'With the phone I hope.'

'I'm not a pervert.'

I shift anxiously in my seat.

'I've got to go soon. I need to get ready,' I say as Felix bounces out of the bedroom.

'Okay, go into the bathroom. I'm going to call you but it won't ring. I want to check we can hear you. Just say *hello, over and out,* that kind of thing.'

I turn the tap on and mutter *testing 1-2-3*. I hear them shriek.

'It only works,' says Sylvie excitedly as she bursts open the bathroom door. 'We could hear everything.'

'You don't have to sound so surprised,' says Felix.

'What if there are some things I don't want you to hear?' I ask. 'How do I turn it off?'

'I haven't got that far,' he says.
That's just great isn't it?

Chapter Forty-Four

As thrilling as a Harvey Davidson is I'm never riding pillion again. It isn't half as thrilling in a Chanel dress as it may be in leathers. I suspect I am the first woman to ride pillion in a Chanel dress and skimpy underwear. I bet Jennifer Aniston has never rode pillion in her life, let alone in a Chanel dress. I should never have said yes. It would have been far more decadent to have arrived in a chauffeur-driven limousine. It might feel liberating having the wind blow in your face but it's not so decadent when it blows up your underskirt. I spend half the journey struggling to stop my silk pashmina getting lodged in something mechanical and throttling me before Ark Morgan has the chance to, and the other half trying to stop the wind blowing up my dress. By the time we arrive my fanny has turned to ice and even worse, the helmet has been pressing my dangly earrings into my face so I enter the party with welts on each cheek. Sam zooms into the hotel's car park. I'm surprised he didn't just jump over the wall like Eddie Kidd. To make matters worse Ark sees us arrive as he's greeting his guests at the entrance. I struggle off the bike. I swear arriving by horse would have been easier. At least I could have travelled side saddle. Sam helps me down, his annoying grin on his face the whole time. He pulls my helmet off and I pat down my hair the best I can and hope I don't look too much like a scarecrow. Sam takes off his jacket and helmet, and looks gorgeous in his tuxedo. He brushes his hands through his hair and smiles at me. Ark doesn't take his eyes off us and I feel my body tremble as we approach the entrance.

'Are you cold?' asks Sam.

Before I can reply Ark Morgan walks down the entrance steps towards us.

'You didn't come in the car Miss Brown?' he asks his voice hard and his cheek twitching.

'I ...'

'I offered to escort Roxie,' says Sam, meeting Ark's eyes.

'Escorted?' repeats Ark. 'Is that what you call it? I think you'll find Roxanne is more used to gentlemen escorting her than Jack the lads on motorbikes. Besides, I had arranged transport for *Roxanne*,' says Ark, emphasising the Roxanne.

I smile nervously.

'It's fine, really. It's a warm evening,' I say.

Although I'm not so sure my cold fanny would agree with me.

'I hadn't realised you and Sam Lockwood were that well acquainted,' he says, giving me a hurtful look.

'Oh yeah,' says Sam lazily. 'We know each other quite well.'

I shoot him a look. That's not strictly true, and it really isn't helping. That's another nail in my coffin. Ark looks at Sam and scowls.

'Are you gatecrashing?' he asks bluntly. 'Because I don't think you are on the guest list.'

'Ah,' says Sam. 'You're wrong there.'

He pulls an invitation from his tuxedo and waves it in Ark's face, his delicious fragrance wafting over me as he does so. Ark studies the invite.

'It's clearly a mistake. I'll have to fix this for next time, but as Roxanne knows I don't hold grudges and like to think I'm hospitable. I hope you enjoy the evening.'

I wonder if Felix and Sylvie can hear this. I wish they'd set something up so they could talk to me too. I'd feel less lonely if I could hear them.

'The dress is perfect,' says Ark, looking at me admiringly. At least he isn't looking at me murderously. That's a good sign.

'Please excuse me Roxanne. I'll see you later.'

He walks back to the entrance to continue greeting his guests. We enter the foyer which is adorned with lit candles. Frank Sinatra serenades us and waiters hover with silver trays of champagne, Pimms and glasses of water. Glass chandeliers hang from the ceilings and sconces and pillar candles adorn the panelled walls. I can't but help be impressed. Sam takes two glasses of champagne and hands me one. We are offered canapés and I find it hard to resist.

'Did Ark buy you the dress?' Sam asks, looking at me curiously.

I nod.

'He left it outside my apartment with some perfume.'

'A bit presumptuous of him don't you think? How can he know your taste?'

I feel a little surge of anger. Is he criticising me?

'I happen to like it,' I lie. 'It's very much my taste.'

In fact it isn't at all and I can almost hear Sylvie gasp and Felix mutter *little liar*.

'Really?' he questions. 'I wouldn't have thought so. Bright colours suit you better if you want my opinion.'

'I don't actually, and you don't know me at all,' I say, placing my glass onto a tray and taking another.

'Champagne is pretty potent stuff,' he warns. 'It might taste like lemonade but it hits you a lot harder.'

'Sorry, are you like my father or something?'

I sound like something out of *TOWIE*.

'I'm not sure I understand why you're angry,' he says picking olives off his canapé.

'I'm not angry,' I say, feeling my hackles rise as he removes another olive.

'You're doing it again,' I say, nodding at the olives.

'I don't like olives,' he says simply.

'So why take a canapé with them on then?' I ask irritably.

'Why does it bother you so much?'

'It doesn't bother me,' I say, taking one myself.

The truth is it is rather disconcerting that he knows me so well. It's quite true that the dress is not to my taste and I do knock champagne back like lemonade. We're encouraged to leave the foyer and are escorted into the banqueting hall where round tables have been exquisitely laid out. I check the table plan and see I am on Ark's table. I search for Sam's name and realise his table is the other side of the room.

He gives me a grin.

'At least I can't drive you mad during dinner. See you later.'

I watch as he walks away and feel suddenly isolated. I'd much prefer him drive me mad over dinner than not be with him. When he is with me I feel secure and safe, although I don't know why considering he's a suspect.

'Let me lead you to your seat,' says Ark from behind me.

I'm a nervous wreck. It doesn't help knowing that Felix and Sylvie are listening to my every word. I've never been a big fan of voyeurism, not that this is voyeurism of course. I'm not going to have sex with them listening am I? I'd bloody kill them if they listened in on that. Not that I'm going to be having sex with anyone in the near future, let alone tonight, and I certainly won't be getting spanked, that's for sure.

'Did you get my perfume?' he whispers.

What he means is did I get the note?

I nod. I don't want Felix and Sylvie to hear the tremble in my voice. I'm perfectly safe while there are people around me. The key is not to be alone with Ark. Who'd have thought it, only a week ago I was desperate to be alone with him.

'Here we are,' he says, pulling back a chair. 'This is Edward.'

The man sitting in the chair next to me shakes my hand.

'Odd name for a woman,' he says as Ark walks away.

'No,' I say, 'I think you're the Edward.'

He frowns.

'Well I know that,' he says, slightly offended. 'Who are you then?'

'Roxie, I mean *Roxanne*.'

I imagine Sylvie is roaring with laughter. I wish I could turn the damn wire off.

'Why didn't he say that then?' he asks, looking confused.

I shrug.

'I'm not sure,' I say.

'Splendid hotel.'

'Yes,' I say, catching Sam's eye across the room. He winks and I quickly look away.

'Lobster, excellent, you can't beat it,' says Edward as a waiter places a bowl of soup in front of us.

Another man sits the other side of me and I turn. Our eyes meet and I feel my heart jump into my mouth. It's Max Walters, one of Ark's regular guests.

'Hello,' he smiles. 'I'm Max.'

'Roxanne.'

He looks curiously at me and I see recognition dawn in his eyes.

'I know you don't I?'

Chapter Forty-Five

'I don't think so,' I say, lowering my head to my soup bowl.

'Yes, your face is very familiar. Have you been on television?'

Not yet, but I could still have a starring role in *Crimewatch*.

'No, I'm not on television.'

'What do you do? That may jog my memory.'

'Do?' I repeat

'As in a job,' he says patiently, dunking bread into his soup.

I stare appalled, is that acceptable at a do like this?

'Or are you a socialite?' he says nonchalantly as if he meets them every day, although come to think of it, he probably does.

'Not exactly.'

Not exactly? What does that mean? I'm as far from a socialite as anyone can be.

'I don't recognise you,' I say, not looking at him.

'It'll come to me,' he says. 'Are you in politics?'

I imagine Sylvie and Felix are rolling around the floor now.

'Absolutely not, they're all a bunch of crooks.'

At that moment Ark leans over my shoulder, his lips close to my cheek.

'I hope you're enjoying the food,' he says and I feel myself freeze.

'I was just saying, I feel sure I know Roxanne from somewhere,' says Max.

'Really?' says Ark, stroking my shoulder.

'It'll come to me,' says Max resolutely. 'It always does.'

Not in the next few hours I hope. Fortunately he is sidetracked by another guest and I'm able to finish my soup without choking on it. Ark circulates and chats with his guests while occasionally looking over to me. Dinner passes in a haze of wine, champagne toasts and a most delicious chocolate cheesecake. Coffee is served and by the time Ark approaches me again I'm pretty tipsy. The dark bristles on his face loom ever closer to mine. My face that is, not my dark bristles. I've drunk too much and I can't think straight. He takes my hand.

'Come Roxanne,' he says softly.

Ooh he's sounding just like Christian Grey isn't he? I let him lead me like a lamb to the slaughter. The waiters clear the tables to make space for the dance floor and the guests mingle in the foyer. My eyes meet Sam's across the crowded room and it really is one of those romantic moments. Our eyes lock and in that instant I realise that Sam Lockwood is the Mr Right I'd dreamt of all my life.

'Do you like the perfume?' Ark asks as the band begins to play.

I'm pulled into his arms and swung around the dance floor to the applause of the other guests and I realise we are the only ones dancing. I sway slightly as I lose my balance. I'm giddy enough from the champagne as it is without him whirling me about like a spinning top.

'A Chanel dress cannot be worn without matching perfume,' he whispers, twirling me so fast that my head spins.

'I prefer you didn't see Sam Lockwood,' he continues before I have a chance to open my mouth. It's just as well because I'm not sure much sense would come out of it right now.

'The night we met at the Fun Palace ...' I begin, trying not to slur my words.

The Master of Ceremonies welcomes everyone to take to the dance floor. I strain to see the woman Sam is dancing with.

'He hates me being with you,' Ark smirks. 'Now he knows what it feels like.'

I have no idea what he's talking about.

'He'll soon learn what it is to lose somebody,' he says menacingly.

Holy shit, I now think I know what he's talking about. This sounds like a possible yellow. He leads me out of the hall and down a long corridor. I hope Felix's bloody GPS is working.

'I love the *yellow* décor,' I say shakily.

'I think you must be colour blind, or a little drunk,' he smiles but the smile doesn't seem to reach his eyes.

'What about the night of the Fun Palace, Roxanne?' he asks pulling me into a dimly lit room and closing the door.

Sylvie

'It's got to be working,' I say desperately. 'Jesus wept Felix, this is not the time for the bloody thing to go wrong.'

'I know that love. I don't know why it's cut out. Could just be lack of signal.'

'Don't you have a bloody handbook?' I ask stupidly. 'She could be screaming *red* like no tomorrow for all we know.'

'I downloaded it you silly mare.'

'Can we phone her, you know, like a normal person?' I ask, clicking into her name before he can reply.

'I wouldn't call Roxie a normal person,' he says.

'Nothing,' I say, worriedly. 'It's not even ringing.'

'No signal,' says Felix, trying to feign calmness but I know he's panicking.

'What do we do?' I squeal, my hand itching to tap 999 on my phone.

'At least we know what she's wearing, a black dress and Chanel No 5.'

'That doesn't comfort me.'

We wait silently but there is nothing. I am about to press '9' when Roxie's voice crackles on Felix's phone.

'Don't you think we should get back? Your guests will wonder where you are.'

'Thank God,' I mumble.

'Come on,' mutters Felix. 'Get him to incriminate himself.'

Chapter Forty-Six

'Don't you think we should get back? Your guests will wonder where you are,' I say, fumbling for the light switch.

Light floods the room and he smiles at me, his eyes glittering. We're in an office.

'I've seen into your eyes Roxanne,' he says pushing me against the desk.

Oh my God, I'm so bloody scared that I can't remember the safe words.

'When?' I ask hoarsely.

'Every time you look at me, I know how you feel. You needn't feel guilty about Lockwood; he's getting what he deserves. I keep warning you, he's bad news.'

'But that night ...' I begin. 'The night our eyes met.'

'Yes,' he whispers, moving closer to me.

I duck under his arm and back away only to hit the wall. He leans forward and presses his hands on the wall, his eyes meeting mine.

'You felt it too, didn't you?'

I'm getting confused. Felt what?

'Was it you?' I ask.

He pulls back from me and smiles.

'And it was always you,' he says huskily, his hand sliding up the inside of my leg.

He groans and I pray Felix and Sylvie didn't hear. I put my hand over his.

'You didn't fly to Munich that night did you?'

He strokes my hair.

'What night?' he laughs.

'The Fun Palace night, the night of the murder,' I say with a gulp.

He stops. His lips close to mine. The door bursts open and for a moment I think Sylvie and Felix must have called the police but instead of the riot squad rushing in shouting *freeze, put your hands above your head*, a slightly drunk woman totters in.

'Oh, this isn't the loo,' she says, making a quick exit.

'The murder, what murder?' Ark asks, stroking my hand as he does so. 'You're not making sense.'

'You met my eyes through the telescope.'

'We looked at the stars on my boat, is that what you mean?'

I shake my head. My brain is getting fuddled. His hand is stroking my throat and I shiver uncontrollably.

'You didn't go to Munich that night,' I repeat.

He sighs.

'The flight was cancelled, my pilot was taken ill. You know how I hate flying; I won't let anyone else fly me.'

'So you went to Clapham instead,' I say, trying to lead him into a trap.

'No, I didn't go back to the Fun Palace.'

Why is this so bloody difficult? It never takes this long in the movies does it?

'So where did you go?' I snap irritably.

'To Fulham, to Maria's for dinner, she's here if you want to check with her.'

I stare at him.

'Maria?' I repeat.

'You've no need to be jealous of her,' he whispers, before his lips claim mine.

I can barely think straight. Ark Morgan doesn't want to kill me. He simply wants to steal me. The door swings open again and he sighs.

'This isn't the loo,' he says irritably, pulling me roughly out of the room and back into the ballroom.

'Let's find somewhere more private,' he says.

I see Max Walters make a beeline towards us and my heart sinks.

'I know where I've seen you,' he says triumphantly. 'You're one of the chambermaids at the Crescent.'

Chapter Forty-Seven

Ever wanted the floor to open up and swallow you? Ark Morgan stares at me as if I've got two heads and Max Walters, realising what he's done, looks mortified.

'What did you say?' thunders Ark.

'Nothing, it was nothing,' says Max, taking a step back. 'I think I'm mistaken.'

'Repeat what you just said,' Ark barks as the ballroom goes quiet.

'He said he recognised me as one of the chambermaids at the Crescent Hotel,' I say.

Well I'm sick and tired of feeling ashamed of being a cleaner. It's an honest living and I'm a good person. There are a few gasps from the guests. Honestly, you'd think I'd just said I was the hotel's resident prostitute. The fact is, chambermaid or no chambermaid, Ark Morgan fancied me and quite frankly I'm as good as any of this lot at Ark Morgan's do. I grab a glass of champagne from a waiter and throw it back. I can hear people mumbling behind me.

'You're a chambermaid?' says Ark with his eyebrows so high that I imagine they could cover his bald patch.

I nod.

'Do you have a problem with that? If I'm guilty of anything it is for not being totally honest with you, and for that I'm sorry.'

Recognition sparks in his eyes.

'Christ,' he mutters. 'You were in the lift that day. I remember you.'

A waiter approaches him with a tray of drinks. He angrily knocks it out of his hand, sending champagne glasses crashing to the floor.

'You're nothing but a deceiving little slut,' he spits.

I gasp. The deceiving isn't far wrong but the slut is a bit out of order you have to agree.

'Whoa, that's a bit strong,' says Sam, handing me a tissue. 'And you're nothing but a two-faced hypocrite and a deceiving bastard, so you can't talk. I think you owe the lady an apology.'

Ark either doesn't see Sam or chooses to ignore him.

'How dare you spy on me for that wanking Lockwood?'

'I haven't been spying on you,' I say. 'I happened to like you and I thought you would never look at a chambermaid, and I wasn't wrong was I?' I say, feeling my face grow hot.

I can feel all of the guests' eyes on me.

'You need to get over your obsession Ark, that I'm forever trying to steal things from you. And I say again, you owe the lady an apology,' repeats Sam, his tone firmer now.

'She's no lady,' says Ark, his eyes blazing. 'And you're an uninvited guest, so you can leave right now.'

'Neither of us is going anywhere until you apologise to Roxie.'

I think it's going to be a long night.

'You're fired,' Ark snaps. 'And I want that dress back.'

He lurches dangerously towards me.

'Now hang on a minute Morgan. There's no need for that. She's done nothing wrong,' says Sam, putting his hand on Ark's chest.

'Take your hands off me,' Ark roars, slapping Sam's hand away. 'Now get out before I have you thrown out.'

Sam grins.

'You know I'm not leaving until you apologise. And I'm more than happy to take your guys on. Good practice for the championship, unless you're offering to be my sparring partner.'

I'm half expecting the band to strike up Eye of the Tiger.

'I wouldn't waste my energy,' Ark says finally.

That's a relief. I've seen Sam beat seven bells out of a monster far bigger and meaner than Ark Morgan.

'That's a shame. You'll have to have us thrown out then. Like I said, I'll only leave after you've apologised, and Roxie can't leave because she came with me.'

'It's okay,' I say, just wanting to get out as fast as possible.

'It's not okay,' says Sam.

He's so bloody minded. I can see from the expression on his face that he would just love to take Ark outside.

'I apologise for calling Miss Brown a slut. That was somewhat uncalled for,' Ark says, his face turning red from the effort of having to say it. 'I would like the dress back and the perfume.'

I can't think why. It's as sweaty as shit.

'I'm not taking it off here,' I say.

Sam grins.

'Aw, now there's a disappointment,' he says.

I glare at him.

'Right, we'll love and leave you then. Thanks for a great do. Fab food as always and brilliant champagne, company leaves a lot to be desired but hey, you can't have it all,' says Sam. 'We'll pop the dress in the post.'

He takes my arm and leads me out. We reach the entrance and he turns.

'Oh, I'm presuming that Roxie does still have her job? We wouldn't want to do you for unfair dismissal would we? She'll be there Monday as usual.'

I wish he'd stop talking for me. We finally get outside and the air feels wonderful. I take a deep breath and turn on him.

'I can speak you know,' I say.

'I noticed,' he grins.

'You didn't have to get involved.'

'I wanted to, and what you saw in him I will never know. All I can say is you have abysmal taste in men.'

'How dare you.'

'I just did, and I was quite right that dress doesn't suit you.'

'You're quite rude, do you know that?'

He nods.

'Of course you could say thank you.'

I scoff.

'Thank you for what exactly? For dragging the whole thing out longer than needed.'

'You wanted me to thrash him, you know you did,' he says arrogantly.

'I did not.'

'Just like you want me to kiss you now,' he says with his irritating grin.

I blush.

'I do not.'

'I beg to differ,' he says huskily as his arms surround me and his hot sensual lips land on mine. I'm in heaven as his tongue explores my mouth with an expertise that Ark Morgan never had. I don't want it to stop. His hand grips my bottom. I encircle my arms around his neck and return his kiss with fervour. I feel drunk on Sam Lockwood. I moan softly and then I remember. If those two haven't turned off that bloody wire I'll kill them.

Chapter Forty-Eight

'Mr Morgan will see you now,' says the gorgeous blonde assistant.

If I didn't know better I'd think this was one of my fantasies. I've never been inside Ark Morgan's office. I've fantasised about it, of course. My heart is hammering in my chest and not out of desire but from a sickening feeling in my stomach that Ark is going to sack me. I walk into the office, clutching the dress and perfume.

He has his back to me. He's facing the window and I'm living the ultimate *Fifty Shades* fantasy. I cough softly but he doesn't turn. Oh dear, this doesn't bode well.

'I've brought the dress and perfume.'

'They're yours,' he says quietly.

'I can't take them,' I say, stepping forward to place them on his desk.

He turns from the window.

'Because Sam Lockwood says so, is that why?'

I shake my head.

'I had the dress dry-cleaned,' I say with a wince.

I couldn't have handed it back if I hadn't. I'd sweated buckets that night. I'm not doing much better now to be honest. He looks at them, a pained expression on his face.

'Won't you at least keep the perfume?' he asks, finally meeting my eyes.

'I really shouldn't,' I say, slowly stepping back and knocking over his row of Ark Morgan pencils. God, this is *Fifty Shades* incarnate.

'Sorry,' I say, bending to pick up the damn things, most of which have rolled under his desk.

We stoop down together and I look into his eyes, narrowly missing a head butt.

'You're not fired Miss Brown,' he says softly.

That's a relief. I've got the mortgage on the new flat to pay. He holds out his hand to help me up. I take it cautiously. I bite my lip and almost expect him to say *I wish you wouldn't do that Miss Brown* but instead he says,

'Sam Lockwood always gets the best. Thanks for coming.'

And with that he turns his back on me and faces the window. I take that to be my dismissal and hurry from the office before he changes his mind about my job.

Chapter Forty-Nine

'Do you think we should wire you?' Sylvie asks Felix.

He shakes his head emphatically.

'I don't want either of you listening in on what I'm up to, thank you very much. Anyway, I wouldn't trust either of you to do it right.'

'Ooh go on,' giggles Sylvie, 'it will be a laugh.'

'I would have thought you'd had enough laughs listening in on me,' I say accusingly.

'We turned it off at the kiss,' says Felix defensively. 'Obviously it took us a while to realise it was a kiss. You could have been drinking out of a bottle for all we knew.'

'I still don't think it's a good idea for you to meet him tonight. It's not like we'll be sitting here waiting to hear from you. What if something happens and you need us?' I say worriedly.

'I don't think Hugh Richards is going to throttle me love. After all, I'm not the one who saw him through the telescope am I?'

'All the same ...'

'It will be fine,' says Sylvie, waving a hand airily. 'He can keep in touch through the *That Night* group.'

It would be awful if while Sylvie and I are both out enjoying ourselves Felix is being butchered to death. I shudder at the thought.

'Don't gay men have some code of honour when it comes to killing their own?' I ask.

'I think you're mixing them up with the Mafia,' says Sylvie, rolling her eyes. 'Although how you've managed to do that I'll never know. I've yet to see a Mafia homosexual in a Coppola movie.'

Sylvie has become an expert on films since she started seeing Nigel Forrest. Neo-Noir films in particular, whatever they are. From what she tells me they don't sound like Woody Allen.

'Anyway, Hugh Richards isn't the killer,' says Felix.

'I have to admit that the guy I saw through the telescope didn't look very camp,' I say in agreement.

'We're not all Julian Clarys love.'

'You know what I mean. He looked too manly to be gay. He had a stance about him that I just wouldn't have thought was gay.'

'I'm trying so hard not to be offended darling.'

'Well, it's not Nigel if that's what you're trying to say,' says Sylvie hotly.

'He does belong to a gun club,' I remind her. 'And he knows someone who lives at Rommel Mansions, plus he has a Starbucks card …'

'Has being the operative word,' says Sylvie.

'He was at the Fun Palace,' I say.

'So was Sam Lockwood,' she argues.

'But he's not in a gun club. That on its own is dead suspicious.'

Sylvie is totally convinced that Nigel Forrest isn't the murderer, although suspicion points to him more than Sam. There is no way a murderer kisses like Sam Lockwood. The memory of his kiss makes me go all weak at the knees. What started off as a horrendous evening ended up being one of the nicest of my life. We'd driven off into the sunset on his Harley Davidson. Okay, more like Clapham and the chippy just around the corner from my flat. All the same, it felt like heaven. I never thought saveloy and chips could taste so good. I guess it depends on who you're sharing them with. I never want to eat chips off a plate again.

'He hasn't been to the gun club in yonks,' says Sylvie, 'and when you meet him you'll know he couldn't murder anyone.'

'Pity he couldn't come this evening,' says Felix. 'We could have judged for ourselves.'

'He's on location, he won't be back until late tonight and then he's taking me to dinner,' she says, her eyes going all dewy. 'But we're all invited to the first night of his play in just over a week. I'm so excited and then you'll all get to meet him and can judge for yourself. You'll see that he couldn't hurt a fly.'

'Well I couldn't hurt a fly either but sometimes I could murder my mother,' says Felix.

'He didn't do it,' she says forcefully.

'Well someone did and Roxie saw it.'

I so wished I hadn't.

'It wasn't Sam,' I say.

Sam wouldn't hurt anyone, except in the boxing ring, not that that makes it okay of course but you know what I mean. It's more expected isn't it?

'Have we covered everyone on the guest list?' asks Sylvie.

'Yes we have,' says Felix. 'Now, I'd better get ready for this boxing match. I'm wearing my salmon pink shirt. I must say I am looking forward to the bare-chested men parading around like gladiators bit. Mind you, that's the only nice bit about it if you ask me. The barbaric bit of bashing each other up I'm not keen on. Can't see what you girls see in it.'

'Are you sure you'll be okay later?' I ask again.

'I assure you love, if I get even a whiff of gunpowder I'll phone one of you two bitches to come and rescue me.'

Chapter Fifty

The bell rings for round six. I fight the urge to jump from my seat and shout like a banshee. Sam's muscular body tenses as he takes a hard right punch to his chin. I wince. It's like I feel every blow. He sways and for one awful moment I think he is going to go down but he recovers and sends a hard punch to the other man's chest. I watch anxiously as they circle each other. My eyes survey Sam's muscular toned physique and I shiver. I can see the lustful looks in other women's eyes as they watch him too. His eyes meet mine and it's like there is no one else in the room. He's my champion whether he wins or not. He gives his cheeky grin and my heart melts. He can do anything to me. I'd never be able to say no. What a shame Sam doesn't have a playroom. Then again ... maybe he does. One lives in hope.

Felix moans beside me.

'Is it over yet? God, I thought that fight scene in *Eastern Promises* was brutal, but this is far worse and much too close,' he says fumbling for his glass of wine.

'Have I got blood on me?' he winces.

I sigh.

'Of course you haven't.'

'There's enough of it flying around.'

My phone vibrates in my jeans pocket. I pull it out and see it is my mum. I'm too afraid not to answer her calls since the last time. She only seems to call with bad news.

'Did you know Sam Lockwood's father owns Lockwood Estates? Stinking rich apparently,' she says without preamble.

'How do you know?'

'Is that our Sylv?' asks Felix. 'Tell her it's worse than an abattoir here.'

'What's that?' asks Mum. 'What are you doing in an abattoir for goodness' sake?'

'I'm not in an abattoir.'

'Just feels like it,' moans Felix.

'I'm watching Sam fight for the championship,' I say proudly.

'Lovely,' says Mum, who detests boxing. 'His father's bigger than Ark Morgan. Your dad googled him, didn't you Martin?'

I hate it when she puts the phone on hands free.

'Only because you nagged me to,' grumbles Dad.

'His father belongs to just about everything. They have a huge apartment in London, a country home in Berkshire, acres and acres of land and all that. They have clay shooting competitions. His father is quite the champion. Isn't that right Martin?'

'Are you sure about that?' I ask, feeling like someone just punched me in the solar plexus.

'Sure about what dear?'

'That Sam's dad is a champion at clay pigeon shooting.'

Felix's eyes widen.

'You can't have better access to a gun than that love,' he whispers. 'They probably have their own gunroom, permits, the lot. You name it, they've got it. They'll have a little arsenal there, a one-family terrorist group.'

I grab a can of beer and quench my dry mouth.

'A gun right on your doorstep,' he persists, shielding his eyes with his programme.

'Okay,' I mutter through gritted teeth. 'It doesn't mean he's the ...' I hesitate when I remember I'm still talking to my mum.

'Everything all right dear? Is Sam winning?'

I can't very well tell her the truth can I? That Sam has become suspect number one again in the *That Night* murder.

'Everything's fine,' I say.

I study Sam, my heart hammering in my chest. His eyes connect with mine and I fight my swoon. Oh God, I don't believe this. What if Sam is the murderer? Does he know I saw him? Is he spending all this time with me because he wants to know how much I know? Does he even know I know it was him? My head begins to spin. Even I don't know what I'm talking about. Let's face it, the evidence against him isn't that heavy. Okay, so he lost a Starbucks reward card and he owns Rommel Mansions. That doesn't prove anything does it? And so what if he went to the Fun Palace that night and his dad is a champion at clay pigeon shooting. That doesn't mean he was the guy I saw do the shooting does it? It only means he has easy access to guns. Oh shit, how many people have easy access to guns? I knock back the last of the beer and slump in my seat. It seems all I do is think about the murder. We should go back to the flat, but Sylvie said it's too dangerous. Murderers always return to the scene of the crime and if he should see me there, then he will know for sure that I saw him on the night of the murder. My only hope is that Felix will find out that Hugh is the murderer and we can all sleep soundly in our beds.

'He's lovely Roxie. Perfect for you,' gushes Mum. 'I couldn't have chosen better myself.'

Oh I doubt that. I know Mum has lousy taste but even she stops at murderers. I click off the phone as the bell goes for the end of round six. Felix exhales and reaches for another drink.

'Don't you think you should keep a clear head?' I say. 'Don't forget you're meeting Hugh later.'

'It can't get more brutal than this,' he says as the bell goes for round seven.

'How many are there?'

'Twelve, I think, unless there is a knock out.'

'I'll be knocking myself out if I have to watch much more bloodshed.'

Sam's opponent flies out of the ring like Rocky and lays into Sam.

'Blimey, who put a firework up his arse?' exclaims Felix.

I jump from my seat, waving my fists around and screaming at Sam.

'Come on, you can do it, come on.'

'I suppose there's one consolation,' says Felix as Sam fights back. 'If Sam wanted to kill someone I doubt he'd need a gun.'

Felix jumps to his feet as Sam throws punch after punch.

'Finish it,' he screams.

For someone who hates bloodshed he certainly seems keen for more. I watch with half-closed eyes. I can't bear it. The poor guy is getting slaughtered by Sam. Everyone is screaming and baying for blood. Before I know what I'm doing I've thrown myself at the ropes.

'Stop, stop the fight. Sam, stop.'

In that moment Sam looks at me and his opponent seeing his opportunity lashes out and hits Sam with such a vicious punch that sends Sam straight to the floor.

'Holy shit,' says Felix.

There are gasps from the crowd and I hold my breath. Oh God, I've only gone and lost him the championship. Why can't I learn to keep my mouth shut?

'Come on love, get up,' shouts Felix. 'It's not over yet. Show us what you're made of. He's all brawn and no brains that other bugger.'

I silently beg Sam to pick himself up. The ref begins to count and my heart sinks.

'I feel like jumping in and shoving him up myself,' says Felix, fidgeting on his feet.

Then Sam is up and I let out a sigh of relief. I mouth sorry but he just grins and throws himself back into the fight.

'Thank God for that. Let's hope he isn't the murdering type darling, because right now you bloody deserve to be.'

I can't disagree.

Chapter Fifty-One

Sylvie

Nigel is waiting outside the restaurant. He doesn't see me so I'm able to drink him in for a while. He's wearing the bomber jacket and faded jeans. It's impossible to miss him. I have visions of walking down the red carpet with him. He's going to be a heart-throb for sure. Move over George Clooney. I've got a lot of work to do before I'll be his Amal Alamuddin, but hey, if Roxie can do it in one day, then so can I. I'm not letting this fish get away. He's the best catch I've ever had and I just know he is my soulmate, my real soulmate. Not like the others. Madam Zehilda got that right. And there is no way he is the murderer, he is much too gentle for that. Hopefully Felix will WhatsApp later to say that Hugh is the murderer and we can all sleep soundly in our beds. That's hoping Felix doesn't get himself shot of course. He's stupid enough. At least he'll stand out in that bright pink shirt of his. That will dazzle everyone watching *Crimewatch*. Stands to reason that the murderer has to be Hugh because I know for sure that it isn't Nigel and Roxie is convinced that it isn't Sam.

Nigel smiles when he sees me.

'You're looking lovely,' he says, kissing me on the cheek. 'But then you always do. I never thought to ask if Chinese was okay with you. I should have checked that you liked it first. I somehow thought if I did then you would too. We seem to share similar tastes.'

He's so perfect for me. I love Chinese food. We enter the restaurant and are shown to our table.

'How was the filming?'

'Brilliant. It's going really well. I've finished my bit. I only hope they keep it in,' he laughs.

'I know they will,' I say, trying not to gush too much.

'Ah,' he says, pulling something from his jacket pocket.

'I've got tickets for the first night of the play. How many do you want?'

'Three, if that's okay. My friends Rox and Felix would love to see it and they're dying to meet you.'

Oh God, what made me say that? That was just a bit too close to the truth. We should never have allowed Felix to go alone to meet Hugh. Hopefully as long as he doesn't say anything about the murder he'll be safe.

'Sure,' Nigel says handing me the tickets.

I stare at the gold lettering that spells his name above the title of the play, *A Night of Madness.*

At that moment my phone bleeps with a WhatsApp message. Oh no. Please don't let that silly arse be in trouble.

Chapter Fifty-Two

WhatsApp

Felix: *Hello lovelies, how's it going? This Hugh seems an unassuming guy. Not my type though, far too introverted. Spends most of the time saying umm and as I'm not fluent in the language of umms, we're not getting very far.*
Sylvie: *That's a relief. I was panicking you were dead.*
Felix: *Did you think I was WhatsApping through a medium?*
Sylvie: *Very funny. He's probably struck dumb from seeing that bloody shirt of yours. Let's face it it's enough to render anyone speechless.*
Roxie: *Introverted? Oh no. Isn't introspection a characteristic of murderers?*
Sylvie: *I don't know. Is it?*
Roxie: *You're the expert.*
Sylvie: *Not on bloody murderers I'm not. I've never ever met one.*
Roxie: *Unless Nigel Forrest is one.*
Sylvie: *He isn't.*
Felix: *We still don't know darlings. There's that little question of Sam's dad's little gun cache.*
Sylvie: *What?*
Felix: *Hasn't she told you?*
Sylvie: *Told me what?*
Roxie: *I haven't had time.*
Sylvie: *That's something I don't have much of either. I'm in the restaurant loo. Nigel will think I've got dysentery if I'm in here much longer.*
Roxie: *It's nothing. Just Sam's dad is a clay pigeon enthusiast.*
Felix: *With his own gunroom.*
Roxie: *We don't know that.*
Sylvie: *Holy shit, really?*

Felix: *We're off to a gay club, Copacabana. I'm hoping if I get a few vodkas into him he'll open up.*
Roxie: *Too much information Felix.*
Sylvie: *I don't want to hear about your sex life.*
Roxie: *I feel sure he's the murderer. Be careful Felix.*
Felix: *Hopefully all will be well and the only murderous thing I'll come into contact with is the burly bouncer on the door, but in case neither of you noticed, I'm wearing my salmon pink T-shirt with a grey waistcoat.*
Sylvie: *If that's pink I'll eat my hat.*
Roxie: *I thought it was purple.*
Felix: *Trust me lovelies, it's salmon pink. I'll report back in an hour to let you know I'm still alive.*
Sylvie: *We should have set safe words for you.*
Roxie: *We still can.*
Felix: *Pink for danger and bright red for get me out of here. I'd better go lovelies, Mr Umm is waiting.*
Sylvie: *BTW, did Sam win the championship?*
Felix: *He got a medal and everything. God, that man is gorgeous, especially when he's half naked. No thanks to Roxie mind you. If she'd had her way he'd have concussion instead.*
Roxie: *Unfair. I just can't stand the sight of blood.*
Felix: *Going, going, gone.*
Sylvie: *Me too.*

Chapter Fifty-Three

Fortunately for me Sam went on to win the championship. I was so proud. The first thing I did was phone my mum. You'd think I'd given birth she was that thrilled. I thought she was going to burst into tears she was that emotional. Sam forgave me for almost stopping the fight. It was Felix who pulled me from the ropes.

'Darling, I don't think this is how it's done. The traditional way is to throw in a white towel, not your whole body.'

He'd sat me back on my seat, plied me with wine and kept a restraining hand on me until the very end. I'm so hoarse from shouting that I can't speak above a whisper. I drop my phone into my clutch and leave the ladies.

Sam is studying the menu when I return to the table. He has the most lovely eyes, Surely I would remember them if I had looked into them that night? Sam doesn't have an evil bone in his body which means the murderer has to be Nigel Forrest, which doesn't surprise me, seeing as he's got access to a gun. You often hear after a murder, that the murderer was a member of a gun club don't you? It stands to reason it was Nigel Forrest. Hugh sounds like a sweetie, so it can't have been him. Poor Sylvie, she will be distraught. I hope she will be safe with him tonight. Maybe I should WhatsApp Felix.

'Penny for your thoughts,' says Sam, giving me his grin.

I smile.

'I was just thinking about ...'

Can I tell him about the murder?

'Everything,' I finish.

I don't think it would be sensible. Not that I have any doubts about him but, well, just in case. Best to keep my mouth shut until we know for sure that Nigel Forrest is the murderer.

'What do you fancy?' he asks glancing at the menu. 'I've ordered some bubbly.'

I look at his bruised cheek and cut eyebrow and feel an urge to kiss them. I've never felt like this about anyone. I'd always dreamt of having these feelings but never believed I would. Darren never really inspired romance.

'You choose,' I say.

I've always wanted to say that. Have a man take control. Bugger women's lib.

He looks up and reaches for my hand across the table.

'I really loved that you wanted to stop the fight,' he says, stroking my hand.

'Really? I thought I was one big embarrassment.'

'No, I liked that you cared about Tom, the other boxer. Do you mind the boxing that much?'

The waitress approaches and he orders lamb cutlets in basil sauce for both of us. She pours the bubbly into glasses and we toast his win.

'I like the danger and excitement of it. It's part of my personality,' he grins.

'I've noticed,' I say softly, sipping from my glass.

He takes my hand again.

'I'd like to show you my house tonight, it overlooks the Thames. It's beautiful. You'll like it.'

I lower my head and watch the bubbles in my glass.

'Your parents won't mind you going out with a chambermaid?'

He laughs,

'My dad was a market stallholder before he made it, and my mum was a cleaning lady. You could look down on them if you wanted. They'll love you. They've seen a picture of you.'

I widen my eyes.

'They have?'

'I took it at the Fun Palace, remember? The selfie?'

'Oh yes,'

He fumbles with his phone for a few seconds.

'Ah, yes here it is.'

He holds it up and I smile, and then I remember and my body freezes.

Felix

Hugh's an okay bloke I'm discovering. He just needed a few vodkas to loosen him up. He is a pretty good dancer too. I may have struck lucky here. He doesn't like to talk much, unless you count his umms. My kind of guy, considering I like to do all the talking.

'How do you know old Ark Morgan then?' I ask.

'Who?' he yells above the music.

'Ark Morgan,' I repeat.

'Oh, I don't really, not well anyway. He supports this Aids foundation I work with, and invited a representative to the do on the yacht, so I got to go. I met him though, nice guy. Is that why you wanted to meet me? Do you know him too?'

'Kind of, I'm doing some research on charities and he gave me some names,' I say, thinking what a bloody weak lie that is. He's bound to see through it. 'We did a thing on 30th May. Actually, I think I saw you there.'

Once you start lying it gets easier. He sings along to the music, and waves his arms around so much that he almost takes my eye out.

'May 30th, can't think where I was,' he mumbles.

I'm sure he'd remember putting a bullet into someone.

'Oh hang on,' he says swinging around. 'Umm, yeah, I remember. I was in the Isle of Wight.'

Isle of Wight? why the hell would anyone want to go there?

'Isle of Wight,' I repeat, 'you sure about that?'

'Yeah, sadly, it was my uncle's funeral. He lived down there. It was a good wake though.'

'You were there overnight?'

'Yeah, whole weekend. I love this song do you?'

Oh dear. How do I tell the lovelies that one of them is with the murderer?

Sylvie

I've eaten so much I feel like a stuffed pig. Still, it was a Chinese, so no doubt in an hour I'll be hungry again. Nigel takes my hand and we stroll towards the embankment.

'It's a beautiful night,' I say.

'Not as lovely as you,' he says, leaning over to kiss me.

This couldn't be more perfect. The Thames lapping below us, the stars shining above us and his lovely warm arms around me and finally his hot pulsating lips on mine. I meet his lips eagerly and feel him push me against the embankment railings. I pull away quickly. I'm surprised there isn't a squelch as I pull my lips from his. I look down to the cold dark water.

'You okay Sylvie?' he asks.

What am I doing? The poor bloke will think I'm nuts. I can't very well tell him I'm suspicious he may be a murderer.

'Sorry, I'm a bit nervous of water,' I say, feeling like a right wally.

He rubs my hand between his.

'You're cold, how about a nightcap to warm you up?'

I feel my phone vibrate in my bag but decide to leave it. I don't want Nigel thinking I'm a wet blanket, scared of this, scared of that, and always peeking at my phone as if I've got someone else on the go.

'That sounds lovely.'

'There's a pub up the road, or we could go back to my place.'

'Oh,' I say, 'Where's your place?'

Please don't say Rommel, please don't.

'Clapham, where else, shall we get a cab?'

Thank God. I nod. A couple of drinks in me and I'll be fine. We climb into the cab and I quickly check my phone.

Felix: *Hugh isn't the murderer girlies. I hate to be the bearer of bad news. He was at a funeral in the Isle of Wight. And yes, I thought it was dubious, so I ran a quick check. Your little Felix has got contacts now. I was thinking I might go into this investigative business full time. Anyway, cut to the chase, there was a funeral and old Hughie did a reading. So ... one of you is with the murderer right now because Clive Marsham wasn't at* *the party. He was on the guest list but not at the party as he'd been in hospital for the past month with some mystery illness. Anyway, simply type RED and I'll call the police. But be sure to have concrete evidence first. We don't want the murderer knowing we know until we do If you get my drift.*

I wait for a response from Roxie but there isn't one. Bollocks. He could have his hand around her throat at this very moment. I turn to Nigel to ask him what the hell I should do when he says to the cab driver.

'Somerville Place, Clapham.'

Felix

I stare at the screen until the words blur. Jesus peanuts, why doesn't one of them answer? How am I supposed to know which one is in trouble? I wait but just keep staring at my own message. Then the ticks turn blue. They've read it. Come on, one of you answer.

'Everything alright?' asks Hugh. 'I'm getting another vodka, do you want one?'

'Not for me, thanks love.'

I need to keep a clear head. I look down at my phone again. This is brilliant. I don't even know where the bitches are. All I know is that one of them is with the fart who murdered the guy in Somerville Place. My hand grips the phone so tightly that my knuckles turn white. What's going on?

I'll give them fifteen minutes and then I'm phoning the police. What choice do I have?

Chapter Fifty-Four

It comes back to me in a flash and there, like a vision, is the memory of Sam at the rifle range. How could I have forgotten that? He was an expert marksman. He didn't miss once. Sam is a man used to handling a gun. I hide my trembling hands and attempt to smile.

'Do you remember that?' he asks.

I can only nod. I am sure if I speak it will come out as a high-pitched squeal. I can hardly breathe. I look at the photo while trying to hide the horror from my face. Can it be possible? I wouldn't feel the way I do when his hand touches mine, or lose myself within him when he kisses me. I would have felt it, surely?

'I remember you were good at the rifle range,' I say, finally finding my voice.

My phone bleeps and I glance at it. It's a new message from the *That Night* group.

'How come you were so good?' I ask.

He gives the grin I have come to know so well and my heart flutters.

'My dad holds clay pigeon championships at their country home in Berkshire. I did a lot of my practice at those. I'm not that good. A rifle range is easy. Don't be too impressed.'

I list the evidence in my head as the waitress places our food in front of us. The lost Starbucks card, the ownership of Rommel Mansions, the rifle range, the handwriting analysis, and the fact that he was at Ark Morgan's do.

'What did you do that night after the Fun Palace?' I ask, forcing myself to sound matter of fact.

'Do?' he says questioningly, looking straight into my eyes.

Did you go on to kill someone in Somerville Place I want to ask. *Get it out into the open. I so need to know.*

I discreetly pull my phone from my bag and check the message. It's from Felix. Please let it say Hugh is the killer.

Felix: *Hugh isn't the murderer girlies. I hate to be the bearer of bad news. He was at a funeral in the Isle of Wight. And yes, I thought it was dubious, so I ran a quick check. Your little Felix has got contacts now. I was thinking I might go into this investigative business full time. Anyway, cut to the chase, there was a funeral and old Hughie did a reading. So ... one of you is with the murderer right now because Clive Marsham wasn't at the party. On the guest list but not at the party as he's been in hospital for the past month with some mystery illness. Anyway, simply type RED and I'll call the police. But be sure to have concrete evidence first. We don't want them knowing we know until we do If you get my drift?*

'If I remember, I went back to a mate's flat and had a few beers,' he says casually, topping up our glasses.

He picks up his phone.

'Hang on ...' he says looking closely at the picture. 'I don't believe it.' He digs into his jacket pocket which hangs on the chair behind him.

'You're wearing the exact same earrings in that picture as this one.'

He pulls an earring from the pocket.

I choke as I fight back a gasp.

'Are you okay Roxie?' he asks, pushing a glass of water towards me.

'What are you doing with an earring?' I force a laugh and knock back the remains of my bubbly.

'Don't worry I don't go around collecting them. Found this one in my mate's flat. He got burgled, kind of.'

Burgled? Jesus, he really is the murderer. He killed his friend, which means he could just as easily kill me.

'It's a common earring,' I say. 'I bought them in Topshop.'

He stuffs the phone and earring back into his pocket.

'I didn't think it was yours,' he smiles.

That's just the problem. It is mine.

Sylvie

I'm seriously considering typing *red* when I remind myself that there are fifty or more flats in Somerville Place and Felix is right, we need concrete evidence before contacting the police, and Nigel living in Somerville Place is not concrete evidence. It's a bloody coincidence though. It worries me that Roxie has read Felix's message but not got back to us. I need to let Felix know I am okay, at least for the moment. I hold up my phone.

'Sorry about this, it's my gay friend, Felix, he's got man problems.'

I quickly tap into WhatsApp.

I'm fine, I think. I'll let you know if things turn sour. We're on our way back to Nigel's flat which only happens to be in Somerville Place. It's not possible it's 104 is it? Rox are you okay?'

I hit send and relax back in my seat. Of course it won't be 104 and I won't be typing *red* either. I really never thought I was the panicking kind but I'm bloody panicking now.

The cab turns towards the flats and memories of the three of us staking out the place come back to me. Then I remember what the old lady at 103 had said and I sigh with relief. Nigel is as far from a bum boy as anyone could get. By the time we pull up outside the flats I am feeling decidedly calm. I'd feel much better if Roxie would message back. If only Hugh could have been the damn murderer it would have made things so much easier. Nigel pays and then hooks his arm into mine.

'I've got some DVDs you'll love. I can't wait to show you my collection.'

I laugh.

'It's usually *etchings*,' I say, following him up the stairs. Each time we reach a landing I pray he will stop but we just keep on going.

'Sorry about this,' he says apologetically. 'The lift seems to be permanently out these days.'

'I know,' I say and then bite my lip.

'How did you know?' he asks with a smile.

'All blocks are like it these days, my friend had the same problem in her old flat too.'

Christ Sylvie, think before you speak. It's not like it takes long.

'I guess so,' he says, opening a door leading to flat 104. I feel my legs give way and have to grasp the bannister to stop myself falling.

'You okay Sylvie?' he asks, putting his key into the lock of number 104.

'I …' I say, barely able to get my breath.

He takes my arm and leads me into the flat. I see the Buddha painting and then everything goes black.

Roxie: *RED*
Sylvie: *RED*
Felix: *What the fuck?*

Chapter Fifty-Five

'How did you get out?' I say hugging a whisky glass close to my chest.

'I said Felix was cracking up and might do something stupid and that he has a tendency to be suicidal.'

'Thanks for that love.'

'I don't believe it,' I say, feeling quite suicidal myself.

'You're right not to darling. I'd never top myself over a man.'

I'm beginning to think I could. It's all too awful for words. I finally fall in love with the perfect man, even my mum is happy and that isn't easy to achieve, and now it turns out everything points to him being the murderer.

'I mean, I don't believe this situation.'

'How did you make your escape?' asks Felix. 'Don't tell me you told Sam I was suicidal as well?'

'I said I didn't feel well,' I say, thinking back to my evening with Sam. He had been so caring and attentive when I'd said that I had a migraine starting. I've never had a migraine in my life. Mind you, I've got a thumping headache now. That will teach me to lie. He'd escorted me home and has sent two texts since. How can someone that caring be a murderer?

'It can't be both of them,' says Felix, dipping two sponge fingers into my jar of Nutella. I can't even face eating one. I feel sick with dread and disappointment. How can I be in love with a murderer?

'After all, you didn't see three men that night did you? Let's look at the evidence,' he says rationally.

It's easy for him isn't it? He's not in love with one of the two suspects.

'Hughie is out of the picture. Well, where the murder is concerned anyway. I'm certainly keeping him in the picture. I tell you, he really is ...'

'Felix, can we stick to the point,' snaps Sylvie. 'I really don't think my nerves can take much more.'

'Sorry, being a bit insensitive.'

Sylvie spoons out a large dollop of Nutella and sucks greedily on it.

'You'd think it was cocaine the way you're going at it,' remarks Felix.

'Nothing is numbing the pain,' she complains.

'Right, back to the evidence. First let's look at Sam. Having an earring in his pocket isn't that damning is it and ...'

'It matched mine,' I say earnestly.

'I know, but like you've said, they're Topshop, and I imagine loads of chicks are wearing them ...'

'But how many chicks leave one in the flat?' asks Sylvie.

'Sounds like you want it to be Sam,' I say angrily.

'Well, I don't want it be Nigel do I?' she snaps.

I can't believe Sylvie and I are arguing over a man.

'He's more likely to be the one,' I say. 'Don't forget that he lives in the murder flat.'

'He may have just moved there for all we know. He could be the new tenant after our one was murdered.'

'We need to find the Where's Wally scarf. We can't do anything without more evidence. When is this play of Nigel's?' asks Felix.

'It's Saturday,' says Sylvie miserably.

'Okay great. You need to get Sam to go with you,' says Felix, looking at me.

I nod.

'You need to get another ticket from Nigel,' he says turning to Sylvie. 'It's the best place to set a trap. A public place with plenty of people around.'

'I've got four,' she says. 'I thought Roxie would want to bring someone, I just hadn't bargained on it being the murderer.'

'We don't know it's Sam,' I say angrily.

'We don't know it's Nigel either,' she snaps.

'We know it's *one* of them,' says Felix, shutting us both up. 'I've gone through the guest list and there is no one else to check. Text Sam that you've got a ticket and ask would he like to go with you.'

Bloody bossy or what?

'I wish you'd stop telling me what to do. In fact, I wish I had never told either of you about the murder. I should have gone straight to the police and ...'

'But you didn't,' interrupts Felix.

'Well, I just know that Nigel couldn't murder anyone,' says Sylvie giving me a dirty look.

'And I know that Sam couldn't murder anyone and besides, if he had been wearing the Where's Wally scarf at the Fun Palace I would have noticed.'

'He was half naked,' Sylvie reminds me.

'Not at the rifle range.'

'But we barely saw him, let alone his scarf,' argues Sylvie.

Felix sighs.

'Well one of them did it,' he says patiently. 'I'm not a gambling man but I would put my money on Sam Lockwood.'

We both gape at him.

'Sam?' I repeat hoarsely.

'He does own Rommel Mansions remember?'

'And that's it?' I say.

He shrugs.

'We need to get his fingerprints on Saturday. Make sure you go for a drink during the interval. Sylvie, you'll need to lift the prints from his glass and see if they match the Starbucks card.'

'Are you telling me I've got to go to the theatre with a bag full of my stuff?'

'If you want us to find out who the murderer is, and we'll also need a sample of Sam's handwriting. I've got a plan for that.'

I sigh.

'It's a night at the theatre, not a Paul Daniels show. She'll be pulling a rabbit out of that bag too at this rate,' I say miserably. 'I don't know why you're accusing Sam anyway.'

'Because he's the most likely suspect from the evidence we have love. Anyway, on the night of the play we will nail who it is even if we have to set a trap.'

Chapter Fifty-Six

The sight of Sam in the foyer sends desire shooting through me. I'm beginning to think that even if he is the murderer it won't stop me feeling the way I do. After all, love conquers everything doesn't it? Okay, that's probably a bit over the top romantic considering the situation. He waves as soon as he sees us and I have to stop myself bursting through the doors to get to him. I'd not seen him since the championship four days ago. He's been texting me regularly, asking how the migraine is. Honestly, who has a migraine for three days? I'm surprised he didn't think I had a brain tumour. Sylvie opens the door and I make my way to Sam and then freeze. Sylvie bumps into the back of me almost sending me sprawling.

'Christ, sorry. It's this ruddy great rucksack I'm carrying. You'd think I was on an expedition to Everest rather than a trip to the theatre,' she grumbles.

I ignore her and groan, 'Oh God.'

Sam is wearing the Where's Wally scarf. That's it then isn't it? I'll have to phone the police and put the man I love in the clink. It's all I can do to hold back my tears. I've secretly dreamt of my Mr Right never believing I would ever find him. Now, here he is standing right in front of me and if he really is the man I saw pull that gun, then I really can't have him. Life sucks doesn't it?

'Keep calm,' whispers Felix. 'You can't be sure of anything yet.'

'It's the scarf, I recognise it. It's too coincidental.'

'Let's wait and see.'

'Hey,' Sam says when I reach him. 'Thanks for inviting me.'

He kisses me on the lips and I have to hold onto his arm to stop my legs giving way. Honestly, I'm useless. Just one kiss and I'd be forgiving him for genocide.

'Hi,' says Sylvie, 'been here long?'

'Yeah, quite a while actually, my mate is in this play so we had a drink before he had to get ready. I was going to get a ticket for you but then you said you had one. Still, all's well that ends well,' he says, giving us his grin.

'Oh,' I say.

'Hello there,' says Felix offering his hand. 'I'm Felix. I'm sure they've talked about me.'

'You're not that special,' says Sylvie

Sam smiles and my heart melts. He's wearing a striped blue shirt over white combat trousers and looks good enough to eat.

'I like your scarf,' says Felix and I nearly die on the spot.

Please say it isn't yours, I pray.

'We went to the rugby, it's my team's colours but I won't bore you,' laughs Sam. 'I wear it whenever I go to a match. I have a thing about lucky mascots. Roxie knows all about that.'

I struggle to smile. Was there a match on that Saturday, the day of the murder?

'Who's your friend then?' says Sylvie, casually steering Sam back to the subject we're all interested in.

'Nigel Forrest, he's making a film actually.'

I don't know which one of us gasps first.

'That's ... He's my friend too,' says Sylvie.

'What a coincidence,' says Felix.

I struggle to understand what this means but nothing adds up so I look at Felix and then Sylvie and their blank expressions tell me they have no idea what to make of it either.

'How's the migraine?' Sam asks.

'I'm fine, I don't know why it took so long to go,' I say, feeling myself blush.

He drapes his arm around my shoulders.

'It's great to see you,' he whispers.

Oh, the feeling is so mutual. Sylvie excuses herself to go backstage to see Nigel, and Sam takes my arm.

'Shall we sit down?' he asks.

'These are great seats,' says Felix enthusiastically. 'We seem to spend our time in the front row, don't we Rox?'

I glare at him. How can he make light of everything?

'I'll let you two lovebirds sit together,' he says, looking at me and raising his eyebrow. I swear I'll bloody kill him after the play. Felix thumbs through the programme and I frantically try to think of a connection between Nigel and Sam and the murder that night. As the curtain goes up it dawns on me. What if Nigel lured the bum boy to the flat? All this time we've been thinking that the bum boy lived there but supposing he didn't, supposing the old girl got muddled. What if Nigel has lived there all along? Maybe the bum boy visited him a lot. Oh God, maybe Nigel owed him money. Actors are always struggling aren't they? I jump as Sam takes my hand and rests it on his knee. I must stop thinking about the bum boy. In fact, I must stop calling him a *bum boy*, period. It's obvious the old girl just got in a muddle. Look at my parents and they're not that old but they get everything wrong.

Music begins to play and Nigel waltzes on wearing a bright pink jacket. He's as camp as a row of tents.

Chapter Fifty-Seven

'At least we know where the bum boy came from,' says Felix as we find a seat near the bar.

'You think Nigel is the bum boy the old lady was talking about?' asks Sylvie.

'We can't be sure of that,' says Felix. 'But most likely. He probably came over as a bit of a lovie to her. I imagine all actors are bum boys as far as she's concerned.'

'He's playing the part of one, so it seems to add up with what the neighbour said and can we please stop using the phrase *bum boy*?' I say, my eyes not leaving Sam's gorgeous body as he queues at the bar.

'She's quite right, I'm feeling very offended,' says Felix.

'Oh, you get offended every second of the day,' scoffs Sylvie.

'I love you too,' he says, blowing her a kiss. 'But we still shouldn't dismiss the gay guy because Nigel is playing one.'

'It occurred to me that maybe Nigel lured the bum ... gay man to the flat so ... so someone could kill him. Maybe it was a business deal gone wrong or something,' I say.

'So Sam could kill him you mean?'

'Well, I still think Nigel ...' I stop as Sam returns with our drinks.

He drapes his scarf on the back of the chair and sits beside me. We all struggle not to focus on the scarf but it's bloody difficult.

'What do you think of the performance? Nigel's good isn't he. We've taken the Michael out of him while he's been preparing for this,' he laughs. 'No offence,' he adds, nodding to Felix.

'I don't get offended love,' says Felix.

Sylvie clicks her tongue and swings her rucksack around hitting Sam's glass and sending his wine everywhere.

'Oh God Sam, I'm so sorry. Let me get you another.'

She takes the glass carefully from his hand and then looks at her dress.

'Oh look, I've got wine all over me. Will you excuse me? Felix will you get another drink for Sam? Are you okay Sam? I'm so sorry.'

'No harm done,' he smiles.

I'm speechless. Felix jumps up.

'Oh right, yeah sure. What was it Sam?'

'Red,' Sam smiles.

Sylvie slides past him, casually taking the scarf with her. I can't believe my friends are so smooth.

'That's one way of leaving us alone together,' Sam smiles. 'I was starting to think you were avoiding me.'

'Oh no,' I say, guzzling my wine like lemonade and feeling my head spin.

'Is everything okay?' he asks, looking at me closely. 'You don't seem yourself.'

That's probably got something to with the fact that I'm far from myself and that right now my friends are lifting your prints and studying your Where's Wally scarf. It suddenly occurs to me that I could warn him, give him a chance to make a run for it. Maybe I could run with him. We would be fugitives together.

'I'm fine, the thing is ...'

'One red wine,' says Felix. 'By the way love, would you mind signing this little card we've got for Nigel. Just a little congrats card. Put a few words if you don't mind. Something like, *Good performance, we should discuss it later*.

I give him an odd look. These two are really something else. My eyes are drawn to the loos. Will I be able to tell from Sylvie's face that the fingerprints match?

'Sure,' Sam says, 'maybe different words though.'

I watch and feel like he's signing his death sentence.

Sylvie

I'm the only bloody woman in the loo with a sodding great rucksack. They must think I'm high maintenance if I need to take a bag this size to the loo with me. I only wish I had time to do something with my hair. I don't even imagine I've got time to pee. The queue moves slowly and I consider dashing into the men's. They never have a queue. They just pull it out do a quick piss and leave. I'm definitely coming back as a man. This lot have probably got Spanx and whatnot to pull down before they even get to their drawers. I'll be here all bloody night.

After what feels like an eternity I'm able to dash into a cubicle. I pull my equipment out and place everything on the toilet seat. I'm dead nervous of pulling the prints. I don't want it be Sam any more than Roxie does. I don't want it to be Nigel or Sam but the fact is one of them has to be the murderer. I try to ignore the rip in the scarf which has frayed so much it looks like a bad haircut, and carefully lift the prints from the glass. I struggle to concentrate with toilet chains being pulled all around me but I eventually do it without dropping anything. I compare the two photos on my phone and flop onto the seat. I so wish Roxie hadn't seen that murder and what's more I wish she hadn't told Felix and me.

Chapter Fifty-Eight

'There's a sushi bar around the corner, does great food. I thought you and I could go there after the performance?' Sam says, handing the card back to Felix and turning to me.

There's a buzzing in my head. The only thing I am aware of is Sylvie marching out from the loo holding the scarf in such a way that I can't miss the rip in it.

'Roxie,' Sam says, but it sounds a million miles away. 'Roxie,' he repeats.

I feel myself slide from the seat and grab his arm for support.

'Roxie, what's wrong? Is it the migraine again?'

I can almost hear my mum saying, *I knew it was too good to be true*, and she'd be quite right. It was too good to be true. Maybe Ark wasn't so wrong about Sam after all.

Chapter Fifty-Nine

WhatsApp

Roxie: *We need to talk about Nigel.*

Felix: *This is not a bloody novel you know.*

Sylvie: *Feels like one.*

Roxie: *Nigel is involved too. He has to be.*

Sylvie: *You do realise our phones are lighting up the whole bloody arena.*

Felix: *You do exaggerate sometimes love.*

Sylvie: *The facts: (a) Sam's prints match those on the Starbucks card. It belongs to him. (b) The scarf is the one Rox cut up. We should phone the police.*

I stare at my phone and my feel my heart sink.

'Everything okay?' Sam asks.

I swear if he asks me that again ... I nod and slip my phone inside the programme and pretend to look at that.

Roxie: *Not yet, it's too soon. Wait till the end of the play.*

That will give me time to decide whether to warn Sam or not.

Felix: *She's quite right though. We need to talk about Kevin ... I mean Nigel.*

Roxie: *There's nothing funny about this.*

Felix: *I never said there was.*

Roxie: *I think Nigel helped lure the victim to his flat so Sam could murder him.*

Sylvie: *So why weren't there three men in the flat that night?*

Roxie: *Maybe he was out of view.*

Felix: *We have to phone the police as soon as the play finishes. We can't afford for either of them to get away.*

Sylvie: *God, Nigel's acting his balls off.*

There are gasps from the audience as the play reaches its climax. I watch mesmerised as Nigel confronts his lover, bursting dramatically onto the stage. I picture the police bursting into the theatre after the performance. We'll be all over the papers in the morning. I sigh and try to focus on the play.

'Explain this,' he shouts, waving the love letter in the air and pointing at a photo on a side cabinet.

'You think I couldn't tell from those photos. You're all over him.'

He's a good actor. I imagine he is going to do really well in films, if he isn't in Broadmoor of course.

'He's great isn't he.' whispers Sam.

I can't take my eyes off him and grip Sam's arm tightly as the play reaches its dramatic conclusion.

'Things aren't what they seem,' says the other actor, backing away.

Madam Zehilda's words slap me in the face. Hang on a minute. Oh my God, is this really happening?

'I won't let you go to him,' Nigel screams before throwing himself at the man and putting his hands around his throat.

Sylvie gasps and I have to stop myself from jumping from my seat. Oh my God, it's the murder scene all over again. The other actor is even wearing a scarf. What's happening? It's like I'm reliving the nightmare. I watch with my heart hammering as they struggle for a few moments. I know before he does it that the other man will pull a gun from his pocket. And then, as though in slow motion, Nigel's lover pulls the trigger. I jump and watch open-mouthed as Nigel falls to the floor. The audience gasp. My phone lights up and I stare at it in shock.

Felix: *Déjà vu or what?*

I'm dumb. I can barely look at the stage. The curtain drops and I nearly fall to the floor with it. The audience are on their feet applauding and cheering. I can barely get my shaky legs to support me.

'You are okay Roxie, is it the migraine?' asks Sam

Sylvie's cheeks are rosy and her eyes wild. The audience are making their way to the exits and we have to keep moving to allow them round us.

'I don't have migraines,' I say.

I'm so exhausted from the stress. I need a giant jar of Nutella and a bucket load of sponge fingers, coupled with a large vodka and a handful of Valium. I'm not coping.

'But I thought ...' begins Sam.

'Have you asked him?' blurts Sylvie.

Sam looks curiously at us.

'I'm missing something,' he grins.

'You didn't murder anyone in Nigel's flat did you?' says Sylvie excitedly.

'Murder someone?' he laughs.

'The night we saw you at the Fun Palace?' she says. 'You went back to Nigel's didn't you?'

'Sylvie,' I say with a pleading look.

'How do you know that?' he asks with a smile.

'Because Roxie here,' chips in Felix, 'saw you through her boyfriend's telescope commit, what seemed to be a murder.'

'You saw our drunken rehearsal?' says Nigel joining us.

'I thought it was real,' I mumble.

Sam looks into my eyes.

'You didn't have a migraine did you? You've been avoiding me?'

'Well it wasn't ...' begins Sylvie.

'Sylvie,' I say quietly. 'I think you've said enough.'

'Was it you lot that broke into my flat?' says an astonished Nigel.

Sylvie pulls a face.

'Well, it wasn't exactly breaking in ...'

'I warned you,' says Felix.

'Roxie was so sure ...'

I thought I'd get the blame.

'And when we found the bloodstain,' continues Felix, 'that sort of clinched the murder for us really. Of course we now realise it was ...'

'Stage make-up,' finishes Nigel.

'You've got a lot of vodka and frozen peas in your fridge love,' says Felix, 'what's that all about?'

He smiles at us all, trying to lighten the tense atmosphere.

Nigel grins.

'Oh well, no harm done. I think you cleaned the place up actually.'

Sam is still looking at me. I'm jostled by a group of people and pushed into his arms. He steadies me and then drops them.

'You thought I was a murderer?' he asks solemnly.

'She also thought Ark Morgan was too,' adds Sylvie, pulling a face at me. 'And Nigel.'

I groan.

'So, that's why you went out with Morgan and why you went out with me?' he says, grabbing his scarf. 'I suppose you did this too.'

He holds up his ragged scarf and I wince.

'I'll replace it.'

He pulls the earring from his pocket and hands it to me.

'This is yours then I presume?'

'Erm ...' I begin but realise there is nothing to say that will stop him hating me.

He places the earring into my hand and turns to Nigel.

'I'll see you later mate.'

And with that he is gone.

'Christ,' says Sylvie.

'You're not letting him go, are you love?' says Felix.

Chapter Sixty

'Jesus peanuts, go after him you silly bitch,' says Felix, shoving me towards the door.

I hesitate for a moment and then bound for the exit. My head thumps. If I didn't have a migraine before then I'm certainly getting one now. My throat is so dry too. I don't think I'll be able to speak if I catch up with him. I burst out of the exit and look down the street. I see the scarf as he turns the corner. I push my way through the crowd that spills out of the theatre and hurry after him. I can't run in my heels without fracturing an ankle. I turn the corner and there he is.

'Sam wait, please wait.'

He turns, looks at me and carries on walking.

'Please wait,' I call, breaking into a run. 'I'll cripple myself chasing you in these stupid shoes. Just let me explain. For God's sake don't be a prick, Sam please.'

He stops and I take a deep breath. I don't do running at the best of times but in bloody heels it's a nightmare. My calves feel like they've been on a torture rack. As I reach him I am overwhelmed with love for him. I stand panting. I bet Jennifer Aniston never has to chase Justin Theroux like this.

'You're so unfit,' he says.

Okay, no need to point it out.

'I know,' I pant. 'Look, I'm so sorry. That night everything looked so real. If you knew how much I didn't want it to be you. I was ...'

'This whole time you thought I murdered someone?'

I shake my head emphatically.

'No, not at all, it was only when you showed me the photo from the Fun Palace and pulled out that earring that you became a suspect, and there was the Starbucks card before that.'

'Have you got my Starbucks card?' he says, his eyes widening. 'I can't believe you broke into Nigel's flat.'

'We didn't exactly break in,' I say with a wry grin.

'You didn't exactly break in,' he repeats. 'What does that mean *exactly?*'

'Sylvie got in with a credit card. She's into crime novels.'

I look closely at him. I think I see him fight back a grin but I don't want to raise my hopes.

'A credit card, you actually got the door open with a credit card?'

'Well, Sylvie did.'

'You left a big water stain on the carpet.'

There is a grin, I'm sure I can see it.

'Well we were doing everything wearing Marigolds so it was a bit difficult.'

'And Ark Morgan?' he asks, taking my hand so I can adjust my shoe strap. His hand in mine sends volts searing through me.

'I was a bit infatuated with him and then I thought he was ...'

'The murderer,' he finishes for me.

I nod. We step to the side as a group from the theatre pass us, his hand holding mine.

'You know you can't possibly work for Ark if you're going out with me.'

My heart leaps. I nod.

'And I'd expect you to be at all my boxing matches.'

I nod again.

'You know I'm crazy about you, don't you?' he grins, pulling me into his arms.

'I'm crazy about you too,' I say.

'Want to come back to my house,' he whispers.

Try stopping me. I see Sylvie and Felix at the corner. If they do anything to bugger this up I swear I won't be held responsible.

'Everything hunky-dory love?' asks Felix.

Sam's lips brush my neck.

'Except you'll never really know if it was a real murder will you?'

He's joking, at least I hope he's joking but as his lips touch mine I realise I don't care if he isn't.

The Dog's
Bollocks
a romantic comedy
by
Lynda
Renham

Pink Wellies
and FLAT CAPS
Lynda Renham

IT HAD TO BE
You
A romantic COMEDY by
Lynda Renham

Coconuts
and
WONDERBRAS
a romantic comedy adventure
Lynda Renham

Fudge
Berries
AND
FROGS' KNICKERS
A ROMANTIC COMEDY BY

Rory's
Proposal
a romantic comedy
by
Lynda Renham

If you enjoyed Fifty Shades of Roxie Brown you will love:

The Dog's Bollocks

On arriving home after a friend's posh wedding, launderette worker Harriet finds her life irrevocably changed as she discovers her flat ransacked and her boyfriend missing. In a matter of hours she is harassed by East End gangsters and upper crust aristocrats. Accepting an offer she can't refuse, Harriet, against her better judgement becomes the fiancée of the wealthy Hamilton Lancaster, with dire consequences. What she had not bargained on was meeting Doctor Brice Edmunds.

The Dog's Bollocks one of Lynda Renham's funniest novels. A cocktail of misunderstandings, three unlikely gangsters, a monkey and a demented cat make this novel a hysterical read. Follow Harriet's adventure where every attempt to get out of trouble puts her deeper in it.

Felix: Just *bumped into Angie, apparently Darren is moving in with her.*

Sylvie: *I hope they'll be very happy together.*

Felix: *If they are I'll eat my arse.*

Sylvie: *Seriously, he may have found his soulmate.*

Roxie: *Can you two stop talking about my ex. Jennifer Aniston never had to put up with this.*

Felix: *How was last night with Sam, love? I want details.*

Roxie: *Wonderful, and you're not getting any.*

Sylvie: *Nigel's invited me to go on location with him - can't wait.*

Roxie: *That's great Sylvie, I'm so happy for you.*

Felix: *Got to dash, meeting Mr Umm at Copacabana in 30 minutes.*

Roxie: *Have fun, x*

Felix: *Going, Going, Gone.*